A former magazine editor, Charlotte Butterfield was born in Bristol and studied English at Royal Holloway. She moved to Dubai by herself on a one-way ticket with one suitcase in 2005 and left twelve years later with a husband, three children and a forty-foot shipping container. She now lives in the Cotswolds, where she is a freelance writer and novelist.

The Second Chance

Charlotte Butterfield

avon.

Published by AVON
A division of HarperCollins*Publishers*
1 London Bridge Street
London SE1 9GF

www.harpercollins.co.uk

HarperCollins*Publishers*
Macken House
39/40 Mayor Street Upper
Dublin 1
D01 C9W8

A Paperback Original 2024
3
First published in Great Britain by HarperCollins*Publishers* 2024

A catalogue copy of this book is available from the British Library.

ISBN: 978-0-00-864294-5

This novel is entirely a work of fiction. The names, characters and incidents portrayed in it are the work of the author's imagination. Any resemblance to actual persons, living or dead, events or localities is entirely coincidental.

Typeset in Birka by Palimpsest Book Production Limited,
Falkirk, Stirlingshire

Printed and bound in the UK using 100% Renewable Electricity at CPI Group (UK) Ltd

This book contains FSC™ certified paper and other controlled sources to ensure responsible forest management.

For more information visit: www.harpercollins.co.uk/green

To my Dad, the shiniest star in the sky.

I shall be telling this with a sigh
Somewhere ages and ages hence:
Two roads diverged in a wood, and I—
I took the one less traveled by,
And that has made all the difference.

Robert Frost

PART ONE

Heaven is louder than you'd expect

CHAPTER ONE

The doorbell rang. He was early.

'Hello, Tom, is it?'

The man nodded. 'Nell?'

'Yes. Hi.' She stuck her hand out. 'Nice to meet you. Sorry to be rude, but I haven't got long, so shall we go straight up to the bedroom?'

He seemed a little taken aback, like he was expecting a cup of tea first, or a preamble about the traffic or the weather. But he followed her dutifully up the stairs regardless. Normally when a man followed her quite so closely, she'd have been worried about the size of her bottom, but in this particular circumstance Nell didn't think it mattered.

'I don't really know how this works,' he said as they stalled in the doorway to her room, 'Shall I lie down?'

'Sure. Take your shoes off though.'

'I'm not a savage,' he laughed, kicking off his boots. His striped socks were like gloves, with each toe nestled into its own little woollen home. It was an unsurprising quirk; Nell had already pigeon-holed him as an artist, or musician maybe. His curly hair covered his collar and he had a thick silver ring on his thumb.

'Nice socks,' she said.

He wiggled his toes in appreciation at her.

He lay down on the bed, his hands by his side. Not unlike the pose of being in a coffin – a thought Nell swiftly batted away.

'It's comfy.'

'Thank you,' she said, as though the bounciness of springs was entirely her own doing.

'Is it a queen or king?'

'I'm not sure, king, I think.' She hoped it wasn't obvious that she was completely making it up; it was cheap was what it was and bought from an address just around the corner, which saved on hiring a man with a van.

'This may sound like a very odd request,' he said.

'Try me.'

'Could you lie down next to me? It's just I want to see if it would feel crowded with two people in it.'

'Why didn't you bring your partner with you?'

'Because I don't have one yet.'

'I feel that you may be doing things in the wrong order,' Nell said, with characteristic frankness.

He smiled. 'It doesn't hurt to be prepared.'

'I like your optimism.' She hopped onto the bed next to him and lay down, imitating his Tutankhamun pose, her own curly hair spilling out all over the pillow. 'So, as you can see, plenty of room for two.'

That was clearly a lie. It was plainly not a king; to call it a double might even have been a stretch. Their bodies were touching the whole way down their arms and legs, while their other sides were hanging slightly off the mattress.

'Cosy,' he said.

They both started laughing. 'Okay, clearly I know nothing about beds,' she said. 'Sorry to have got you here under false pretences. Totally understand if you report me to Facebook Marketplace for being a fraud.'

'Not a fraud. You said you were selling a bed. You are indeed selling a bed.'

'Yes. True. And king-sized does not actually refer to its technical size, what I actually meant was that it was sized for a king. A very small one.'

'Henry VI became king when he was only nine months old,' Tom said, 'So he'd have been very short.'

'Exactly,' Nell replied, 'I clearly was referring to him in the advert.'

'To be honest, he'd have found this huge.'

'Too big really. They'd have had to have put cushions all around the edge to stop him falling out.'

'Or pool noodles tucked under the sheets,' suggested Tom.

'Oh, that is clever. Very clever. Were they invented then?'

'Pool noodles?'

Nell nodded beside him. They were both still lying flat on their backs looking up at the ceiling.

'Not sure. But flatpack beds didn't exist then either, so it's a bit of a moot point.'

'True, true.'

'So. . .' Tom started, 'Where are you moving to then?'

Nell had been asked this by pretty much everyone she'd sold her belongings to over the last month. She'd always lied, or said something vaguely truthful like, 'I'm not really sure,' which wasn't a fib, no one really knew for sure where they were going after, did they? But there was something about lying down on a bed with your hips touching someone else's that required honesty so Nell replied, 'I'm actually going to die next Monday so I won't be needing it.'

'What?' Tom exclaimed, immediately shifting onto his right side so he was facing her. 'Say that again?'

'I'm going to die on Monday. And I'm selling everything before I go, so it's nice and neat for my family and I don't leave them with the task of doing it after I'm gone. My dad is far too busy playing golf and my mum doesn't like driving on the motorway.'

Nell was still lying on her back, but she could sense his brown eyes narrowing in confusion at her, boring into her from her left. 'Don't stare at me,' she said, still looking up at the ceiling. 'It's weird.'

'Are you ill?'

She shook her head.

'Are you going to kill yourself?'

That was a very blunt thing to ask, and should she have been feeling that way, she wasn't sure that would have been a particularly tactful way to inquire about the state of her mental health, but she'd met too many people along the way who smothered their words in honey, so actually appreciated his candour.

'No. If I tell you, you're going to think I'm mad, so I'm not going to tell you.'

'Tell me.'

'No.'

'Tell me.'

Nell moved her head from side to side. 'Nope.'

'Please.'

'Don't you have somewhere to be?' she asked.

'Nope.'

'That's sad.'

'Do you?' he countered.

Nell shook her head again.

6

'That's even sadder. You're the one with six days left to live. Not me. I can afford to dick about a bit.'

'If you're going to tease me—'

He propped himself up on his elbow facing her. He smelled of shower gel and peppermint. 'I'm not teasing you. Please, tell me.'

'Okay. If I tell you, you can't judge me, or laugh, or mock me.'

'Deal.'

She hesitated. She hadn't told the full story for years, just edited highlights. It had only ever been received with mirth and mockery, but there was something about Tom's intensity and kind eyes that made her sigh, and then she started talking.

It wasn't like she was expecting the clairvoyant to live in an old Romany caravan with peeling paint and fold-down wooden steps, but she wasn't quite prepared for the forgettable three-bed semi in an unassuming Sydney suburb with a kid's tricycle in the driveway next to a ten-year-old Volkswagen Polo. And the mystic was wearing jeans. No tie-dye, no kaftan, just high-waisted stonewashed denim paired with a stained Sydney Sevens rugby shirt. 'Call me Mandy,' she'd said, hoicking the source of the stain onto her hip and sticking a dummy in its mouth. She'd ushered them in, past a heaving coat rack and a cat litter tray that definitely needed emptying. 'Come in, come in, go through and make yourselves comfy while I put this one down for his nap.'

Teenage Nell and her boyfriend Greg went 'through' but instead of emerging through the ajar door into a Bedouin tent with billowing drapes, they were in her garage with the exposed pipes above their heads. Fabric was cheap, Nell remembered thinking, it wouldn't have cost much to pin up

7

a few bits of chiffon. There was a bike rack on the wall and a couple of old boxes presumably from Mandy's last house move as one had 'playroom' on it and the other 'kitchen fragile' scrawled on the side. There was already a camping table and chairs set up in the middle of the garage, above an old oil stain on the concrete floor. Mandy hadn't even bothered to light a candle, and they'd passed lots of discount home stores on the ring-road going there so it wasn't like she hadn't had the opportunity to buy a tealight or two. Mandy came in then, holding a crackling baby monitor, and placed it in the middle of the table where a crystal ball should have been but wasn't.

'So, is there anything in particular you want to know?' she asked, quickly glancing at her watch.

Greg sat on the edge of his chair next to Nell, his newly tanned face open and eager to know more, to know everything. His index finger was tap, tap, tapping on his knee under the table. Nell knew Greg's face and reflexes better than her own. At nineteen he didn't have the laughter lines and deep set wrinkles his face would inevitably eventually wear, but his face was peppered with little reminders of past escapades. The tiny hole near his left eye from a chicken pox scab he'd been warned by his mum not to scratch. The two-centimetre sliver of white on his chin he got showing off at the skateboarding park when they were thirteen, his chipped front tooth from a ski trip when they were sixteen. But more than these physical features, Nell knew his expressions. He was grounded, trusting and the driving force behind all of their adventures. It was him who had made the first move in turning their friendship into more two years before, him who suggested this year of travel after their A levels, him who convinced Nell to aim higher for a better law degree at a better university for September.

It was as though he'd had both hands on her back pushing her forward ever since they started secondary school. Even going to Mandy's that day, *especially* going there that day, had been due to his contagious excitement bubbling over at the hostel the night before when they were told about this mystical woman with all the answers.

So far though, Nell thought, the answers seemed to be somewhat vague. There was apparently going to be travel in their lives. Considering that they had trouble squeezing past the coat rack in the narrow hallway because of the massive rucksacks on their backs, had peeling sunburn on their noses and shoulders and both sported English accents, she understandably felt a little let down. Also, the letters M, B, L, P, S, A, E, T and perhaps C, H and G were going to be very important in their lives. There was a mother figure, who might not be a mother, maybe an aunty, or grandmother, even a sister maybe, or cousin, either in this life, or the next, Mandy couldn't be sure. Greg nodded excitedly at Nell, mouthing, 'Mum's called Patty!'

Nell smiled and nodded encouragingly at him. 'Yep.'

Mandy's eyes closed, and she was swaying slightly from side to side making little humming noises. This wasn't right, Nell thought. They shouldn't have come. She suddenly felt uncomfortably hot. 'I've changed my mind,' she whispered, leaning in close to Greg, 'We should go. I don't want to know.' Greg didn't move, so Nell nudged his knee with hers. His wide eyes were trained in awe on Mandy, he was even swaying in time with her as though entranced. The baby monitor gave a little crackle.

Nell leaned down and picked up her rucksack; she'd had enough, this was too weird, and she was now feeling unbearably flushed and clammy and needed some air. Mandy's eyes shot open and with no warning or fanfare gave the two teens each the date of their deaths: 29 July 2089 for Greg, 16 December 2024 for Nell.

Nell was now lying on her side facing Tom, their noses a few inches apart.

'She said it just like that?' Tom asked, his eyes wide.

'Just like that. It was what we'd gone there for. Lots of people at the hostel had been talking about her, she was well known for this party trick. It had seemed like a really good idea when we were three bottles of beer and a couple of joints in the night before, but in the cold light of day, I knew that we never should have come. And knowing, changed everything. . .'

'But you said yourself that she didn't get anything else right, why would you believe her on this bit?' Tom asked.

Nell paused. Remembering was making her heart hurt.

'I'll be a hundred-and-three!' Greg had said excitedly as they picked up their battered rucksacks and left the garage via the side door, standing to one side to let their friends from the hostel, Sophie and Hayley from Dublin, who had been patiently waiting outside the door for their own magical predictions, go in.

'I'll be thirty-eight,' Nell said to Greg. 'That's not old. I mean, that's old, but it's not a hundred-and-three old.'

'It's ages away. We're nineteen for Christ's sake, and you're not going to cark it for another nineteen years! That's double the time you've been alive, that's loads of time!'

'I'm not sure I believe any of it anyway,' Nell said, clipping the belt of her rucksack around her waist. 'She didn't seem very professional.'

'What were you expecting? A painted wagon on wheels?' Greg laughed.

'No,' Nell replied, a little affronted. They sat down under the shade of an old sycamore tree in Mandy's back garden just beyond her living room while they waited for Hayley and Sophie to finish. The irony wasn't lost on Nell that this tree would outlive her, unless Mandy ever wanted an extension off her lounge and the planning application was accepted.

The garage door swung open after about ten minutes, ricocheting noisily off the wall behind it. 'It's all a crock of shit, Sophie,' came the loud voice of one of the two Irish girls as the door of the utility room crashed open.

'What an asshole,' puffed Sophie.

'I can't believe we paid her for that.'

'She shouldn't be allowed to peddle such crap. Wouldn't even give us our money back,' Hayley seethed.

'She's a psycho.'

'Flaming psycho.'

Greg and Nell were quiet as they joined the other two stomping along the narrow pavement, sometimes in pairs, occasionally falling in line behind each other as they navigated the narrow pathway with other people walking the suburban streets of northern Sydney.

'How long did she give you two then?' Hayley eventually asked.

'Til I'm thirty-eight,' Nell replied glumly.

'A hundred-and-three,' Greg added, having the good grace and social awareness to at least sound apologetic and far less jubilant than before, sensing the time for joyful celebration was not now, although Nell could still see his eyes dancing with this new information.

'So much for the luck of the Irish, I'm apparently going to meet my maker when I'm forty,' Hayley said.

Sophie was quiet.

'Sophie?' Greg prompted. 'Tell us your date of doom?'

11

'Next month,' Sophie said quietly. 'The seventeenth of January.'

'It's all a load of horseshit though,' Hayley swiftly said.

'Course it is,' they all agreed.

By the time the four of them had made their way back to the hostel to dump their rucksacks on their beds, they'd stirred themselves up into a collective simmering rage. 'I can't believe someone could prey on young people like this,' they said, completely and conveniently forgetting that they'd sought the soothsayer out themselves, tracked her down to her small garage off her kitchen using two adjacent pages of their city map and happily handed over the money they'd just earned fruit picking in Queensland to hear the date of their demise. Had they all been given dates like Greg had, far off in the distance hovering somewhere above the horizon, the cacophony of fury would either be replaced with giggles and banter, or completely forgotten about, sliding into the memories of their travels alongside snorkelling and trying barbecued crocodile. If any of them had even considered that they might not reach pensionable age they wouldn't have gone.

Mandy's forecast was never mentioned over the next few days as they all did a really convincing job of *having a really great time*, but Nell studied Hayley and Sophie when they weren't looking and she knew she caught glimpses of wistfulness or anxiety that was a sign that she wasn't alone in being unable to let it go. She'd tried talking to Greg about it, not during the day when the sun was high and invariably, he was too, but when dusk fell and they'd curl up together on a hammock, Nell with her head on his chest as he stroked her hair. 'I'm sad,' Nell confided one evening.

'Why? Aren't you having fun?'

'I keep thinking about what Mandy said.'

'Oh God Nell, don't even think about it. I'm not.'

'You're going to live until you're pissing your pants in an old people's home, I'm not even going to see my fortieth!'

'Course you are! It's all a load of nonsense! You don't actually think that it's true?'

'You seemed pretty convinced by her.'

'No, I didn't, it was just a bit of fun, seriously Nell, don't give it another thought. Now kiss me.'

The four friends spent Christmas on the beach eating freshly caught barbecued fish and drinking beer. Greg's Grade Six guitar skills came in useful when a fellow traveller left behind his ukulele in the hostel and whenever the humour dipped, Greg would provide a suitably upbeat mood enhancer that made them all momentarily forget the ticking timer. As the days marched on towards 17 January, Nell thought that Sophie seemed, if anything, more and more buoyant about life.

'We should go cliff jumping,' Sophie said one morning. 'There's one about an hour away, it's the best spot in Australia apparently.'

'Maybe not tomorrow though, eh?' Nell laughed nervously.

'Why not? It's meant to be fine all day.'

'But it's the seventeenth.'

'Which is exactly why we should go,' Sophie said, 'Prove once and for all that that charlatan was wrong.'

'We can do that by going on the eighteenth,' Hayley said. 'We all know that Mandy was a complete con-artist, but maybe we should just lie low tomorrow, go to the beach or hang out around the hostel for the day.'

Nell felt grateful that Hayley voiced what she was thinking. If she was in Sophie's position, she'd stay in bed all day tomorrow until midnight. Not that there was anything in Mandy's proclamation, but you could prove that she was a liar by waking up on the seventeenth, having a stretch and going for a nice soft, easily chewable breakfast, not by flinging yourself off a cliff into the rock-strewn sea below.

But Sophie was adamant. She'd show Mandy up for what she was.

Nell didn't know at what point in retelling the story to Tom she'd started crying, but was suddenly acutely aware of lying on her bed next to an absolute stranger bawling her eyes out and telling him her innermost secrets.

Tom reached into his jeans pocket, pulled out a clean folded tissue and gave it to Nell. 'What happened to Sophie, Nell?'

Nell sniffed. 'Hayley didn't come back to the hostel after the accident. She phoned the hostel and got me and Greg to pack up her and Sophie's rucksacks and to send them on to Ireland.'

'Sophie died?'

Nell nodded.

Tom let out a low whistle, 'Shit.'

'And that's why I need you to buy my bed.'

CHAPTER TWO

It was funny. There were so many things that Nell would never have done if she wasn't going to die. Sleeping with the guy that bought her bed was the latest.

There was something wonderfully liberating about not playing by society's rules, casting off any lingering inhibitions and just giving into any whim or urge that took your fancy. Liberating, and also a little seedy as straight afterwards he counted out eight ten-pound notes and left them on her bedside table before he set to work with a screwdriver to dismantle the bed, ready for the man with a van to pick up a few days later.

'It's been an unusual afternoon,' Tom said, as he wrapped a stripy scarf around his neck while she opened the latch on the front door to let him out.

Nell nodded, 'Yes.'

'I guess you have quite a few of those.' He blushed, suddenly realising how that sounded and quickly countered it with, 'I mean, spur of the moment things, carpe diem and all that. I don't mean that you do *this* often, I mean, you might, I'm not judging, each to their own, I just meant—'

Nell opened the door wide, 'Bye, Tom,' she smiled. 'Thank you for the last three orgasms of my life.'

'I wouldn't be so sure about that. You still have six days.'

'Bye Tom.'

Six days. Six nights. The problem with living like there's no tomorrow was that making plans wasn't one of Nell's fortes. Getting a bit bored of yoga in the Himalayan foothills? Check out immediately and head for a dance party on the beach in Pattaya. Wonder what life was like in the Brazilian rainforest? Stop sitting there and grab some mosquito repellent. The only thing that had ever stood between Nell and her latest flight of fancy was money, and she'd earned it in whatever legal way she could – pot-washing, cleaning, nannying, answering phones, driving an Uber, dressing up as an elf in a shopping mall at Christmas in Albuquerque (ending up there purely because the name had always appealed to her, and if she was being truthful, she thought New Mexico was the renovated part of Mexico).

She'd write a list. She'd never written a list before. She hunted for a pen. It hadn't been sold – yet – so there must be one around somewhere. Right, pen found, and some paper. *We are cooking with gas*, Nell thought with a satisfied smile as she sat down on the floor to compile her last ever bucket list.

Floorboards weren't meant for bottoms. They were meant for rugs and the feet of people and furniture. It had definitely been a mistake to sell the sofa so far in advance of moving out but Nell had honestly thought it could take a couple of weeks to get a buyer, it was third-hand already after all, had a small burn mark on one of its arms and was faded from direct sunlight on the other side, and the landlord was very clear the flat had to be completely empty when she gave the key back.

'When's your new one arriving?' the woman who picked it up said, taking in the empty lounge.

'I'm not getting a new one,' Nell replied. 'I don't need a sofa where I'm going.'

'Oh, is your new place fully furnished?'

'Something like that,' Nell smiled.

In hindsight, she should have sold it a few days later. She wasn't going to make the same mistake with her phone or clothes, she thought, as she sat on two folded up towels to stop getting even more splinters in her behind. The flat seemed really quiet. She'd sold the television earlier that morning. Not that she watched it much, after so long abroad she didn't have a clue who anyone was anyway and those she did recognise now had wrinkles decorating their faces and salt and pepper hair, which was very disconcerting. When she wasn't looking her family had got older too. That was the biggest shock moving back to England. Not the borders of towns that had swallowed up the countryside, nor the fact everything cost five times more than it did when she left. But them. Her sister was now a mum, her own mum was past retirement age, when did these things happen? She hadn't told her family she was back in the country; they'd have wanted to see her, and it would have been too hard saying goodbye knowing there wouldn't be a next time. She should have come back more when she could have done.

Nell sighed and looked around the sparse room. It had only been home for the last month so it wasn't as though she'd created many memories in it, but it represented the life she could have had, had she chosen to stay in one place, to put down roots. Would she have been happy, she wondered. With one job, one home, one partner? Getting bread from the same bakery, waving to the same neighbours, opening and closing the same front door every day?

Stop it, she told herself. *The past is gone. Think about the future while you still have one.* First thing she had to do was to go dancing. She loved dancing. Not the side-stepping, pointy fingers dancing her sister Polly did, but actual dancing, where the music flooded every cell of your body, and your eyes closed, and your limbs had a mind of their own. Admittedly, in the past, her limbs may well have been helped to achieve that level of liberation with a chemical boost, but that was the kind of dancing she wanted to do once more before next Monday. Monday. Why did she have to die on a Monday? It's such a nothing day. And it was December at the peak of flu-season so the undertakers were bound to be busy dealing with a backlog from the weekend.

Laughing. She wanted to laugh. Big ugly tear-wiping belly laughs.

Chicken chow mein. She definitely wanted one of those. She should make a menu of things she wanted to eat this week so she didn't waste a meal time having a microwave meal.

She should go and see her family. *Should should should.* She still had six days to make the pilgrimage down to the South coast and surprise them. She chewed her bottom lip imagining the reunion and smiled, then pictured the inevitable moment of leaving them and flicked the thought away. No, this week was not a week of goodbyes, it was a week of joy.

Nell turned on her phone to see what was happening in London for the rest of the week to help her plan it out. Tuesday was very quiet. No doubt pandering to all those still getting over the highs of the weekend. Looked like she'd have to stay in and stare at the space on the wall where the TV used to be. But thankfully it picked up from tomorrow onwards. She started scribbling down the names of clubs and comedy gigs she would spend the last week of her life going to. But for tonight, there was no shame in finishing off the last microwaveable meal in the freezer, it'd be a pity for it to go to waste, and the microwave was being picked up tomorrow morning. This chicken jalfrezi would be a last hurrah for it.

The comedy club the next evening was in a big room at the back of a pub in Balham, which took Nell to a part of London she hadn't ventured to before. Normally she relished unexplored terrain, and definitely wasn't a stranger to solo expeditions, but she suddenly realised, looking around at the people in the queue in front of her and snaking behind her, that she was the only one there by herself; everyone else was in couples or with friends. She had a sudden pang of loneliness, and almost stepped out of the queue and retraced her steps back to her flat. She *has* friends, she told herself sternly, they just weren't here. Her wide smile, her infectious enthusiasm for life, her hunger for new experiences made her a joyful companion for other people's brief adventures before they retreated to the real world. She had over 700 friends on Facebook who were scattered like confetti around the globe; she was tagged in photos from every continent, and yet, here she was, on a Wednesday evening, waiting to be let into a comedy club, where she would sit alone laughing. And suddenly she couldn't think of anything sadder.

The first comedian was okay, too many f-words for Nell's liking. Not that she was a prude, far from it, in fact she celebrated the use of a well-timed vulgarity, but this comedian managed to use the f-word as a verb, noun and adjective in the same sentence, which Nell thought was overkill. The second was marginally better, she managed to sniff-laugh, rather than belly-laugh, but a sniff-laugh was better than no laugh. She got up between this act and the next to get another beer, and was still paying for her drink at the bar at the back of the room when the next comedian came on.

'I went to buy a bed yesterday and ended up having the most incredible sex with the woman who sold it to me.'

Nell froze with her back still to the stage as the whole club around her roared with laughter, applause and wolf-whistles. Her body completely stiffened and she felt a rage start simmering in her stomach.

'Whoa, whoa, this isn't a look-how-virile-and-charming-I-am story, but thank you, I must admit, I do feel pretty charming and virile today. Although I think I've strained a muscle in my back. But it was totally worth it.'

More applause and whoops from the audience. Nell received her change back without even acknowledging the barman, her hand shaking with undisguised fury.

'This woman was incredible. Beautiful, I mean breathtakingly attractive, she had this mad curly hair that fizzed out at all angles, stunning green eyes and she was just cool, you know? It was the best afternoon I've had for years. I mean she must have been pretty amazing, I ended up paying eighty quid for a really crap bed that I can't fit in. So, what's the problem, I hear you ask?'

'So, what's the problem?' a man heckled near to Nell's right.

'Thank you sir, exactly, what is the problem? It's a great story to tell the grandkids, right? Wrong. This fabulous woman, the creature of my dreams, is going to die next week.'

The whole audience collectively gasped. Nell tightened her grasp on her beer bottle, she still hadn't turned around to face the stage, standing resolutely facing the bar instead.

'Now before you start judging me, having a one-night stand with someone on their deathbed, calm down, she's fine. The date of her death was predicted by a clairvoyant when she was a teenager, and she's lived her whole life believing it.

Which I'm quite pleased about because there's no way she would have shagged me if she didn't think she was going to die, so thank you Mrs Clairvoyant, you've done me a solid.'

More applause and whistles.

'But it did make me think, about life and how we live it. If you knew you only had a week to live, what would you do? I mean, for starters you wouldn't be in a room in the back of a pub in South London listening to a thirty-six-year-old bloke wax lyrical about having the best sex of his life, would you? You'd be having tea at The Ritz or scaling a mountain. Shearing a sheep. Painting a sunset.'

Nell had had enough. She'd stood there, seething, listening while Tom turned her life into a stand-up routine and strangers laughed at her. Well screw him, and screw them, she wasn't going to stand there for a minute longer. She slammed her bottle down on the steel-topped bar with such ferocity it made a massive clang, making everyone turn to the back to see the source. Tom paused in his routine and peered through the lights and the gloom to see what everyone was staring at. Nell didn't care, she strode to the exit, pushing past men, women, loudly scraping empty chairs across the floor.

'Something I said?' Tom laughed from the stage.

'Don't mind me,' Nell said loudly, making sure her voice reached the stage, just moments before the spotlight swivelled to illuminate her, making her wince in the bright light. 'I just remembered that I have to go and paint a sheep.'

It wasn't until later, as she sat on the tube heading home and the adrenalin and anger had filtered away that she realised what she'd said – *paint a sheep* – and did the first proper belly laugh of the evening, not giving a damn what anyone else on that train thought.

*

Tom called round two days later on Friday afternoon while she was out at The Ritz having afternoon tea. She had to thank him for the timely reminder that she'd never done that before. And it seemed fantastically fitting that she used his eighty pounds to pay for it. She did feel a bit bad because she had made a pledge to herself that all the money she raised from selling everything off would go to a local children's charity, but she reasoned if you couldn't indulge in a spot of self-love three days before your death, when could you? She'd had tea by herself plenty of times, lunches and dinners too, but the 'table for one' request definitely raised some eyebrows at The Ritz. And as she sat there, surrounded by couples and daughters with fathers, and sons with mothers, and friends and sisters, she found herself wishing she had someone to gush over the macarons with. Maybe not the macarons; it didn't matter how much she tried to like them, they were just colourful cardboard. But if they were there, her mum, and sister Polly, in these plush surroundings with Nell, it would have been awkward and tense. Polly would bat barbed comments her way the whole time about Nell being the prodigal child while her mum would make all the right noises and nods but have half an eye on her watch and half a mind on avoiding the rush hour traffic. They'd both exchange knowing glances when Nell would ask for soy or almond milk with her tea, while inwardly thinking how travel had made her uppity.

Once she had run through that scenario in her head, she was much happier being alone. And as the afternoon wore on, she realised that the glances from other diners that she assumed were ones of pity, were actually ones of envy – absolute unfiltered jealousy at being able to enjoy the tray of treats in peace. By the end of it, she was enjoying herself so much she even finished the macarons.

The note was pinned to her front door when she got back.

I'm an idiot. You are lovely. Please let me take you out for your last supper. Tom

She tore it down, screwed it up, walked across the road where there was a skip in a neighbour's driveway and threw it in among the rubbish before brushing her hands off and heading back inside to change into her dancing clothes.

On her last couple of days before D-Day, Nell was rushed off her feet. She had to take the final few bits and bobs lying around the house to the charity shop, hand back her key to the landlord, cancel her phone contract, shut down her bank account, tell the council she'd moved out, get her roots done – 'no, not going away on holiday this year' – use the last remaining points on her Tesco clubcard, and write the damn letters.

She'd been putting this off for weeks, but it was the final step in cleansing her mind and closing the door on this crazy life, so she knew she had to do it. It had started with just the one to her mum, thanking her for all her love and support and apologising for being absent when she should have been present.

I didn't know how to love you, and then leave you, so I just stayed away. You can't miss what you never see. But you deserved more. And I'm sorry. I also couldn't bear to see you broken after Dad left. You've always been so strong Mum, and I want you to know that you can be again. You don't need to be with a man to be happy, you are enough.

Wiping away her tears, Nell knew she now needed to write the one that would make her angry, not emotional. *Dear Dad*, she started, pressing her pen down with such force the nib was in danger of snapping clean off. *Goodbye you selfish fuckwit.* Yes, that was good, thought Nell. It said everything she needed it to. But was it how she wanted to be remembered? Probably not. It did mean that honesty would be her legacy, but definitely at the expense of eloquence and compassion. She started again on another sheet.

Dear Dad, While I can't always understand your life choices, I do recognise the fact that they were yours to make. To use an analogy I hope you'll understand, when you tee off with someone aiming for the fairway, you may well hit the rough, but it's very poor form to abandon them in the middle of the forest in order to get to the green with someone from another team. Not to mention riding off in the golf buggy with your new buddy towards the clubhouse while your original partner languishes in the dark wood before dying heartbroken and alone. Just a thought. Speaking of dying, by the time you read this, I will have done. You were a really excellent dad for the first thirty years of my life, before you started playing golf.

Yes, that was perfect. A little obtuse, but not rude, and she figured that her dad would get the metaphor. If he didn't then, at least she'd given him some sporting advice. Her sister was next, and this was the one that was bothering her the most. How confessional could she be? This was the biggest secret she was carrying, and she couldn't go to her grave with it still buzzing round her head like an annoying malaria-laden mosquito ready to cause untold damage at any point in the future. But then, if she exploded the secret now, that would do immediate damage. Nell tapped the pen on the table as she considered all the options.

Dear Polly, Darling Polly. My partner in crime, my best friend for our entire childhood. My goodbye to you is probably the hardest one I have to make because I honestly thought that we'd be old women together, but the universe had other plans for us. I see how you are with Bea when we video call and it makes my heart burst. You're such a great mum and I'm so proud of you and I'm so sad that I won't be around to see her grow up. I don't know how to say this next part without blowing your whole world apart, but I'm your sister, and I love you and so I have to. It's about your husband.

When Nell finished writing that letter her heart hurt, but her head felt clearer. Had she changed the order of the letters she was writing, she might not have poured quite so much into the final two she had left to write, but after the depressing revelations of the last two letters, Nell needed to end on a high.

Dear Greg, It's been nearly twenty years since I wrote those two words, the last time I think was in your Christmas card that I wrote but never gave you, in which I told you that you were my soulmate and I couldn't wait to spend the rest of my life with you. I meant every word of that, and had it not been for this cruel twist of fate, we would hopefully be blissfully happy still now. I have thought of you every day since we were eleven.

Was that too much, Nell wondered. It wasn't strictly true, he'd flitted into her mind once a month or so in the last few years, but only when she'd met another Greg or heard their song on the radio, but that didn't have the same gravitas.

Who knows, had things been different, we might still be adventuring together; you were, quite simply, the love of my life.

It did feel slightly disingenuous to write something along the same lines to another man, but in the spirit of cleansing mind and body, purging it of all unsaid thoughts, it had to be done. Something about the earnestness of the note he'd pinned to her door had been bothering her over the last day or so; his apology seemed really genuine, and after replaying his comedy set back in her mind, she realised he had actually been pretty complimentary about her.

Tom, hello from heaven. Or hell. It's a 50/50 which one I ended up in. It's an odd thing, writing the last letter I will ever write to someone I only met a week ago and spent the grand total of three hours with. But I guess that's yet another example of how your life can change in a moment if you're open to it. I really liked you, Tom, and felt that we had a real connection. Despite you turning my life into material for your show, you have kind eyes and a kind soul, and had things been different, I would have liked to look into them both a bit more. And, you were right, the sex was incredible. Your path crossing with mine six days before I died was one of fate's crueller twists. Live life to the fullest my friend, and see you on the other side, when maybe we could start again from where we left off. . .

She popped all five envelopes into the post box outside the Co-op, opting for second-class stamps so they would definitely arrive on the relevant doormats after her death and then shut down all her social media accounts. She decided against leaving a final post on each one; she briefly considered leaving an enigmatic one of a sun setting, but she'd posted so many of those in the past it might have been too cryptic to decipher and people would just think she was off on her travels again. So, she did with her social media what she'd so often done at parties, and just slipped away without fanfare.

CHAPTER THREE

The tealights were causing Nell something of a dilemma. On the one hand, dying by candlelight was absolutely something she would like to do, but then again, dying *because* of candlelight absolutely was not. And the hotel had not scrimped on fabric in this suite. It had taken Nell at least four minutes of what was left of her life to remove all the cushions and bolsters from the bed. There was even a throw on top of the throw. She wondered if she should light the candles now, far away from the curtains, fourteen cushions and deep-pile rugs, wallow in the lovely ambiance for a bit, then when she saw the white light coming for her, she could quickly blow them out. She'd hate to be the cause of the whole hotel going up in smoke. It was bad enough that they were going to have to deal with a dead body tomorrow, dealing with fire departments and insurance companies for months on end really wouldn't be fair on them. Not to mention the risk to others; she'd seen families with young kids checking in at the same time as she did. She sighed. She should have brought electric candles. Next time.

Next time, Nell scoffed. There wasn't going to be a next

time of anything after tonight. She'd even just finished her last meal. Vegetarian quesadillas. It wasn't her first choice if she was being honest; whenever she'd watched a true crime documentary about death-row inmates, she'd always conjured up a mouth-watering pyramid of prawns as hers, but it was a well-known fact that seafood caused the most food poisoning episodes, and curled up in a ball on the bathroom floor leaking from both ends was definitely not the way she wanted to go. For that reason, anything involving chicken was out too. Or cream. She also didn't want to die choking, so all hard textures and windpipe-sized options were eliminated too, leaving her with either the quesadillas or a club sandwich, and she just couldn't bring herself to order a sandwich for her last ever meal on earth, she might as well have packed a loaf of Hovis and a packet of wafer-thin ham and saved herself the money. It wasn't until she'd finished her last supper that she realised that quesadillas were basically a Mexican sandwich and she felt a pang of disappointment in her choice.

Not knowing how it was going to happen was the worst thing. She had assumed it'd be a heart attack or a stroke in her sleep. But she'd had angiograms and CT scans, and every part of her body prodded, poked and photographed – inside and out – and she was in perfect health, despite having never taken a multivitamin; there was no point when you've known the date that you're going to die for nineteen years. And that day was today.

She'd had nineteen years to prepare for the perfect death and despite beaches, forests and meadows all being considered as the location of choice at one time or another, a deluxe river-view suite at a top London hotel won out in the end. She'd also chosen glamour for her attire. Nothing screamed a life well lived more than being found in an expensive hotel room wearing a designer ballgown. The rented dress was covered in thousands of hand-sewn beads and had a hula hoop sewn into its hem. It was extravagant, over the top, and would absolutely have gone down a storm at the Met Gala, and it certainly raised quite a few eyebrows at the reception downstairs when Nell checked in wearing it. It weighed almost more than Nell did, was utterly impractical, and yet she loved every centimetre of it. She'd made sure to pin the name and address of the company she hired it from inside the dress's hem so it would find its way back to them tomorrow.

She caught sight of herself in the mirrored doors of the wardrobe and did a little twirl. Then realised with a jolt that she'd never actually owned her own wardrobe. Wardrobes didn't fit into suitcases, and they also suggested ownership of crease-able clothes which she had deliberatively swerved ever buying, which made her realise that an iron was an item she'd never purchased either. Now she came to think of it, there were loads of everyday things that she'd never had reason to buy: vacuum cleaners – she'd never lived anywhere with carpet before being in London, just tiles, and her last rented flat had one provided by the landlord; lawnmowers – she'd had gardens, a lovely handkerchief-sized pocket of grass in Phuket and a larger one in Ubud in Bali, but for the cost of a smile and a plate of her legendary Rocky Road her neighbours always let her borrow their mowers. She wouldn't say that her life had been the poorer for not having wardrobes, irons, vacuum cleaners and lawnmowers in it, but they were all part of the 'should own' list, especially by the age of thirty-eight.

'Should' was the word Nell despised the most. It was loaded with expectation, of judgement. You *should* be settled down by your age, you *should* start putting down roots, you *should* call your mum more. She wondered if there were any countries where the notion of 'should-ness' didn't exist – if there were, she *should* have moved there.

Nell lay back on the bed looking up at the ceiling. There was no damp patch, so a bathtub from the room above was unlikely to crash through the ceiling and squash her, and the chandelier wasn't positioned over the bed, so that wasn't going to fall on her in her sleep either. This wasn't mentioned on the hotel website, but annoyingly there was a big mirror positioned right above the bed, which was odd as it really didn't seem like *that* type of hotel, but it also meant that when the moment of her demise did come, she'd have to remember to shut her eyes because she really wouldn't want to see it. She also hoped it was screwed in well, or it could be that which ended her.

Seriously, how might it happen? It was driving her mad. She had no intention of leaving this room, so it couldn't be a traffic accident and she had unplugged all the appliances so electric fires were also out. Not knowing was impacting even the simplest decisions, like whether she should have a shower or a bath. She was veering towards the former in case she drowned, although she would say that she was pretty adept at not drowning in baths, but there was a first time for everything and sod's law would suggest today would be the day for her to forget how to bathe. Although there was a large glass jar of fresh rose petals next to the bath, ready to be scattered on the water that looked glorious and sorely tempted her to turn the taps on. But the bathtub was a Jacuzzi, with hundreds of little jets, and while none of them were large enough to suck her into a drainage vortex, they were certainly the size of a toe or finger, which definitely had the potential to cause a fatal accident. Nell once did a history project at school on parish registers, and people did die of very strange things. 'Burned by beer', was one that stuck in her memory, as was 'killed by a corner', which threw up all sorts of questions. One unfortunate soul, aged just forty-four, died of 'stoppage' and, as she didn't know what that was, couldn't deliberately avoid it, so stoppage was still firmly in play too.

After her shower and back in her dress, she walked to the window, being careful not to get too close. She didn't want to smash through it and fall all seven storeys to the busy London street below. She pulled back the curtain and looked out. Cars, people, noise, life. Hundreds of people just merrily going about their lives, planning what to eat tonight, what movie to see tomorrow, which friends to see at the weekend, where to spend Christmas in a couple of weeks' time, where to go on holiday next summer. Time just stretching ahead of each of them as they lazily traversed through their days, completely unaware that planning tomorrow's movie might be a complete waste of time. Across the skyline she saw the London Eye slowly rotate, filled with tourists box-ticking their city-break itinerary. She'd read somewhere that there'd been more than 5,000 proposals on the London Eye. Was one happening now? At this exact moment were two people so sure that there was no one better for them in the entire world that they'd agree to walk the rest of their days side by side?

She envied them. She envied their ease of living. She envied their certainty that next July it would be a week in Santorini, followed by a fortnight in Thailand the year after – give them more time to save, made sense. She envied the couples that planned to have kids, 'In five years or so, once we have a bigger house.' She envied the long engagements, the investment in hobbies, the putting down of roots, the making of plans, but most of all, she envied the ones who weren't alone.

'Are you absolutely sure that you wouldn't like me to be with you?' Hayley had asked when she called two days earlier for their last goodbye before Nell sold her phone and gave the money to charity. Sharing that moment in Australia as teens, going through Sophie's death together and bonding over the horrible realisation that the prediction was true had cemented their friendship and they'd regularly met up over the years in weird and wonderful locations.

'Absolutely. Look, it's not as though this is unexpected,' Nell said. 'I'm not scared or anything, it is what it is. I've had a massive life. Much bigger than most. And now it has to end.'

'We could watch movies all night and get really drunk.'

'Alcohol kills around 25,000 people in England every year,' Nell recited. She knew the statistics for most, if not all, accidents and misadventures. She was a risk assessor's dream.

'Anyway,' Nell continued, 'if you're with me, you'll get stung with the hotel bill, so I won't choose the most expensive room if I know you'll have to pay for it, I'll choose the standard twin in a hotel next to a motorway or something, and that doesn't have the same ring to it. I want to do it this way.'

Hayley sighed. 'Fine then. But if you change your mind you need to let me know by tomorrow lunchtime for me to get on a plane on time.'

'I won't, but thank you.'

'And you're sure they'll do a Zoom link for the funeral?'

'Yep, it's all there in the pack I prepared.'

'Okay. Bye chick. See you on the other side in a couple of years. Love you.'

This goodbye was the hardest to say. Nell didn't know if it was because Hayley was the only one who got it. She was there when they were told; she believed it too. She knew that this was her fate, no one else had even said goodbye or good luck or expressed any type of emotion at all about it because they fully expected her to wake up tomorrow and have a good laugh about the fact that she'd spent twenty years prepping herself for a non-event.

Well, this would show them.

CHAPTER FOUR

Nell had now been in this hotel suite for thirty-five hours, and largely awake for the majority of them. She'd wanted to check in and be prepared from the time Sydney tick-tocked into the sixteenth, just in case Mandy's prediction referred to antipodean timing. It didn't appear it did, as Australia was now firmly into 17 December and Nell was still alive. Knackered, but alive. So, it must have been England's timing, which made more sense. It was now 7 p.m., only five hours left to go. The dress was a bit scratchy if she was being honest, and more than once she'd wondered if this dress might actually end up being the death of her, which would be a level of irony she'd yet to experience. A bruise was already forming on her left thigh after falling into the bidet trying to lift the dress up to have a wee and she'd never known a bout of hiccups to be painful before, but the corset was restricting her ribcage so much every hiccup had her wincing in pain. And she couldn't even loosen it as it had a zip at the side and not just laces down the back. Her boobs, however, looked astonishing. She sighed. First the quesadillas let her down and now this. But she was determined to be found in this dress, so she persevered.

She turned on the television. No point watching a soap in case it ended on a cliff-hanger. Home and garden makeover shows held zero appeal for her, always had done as she moved from short-term rental to short-term rental. She watched about ten minutes of a football match between Arsenal and a random Spanish side before flicking over to a re-run of an American sitcom she used to follow when she lived there, but the jokes didn't seem so funny and the canned laughter masquerading as the audience was actually quite annoying. She flicked the television off and threw the remote onto the bed beside her. She picked up the other remote, the one that controlled the blackout curtains for the windows and pressed the arrow pointing right. They whirred into action, slowly blocking out London. She pressed the arrow left then, making the city once again come into view, and alternated her thumb over the two arrows for a while, *first you see it, now you don't*, which took care of another four minutes or so.

Eight p.m. She yawned. She'd had to replace the tealights twice as they'd burned themselves out, thank goodness she'd bought the big bag. Winter berries. It smelled like Christmas, which was ironic because she'd deliberately written in the 'special requests' part of the online booking form for the hotel that she didn't want any Christmas decorations in the suite, and it was testament to quite how much this suite was costing that the hotel acquiesced and dutifully removed the garlands and ornaments that had taken the housekeeping team hours to put up a couple of weeks before. It's not that Nell didn't like Christmas, she did, but a patent reminder that she wouldn't see the one that the decorations were put out for was understandably too much.

Would her mum still celebrate it this year, she wondered. She had only spent a handful of Christmases with her in nearly twenty years, so it wasn't as though there'd be a Nell-shaped hole at the Christmas table or a stocking with her name on it hanging on the fireplace. She'd never been upset or disappointed when Nell had sent an email saying she couldn't come home this year from Indonesia or Polynesia or Nova Scotia – that was a weird Christmas, she'd taken a three-month contract with a live lobster export firm, and rather than working in the office, where she thought she'd be, it had been her job to wrap their claws up before packing them in crates. She'd apologised to every one of them while doing it. The guilt was too much in the end so she only lasted two weeks but then was stranded there for Christmas so celebrated it with her former colleagues, and the only thing on the dinner table was lobster. She hadn't eaten it since. They'd always had turkey growing up. Other people said that turkey was dry and tasteless, but her mum used to faff around for hours with brining buckets and marinades and it was absolutely delicious. Now *that* would have made a great last supper.

Nell had felt like she should go back home for the first Christmas after her dad had left, and it was the most depressing few days. Her mum still bought the magazines with the ideas for Christmas crafts and lavish garland arches in them, but the only concession to Christmas she ended up making was using the posh tablecloth and putting crackers on the plates. Nell realised now that she could have helped her spruce the house up a bit. She had a holly bush in the front garden, there was nothing stopping Nell from nipping out in her slippers and slicing a few stems off it, but she didn't. She just sat inside looking at the same fake tree they'd had for years feeling more than a little disappointed with her mum's lack of enthusiasm, making so little dispensation to how difficult it must have been for her mum to just get up on that day, let alone pull a cracker. Why did it never occur to her to come home and keep her mum company each Christmas since that first one? All those years Nell had spent Christmas around a table with strangers while her mum spent the day alone watching re-runs on television and eating leftover turkey from a Tupperware for days. It was hard thinking about it, feeling the familiar pull of family on the one hand and the persistent tug for pleasure and adventure on the other.

In some ways Mandy's prediction opened the world up to Nell and gave her an excuse to opt out. She'd often thought about what her life would have been like if she hadn't been told this. If she and Greg had never heard of Mandy, or sought her out. She'd have returned from her gap year; the tan would have faded along with her newly discovered zest and she'd have lived the rest of her life with that gap year being the most exciting thing about her. *'I spent a year abroad when I was eighteen.' 'You never did?' 'I did.' 'Gosh, how exciting.' 'It was.'*

Thinking about Christmases past was making her feel sad, so she blew out all the tealights and instead lit the candles the hotel had provided. They were the posh ones with the white and black labels and little black ribbons tied around them. She looked at the label, Lime and Basil. She breathed the scent in. Fresh, citrussy and herby. Not festive in the slightest. No memories or regrets conjured up at all. That'd do.

She had promised herself that she wouldn't do this: second guess every life decision at the eleventh hour. Or – she looked at the clock – eighth and a half hour. *It is what it is.* She'd made her choices. *I am what I am.* Gloria Gaynor suddenly popped into her head, unannounced, but actually very welcome and timely too. Music. She needed music. That's what was missing from this moment. If she was going to pass through the pearly gates imminently, she needed music to get her there, well, not get her there, but accompany her there. Had anyone died through listening to music, she wondered. Maybe if it was loud enough. She put the volume dial midway, on fifteen, just to be safe. The hotel was so fancy it even had its own iPad with Spotify on it, so Nell spent the next hour working her way through every Seventies soul, funk and Motown classic she could, occasionally veering into rock and roll territory, but the dress prohibited any twisting and shaking, so she reverted to just jumping, while hoping the room below was vacant. This dress was definitely going to need a good dry clean; she felt bad that she'd given away all her money and wished that she had twenty quid left to pin to the note to pay a bit towards it.

At some point during the danceathon, she'd opened the mini bar. She actually didn't know why it had taken her so long having looked at it longingly for the last thirty-seven hours – perhaps the death-by-alcohol statistics that she knew by heart had stopped her. But a couple of units to loosen her up wouldn't hurt. She'd tried for years to like whiskey, and her persistence had paid off a couple of years ago in India, where everyone seemed to drink it and Nell thought it rude to say no. Thinking back to the morning after that first night of whiskey where any movement made her eyeballs burn, she probably should have said no, but as far as hard liquor went, moderation was key, so Nell limited herself to four of the little bottles in the hotel mini bar. And one of those half bottles of champagne, because why the hell not.

Breathless and bone-achingly tired, Nell collapsed back onto the bed. That was fun. She yawned and looked again at the clock. Ten-thirty. Potentially an hour and a half left. There was always the chance that Mandy was referring to West Coast American timing, which would give her an extra eight hours. That was unlikely, but not impossible. Perhaps the person before Nell into the mystic garage was Californian and Mandy simply hadn't adjusted her internal time clock. There was no actual way that Nell could stay awake for another nine and half hours. She was starting to see double she was so tired, although that could have been the alcohol. Anyway, she thought, if she had another nine and half hours, she could afford to close her eyes for a little bit, and still have a few hours left when she woke up to Seize the Day and Live Life Large and all those other life-grabbing maxims. She yawned again, and gradually went to sleep, slowly mumbling, *I am what I am.*

CHAPTER FIVE

Heaven was louder than Nell expected. Less harp and more drone. Like an engine of a hovercraft, or a lawn mower. Or a vacuum cleaner. Yes, a vacuum cleaner, knocking against skirting boards. But why would heaven have skirting boards? Of course, there was always the option she could be in hell, a place she'd never really entertained the idea of, but listening to this incessant throb interspersed with sharp bangs every few seconds would definitely be a form of torture.

She gingerly opened her eyes, expecting to be hit with either the blinding light of white clouds or the blazing orange of the other place, but it was completely dark. Maybe she was trapped in the halfway holding house while they went through her files. No doubt the one time she slipped two magazines through the self-service till but only paid for one would count against her. As would the time she told the *Big Issue* seller she didn't have any change only to spend three pounds fifty on a caramel latte a few minutes later. In her defence she did already have that month's issue, but a lie was a lie. But then there was that goat she liberated from being slaughtered by opening the back gate of the small yard her hostel room overlooked in Oman. It was the eve of Eid Al Adha and the whole city of Muscat was alive with the bleats of the animals experiencing their last days. Nell bet that their last meals were more exciting than a sandwich. Next door's goat had a heart-shaped black splodge on its back and she'd watched it for hours out of her first-floor window until on the spur of the moment she crept downstairs, unlatched the back gate and smiled in joy as it gambolled to freedom down the moonlit street. That must be a tick in the heaven column surely. Thinking about it though, that may have been construed as wanton theft or destruction of property. . . But you definitely couldn't argue about the selfless philanthropy of the well-building project she'd been involved in a few years ago in Burkina Faso. It took months for the blisters on her hands to heal. Only good vibes there. And as long as the guards on the pearly gates didn't examine that the motive behind her staying in Africa three months longer than she'd planned to was the incredible jawline of Sebastian, the mission leader, then she was all good.

God, was she really a horrible person? She guessed God would tell her that soon enough.

Purgatory did smell nice though, which hell wouldn't. Less rotting corpses and barbecues and more citrussy, and what else? She took a big sniff in, wrinkling her nose up, some sort of herb maybe. Lime and Basil. *Lime and Basil*. Nell suddenly lunged to her right, not actually knowing whether she wanted the bedside cabinet to still be there or not. Her hand flapped around in the dark like a desperate fish washed up on a beach until it knocked something onto the floor. The remote for the curtains. No, no, no, no. People didn't need remotes in heaven. Without missing a beat, Nell reached down to retrieve it, fumbling with the buttons, pressing all of them until the monotonous hum of the electric curtains accompanied bright shafts of light bathing the plush suite in offensive sunshine.

This wasn't heaven.

She didn't die.

She didn't die.

She didn't die!

Her breathing was ragged as her thoughts raced. She was alive. She'd survived the night. She turned the TV quickly on to check the clock on it: 10.30 a.m., 17 December. It was definitely tomorrow. In every time zone. And this was definitely earth. Catching sight of herself in the mirror above the bed, she took a sharp intake of breath; she was definitely still wearing a rented three-thousand-pound ballgown that definitely wasn't designed for daytime.

'Housekeeping,' came a voice from the other side of the door, followed by a sharp rap on the wood. Nell froze. This wasn't meant to happen. Housekeeping was meant to unlock the door, find her laid out serenely against the feather-filled pillows and the million-thread Egyptian cotton sheets, pause for a quiet moment of reflection and then alert her family who would have felt so bad that they never took the premonition seriously. The hotel would have given the poor unsuspecting cleaner the rest of the day off and in time, this would have been a regular anecdote to tell and retell among their friends.

'Housekeeping. Madam, are you there? You have missed your check-out time.'

Ordinarily the irony of that statement would have had Nell howling with laughter, loving, as she did, a good pun more than the next person, but she was stunned into silence, laid out on the bed, frozen to the spot, her eyes wide and unblinking at her reflection on the ceiling. The sound of a key in the lock broke the trance and catapulted Nell into action. She sprang off the bed, tucking one of her breasts

41

back inside the evening gown just in time as a cleaner and what Nell guessed to be one of the management team came into the bedroom. One look at the lady whose job it was to service her room made relief flood through Nell that she was finding her very much alive. This woman must have been about eighty and the shock may well have pushed her into joining Nell on the other side sooner rather than later.

'Terribly sorry to interrupt, Ms Graham, but check-out time is ten o' clock, and I'm afraid we need to prepare your room for another guest.'

'Gosh, I'm so sorry,' Nell gushed, immediately leaning down and picking up her handbag from the floor, suddenly acutely aware of the optics of bringing nothing but a near-empty clutch to a hotel for a two-night stay. 'I must have overslept, if you could just allow me a few minutes to, um, get changed, and pack my things that would be great.' She sounded very convincing, as though a whole wardrobe of clothes and bathroom of toiletries were just waiting to be packed into one of her numerous invisible suitcases.

The manager smiled. 'Of course. I will go and prepare your bill now. See you downstairs shortly.'

'Take your time, madam,' the housekeeper whispered kindly making Nell's relief levels soar even more, 'I have three other rooms to do before yours.'

As soon as they left the panic set in. She had nothing to change into, no money or card to settle the bill with, and a quick desperate peer out of the seventh-floor window confirmed what she already suspected, no means of escape.

She should call someone.

But she had no phone.

The hotel had a phone.

The only number she knew off by heart was her mum's landline.

Was that odd, not knowing anyone else's number off by heart?

That did sound odd, most people had a few friends' numbers memorised.

Life's too short to memorise numbers.

Nell shook her head, trying to physically dispel the familiar mantra that had governed the last twenty years of her life. She quickly dialled her mum's home phone in Hove. It rang three times and clicked onto the answer machine.

Nell slammed the phone down. Dammit. Dammit. How was she going to do this? How the hell could she sneak out of the hotel, without paying, while wearing a bright purple ballgown wider than the average doorway, that announced its arrival through the sound of swooshing fabric a fair few seconds before the body wearing it materialised? She had no idea, but had no choice other than to give it a go.

Nell wished her dress was quieter as she ran barefoot down the corridor, passing an older gentleman who winked and said, 'Good party?'

She skidded to a halt and replied, 'Absolutely smashing, thank you,' before slowly walking off whistling. Once he was out of sight she quickened her pace, gathering up her skirt and running. She paused before every corner, flattening her back against the wall and gingerly peering round it to see if the coast was clear. The theme tune to *Mission Impossible* popped into her head and she couldn't help herself momentarily playing the role of a beautiful, albeit overdressed, assassin on a submarine. She stopped short of making a gun out of her fingers as she stopped before another corner, which was fortunate as the bedroom door Nell was leaning against suddenly opened behind her, making her stumble backwards into the arms of another housekeeper.

'Can I help you, madam?'

'No, thank you, thank you, all good. You do a great job by the way, thank you for the chocolate on my pillow. Lovely touch.'

The stairs would be a much safer choice than the lift that opened with a grand 'ping' straight into the cavernous entrance lobby. Her hair was wild around her shoulders; she hadn't brought a hairbrush with her, mainly because she no longer owned one, dropping it into an ironically named 'bag for life' along with her last few items of clothing, her toothbrush and toothpaste, a half-full pack of sanitary pads and the last book she read (she had to skip a few chapters to make sure she got to the end by Saturday) and she gave the bag to a homeless lady outside the tube station, who seemed delighted with most of its contents and tipped the ones she wasn't pleased with into a bin next to her before Nell's back was even turned.

She reached the stairwell, still carrying her shoes in her hands. She had a flashback of a moment eerily similar more than two decades earlier, sneaking out of Greg's hotel room after their lower sixth ball and back to her own bed before her parents noticed she was missing. Her dress was far cheaper and skimpier then, but the gripping fear of being caught was exactly the same.

She ran down the stairs, jumping the bottom three steps on each stretch. She'd just passed the sign for level three when Nell heard voices in the stairwell below her, a female upper-class, cut-glass accent bemoaning the lack of fresh watermelon juice at breakfast, then a deeper male voice telling his companion that he'd definitely mention it on the TripAdvisor review. She stopped, deliberating whether to run back up the stairs or continue down them, meeting the pair on the landing below. Their voices were getting louder now. She had about five seconds to make a choice. She smoothed her hair down as much as she could, took a deep breath, lifted her chin up, stuck her boobs out, puffed out the voluminous evening gown and glided down the stairs as though it was the most natural scenario in the world.

'Good morning,' Nell shrilled at them in a manner that she hoped would make the couple feel that they were decidedly underdressed for this time of day.

'Morning,' the woman returned with a pinched smile. The man just nodded. Nell had got about three paces past them before hearing her name called.

'Nell? Nell Graham?'

Nell turned slowly back around. The man clearly knew her, but she couldn't place him at all. Tall, thin, good-looking but with a pale pallor to his skin, he could have been anywhere from forty to fifty judging from the eye-bags under his eyes. Smartly dressed in a black suit with a grey tie, he certainly didn't look like anyone she would know. Most of the men she'd spent time around barely owned closed-toe shoes, let alone the shiny leather lace-ups this man was sporting. In fact, apart from the hotel manager she'd just spoken to, and Tom, she couldn't remember the last time she had a conversation with a man who didn't have long hair and a beard.

The woman tugged at his arm. 'Come on Greg, we're going to be late.'

'Greg?' Nell replied incredulously. 'Greg Gage? My Greg?' She did not just say *my* Greg out loud.

The woman tightened her grip on the man's arm. '*Your* Greg?'

Oh God, she did.

Greg's face erupted into life, his smile wide and instantly familiar to Nell as he gasped, 'Jesus, Nell, how on earth are you?'

'Oh my God, Greg, last time I saw you, you had long hair and a beard.'

45

He touched his clean-shaven chin with his hand and gave it a rub, 'Yeah, it's been a while since I had that. You haven't changed though,' he laughed, taking in the full magnificent ensemble in front of him. 'But then life's too short to not wear ballgowns on a Tuesday morning, isn't it Nell?' he said winking at her and laughing.

'There's a funny story about that actually—' Nell started but the woman cradling Greg's arm with such a ferocity it was a wonder he still had feeling in it, interrupted her with a deliberate cough.

'Oh, Nell, this is Daisy Ashford, my—'

Nell winced as he finished his sentence with 'colleague' at the exact same time Daisy said 'girlfriend'. That was unfortunate. Daisy's grip on Greg's arm was decidedly looser now.

Greg ploughed on. 'Daisy, Nell and I went to school together. God, it must be nearly twenty years.'

'Eighteen. To the day.' Nell replied, her words casting a shadow over the hallway as they both remembered the last time they saw each other. He'd stood in the doorway of the flat they shared, between her university in York and his in Leeds. He stood there shaking his head as she rushed around unpinning her posters off the walls and taking her drying underwear off the hall radiator to push them in the top of her rucksack, both still reeling from the night before. They shouldn't have opened the third bottle of wine. Bad things happened when a third bottle was in play. What started off as a joke, toasting the date she would one day die, turned into vague melancholy by the second bottle but morphed into desperate moroseness by the third. Everything he'd said made it worse.

'Come on Nell,' he'd said. 'Cheer up, either it won't happen and you'll waste the next eighteen years thinking about it, or it will, and you'll have wasted the last eighteen years of your life thinking about it!'

'You can't possibly understand!' she shouted. 'You're going to live forever, you have no idea what it's like to have a stopwatch hanging over your head counting down the days.'

'You're crazy,' he said, shaking his head. 'You've lost the plot. You're actually insane. You're going to throw away your life because of what some weirdo said to you?'

'But Sophie—'

'Sophie made her own stupid choices that had nothing to do with the prediction. You can't base the way you live your own life on the mistakes that she made.'

'You can't know that for sure, what if it didn't matter what she did that day?'

'It wouldn't have happened if she had just laid low that day,' Greg said angrily.

'But if it was always going to happen,' Nell countered.

'It wasn't always going to happen!' Greg exclaimed. 'How many healthy twenty-year-olds die while reading a book in bed? None. How many die from flinging themselves off high cliffs? Considerably more. It had nothing to do with dying on a specific date some random woman predicted, but everything to do with taking risks and being stupid just to prove a stupid point, stupid, stupid, stupid girl.' Greg sunk onto the bed. 'She was a stupid girl. What a waste. What a fucking waste.'

'But what if—'

Greg shook his head furiously, 'I'm not going to stand by watching you do this to yourself. I love you. I love you so much it makes me so angry to see you ruin your life over this. I'm not prepared to spend the next eighteen years listening to you talk about this and watching it eat away at you.'

'What, so you're going to leave me?' she retaliated, her eyes flashing.

'No. I'll never leave you. I want you to stay with me forever, but I can't go through my life hearing you torture yourself with this rubbish. If you stay, I never want to talk about this again. This date means nothing. It's just another day in the year. We won't talk about it; we won't even think about it. It's nothing to us. We'll carry on with our lives, we'll get married, we'll have children—' He put up his hand then to stem the retort he knew would be coming soon. It always came whenever the subject of children came up, that Nell didn't want them because of leaving them without a mother, of it being too hard to go.

'If you stay, that's it, Nell. This has to stop.'

'I can't,' Nell said quietly, sadly. 'It's all I think about.'

'Don't you want to be free of it? To say today that that's it, and you won't think about it again?'

'Of course I do, I wish we'd never seen her! But now I know, I can't just forget about it. And if you can't understand that, then. . .' she slowly breathed out, realising the enormity of what she was about to say. 'Maybe we should go our separate ways.'

Greg shook his head in disbelief. 'You're really choosing some random woman's nonsense over us?'

'I believe her Greg, I absolutely believe that I'm going to die in eighteen years' time, and I know that's going to affect every decision I make from this moment to then.' Any hint or sign of uncertainty in what she was saying had gone, replaced with a sad, but honest realisation of the truth. 'You're going to live for another eighty years Greg, eighty years!' She took his hands in hers and looked straight into his eyes. 'You need to find a wonderful woman to grow old with, to raise a family, you'll even get to meet your great grandchildren! That's incredible, and I'm happy for you, but I won't.' Her voice started cracking, 'By the time you join me on the other side, I'll have been there for more than sixty years!'

Greg's eyes had filled with tears, which he made no attempt to brush away as it would mean letting go of her hands. 'So that's it? After everything we've been through, that's it?'

Nell nodded, pulling him closer for one last hug before their paths, which had been running side by side for nearly a decade, suddenly took them in opposite directions.

Recognition dawned on Greg's face as the three of them stood in the hotel's stairwell.

'You didn't die,' he said finally. 'It was meant to be yesterday, wasn't it?'

'I didn't die,' Nell repeated.

'So, this is the first day of the rest of your life?' Greg said. 'Well, you're certainly dressed for it.'

CHAPTER SIX

Daisy was clucking next to Greg. Actually clucking with her tongue, as though Greg was a pony she was trying to break in but he'd stubbornly stalled and she was attempting to get him to move. 'It's been lovely to meet you, Nell.' Her face was saying the opposite. 'But we are already late for the conference, so we really must be going.'

She pulled on Greg's arm so hard it almost came out of his shoulder socket.

'Sorry to hold you up, you should go,' Nell said apologetically, stepping away from them. 'It was nice to see you again.'

'Wait, wait, I can miss the first session. Daisy, why don't you go on ahead, I'll message Gareth and tell him I'll be along later.'

It's lucky Nell was evidently immortal because the look Daisy gave her before striding away would have struck a weaker woman down dead on the spot.

'God, this is insane,' Greg said once Daisy had gone, running his hand through his now cropped hair. Nell remembered braiding his hair; it was so thick she used a whole pack of thirty hair bands on it once.

'Shall we get a coffee down in the lounge?'

Nell hesitated before saying, 'I can't. I can't go past reception.'

'Why?'

He'd understand. He was more rule-breaking and rebellious than she ever was. He had his nipple pierced, for goodness' sake; you couldn't get more liberated than that.

'I stayed here last night and the night before because I thought I was going to die and I wanted to die in a lovely place with fancy chocolates on my pillow and ten different types of coffee pods for the machine that I couldn't even work out how to use in the end, but then it turns out that I didn't die and so now I need to pay six grand which I can't because I gave away all my money.' She managed to get through all that without taking a breath and now studied his face for any indication of how that revelation went down.

'You what?'

'Which part of that didn't you get?'

'Jesus, Nell. Don't you need to give your card details when you check in?'

She nodded. 'I did. But then I cancelled my card so the money never went out.'

'So, the plan was to con the hotel into a free room, and I bet you ordered room service too, and then you were just going to let some poor cleaner find you?'

This was where the plan got sticky. When the housekeeper, Christina, came back to clean the room, she and Nell had had a lovely chat. She'd even shown Nell pictures of her two grandsons back in Manila on her phone, and if Nell didn't already feel bad enough, Christina's screensaver was a picture of Jesus on the cross.

'I didn't really think that part through,' Nell admitted. 'Anyway, all's well that ends well, I'm not dead.'

'And this. . .?' Greg waved his finger up and down, pointing at her gown.

'Is rented.'

He exhaled. 'You weren't planning on paying for that either?'

'I actually paid for it in advance I'll have you know,' she said, her cheeks still flaming.

'What's your plan now?'

'I haven't really got one. I sold everything or gave it away. I literally don't own a single thing.'

'Well as far as I can see you have two options. One, you can be honest, and offer to pay back the money in instalments.'

'For the next hundred years. What's the other option?'

'I pay it for you and then you pay *me* back in instalments.'

Who had six grand just sitting about in their bank account? Turned out Greg did. Nell grimaced. 'Neither option is looking attractive right now Greg, I'm not going to lie. There is always the third option.'

'Which is?'

'I find the back entrance of the hotel and try to escape through there and hope that karma isn't a thing or it is going to bite me one day.'

'That is a very bad option that should be immediately struck off the list of options.'

'Oh come on, you stole salt and pepper pots from every café or restaurant we ever ate in.'

Greg looked horrified. 'I did not!'

'You did! You even stole more after you left your favourite hoodie, the one with the fox riding a skateboard behind, in that café, and then had more room in your rucksack.'

'That is a barefaced lie!' Greg exclaimed before rearranging his face to greet an older couple walking down the stairs past them on the landing. 'Good morning, lovely day.'

Nell had to press herself up against the wall for them to get past her.

'Lovely dress dear, have a nice time at your party.'

Nell smiled. 'Thank you, thank you, I like your hat.'

They waited for the door on the landing below to close before Greg hissed again, 'I've never stolen anything in my life.'

'You must have blocked it out, the guilt probably got too much for you.'

'They're going to start looking for you, you know. They'll have your details on the booking form, they'll know where you live.'

'I don't live anywhere. I moved out on Sunday morning before checking in here.'

'The landlord will give them your forwarding address.'

'I don't have one, remember? I'm meant to be dead.'

'So where are you going to go now?'

Nell shrugged. 'I have no idea.'

'You can't even go to your mum's because she's away.'

'How do you know that?'

'She put it in her Christmas card.'

'Her what?'

'Her Christmas card, it arrived last week. I hope she's got a burglar alarm though because it was in her annual round robin that she was going on a cruise for three weeks over Christmas and she sealed the card with one of those gold address labels so let's hope none of the cards fell into the wrong hands.'

'What is she doing sending you a Christmas card?'

'She has done every year. I send her one too. She also remembers my birthday and even puts a tenner inside the card.'

'Sorry, my mum sends you ten pounds every birthday?'

'Yes.'

'You're thirty-eight.'

'I know.'

'We broke up nearly two decades ago.'

'I know. She said I'm like the son she never had.'

'She doesn't even send me ten pounds.'

'She never knows where to find you. You should call her more.'

Oh my goodness. Nell had forgot how infuriating this man could be. 'I need to get out of here, nice to see you, Greg, good luck with Daisy, she seems. . .' Nell searched her brain for a suitable word. 'Efficient.'

'Where are you going to go? You've got no money, no phone, no clothes apart from this ridiculous—'

'Fabulous,' Nell interrupted.

'—dress. What are you planning to do, assuming you get out of here without them calling the police, which would certainly solve your problem of where you'll be staying for the next few months.'

'When did you get so uptight?' Nell said, hands on her hips.

'When did you get so, so inconsiderate?'

'Spontaneous.'

'You're not going to make it out of here.'

'Watch me. Goodbye Greg.'

Nell's swoosh away from him was so satisfying she broke out in a big grin as she walked away, and in perfect could-be-in-a-movie timing the door to the lift opened with a jubilant 'ping' as soon as she pressed the button to call it.

The doors were closing when one of Greg's shiny brogues stuck in the door to open it again. 'Wait. I can't believe I'm saying this, but if you're going to do option three then you're going to need some help.'

He pressed '-1 STAFF ONLY', which opened into a wide

service corridor lined with lino. After a quick surreptitious peek in both directions to ascertain it was empty, they ran towards the sound and smell of the kitchens. With one arm around her shoulders and the other hand held up to his ear as though he had an earpiece in, Greg whisked her through the kitchens like she was Lady Gaga evading the paparazzi on her way to play at Wembley. They walked quickly past the chefs prepping for lunch, through the pot-wash and the food storage area, Greg saying the occasional, 'Coming through, mind your backs,' to any staff they passed, until they emerged into the bright sunshine through a propped open door by the bins.

'Thank you,' Nell gushed. 'That was inspired. How did you know where to go?'

'A year or so after we broke up I worked for an agency doing silver service for weddings through university, and I did a few here.'

'You were brilliant! I can't believe we got away with it.'

'You made me an accomplice. Thirty-eight years of living a squeaky-clean life ruined.'

'I won't tell if you don't. Right, I need to sweet talk my way onto a bus.'

'You can't go on a bus in that. Where are you going anyway?'

Nell hesitated. Hayley lived in Dublin, her mum was seemingly away, she couldn't remember Polly's address and everyone else she knew were in different time zones.

'Why don't you phone someone?'

'I don't have a phone.'

'Here,' Greg said, fishing in his pocket, 'use mine.'

'I don't know anyone's numbers.'

As the reality of her dire situation hit home, she could feel her breath getting shallower, not helped by the corset. 'Let me think, let me think,' she said, putting one hand on her head to help warm her brain up. She started pacing outside the hotel bins, she couldn't think clearly at all. It was mid-December, zero degrees at night, she'd freeze to death. There was a group of homeless people under the bridge who always had fires lit in barrels, she could go there. It would be a sea change from the deluxe suite with a river view and a rather crappy start to the first day of the rest of her life, but at least the only way was up from there.

Greg could sense Nell spiralling, 'Look, I'm staying here until Thursday, I'm at a conference. As long as you're gone by Thursday morning and don't leave a single thing out of place, you can stay at mine for a couple of nights until you get yourself sorted out.' He fished in his pocket for a key. 'Here. Have you got a pen and I'll write the address down.'

Nell looked at him as though he was stupid and gestured to her balloon-like ballgown. 'No pockets.'

'Oh, yes, okay, so will you remember this?' He told her the address, and the code for the alarm and gave her a fifty-pound note for the taxi and some food.

'There's some food in the fridge and clean bedding in the wardrobe in the spare room.'

'You have a wardrobe?' Nell said, impressed. 'You are grown up.'

Greg put his head on the side trying to work out if she was joking or not.

'I can't accept this though, it's too much.'

'From where I'm standing, you don't have any choice.'

He was right. She didn't even own the clothes she was standing up in. 'Are you absolutely sure?'

Greg nodded. 'Do you want me to call you a cab?'

'That would be weird, my name is Nell.'

Greg rolled his eyes. 'So, two nights. Out by Thursday morning. Leave the key on the counter, I have a spare.'

'Got it.' Nell stuck her arm out for a passing lit-up taxi, who stopped immediately; the chance to pick up an A-lister outside the back of one of London's top hotels was too great an opportunity to pass up. Nell rolled herself into the back seat and stuck her thumb up at Greg out of the back window as the car moved away from the kerb.

Greg lived in a Victorian terrace, which surprised her. Admittedly it was in a very smart part of London, and if the tube station had been any nearer to it the ticket machine would have been nestled happily next to his fridge, but even so. His sharp tailored suit, shiny shoes, posh girlfriend, conference at a posh hotel, all pointed firmly towards a glass duplex along the river, not an unassuming two-up, two-down. Next door had a pair of bay trees flanking their tiled entrance which was a nice touch. Greg's concrete front path and plain front door looked a little forlorn in comparison. Nell pushed the front door open and the deliberate minimalism continued inside. A white hallway led into a large white living room with a massive flatscreen television mounted above the fireplace opposite a navy velvet sofa that screamed 'sit on me' with its sumptuous deep cushions and matching footstool. But that was it, apart from the elaborate ceiling rose and beautiful cornices – though they weren't Greg's doing, they belonged to the house. Nell wandered through to the next room, obviously once a dining room, and now a rather high-tech home office, with three monitors set out like theatre dressing table mirrors on a wide desk. All that was missing was lightbulbs all around them. What did he do for a living that necessitated three computer screens? Maybe he just didn't know that you could open multiple tabs on your computer at once.

There was a nod to decor in here at least, with a framed painting on the wall. Nell recognised it instantly as the

Aboriginal art he bought when they visited Alice Springs together, a month or so before they met Mandy.

'How much!' Nell had exclaimed at the time when Greg said he wanted to buy it.

'It speaks to me,' Greg had said, trying to justify spending two weeks' hostel money on the canvas filled with intricate dots. 'I love it. And I have to have it. And you're just going to have to spend every day for the rest of your life looking at it.'

She liked the fact that the only painting he deemed worthy of banging a nail in the wall for was one that he bought when she was with him. It showed that despite appearances, maybe he hadn't changed that much.

The kitchen at the back of the house debunked that thought with its futuristic glossiness. No handles, no open shelving, just black and stainless-steel shininess, and a coffee machine with real beans in the glass box on top of it. No Nescafé here. Nell opened his fridge noting the speeding fine stuck to the outside of it with a magnet. Six bottles of yellow-labelled champagne stacked at the bottom. An unopened pot of red pepper hummus, a jar of olives and a neat stack of ready meals, but not the ones you'd find in the freezer compartment at the local supermarket, these were fancy ones in artisan brown boxes, the type that got delivered every week to your door via helicopter. Nice. Nell closed the fridge door and realised she didn't have a clue who this Greg was anymore. They used to boil noodles inside the hostel's kettle because they didn't own a saucepan. Nell still didn't.

Nell went upstairs then: two bedrooms, equal in size, both painted white, both with the exact same furniture, same bed – definitely king-size, it was double the size of the one that she'd sold Tom. *Urgh Tom.* Obviously, Greg had gone into the bed shop, found a style he liked and just got two of everything.

Easier that way. More efficient. Nell bet Daisy approved. The only way Nell knew which was Greg's room and which was the spare room was that there was a glass of water on the nightstand next to the bed in the room overlooking the road at the front. There were literally no personal touches or distinguishing features at all. He did own two wardrobes though, so well done him.

Once she'd figured out how to de-robe, as the zip seemed to be a bit stuck, she had a quick shower standing under a square panel on the ceiling that must have been a square foot in size, all the while thinking about her next move. Since waking up, she hadn't had time to think about anything other than logistics: how to get out of the hotel, how to get across London, how to get out of the dress, so the enormity of even waking up that morning hadn't even hit her.

That would come though.

CHAPTER SEVEN

The taxi to Greg's was eighteen pounds but Nell had rounded it up to twenty. Those extra two pounds would have really come in handy but she'd never not tipped a driver, whether it was a Thai tuk tuk or a Brighton beach donkey, and she wasn't going to start being frugal in that area now. This left her thirty pounds. She hadn't eaten since last night's disappointing quesadillas, which was approximately eighteen hours ago, but more pressing than the gnawing hole in her stomach was the fact that the only item of clothing she owned was the pair of knickers she'd now been wearing for three days straight and her heels. There were ways of making money of course where only pants and heels were needed, but she wasn't yet that desperate. She couldn't even order something online to be delivered because she only had cash and no bank account.

The wardrobe in Greg's spare room was full of winter coats. Evidently Greg was now a skier because he had all the kit. He also had full leathers in there and a couple of helmets so there must be a motorbike currently sitting in the hotel's car park as it wasn't outside. That was odd, he'd always said they were too dangerous, point-blank refusing to even hire mopeds when they were travelling. Nell went into Greg's room and opened the top drawer of his chest. She didn't feel any guilt about it, it was Greg. There were perhaps twelve, maybe fifteen, carefully folded trunk-style boxer shorts, one of those would do nicely. She took a pink shirt from the wardrobe; it was still in the clear plastic covering from the laundry service. Nell could tell it was expensive because the inside of the collar and cuffs had a flowery design and a label in the neck that wasn't M&S or Next. His three-monitor job obviously paid a lot. She had to roll the sleeves up to be able to see her hands, and the pair of jeans she found also hanging up – *who hangs up jeans?* – definitely needed a belt and a few folds up of the hem. She glanced at herself in the mirrored door of the wardrobe. She looked like she'd been shrunk in the wash, but it would do. She grabbed one of the leather jackets and headed out.

Unlike the part of London that she'd been renting in, where every second shop was a charity shop, seemingly Greg's neighbours favoured antiques and loaves of sourdough. It was only about fifteen minutes' walk from the dress rental company though, which was good because any longer holding the gown and Nell's arms may have fallen off.

'Thanks ever so much,' the lady who took the dress off Nell said. 'Was it a successful night?'

Nell put her head on one side to fully consider the question. Was it a successful night? Well, she didn't die at the end of it, which by most would make it pretty successful, but then the whole point of the night was to, so by that reckoning it was a failure.

'It was. . .' Nell paused, searching for the right word. 'Life-changing.'

'Oh well, that's marvellous.'

After dropping the dress off, Nell must have walked for

miles before spotting a Barnardo's, and this was definitely in a different postcode – no sourdough here, but she had passed three different Turkish barbers.

She figured she could spend twenty pounds on kitting herself out in this charity shop and still have money to feed herself for a couple of days, as long as she stayed away from the bakeries near Greg's house.

Half an hour later she approached the till, laden with three T-shirts, a pair of cargo trousers, a pair of jeans, a jumper with a giant daisy on it, because it made her smile with the irony of it, a duffle coat and a pair of trainers. She did ask if they had any underwear, but the volunteer smiled kindly at her, and said, no, second-hand knickers weren't really popular, but the pound shop next door sold them. Bingo. On the cash desk was a little basket with new Fairtrade socks in, each pair sporting little woollen pockets for toes, exactly the same as Tom wore when he'd come to buy Nell's bed. Nell laughed to herself with the memory of how utterly surreal the whole experience with Tom was, and on a whim, picked up a pair and put them in her basket and handed it to the lady behind the till, still smiling.

The total was sixty-five pounds. Nell hadn't thought to look at the prices as she was gathering items up; it was a charity shop, she assumed everything would be pennies. Then she realised that the last time she'd been in one in England was 2006, and there might have been a little inflation since then.

'Here's the thing,' Nell confided in the volunteer, leaning in closer over the counter, 'I'm wearing my ex-boyfriend's clothes right now because I literally do not own a single thing. And I know people say that, don't they, *oh I haven't got a thing to wear*, but I actually don't have a single thing to wear. I sold or gave away every worldly belonging because I thought I was going to die yesterday, and then I didn't.'

'Ooo, I read a book about that once, these four siblings who all got told the date they were going to die on and then one didn't.'

'Well, that's happened to me!' Nell said excitedly. 'I honestly thought that was it, me done, so I closed down my life, and now I have to start again. From scratch. Starting with these clothes. So please, please, let me buy them for twenty pounds, because I've only got thirty left and I haven't eaten since yesterday.'

The woman's mouth twitched. Nell could tell that she was considering it.

'Tell you what,' the woman said. 'That shirt you're wearing is a Paul Smith. I could get thirty pounds for a Paul Smith. If you put in your twenty, and donate the shirt, then I'll let you have it all.'

'This shirt?' Nell tugged on the front of it.

The woman nodded. 'We sold one just like it a couple of weeks ago. I'll put it in the window, it'll go within the hour.'

To be honest, it was unlikely Greg would miss it. There were at least twenty shirts all hanging up in their plastic coverings in his wardrobe, and a few of them were pink. Nell bit her bottom lip. But then again, he was doing her a massive favour letting her stay at his, she should repay him with kindness, not grand larceny.

But on the other hand, it wasn't as though she would be selling his shirt to pay for drugs or entry to a theme park, these were things that she really needed.

Out of the corner of her eye she spotted a book displayed on the top of a bookshelf and she had an idea. 'Tell you what, if you throw in that book too, then we've got a deal.' Nell stripped off in the little back room where the volunteers unpacked the donations, trying not to knock over a china tea set or any of the piled-up bin bags as she did so. The new T-shirt was a perfect fit, and the daisy jumper was lovely and soft. This was a good decision.

All in all, it was a successful shopping trip. The pound shop did indeed have a set of five briefs for a quid, which was a billy bargain, and the stallholder on the market stand loaded her up with funny-shaped fruit and vegetables he wouldn't be able to sell for a fraction of their chalked price. She knew that Greg had kindly told her to help herself to his food in the fridge, but she wouldn't. He'd done enough. Especially now.

The lights were on in the living room window as Nell approached Greg's house. That was funny, she thought, she could have sworn she turned them off. It wasn't his electric bill she was worried about – he could clearly afford it – it was the fish. She'd shared a dorm room in a hostel in Brazil once with a Canadian woman who worked for an environmental agency, who told her that *electricity uses coal, coal produces mercury, mercury gets into water, fish eat it, they die. Or we eat the fish and we die. It's a lose-lose situation.* That'd stayed with Nell for years and she'd even been known to pee in the dark sometimes.

As she put the key in the lock, she could hear a loud droning noise from inside, not unlike the vacuum cleaner sound she'd woken up with that morning. That morning. How was it still the same day? Nell had absolutely nothing on her that she could use as a weapon. As she gingerly walked along the corridor though, towards the increasing noise, she was also met with the smell of roasted coffee beans and expensive aftershave.

'You're back,' she exclaimed, seeing Greg standing at the coffee machine. 'Why are you back? I thought you had a conference?'

'I skipped the afternoon session, I couldn't concentrate knowing you were here, and you might not know how things work, and so I thought I'd hop on the tube, come back and just show you a few things.'

'You didn't need to. I'm good. I've done a bit of shopping—'

'I can see. Nice jumper.'

'Thanks, I thought it was ironic, as I'm meant to be pushing up daisies myself by now, but guess I probably don't like Daisies as much as you do. . .' Nell waited to see if her joke would land. It didn't.

'Oh, and I got you something.' She fished in the charity shop carrier bag. She pulled out the book and gave it to him. 'To say thank you.'

He turned it over in his hands. 'The Hitchhiker's Guide to the Galaxy,' he read.

'A cup of tea would restore my normality,' Nell said, quoting from the book.

'I'm making coffee, would you prefer tea?'

'It's a quote, from the book. We used to say it every morning when we woke up.'

'Did we?'

'It was your favourite book. You were really sad when you left it at that place in Queensland.'

He shook his head, 'I don't remember. Thanks though, I don't really have much time for reading these days.' He put it down on the worktop.

Nell suddenly realised that was what was missing from the house. Books. There wasn't a single one. Not even a cookbook. Everyone owned at least one Jamie Oliver.

'Well, there you go,' she said brightly. 'You can kickstart your reading addiction with an old favourite.'

'So did you want a tea?'

'Coffee's great, thank you. So, what do you spend your time doing if it's not reading?'

'Work mostly. Or running.'

Two of Nell's least favourite activities.

'And what is work?'

'Finance.'

'Ah, the movements of small green pieces of paper.'

Greg looked at her quizzically.

Nell motioned to the book on the counter. 'Another quote.'

'Oh, okay.'

'And is finance rewarding?'

Greg shrugged. 'I don't have a mortgage, and I've got a number of ISAs if that's what you mean?'

It wasn't. Nell just smiled politely and thanked him for the coffee he held out to her.

Nell followed Greg through to the lounge, blowing on her cup as she walked. 'Daisy seems. . . nice.' She didn't mean to leave a pause there, now it sounded sarcastic.

'She is.'

'How long has she been your colleague stroke girlfriend?'

'She's not my girlfriend.'

'She said different.'

'We're working on a project together.'

'I bet you are.'

'No, we are, a really big one.'

Nell grinned. 'I remember.'

Greg looked confused for a moment then went beetroot red and almost spilled his coffee. 'So, um, what's your plan? I mean, you can still stay here for a couple of days to work it out.'

Nell shrugged. 'I honestly don't know. Everything I have done in the last eighteen years was leading up to yesterday, I haven't even considered today onwards.'

'You honestly really hadn't? You believed that woman so much that she dictated the rest of your life for you? I mean, I know you did at the beginning, that's why we – well, why we went our separate ways, but you kept on believing it?'

Nell nodded. 'I did. There wasn't a shred of doubt in me.

That's why I've packed my life full of travel and weird and wonderful experiences. If I was going to die young, I didn't want to have anything left on my bucket list.'

'You've done everything you wanted?'

'Yep. Well apart from have kids, but having them would have made dying much harder.'

'In what way?'

'If I knew I was leaving people I really loved.'

'But what about your family? They love you.'

'I'm sure they do. And I know they'd have been sad, but I don't get home very much, so it's not as though they'd have missed me being around.'

'Do you think that you would have been around more if you didn't have this date hanging over you?'

'I honestly don't know. I have loved travelling, I have loved the life I've had, but if you're asking me would I have done it like this if I knew I had this lovely long life stretching ahead of me? Probably not. I would have settled down with someone – you and I might even be still together; can you imagine that!'

There was a moment then when Greg appraised Nell sitting there barefoot and cross-legged on his expensive sofa, wearing her eclectic charity shop finds, her curly hair wild and untamed, looking so at odds with the immaculate surroundings that it was absolutely unfathomable.

'But you know what this means though Greg?' Nell said. 'If my prediction didn't come true, you might not live 'til you're a hundred-and-three. That would be a bummer for you. If you believed it, which you don't.'

Nell was too busy sticking her finger around the bottom of her coffee cup to get the last of the froth out to witness Greg's face draining of all colour as the enormity of her words hit home.

CHAPTER EIGHT

'What was the conference about?' Nell wasn't particularly interested, but she had to say something because Greg had gone a bit of a funny colour and was just staring into space. The easy way that they'd always communicated in the past, bantering back and forth, was taking its sweet time reappearing.

'The heterogeneity of stock price responses to policy shocks,' Greg replied blankly.

'Oh.'

'Do you even know what that means?'

Nell was annoyed by that. She might be wearing someone else's clothes and sleeping in someone else's house but she wasn't stupid. 'Yes,' she said, as though in fact he was.

His pregnant pause suggested that he wanted her to explain it.

'It means how the stock market is varied in its approach to dealing with impromptu changes in the law that could affect the economic landscape.'

Greg gave a low whistle, 'I'm impressed.'

'And also, very patronising. Unlike some around here, I read. A lot. I know a lot of long words, that people like you throw about to make themselves sound really important, but actually it's really unnecessary and pompous.'

Greg laughed. 'People like me?'

Nell nodded. 'People like you.'

'And what are people like me like?' His voice had a tinge of familiar playfulness about it, which made Nell keep going.

'You finished university top of your cohort, joined an investment firm on a graduate scheme, got promoted through the ranks pretty quickly thanks to your love of early mornings and charm. You may have moved to other financial firms in the city, but probably not, people think highly of you where you are, so you stay for the bonuses. You've had a goal in sight, probably six- or seven-figure sum in the bank that you'd like to get to, maybe a title in a company, some sort of vice president role, and you don't deviate from that aim. Ever. You're like those clockwork toys that have a little key at the back that you wind up and they go really fast in a straight line until they run out of power and break down.'

'That's what I am?'

'Everything that I've seen today suggests so yes.'

'Everything you've seen? What here? In my house?'

'Yes. It is the epitome of functional luxury. Everything is expensive, but nothing is joyful. Where's the stuff that lifts your spirits?'

'My coffee machine lifts my spirits. So does the champagne in the fridge.'

'Caffeine and alcohol don't count. I'm talking about books and art. Actually, I take that back, I saw your Aboriginal art in the dining room. I'm pleased you've still got that.'

'It's covering a damp patch that I haven't got round to fixing,' Greg said. Nell might have been imagining it, but she was sure Greg blushed a little at her mentioning it.

'Well, whatever the reason behind it, you've got one

painting, and now you've got one book. You're a verified culture vulture. Congratulations.'

'I'll have you know, I am very cultured. I watch art house movies and things all the time. . .' He nodded his head towards the huge television mounted above the fireplace.

'Well then, you're cleverer than I thought because it's not connected to anything. I tried to watch it earlier and when you turn it on it talks you through the initial set up.'

'I'm not here much. But I go to cinemas. And theatres.'

'What was the last play you watched?'

'What, you want me to run through them all now?'

'Not all, just the last one.'

Greg paused. It would have been quite obvious even to someone who didn't know him that well, and Nell knew him very well, that he was frantically trying to remember what was on any of the billboards outside any of the theatres he walked past every day on his way to his office.

'*Hamilton*!' he finally announced jubilantly.

'You've seen the musical *Hamilton*?'

Greg nodded.

'The one about the Formula One driver?' Nell asked innocently.

Greg nodded again, pleased with himself. 'Yes.'

'Wow, that must have been noisy.'

'It was, but really informative.'

'Well then, I take it back. You're clearly a man of the arts.'

'Since we're finished with my character assassination, let's talk about you.'

'Me?' Nell asked, 'What do you want to know?'

'Where did you go after you left our flat? Because you didn't go back to your university course.'

'How do you know that?'

'I went to York. I spoke to your tutor. You just vanished.'

'You went to my university?'

'Yes. You weren't answering any of my calls, your parents didn't know where you were, so I went to York and stood outside your lectures every day for weeks. You never turned up. You just dropped out without a word to anyone.'

Nell shrugged a little sheepishly. 'I didn't think that a career in law was for me in the end.'

'What was for you?'

'Seeing the world.'

'For nearly twenty years?'

'It's a big place.'

'What's the longest you stayed in one place?'

'I was in Bali for a couple of years.'

'What made you stay so long?'

'It was heaven.'

'So why did you leave?'

Nell paused as she considered the question. It was the same reason she ever left anywhere she'd been for too long. She'd started to care about people and them about her.

'I got sick of the rain,' she replied.

'So naturally you moved back to England? That doesn't make sense.'

'It was easier. For everyone. For it to happen here.'

'Ah yes. Of course. How considerate of you.'

There was definitely an undercurrent of something in Greg's words and tone. What was it? Jealousy? That she'd lived a life he might have wanted had he not fallen onto this hamster wheel of corporate finance? Resentment? That she'd chosen this life over one with him? Surely not, that was years ago, he must have moved on, but then her being there might have brought all his old feelings bubbling to the surface. Nell studied his face. He was giving nothing away, but he didn't look particularly happy. If anything, he looked exhausted.

'Are you okay?' she asked.

'I'm fine, why do you ask?'

'You look tired.'

'I am tired.' He yawned as if to prove he was telling the truth. 'There was a boozy dinner last night, then I got up early to have breakfast—'

'I met you on your way back from breakfast at 10.45, remember; it's not as though you got up to watch the sunrise from the roof.'

'I went to the gym before breakfast and ran ten miles.'

'I've never understood why people do that,' she said. 'Standing on a machine, staring at a wall, running. Why couldn't you run outside in the fresh air?'

'The fresh London air?'

'The park wasn't far from the hotel, surely it would be more fun to run around that?'

'It's not about fun, it's about maintaining cardiovascular health.'

'So, if you don't run for fun, or watch TV for fun, or read books for fun, apart from the odd musical about car racing, what exactly is it that you do for fun?'

Greg stood up from the sofa, 'I'm not talking about this. You can't just waltz back into my life and pick holes in how I choose to live it. I'm perfectly happy and don't need you with your unwashed hair and ridiculous flower jumper lecturing me on what a life well lived looks like. Because from where I'm standing, it really should be the other way around.'

Nell sat on the sofa after he left the room, chewing her bottom lip. Had she done that? She didn't mean to do that. If she'd learned anything from twenty years traversing the globe it was that everyone was different. She'd always tried really hard not to force her opinions on anyone before. But this was Greg. And they could always be open and honest with each other. Except, she realised, they obviously couldn't anymore.

'I'm sorry,' she said, walking slowly into the kitchen where Greg was washing their coffee cups in the sink. 'I didn't mean to be judgy about how you live. You have your life quite clearly set up for you the way that you want it and that's great and none of my business. But for the record, I washed my hair about two hours ago and this jumper is not ridiculous, it's ironic and uplifting and remarkably soft.'

'I shouldn't have said that about you not washing. You've always been very clean,' Greg replied, still with his back to her.

'Look, we've clearly made some different life choices, and that's cool, but we're also clearly happy with those choices, so let's stop comparing lives and just enjoy hanging out together again.'

Greg's phone vibrated on the counter. They both glanced over at the illuminated screen. Daisy.

'I'll leave you to get that, I'll be upstairs unpacking.' She turned round at the doorway. 'That was a joke. I have nothing to unpack. But I'll still be upstairs.'

'It's okay, I'm not going to get it. She's already rung twelve times since I left the conference.'

'It might be important.'

'It's not important.'

'She sounds a bit psycho.'

'You're doing it again.'

'What?'

'Judging my life choices.'

'I thought she was just a colleague?' Nell asked innocently. 'Everyone slags off their colleagues. If she was just a colleague you wouldn't be so twitchy.'

'Who's twitchy? I'm not twitchy.'

'You seem twitchy.'

'I'm sorry, but I can't take you seriously in that jumper.'

'I don't have another one.'

'Did you pay money for that?'

'Sort of. Yes.'

'We need to get you some more clothes.'

'No, *we* don't. You've done enough. I can sort myself out from this point.'

'With what? You don't have a thing to your name. How are you going to start your life again?'

'I don't have all the answers at precisely this moment, Greg, I'm still thinking about it.'

'You need to write a list.'

'I'm not a list-making type of person,' Nell shuddered as she remembered the last list she'd written which took her straight to the humiliating comedy club. 'If you have a laptop I can borrow I can send a few emails out to some friends and make some plans.'

Greg nodded. 'Good idea. I'll set you up in the dining room on my computer.'

'Which one?' Nell said under her breath as she dutifully followed him out of the kitchen.

It was on the third try of her username and password not working that she remembered that she'd deleted her account on Sunday morning in an internet café before heading to the hotel. It flooded back to her, Hotmail asking her in a very serious tone if she was absolutely sure that deleting her account PERMANENTLY was what she wanted to do. ARE YOU SURE? it screamed as her finger hovered over the button. Yes, yes she was. She definitely wanted to erase twenty-five years of emails and contacts because they would hold no value to her on the other side, and possibly some reputation damage to some people still living, so yes. A resounding yes.

'Noooooooo,' Nell sobbed, her head falling onto the desk.

'What's wrong?' Greg rushed in from the living room, where he'd been trying to install the television.

'I forgot that I deleted my account the other day.'

'What did you do that for?'

'I was pretty certain that heaven doesn't have wi-fi.'

'What about your Facebook or Instagram accounts, can't you contact people that way?'

'Gone. All gone. I literally erased myself from the planet.'

'You can start again, make new profiles and search for people and direct message them. It would take a few minutes to find them.'

'Oh my God, you're a genius.'

Greg didn't say out loud that he knew that. But it was pretty clear from his smug expression as he walked back into the living room that he fully agreed with her.

CHAPTER NINE

'You're not dead!'

Hayley was shouting so loudly Nell had to hold Greg's phone well away from her ear.

'You didn't die! You're still alive!'

Nell didn't know how many other ways Hayley could proclaim the fact. 'Yep. Still here.'

'This is amazing! I mean, obviously *I* think it's amazing, but do you? I mean by the end you really wanted to.'

'I wouldn't say I wanted to exactly, but I was ready for it.'

'Oh my God.' Hayley's Irish lilt completely changed from jubilation to sheer shock. 'Does that mean that I won't die either? I've only got two years left until my date.'

'I have no idea,' Nell replied honestly, 'but I'm starting to think that Mandy just made up the dates on the spot.'

'But what about Sophie?'

Nell had thought a lot about Sophie as she was trudging round London earlier looking for a charity shop. Maybe Greg had been right all those years ago, and Sophie's death had been her own doing, or undoing. It wasn't fate or predestined or written in the stars, it was just misadventure and really bad luck.

'I don't know,' Nell admitted. 'But don't start selling all your stuff that's for sure.'

'God Nell, your stuff. What are you going to do?'

'That's one of the reasons I'm calling actually, I—'

'I could have a baby!' Hayley interrupted, shrieking. 'I'm going to call Dean right now and ask him to marry me, and we're going to make a baby!'

'Well, I mean, maybe think about it a bit first. Maybe write a list.'

'Oh my God Nell, this is brilliant news! We only broke up because he wants kids and I didn't, but now I can, oh thank you, thank you! I've got to go and call him. Love you, love you, brilliant news, call me again really soon yeah? Bye!'

The phone went dead in Nell's hand.

'So did she say you could go and stay with her?' Greg asked when Nell walked into the lounge.

'No, she's going to be a bit busy.'

'Was she happy?'

'Ecstatic. She's going to get pregnant to celebrate.'

'Wow. That's next level happiness.'

Nell smiled at Hayley's first thought after getting her death sentence reprieved, but it wasn't surprising, Hayley had always been obsessed with babies and procreation, squealing with her Irish drawl, 'Oh my God, your kids would be so frickin' cute,' when she'd first met Nell and Greg in the hostel. She was right, they would have been: all blonde hair and long limbs. Her and Tom's baby on the other hand would emerge with a mass of dark curls and a steady stream of one-liners. Why was she still thinking about Tom? She'd never given any of her fleeting lovers this much airtime in her brain.

'Do you have any idea how to tune a TV?' Greg asked, interrupting her thoughts, with one hand behind the screen and the other feeling along the bottom for any buttons.

'Tune it? It's not a piano. Where's your remote control? Do you know, in the hotel room they had electronic curtains. I mean, they were fantastic, don't get me wrong, but how lazy do you have to be that you can't get up and open your own curtains?'

'It's not laziness though, is it, it's luxury, providing things that the guest doesn't even know they want.'

'True, true. Every time I have to draw my own curtains from now on I'm going to feel a bit let down. Here, let me have a go.' Nell pressed a few buttons on the remote and the screen sprang into action. 'Okay, put in your password and you're good to go. But seriously, why did you buy a TV this big if you've never used it?'

'Every house needs a TV. And I thought I'd spend Sunday afternoons watching old movies or sport, but I never have because I've always got some work to do.'

'On a weekend?'

'Weekend. Evening. Christmas Day.'

'Shut up, you do not work on Christmas Day.'

'I know you don't really get it, but my job is really important.' Greg started scanning through the channels, really pleased with his new toy.

'I don't doubt it, but do you enjoy it?'

'I enjoy what it gives me.'

'I didn't ask that. Do you wake up in the morning and think, "yes! I'm going to work!"'

'No one does that. That's why it's called work.'

'You wanted to be a teacher,' Nell reminded him.

'And earn a tenth of what I earn now?'

'Money isn't everything.'

'You're only saying that because you don't have any.'

'So surely I'm living proof that you can have a really great life without a massive bank balance.'

'But how much easier would it have been with money? Think of all the times on our gap year that we had instant noodles for dinner, wouldn't it have been a better experience if we could have had steak or sea bass?'

'We loved instant noodles! We also had fresh coconut water every day, mangoes we picked ourselves.'

'Or stayed in nice hotels rather than crappy hostels?'

'But we'd never have met any of the people we met along the way if we were in sterile hotel rooms alone.'

'You can't possibly say that you wouldn't have preferred to get taxis instead of buses and overcrowded trains?'

Was he actually serious? Some of Nell's fondest memories of living abroad were these adventures. The camaraderie of shared tales in the hostels, eating street food out of cartons, talking to locals on ten-hour train rides. He used to love that too. Nell remembered him once teaching a young Thai boy to play backgammon on his little magnetic travel set on a 250-mile journey meandering south. They played for hours, every time Greg would say, 'Okay, just one more,' holding his index finger aloft to reinforce the point, the boy would nod excitedly and then immediately set out the pieces again for another game as soon as it ended. Greg ended up giving the boy the set when the train finally pulled into the station, and the boy clutched it to his chest like it was the best gift in the world. How could Greg say now that he'd have preferred to do that journey alone in the back of an air-conditioned taxi?

'What time are you going back to the hotel?' Nell asked. It's not that she wanted him to go, but it was upsetting seeing not only how much he'd changed, but also how he'd rewritten their memories, turning the extraordinary and fun into a tale of hardship and woe. Was this how he'd repainted it for everyone else? Telling his new financier friends or Daisy about his god-awful time abroad, where he slummed it for a whole year with a woman who didn't wash. But it wasn't just the year he was making a mockery of; it was her life. Up until a month ago, she was still getting around in a third-class train carriage sitting on a wooden bench for hours, and sleeping in shared dorms, and for the most part loving it. Of course, communal toilets and drunk backpackers half her age had, on occasion, made her wonder if she was still cut out for it, but those moments were fleeting and absolutely never being voiced out loud to Greg.

'I've ducked out of the rest of the day; I thought maybe we could grab some dinner together?'

'I'm actually really tired, Greg, you should go back to the hotel. I just want some soup and then a ten-hour sleep. I've got a big day tomorrow planning how to start my life again.'

A look of disappointment flashed across his face, replaced almost immediately with a smile. 'Absolutely, of course. Shall I order some soup?'

'Order some? I bought some vegetables from the market. I'm going to make it.'

'Make soup?'

'Yes, Greg. Make soup. I assume you have a saucepan?'

'Yes, I have a saucepan.' Of course he did, Nell thought, how else would he heat up the meals from his meal plan that were carefully curated based on his metabolic rate and blood type and delivered every Sunday and Wednesday nights? He walked back into the kitchen to retrieve it from the cupboard.

'I could stay and help?' he offered, also getting out a chopping board and an array of sharp knives and vegetable peelers.

'I'm sure the heady world of financial services, not to mention your colleagues, are missing you.'

Greg clearly didn't mistake Nell's inflection on the word

colleagues because he followed his offer of help up with, 'Daisy is honestly just someone I work with.'

'Look,' she said, picking up a peeler and waving it at him, 'I realise that my experience of work and yours has been vastly different, but can I offer you some friendly advice about humans?' She took his silence for agreement. 'Daisy likes you. In a non-colleague way. Whether you like her back is your own business, but either way put the poor girl out of her misery. Invite her out for a date or tell her that you're not interested. Life's too short to—' Nell stopped in her tracks. *Life's too short* to not say what you really think. *Life's too short* not to be happy every day. *Life's too short* not to cram it with fun, and books, and art, and people and experiences. Except for Greg, up until today, life wasn't short, was it? Life was long. He'd had all the time in the world to put off today what could be done tomorrow, or the next day. He might ask Daisy out, might not, he'd see. No need to decide now. He might read a book soon, or not, see how he felt. Plenty of time for that later. Of course, he hadn't filled his life with the same sort of adventure she had, because he had no need to. He had a forty-year retirement to save for and fund and then fill. There was loads of time for touring South America or the Indonesian archipelagos, now was the time for stacking the pounds up in the bank's vault, investing in property, savings accounts, pension pots to keep him warm in his twilight years. It all suddenly made sense. They'd both made the choices they had, followed the path they had because of their predictions. It was so obvious that for all of Greg's bluster about Mandy's lack of credentials, he had believed her as much as Nell had. That could be the only explanation for this seismic personality shift.

'You okay?' Greg interrupted, bringing Nell back into the kitchen.

'Yes, yes, absolutely. Sorry, miles away. Right, well if you're going to be my sous chef and hang out with me instead of at a fancy hotel, you'll need to wash your hands and maybe change out of your suit. I feel like I'm your hired help, not your oldest friend.'

Greg was still smiling at what Nell said as he changed into jeans and a T-shirt upstairs, noticing that there was an empty hanger in the wardrobe. One shirt was missing. He made a mental note to call the dry cleaners tomorrow. But right now, he had soup to make with his oldest friend.

Soup and champagne wasn't a normal combination for Nell. In fact, it might have been the first time she'd had that particular blend of food and beverage. It was also likely to be the last as she had precisely three pounds eighty to her name, and that wasn't even hers, it was left over from Greg's handout earlier that morning. With every fizz and pop of the bubbles on her tongue Nell was reminded quite how dire her future was looking, while also knowing how lucky she was to have one. It was an odd mix of feelings: terror with relief. She didn't know where she would be right now, or sleeping tonight, had she not bumped into Greg at the hotel. She was quite adept at talking her way onto strangers' sofas, possibly not in London though. But she'd always had the comfort of knowing that she could afford a hostel or a short-term let if she really needed to; not having any money at all to fall back on was really troubling.

'Penny for them.'

'I was just thinking about how lucky I was to bump into you today of all days.'

'Knight in shiny shoes?'

Nell smiled. 'Something like that. But seriously though, thank you. I really appreciate you helping me out today.'

'You're welcome.'

'I wouldn't have blamed you if you just kept walking after recognising me though.'

'My mouth called your name before my brain engaged. If I'd thought about it, I might not have stopped you.'

'That's understandable.'

'I would have regretted it later though.'

'Would you?'

'Of course. You might have left me a broken shell of a man, but you're still one of the most significant people to have been in my life.'

'A broken shell of a man?'

'I literally didn't wear trousers for a month after you left. Just sweatpants.'

'I'm sorry.'

He shook his head, 'Don't be. I told you to go. I gave you the ultimatum. I should have been supportive of what you were feeling rather than try to snap you out of it.'

'Sounds like someone's had some therapy,' Nell smiled.

'Not therapy, just nearly twenty years to think about it.'

'We were really young. It was a lot to process.'

'You processed. I blocked it out, never thought about it again.'

'If you say so.'

'What's that supposed to mean?'

Nell shook her head. 'Ignore me.'

'No, what did you mean, *if you say so.*'

'Look at me. You were exactly like me back then. We thought the same, spoke the same, dreamed the same, wore the same sort of clothes, you even had longer hair than me at one point. We took so much pleasure in not planning, being mindful, living for the day.'

'We were nineteen, for God's sake, you're literally describing every nineteen-year-old on the planet.'

'But you've changed beyond all recognition. And I think Mandy's prediction had a hand in that.'

'In what way?' Greg stretched out his long legs in front of him. They'd been eating on the floor of the living room around the coffee table, and now their bowls were empty, drained of the last few drops of soup. They were both leaning back against the sofa, sitting on the floor side by side. If Nell had been facing him, with his expression clear to see, she might not have carried on this line of thought.

'I think consciously, subconsciously, whatever, you started living a life befitting someone who was going to be around for a very long time. You've never married, or had kids. Probably because choosing the right partner when you know you could be stuck with them for decades upon decades put you off—'

'You haven't either.'

'Not talking about me, and we spoke about my reasons earlier. You work yourself to the bone to fund your forty-year retirement, you shun any kind of frivolous fun because now's not the time for that, and you don't look after yourself because you think that your health is a given.'

'I'm fitter than most men my age. I run ten miles every morning.'

'Yes, but you skip meals, you only sleep with the help of the sleeping tablets in your bathroom cabinet—'

His head swivelled questioningly to the side.

'I was looking for a refill for your hand soap, and yes, I saw them. And you seem to only hydrate with either coffee or champagne. I'm willing to take a punt on the fact that this was the first homecooked meal you've had in years. Am I right?'

'The soup *was* delicious.'

'Amazing what a few misshapen vegetables can produce. Never underestimate the weird ones.'

'Is that your motto for life?' Greg teased.

'It has served me well. And led me to you on the first day of secondary school.'

Greg dunked his index finger into his champagne flute and flicked it at her.

'Look, I'm not saying this to be rude or mean,' Nell continued, 'but I *know* that what Mandy told us has shaped the whole of my adult life, and I just want you to consider that actually, it may have done the same to you.'

Greg did a good job of arranging his features to look amused at what Nell was saying, but inside his blood and brain was fizzing, because this wasn't a revelation to him. It was something he knew to be absolutely true.

'Have you still got your tattoo or have you had it lasered off?' Nell asked.

'I've still got it.'

'Show me.'

Greg lifted his index finger to show the tiny C inked on the side of it between the knuckle and the first joint. Nell put her finger alongside it, where her backwards C joined with his to make a little heart. They'd had them done on Valentine's Day when they were in the upper sixth, thinking the gesture the peak of romance. 'I'm only saying this from a place of love, Greg, but you need to start living for the now.'

'And you need to start planning for the future.'

'I could mentor you in how to enjoy life.'

'And I could teach you all I know about financial independence.'

Nell grimaced. 'To be fair my challenge for you sounds a lot more fun. Can't we both just do that one?'

CHAPTER TEN

Greg's double glazing wasn't as thick as the hotel's, so Nell woke the next morning to the sound of sirens and shouts reminding her instantly where in the world she was. The duvet was so thick and fluffy though she just pulled it up over her ears, rolled over and fell back into a dreamless sleep. Or that was the plan. Instead her unconscious thoughts pummelled her with the reality of her situation, forcing her to trudge barefoot through the streets of London, which had transformed themselves into those of Oliver Twist's city: dark winding cobbled streets with bawdy inns and beaky-nosed gents in top hats, throwing a coin or two her way as she hobbled along, pulling her shawl closer to her as the wheels of a passing carriage splashed mud all over her bare legs and patchwork skirt. A rat scuttled past in the gutter and a stray dog had its head in a bin looking for scraps. Nell's stomach growled with hunger at the thought of food, not helped by the smell of warm toast drifting through the air.

'Wakey wakey, sleepyhead.'

Thank Christ for that, Nell thought as she opened her eyes gratefully at Greg standing next to her bed with a steaming hot mug of tea and a plate of toast. 'What time is it?' she asked, reaching up to take her breakfast from him.

'Almost eleven.'

'Eleven? In the morning?'

He laughed. 'Yes in the morning. We didn't get to bed until after midnight, you were obviously shattered.'

They'd had a lovely evening, in the end, once they'd unanimously, and silently, agreed not to mention life choices, or death, again. They'd watched a film, one neither of them had seen before. Nothing highbrow, or critically acclaimed, just two hours of mindless action, bad jokes and unlikely happy endings, but it was perfect. Greg had run out to the Sainsbury's Local around the corner and got a couple of bags of different flavoured popcorn – salt, sweet and caramel – a bottle of red and white, and a bag of seedless grapes. Nell guessed that the last item was a panic buy, not having a clue what she would actually like to eat while watching a film, or indeed, what he would, as it had never really happened before. In the end they ate and drank all of it, which was perfect.

'You should have woken me earlier,' Nell yawned, 'I've got loads to sort out today.'

'You needed to rest. Anyway, I've got a plan.'

'Shouldn't you be at work?'

'I've told them there's a family emergency.'

'You didn't need to do that. You might get in trouble.'

'I haven't taken a day off in sixteen years, Nell. One day won't get me fired.' The letter box clanged downstairs. 'Right, I'll get the post while you eat your breakfast and get changed, then we'll sort out your life.'

Nell smiled gratefully at him and bit into one of the triangles of toast before her blood ran cold as she suddenly remembered the handful of letters she had posted on her way to the hotel a few days before. She threw back the duvet and ran barefoot in just a T-shirt out onto the landing. Greg was standing at the foot of the stairs by the front door, casually leafing through the envelopes. He put a couple on the hall shelf for later and started opening another one.

'No!' Nell yelled, hurling herself down the stairs and throwing herself onto Greg's back, frantically reaching round him to try to grab the letter that had her handwriting on the front of it. He tried to shrug her off, completely bemused why she was wrapped around his neck.

'What are you doing?'

'Don't read that! Give it to me! Greg! Give me the letter.'

He held it up higher, out of her reach. 'Is this from you?'

'Greg, please, give it to me, don't open it.'

'When did you send it?'

'Before. Oh my God, please, just give it to me and forget about it.' She was still clinging onto his body with one arm while the other was outstretched trying to grab it from him.

'It must be important.'

'It's not, it's rubbish, the ramblings of a madwoman. Please, just give it to me.'

As Greg shrugged his shoulder one final time, Nell slid off his back and watched miserably as he stuck his thumb along the envelope's seal and unfolded its contents. Two pages, front and back. He raised his eyebrow at her, smiling, 'Well what do we have here?'

There was no point Nell making one final plea; he wouldn't listen. She sat down glumly on the second step of the stairs and watched his eyes move from left to right over the page. He reached halfway down the first page when he looked up at her for the first time. She closed her eyes. She knew the part that he must have got to.

'I was the love of your life?'

Nell winced. It seemed perfectly acceptable wording when

she was writing it, absolutely certain in the knowledge that she wouldn't be around to witness the reception of it. And it was sort of true, she had loved him. She'd loved others, many others, but they'd been fleeting love stories, moving in and out of her life without fanfare. He'd been a mainstay for almost a decade, first as her friend who taught her skateboard tricks, and then as her first boyfriend who taught her other sort of tricks. She felt she needed to tell him how important he was to her in this letter, but this was never designed to be read while she was still here, on earth. This was a love letter from the grave, a romantic postscript, a missive for him to sigh wistfully over about the one that got away. It was meant to leave him with a nice warm glow to carry with him, not stoke up some dying ember into a fully-fledged inferno.

'I had no idea that you still felt like this,' he said finally, turning the sheets over in his hand.

How could she tell him she didn't?

'I mean, stranger things have happened, haven't they?' he said. 'You hear of things like this all the time, don't you? First loves reunited years later. I've got to admit that I've thought of you often over the years too. I mean, I don't know if I still feel the way that you do, but I absolutely see that I might be able to in the future, if that's what you really want?'

Nell bit her bottom lip and hugged her knees on the step.

'Wow. Sorry, it's just a lot to take in.' Greg smiled kindly at her, mistaking her body language for shyness. 'Thank you for being so honest about your feelings, it's given me a lot to think about.'

This was excruciating.

As she sat there on the stairs, watching Greg's retreating back going into the kitchen, his gait much jauntier than before, Nell felt like she was going to be sick. She'd find a way to let him down gently in a bit, but more pressing than that were the other four letters that she'd posted on Sunday, which would also have been delivered that morning. . .

PART TWO

Memory Lane is full of potholes

CHAPTER ELEVEN

There were twenty-seven different types of desserts on the ship's dining room buffet table. Twenty-seven. Jenny thought that was an odd choice the pastry chef had made. Why not thirty, or twenty-five? She thought about saying as much to her boyfriend Ray but he wasn't really a pudding sort of fellow and would give her that look he so often did, which made her feel like she was growing a nose out of her forehead. She helped herself to a small piece of vanilla cheesecake, carefully scraping the chocolate curl off onto the side of her plate – it really didn't look like it was worth the extra forty or so calories – and went back to their table. You had a choice on these cruises, whether to sit at a table for two or be paired up with other couples on a bigger table. They always sat alone. Jenny thought that was quite romantic on their first cruise, back – what – nearly five years ago, Ray wanting her all to himself as they meandered down the Nile. But circling the Canaries, the Greek Isles, Norwegian Fjords and most of the Caribbean sitting at a table for two wasn't romantic at all. It was pretty damn lonely.

She looked longingly across at the big round table of four couples a few feet away, total strangers to each other when they embarked on the *Emerald Princess* a couple of days ago, and now laughing and toasting each other, and looking for all the world like childhood friends reunited with the sole mission to drink the boat dry and laugh their way through the fortnight.

'Maybe we should sit with other people tomorrow?' Jenny said, timing the question as perfectly as possible between his last swig of dessert wine and first of brandy.

'Why would we want to do that? Making small talk with a bunch of people we'll never see again? No thanks.'

'Marge and Barry still see the couple they met on the P&O Balearics cruise, they even went camping together this summer, had a lovely time.'

'You hate camping, left that caravan in Weymouth after just one night and booked into a Premier Inn for the rest of the week. Cost us a fortune. And they ran out of bacon at the breakfast buffet.'

'I'm not saying we have to go camping,' Jenny said through her teeth, 'just that we might hit it off with another couple and become friends.'

'I've got enough friends.'

Jenny sighed. God, he could be irritating sometimes. She found herself wondering, as she often did these days, whether she might actually have been happier staying by herself after Tony left. If she was on a cruise alone at least she could have joined the adjacent table who had now all ordered a tray of some sort of flaming cocktails. Mind you, Ray once singed his bushy grey moustache when he lit a cigar at his grandson's christening, one corner of it even still had a strange orange tint to it, so actually it was probably for the best they weren't on that table.

Tell you what though, she thought, Tony used to love a nice cocktail. One time in Cornwall when the girls were small,

Tony had one too many gins at dinner and couldn't even take his socks off. She'd found it so funny, him sitting on the bed in the caravan trying to work out how to take them off. She'd laughed until tears were rolling down her face, and he had joined in too until they both fell back on the bed. If she remembered rightly, they'd even woken the girls up with their laughing; the two of them standing in the doorway, Polly first with Nell just behind her, clutching their teddies, eyes wide at the sight of their dishevelled, drunk parents before jumping up and joining them in the double bed where they all fell asleep. She wondered if Tony remembered snippets of the past like this? And if he did, if moments like flitted into his brain uninvited, the way they did with her, a bittersweet reminder of how happy they used to be. Would he try to flick the memories away or would he allow them to linger awhile, and be happy reminiscing?

'We're docking at Antigua tomorrow,' Ray said. 'Not sure I fancy getting off to be honest, we're a bit too old for all that snorkelling nonsense and once you've seen one Caribbean island you've seen 'em all, haven't you?'

'What a ridiculous thing to say, Ray,' Jenny retorted crossly, 'that's like saying that France is the same as Spain; they're totally different, with different cultures and history and people. Honestly you do say some silly things sometimes.'

'Pardon me for breathing,' Ray huffed, sitting back in his chair and shaking his head.

'And if you thought that, why on earth did you suggest this cruise in the first place?' Jenny asked.

'Because it's been raining in England every day for the last three months, it's dark when we get up, dark when we're eating our tea, the house is feckin' freezing because you only let us switch the heating on when you can see your own breath, and you hate Christmas.'

'I don't hate Christmas, whatever gave you that idea?'

'You made a lasagne for last Christmas Day dinner.'

'You love lasagne.'

'I do love lasagne, but not on Christmas Day.'

'You had thirds.'

'This isn't about the lasagne, Jenny. I thought getting away over Christmas would be a good thing. On the years Polly and her kids don't come over, you don't even bother getting a tree.'

'Christmas is for the kids, isn't it. No point going in for all that when it's just the two of us.'

'Yeah but you don't need to treat it like any other day, and have things like lasagne.'

'I'll have you know that lasagne takes ages to make. It's not as though we had beans on toast. I stewed that ragu for two hours.'

'Excuse me, Mrs Graham?'

Jenny's head swivelled to her right side where one of the waiters stood holding a small envelope. 'You've had a phone call that I believe is quite urgent.'

Jenny felt her knees wobble beneath her as she shakily made her way to the concierge office to use the ship's phone to call her daughter.

'Polly?'

'That was quick, I only left the message about twenty minutes ago.'

'What's wrong?'

Jenny could hear her daughter's slow intake of breath as she tried to find the right words. 'You've had a letter from Nell.'

'And?'

'And I think you'd best come home.'

*

Tony checked his watch. Eight forty-five. Five of his mates would just be getting into their buggies, preparing to tee-off on the first hole of the Monte Rei golf course in the eastern Algarve, while he was getting ready to sit in a sodding assembly hall to listen to someone else's child murder the first verse of 'Once in Royal David's City' before sitting through countless more massacres of festive favourites until the blink-and-you-miss-it-moment that Ruby would appear to give a quick wave, mouth the wrong words to 'Away in a Manger' and then demand a McDonald's lunch. He'd said as much in a heavily watered-down version to his young wife when he realised the date of the pre-Christmas golf trip coincided with his five-year-old daughter's first nativity, but the ensuing ugly glare of disappointment and days of disgusted head-shaking cemented that there really was only one option for that date, and it didn't involve an engraved personal souvenir bag tag on completion of play.

'Ready?' Katie said brightly, putting one arm through her fur gilet before zipping up her high heeled boots.

'Yep. How long do you think this will go on for?'

'I don't know, the reception one last year was about an hour.'

'An hour!'

'Yes, Tony, an hour. Do you have somewhere else you'd rather be?'

The pause indicated that they both knew that the answer was yes. 'It's just that there's a flight to Faro from Gatwick at midday, so if I leave school at nine-thirty I should make it. So I can do the play and the golf.'

Katie did the steadying breath she relied on a considerable number of times a day to stop herself from picking up the antique hat stand, wielding it like a pugil stick and charging with it straight at her husband. 'I'll wait for you in the car,' she said icily.

Katie was already settled in the passenger seat of her Land Rover Discovery when the postman whistled his way up their driveway, cheerily handing over the post to Tony who flung it unopened on the dashboard before heaving himself up into the driver's seat and revving the engine.

There was the usual smattering of dads at the concert, being scheduled at the deeply inconvenient time for most parents of 9 a.m. on a Thursday morning. Tony didn't need to worry about angry bosses or rearranging Zooms or anything like that, not anymore. His early retirement five years ago meant a life of leisurely lie-ins, lunch at various gastropubs and minibreaks at Europe's finest golf resorts, or at least, it was supposed to. Tony looked around the busy school hall. Katie was chatting with some other mums who Tony didn't recognise, which wasn't a surprise, he didn't know any other parent in Ruby's class. He sighed and tried to block out the noise of the recorder emanating from the little kid with inch-thick glasses standing next to an overly encouraging, but very pretty, music teacher accompanying him on the piano. Maybe they ought to rethink Ruby taking up an instrument, if only to be able to have a one-to-one with the music teacher at the next parents' evening.

'Which one's your grandchild?'

Tony snapped out of his hypnotic state and looked at the grey-haired man sitting uncomfortably close to him on a plastic assembly chair.

'I'm sorry?'

'Jacob's ours, in Year One,' the man said smiling. 'It's a lovely age, but we're glad to give him back at the end of the day.'

Tony shuffled uncomfortably on his chair. Not the first, nor the last to make this understandable assumption, but it didn't make explaining it any easier. 'Um, it's Ruby, also Year One, and she's my daughter.'

'Oh, good God, wow, well done you. Sorry for assuming.'

'No, no, easy mistake. I was fifty-eight when we had her.'

'Golly. Bet that keeps you young, eh?'

Tony chuckled along, while recognising the absolute opposite was true: becoming a father again had aged him beyond anything anyone would consider reasonable. The months leading up to Ruby's conception had been absolutely exhausting; it had been decades since such stamina was demanded of him, and the prize at the end used to be a nice cigarette and another bottle of wine, but Katie had the two of them on some god-awful low-carb vegan diet rich in leafy greens and antioxidants and alcohol was an absolute no-no. He used to sneak in a few units here or there when she wasn't looking, but the fear of being caught outweighed the pleasure so that was another vice swiftly and unceremoniously consigned to the memory box.

'I think it's about to start,' Katie said, sliding into her seat, and hovering her finger over the video button on her phone in anticipation. Tony folded his arms and closed his eyes.

The sugary treats the teachers had used to bribe Ruby's class into good behaviour on their final morning of school before the holidays started to kick in around mile one of their seven-mile journey home, which had Tony gritting his teeth and clenching the steering wheel as his daughter writhed and screamed from the back seat and his wife, seemingly oblivious, added to the noise in the car with guffaws and screeching while on her phone. He swung into the driveway at such a speed that the pile of post from the dashboard flew straight off it, straight into Katie's face. 'Christ's sake Tony, what's wrong with you?'

Where should he start?

He waited until Katie and Ruby had slammed their doors

and were walking up the path before he even moved. Thirty seconds of complete peace before one of them would shout for him. How was he going to get through the next two weeks of the Christmas holidays? The noise. The mess. The promise of something unsavoury always lurking in the downstairs toilet. The incessant WhatsApp messages from the Algarve reminding him of a road not taken. Stupid man. Stupid, stupid, stupid man.

'Tony!' Katie shouted from the front door. 'Are you going to sit in there all day?'

'Coming darling.'

He gathered up the post from the passenger's seat and wearily took it into the house.

*

Polly wasn't in the habit of opening other people's post, but she had recognised her sister's handwriting instantly, not that she'd seen it that much in recent years. She didn't think her mum would mind her reading it, she'd asked her to before when she couldn't be bothered going upstairs to fetch her glasses. Polly honestly thought it was going to be one of Nell's usuals: a list of places with complicated names that her sister had recently been to, a few platitudes thrown in of 'you'd really like it here,' 'I wish you could see how blue the sea is' yadda yadda yadda, but it wasn't. The finite tone of it, the apologies, the outpouring of regret, of love, of honest truths, and of goodbyes, was absolutely heart-breaking.

There was no doubt in Polly's mind that Nell absolutely believed that her death was about to happen when she wrote this. She'd spoken about it over the years, less recently, but lots at first, especially when she and Greg had split up, seeking validation from her sister that she'd made the right decision, and even when Polly said no, emphatically told Nell that she was insane to trust a random Australian woman over her friends' and family's opinions, Nell had been steadfast in her belief in this prediction. Polly immediately reached for her phone and dialled Nell's number. It wasn't recognised. Her heart started beating a little faster as she tapped the Facebook icon on her phone, followed by Instagram, only to find her sister's accounts were gone. Polly started to feel a little lightheaded and had to sit down or her legs were in danger of buckling under her. The letter was dated four days ago, if she hadn't died, she'd have called them, telling them to ignore the letter, to throw it away unopened; she wouldn't have let them read this if it wasn't true, wouldn't let them believe she was gone if she wasn't. Polly phoned the cruise-line on autopilot without really thinking it through, not stopping to consider whether interrupting her mum and Ray's cruise with this news was absolutely necessary, but she knew that she couldn't go through what must happen next alone. There would be so many logistics to sort out, at some point they'd get a call about her body being repatriated from goodness knows where, a funeral to sort out. God knows how you go about doing something like that, not that Nell had ever gone in for any of the God-stuff, which was ironic considering how blindly she'd always believed that this was her fate.

Polly chewed her nail. Maybe she should have waited to call the ship. She didn't mean to blurt it out the way she did, no wonder her mum reacted that way, needing the ship's concierge to take the phone off her and summon the liner's medic to sedate her. This was typical Nell though, causing this much distress from afar, she'd been doing it for years.

As Polly walked back to her own house, just a ten-minute fast walk from her mum's, she passed the bus stop she and Nell had stood at every morning before school, huddled in their matching fur-lined parkas with their skirts rolled up to fashionably indecent lengths. She passed the house on the corner with its front garden adorned with expensive-looking fake grass which Nell had once vomited on after too many Malibu and Cokes in town when she was fifteen and Polly was sixteen. The next day they'd seen the woman who owned the house hosing it down, which made them laugh for the whole bus ride. There was the newsagents where they used to spend their allowance on celebrity magazines and sweets; the hairdresser's Nell had a Saturday job in; the sharp bend in the road where Polly had once come off her bike after going too fast and scraped her legs and elbows something terrible, so Nell had given her a piggy back the whole way home, despite Polly being a year older and a few inches taller. *Don't cry. Don't cry.* Polly blinked furiously to stem the tears that were threatening to fall.

The church she got married in was on the next corner, and the wave of sadness was rapidly replaced by the familiar feeling of disappointment when she remembered Nell's last-minute no-show at the wedding due to the Icelandic volcano's ash cloud halting all UK flights. It wasn't Nell's fault, of course it wasn't, well, not really. It was a natural disaster, unavoidable, although, Polly reasoned, if she was being pedantic about it, which wasn't really in her nature, Nell could have booked flights to arrive a few days or a week or so before the wedding rather than the day before, but she hadn't, her sister had left everything to the last minute, as per usual, and then got stranded in whatever paradise she was living in at the time. Same for Beatrice's christening. Polly had sent the save the dates out months in advance, but Nell hadn't checked the UK's Covid test requirements correctly and rocked up to the airport with the wrong test certificate. Again, had she organised herself properly and maybe, just maybe, left herself more than twenty-four hours, she could have fulfilled her godmother duties in person. Thankfully Polly's friend Lauren was able to step in; she was a much more reliable godparent anyway, had never forgotten a birthday or Christmas, and had even set up a savings account for Bea. Nell never would have done any of that. She only asked her because she was her sister, and it was expected. She would have been rubbish at it. And Nell had never liked Damian, she'd told Polly that on more than one occasion before she'd married him that she didn't trust him. Jealous. That's what she always was. She saw how together Polly was, how sorted her life was, how she'd done everything you were meant to do, in the order you were meant to do it, and it shone a giant spotlight on the fact that Nell hadn't.

Polly let herself into her own house, gently simmering by now, her emotions a confusing blend of mind-numbing sadness alongside the ever-present quiet bubbling of resentment at always being the one left behind to pick up the pieces. She picked up the post from her doormat, before stepping over Damian's running shoes and bent down to pick up a safety pin, *all day long you'll have good luck*, and straightened up, shuffling the letters until she came to one that made her stop still in the hall.

*

Tom checked the rota on the fridge and sighed. He knew Thursday wasn't his day for cleaning the kitchen, it was there in purple gel pen in Heidi's handwriting. He didn't know why four people sharing a house needed a rota in the first place, not if you were all fully functioning adults. It was just common sense. Use a saucepan, wash it up, dry it up, put it back in the cupboard for the next person to use. Spend a long time in the bathroom contemplating your life and expelling last night's dinner from your body, use the toilet brush and squirt some air freshener about. It was just common sense. He'd suggested a kitty system for the basics: milk, tea bags, loo roll, that type of thing. They'd all agreed, 'great idea mate,' Heidi had even decorated an empty jam jar with glitter for the purpose, but four months in and he was the only one ever to add anything to it. It was just common sense, and the complete lack of it in this house was driving him absolutely bonkers.

He did, however, have the emotional intelligence to recognise that his tolerance levels were always at their lowest before or after Arlo's visit. Before, because he was hyper aware of wanting this to be a place Arlo liked visiting, and no one wanted to visit somewhere with cockroaches in the kitchen, and after, because dropping him back at his mum's house – the house Tom was still paying the mortgage for – made the differences between their two homes as dramatic a contrast as night and day. It was so deeply unfair that it was she who had the affair, and yet it was him who had to label his milk with a sharpie, and *him* having to set his alarm at 5.45 every morning just to be the first in the shower, and *him* having to leave passive aggressive notes for his housemates on various items around the house, like, '*Help! I'm nearly empty, fill me up with your milky goodness*' on the refillable milk bottles, or '*Oh no! I only have enough for three more poos before disaster strikes!*' on the dwindling loo roll.

It wasn't even the mess or lack of organisation that did his head in. It was the noise. In the home he used to share with Leah and Arlo, the noise was good noise, if that made sense. The sound of cartoons on the TV would soon be accompanied by his son's delicious giggles; the hum of the extractor fan meant that dinner was cooking; the radio station was always tuned to the station he and Leah liked; the front door closing meant that she was home safely. Here, in this four-bed semi that masqueraded as Piccadilly Circus, every sound was an intrusion. House music from one room, weird French gangster rap from another, Noughties garage from the third room, and very loud huffing and puffing from Tom's. He'd bought noise-blocking headphones for the daytime, expensive foam earplugs for the night, and he still had cause to grind his teeth together upwards of two hundred times a day.

He'd been particularly impatient this last week; he just couldn't shake the thought of the woman he'd bought his bed off. Nell. She would have died three days ago now. There had been no reports about it, in the paper or on the news, but then why would there have been? He didn't even know her last name to find out when her funeral was going to be, he'd have liked to have gone. He still felt a bit sick whenever he thought back to that night at the comedy club. The fact that she'd heard his set and thought that he was the type to turn his lovers into material. *Lovers*, he laughed at the thought. Nell had been the first person he'd slept with since Leah. He'd royally screwed that situation up, and she was so nice as well. Kooky, but he could tell she had a lovely soul. And now she'd gone and what's worse, she'd died hating him.

'Tom?' came a call from one of his housemates from the hallway. 'You've got a letter. I've put it next to the breadbin, and by the way, we've run out of bog roll.'

CHAPTER TWELVE

'Oh God,' Nell moaned into her knees as she slowly rocked back and forth. 'No, no, no, no.' She didn't know what was worse: the emotional, tear-stained goodbye her mum would be receiving, in which she revealed that her boyfriend Ray was really, *really* boring and her mum deserved better in her twilight years; the bordering-on-teenage-daughter-levels-of-belligerence tirade penned to her dad in which she blamed him for everything just shy of the Russian invasion; the toe-curling 'if things were different' love letter to Tom or the fact that she'd just told her sister that in the interests of abject honesty, her husband had once tried to kiss her and she was pretty sure he was having an affair with her friend Lauren.

No, no, no, no, I'm meant to be dead, I'm not supposed to be here to witness the nuclear fallout from my deathbed revelations.

'Coffee?' Greg called cheerfully from the kitchen,

'Arsenic?' Nell replied numbly.

She couldn't even call each of them to tell them to throw the letters away without opening them; all her contacts were on her phone, which she'd wiped and sold, her parents didn't have social media and she didn't even know Tom's last name, just heard him say the address over the phone to the man with a van he'd hired to put the bed in. There was a small chance that he might not have even received it; did Royal Mail even bother trying to deliver letters addressed to people like 'Tom with curly hair'? There was probably a whole garbage bin reserved for letters like hers in the sorting centre. And didn't Greg say that her mum was on a cruise? Her letter would be on the doormat for weeks.

Nell started to perk up with the thought that this could all be turned around. Her dad was bound to be away at a golf resort somewhere, and Katie wasn't the type to open his post in his absence. Actually, who was she kidding? Katie might be the type to do that, Nell didn't know what 'type' Katie was as she'd never met her, but in her mind her wicked stepmother probably just had new acrylic nails put on ready for Christmas and wouldn't want to risk breaking one by opening an envelope. Okay, Nell started to relax, that was potentially three out of four letters she could intercept. Which just left Polly's. It was highly unlikely that Polly had had time to open her post yet, she would have just done school drop-off, just about to start a PTA coffee morning/aerobics class/online degree in aeronautics. All was definitely not lost.

'Look Greg, I know you've done so much for me already,' Nell started, leaning against the doorframe of the kitchen for moral and physical support. 'But can I borrow some money for the train?'

'Where do you want to go?'

'Hove.'

'But your mum's away, remember; I don't think she's back until New Year's.'

'It's Polly I want to see.'

'Polly?'

'Polly, my sister. I think I can remember where she lives, it's just round the corner from Mum's. I've been there once and I need to go as soon as possible.'

'Today?'

Nell nodded.

'I guess I could call work and take the day off, I'm owed loads of lieu days from always working on bank holidays.'

'Honestly, I don't need you to come too, just drop me at the station.'

'Look, for some bizarre reason fate has brought us back together again. My conference wasn't even meant to be at that hotel, did I tell you that? We were supposed to be at one in Victoria but they had a leak right through the ballroom and my company rebooked last minute. Now if that's not a sign of serendipity I don't know what is. Don't you think it's weird that when you needed help I showed up? I think that's really weird.'

'Please Greg, it's important, I need to go to Hove as soon as possible.'

'I'll take you then, we can drive.'

'Honestly, I'm happy getting the train.'

'No, no, it's fine, I'd like to. We could even make a day of it, have a nice lunch somewhere.'

Nell nodded noncommittally, she could only think about one stage of the plan at a time, not that the plan was any more formed than: somehow get into Polly's house and destroy the letter. Somehow get into her Mum's house and destroy the letter. Somehow remember what the heck she wrote on the front of her dad's envelope and destroy the bloody letter. She had no idea what to do about Tom's. The thought of him reading it this morning made her feel completely sick.

'Have you just had it cleaned?' Nell asked Greg, peering over her shoulder into the immaculate back seat of his Audi.

'No, I just don't use it that much.'

'Is it new?'

'Three years.'

'Where's your stuff?'

'What stuff?'

'You know, snacks, tissues, hand gel, sunglasses, magazines, umbrellas, change of shoes, a jumper, old scratch-cards, chocolate wrappers, water bottles, that sort of thing.'

Greg looked absolutely horrified. 'Jesus, remind me to never get in your car.'

'I'm currently wearing everything I own. If I had a car, I'd be selling it. Or sleeping in it. Seriously though, why do you have a car when you have your motorbike?'

'I don't like riding in the rain.'

'What about dancing in it?'

'What?' Greg was scrunching up his nose while looking in his side mirror before pulling out.

Nell waited for him to successfully navigate a couple of very narrow streets with cars parked either side before saying, 'So, talk to me about the motorbike.'

'Hang on, how do you know I have one?'

'I saw the leathers in your wardrobe.'

'You were snooping?'

'It's a wardrobe. It's not like I rifled under your mattress. Anyway, I needed to change out of the ballgown.'

'Ah yes, the ballgown. Why exactly were you wearing that again?'

'It was all part of the perfect death. Don't change the subject. Motorbikes. You've always hated motorbikes, wouldn't even hire a moped in Bali, called them death-traps, so why the change of heart?' As she was talking the penny dropped, it was all making sense. He knew he wasn't going to die on one, or at least, not for another five decades, so why not enjoy the throb of a Kawasaki between his legs when it held zero risk-factor.

'I don't think I was ever *that* against them,' Greg said. 'If you've had the proper training, they're very safe.'

'Uh-huh.'

'What's that supposed to mean?'

'Nothing, nothing at all. And you don't suppose you had this change of heart after your own death-date prediction?'

'Don't be ridiculous.'

'It's not raining today. Why didn't you suggest taking the bike, it'd be quicker?'

Greg shrugged. 'I don't have a spare helmet.'

'You have two in your wardrobe.'

'You're quite the Miss Marple, aren't you?'

'I think you've bottled out of riding it because now you know you're not infallible and have just the same probability of dying on it as any other person, you're probably already hatching a plan to sell it.'

He crumpled his face up in an attempt to show how wrong she was, 'Uh. No, that's not it at all.'

'You've posted the advert online already, haven't you?'

'No!' he said with exaggerated denial.

'What else have you done or not done because of what Mandy said?'

'You're barking completely up the wrong tree, what she said has not impacted my life in the slightest.'

'If you say so.'

'Look, if you want to believe that I've been affected by her too to make yourself feel saner, then fine, believe it, but I honestly haven't thought about her, or her crackpot predictions in years.'

'Fine.'

'Fine.'

Nell stared out of her window, while Greg kept his eyes trained ahead, sticking resolutely to the speed limit and checking his mirror every thirty seconds or so, just like the highway code told you to. He hadn't mentioned the letter again, which was a relief. She wasn't sure how she would have felt if this situation was reversed and she'd just received a note from him proclaiming she was the love of his life. Gratitude? Closure? Regret? And then there was the letter to Tom, that was the one that might have hit the hardest with the least chance of redeeming as she had no clue what his address was; she'd screwed up the paper it was scrawled on before leaving her flat. It was in Southwark, but that was as much as she remembered. She was probably giving herself too much credit that she'd even had an impact on him, making love to women from Facebook Marketplace might be a weekly hobby, like CrossFit, just with more oxytocin and less clothes involved. She'd probably imagined the chemistry between them anyway, it wasn't as though her mind was completely clear and coherent enough to correctly interpret signals, was it? She'd already had one foot in the afterlife after all. He'd probably got the letter this morning, vaguely remembered it being a pleasurable way to spend a midweek afternoon and given himself a little high-five for clearly having such a long-lasting impact on a dying woman, not to mention giving him valuable material for his show. She didn't even really know why he was one of the recipients of her five final notes, surely there had been other people over the years that deserved one more than him?

Nell hated silences. Which was odd for someone who had travelled alone for the majority of her adult life. But she wasn't going to speak first. Nope. She was just going to keep looking out of her window as though the M23 held the best vistas outside of the Whitsunday Islands. Nell puffed her cheeks out as she exhaled loudly.

Greg glanced at her. 'What are you thinking?'

That I'm glad you spoke first. 'Just how pretty England is.' Nell had learned over the years that you should never say anything rude about the country you're visiting, not even if you've heard locals say the same thing. Except, she realised, with another loud sigh, she wasn't a visitor here. This was where she was from and this was where she'd ended up. Gosh, that was depressing, she thought as they passed a couple sitting on picnic chairs eating their lunch on the hard shoulder of the motorway. But if she had chosen to spend her death-date somewhere exotic then she'd have been completely alone, in a foreign country, dealing with waking up with no money, no belongings, and trying to rebuild a life from scratch. Maybe Greg was right, this was serendipity that brought her back here to him, so he could help her do it.

'Do you come back to Hove often?' Nell asked, wondering if this was where they might have gravitated back to one day had they stayed together. If conversations about where their kids might be happiest would have led them back to where they had grown up, breathing in the ocean air, hunting for the most interesting stones from the shingle beach, getting pots of ten-pence pieces for the arcade. They might have even bought a beach hut – priciest per metre real estate you could get apparently – she'd have caved into Greg's persistence, she always did. They'd have to have gone there most afternoons after school when it was sunny and every day in the summer to make it worth it, but she'd have cultivated homemaking skills that she didn't currently have need for to make it cosy and nice. It was funny, she thought, it wasn't just the things you had or didn't have that were different depending what life path you choose, but also the things that you had to learn. She knew how to make friends within a couple of minutes, how to fall asleep sitting down and how to make a sarong work for a beach in the morning, a restaurant in the evening and a hammock at night, but she wouldn't have the faintest idea how to make a home a family would want to live in.

'Every couple of months.'

'Sorry?'

'You asked how often I come back to Hove?'

'How much is a beach hut nowadays?'

'You're not allowed to live in one if that's what you're thinking?'

'I'm not, I'm just wondering.'

'About twenty-five grand, I think. They go like hot cakes.'

'Twenty-five grand? Nell spluttered. 'I've lived on half that for a year!'

'They're actually really useful if you have kids, you can keep their buckets and spades in them so you don't need to keep lugging them down to the beach each time you go—'

'A personal sherpa to carry all your stuff to the top of Everest costs about four grand. I'm pretty sure they'd be happy carrying a bag of plastic buckets to the beach at the end of the road for you for a tenner.'

'They're good to shelter in if the weather turns.'

'If the weather turns, what are you doing on the beach? Go home.'

'You can have a little kitchen in them, make a cup of coffee or a sandwich whenever you want.'

'The seafront's got loads of cafés, why would you need to make yourself a coffee in a shed?'

'Why are you arguing with me about beach huts?'

'I'm not arguing, I just can't really understand why anyone would pay twenty-five grand for one.'

Greg shrugged while doing a mirror, signal, manoeuvre to finally overtake a truck doing twenty miles under the speed limit after driving behind it for the last three miles. 'I always thought it would be a nice thing to have, if you've got kids.'

'Do you want them? Kids?'

'I've got no idea, possibly, probably. One day.'

'Best put your name down for a beach hut now then. Apparently they go like hot cakes.'

'Why are you cross?'

'I'm not cross,' Nell replied.

'Grumpy then.'

'I'm not grumpy either. I just really need to get to Hove as soon as possible.'

'Why the rush?'

'Look, I sent other letters too, and I was a bit. . . honest in them. Now I need to try to intercept them before they're read.'

'What did you say?'

'I don't want to think about it. Nonsense ramblings of a woman on her deathbed wanting to get the last word.'

'Nell. . . what did you say?'

'Oh look, a magpie, did you salute it?'

'Nell.'

'I said things that if I knew I would still be here today I wouldn't have done. Let's just leave it at that.'

'Is that how you feel about the letter you wrote to me? That it's nonsense?'

Tread carefully, Nell told herself, remembering the countless times Greg had thrown his school bag over one shoulder and indignantly marched off, pride hurt at a comment she'd airily thrown away. He'd been so kind, opening his house up to her, giving her money, driving her down here, and the wrong reply might see him literally slamming on the brakes and demanding she tuck and roll out of the car onto the hard shoulder. Anyway, she didn't really know how she felt about him. Not yet. She must have been harbouring some sort of lingering longing or his wouldn't have been one of the last five letters she wrote. 'Of course not,' she said honestly. 'I

114

might not have been quite so forthright as I was, but it wasn't nonsense.'

'Because us bumping into each other like this, I don't think it was an accident,' Greg continued. 'And maybe you're right, we should give things another go.'

Give things another go? Did she say that?'

They passed a road sign which was the perfect conversation-changer. 'Oh wow, we're at Crawley already,' Nell gushed, 'I love the A23, it's such a great road. Do you remember when we had that school trip to the Natural History Museum and we had to keep pulling in all along this road for Laura Allen to be sick?'

'Ah, we're going down the deflection route, are we? Okay, that's fine, if that's how you want to play it.'

'I'm not playing anything; we're literally going down memory lane. Have you got any music?'

Greg sighed, remembering that this was what it was like to have Nell in your life. 'Plug my phone in to Spotify.'

'Ooo,' Nell said, looking through Greg's playlists, 'your music taste has not got better with age.'

'What are you talking about? We loved the same music.'

'Twenty years ago. I'm pretty sure that my tastes have evolved.'

Nell was finding it difficult to pick a song that didn't have a formative memory attached to it. So many of the songs she'd hastily switched off over the years when they came on the radio were all on his playlists. Even the song they'd said they'd have as their first dance. Was it that he enjoyed torturing himself or did he simply not remember its significance? She looked sideways at him to gauge his response as she pressed play on it. He started tapping his fingers on the steering wheel as the bittersweet melody of Aerosmith's 'I Don't Want to Miss a Thing' started filtering out from the car's speakers.

'Oh, I love this song, haven't heard it for ages, good choice.'

Nell watched him incredulously as he continued to part hum, part sing the lyrics, even closing his eyes at the traffic lights to really belt out the chorus without the tiniest hint of wistfulness that had fate dealt them a different hand, they'd have once twirled around a ballroom floor to it. Was it a Mars Venus thing? Or a Greg and Nell thing? Greg and Nell, Nell and Greg. *Where's Greg? I don't know, ask Nell. Have you seen Nell recently? Oh, she's probably with Greg.* She'd floated the idea of calling themselves Neg for a while, but it never caught on. It had taken her years to fill the part of her life that he had once inhabited. Years loaded with other men, sometimes women too, in countries as far away from their one-bedroom flat as it was possible to be, yet whenever she got a whiff of his aftershave, or heard this song, all her hard work at making him fade from view was gone. Yet here he was, merrily listening to it with as much emotion as a table lamp.

'What's that sigh for?' he asked.

'Nothing. Just thinking about what I'm going to say to Polly if she's there.'

'Doesn't she work?'

'I've got no idea. We've sort of drifted apart a bit to be honest.'

'Your fault or hers?'

'Hers. And maybe a bit of mine. Okay, maybe a lot mine. But also, hers.'

It was never really Polly's fault, Nell knew that. It was Nell's own disorganisation, her inability to fuse what was happening 'back home' with what was taking place right in front of her. Receiving the various invitations over the years from her sister had been a painful reminder of what she'd left behind. And she absolutely could have booked flights there and then on reading the save the dates. Nothing had ever stopped her from altering whatever flimsy schedule that was only ever half-formed in her mind to accommodate a family occasion, but she never did. She never bought a diary, never made an online calendar to remind her of these milestone events, she just allowed them to float in her mind along with choices about what to eat that day, where to sleep, whether to head east or west next, knowing that she could RSVP another day, make the bookings tomorrow, or perhaps the day after that. And it wasn't as if she'd be missed at these things anyway. It was duty that put her on these invite lists, shared DNA, not a yearning need for her to share the moment. She'd have been an embarrassment anyway, rocking up with clothes that would never grace the trend pages of women's magazines, with hair that hadn't been professionally cut or styled in two decades, trying desperately to blend with Polly's friends, who all looked like Boden models. She'd once heard Polly attempting to explain away her sister's appearance. 'She's a bit bohemian', 'She's opted out of society a bit,' 'She's something of a *free spirit*'. She was right on all counts, Nell thought, but there was no denying that as the years passed, Hove, and Polly, seemed so much further away than just a flight.

'Can you speed up?' Nell urged, glancing at her watch for the fiftieth time.

'The speed limit's fifty.'

'I saw your speeding fine on your fridge. If you get another one I'll pay it.'

'With what money?'

He had a point.

'Anyway, speeding is dangerous.'

'Ah right, yes, thereby increasing the risk of death, which you wouldn't have given a flying feather about a few days ago, I get it.'

117

'I wish you would leave that alone; it's really starting to annoy me that you think I care about that.'

'Prove it by overtaking the car in front.'

'No!'

'Prove it, prove it,' Nell chanted.

'Stop it, or I'll pull in and you'll have to hitchhike the rest of the way.'

Nell smiled to herself; she'd forgotten what fun it was to bait him.

Nell prided herself on her good memory. She could still recount at least half of the 302 metro stations in Seoul despite it being a few years since she'd last visited, not to mention her childhood home phone number and the car registration plates of every car her parents had ever owned, but faced with a long line of identical semi-detached houses on Polly's road, Nell's cognitive recall abilities totally failed her. She tried to conjure up the front of the envelope she'd written the address on earlier in the week, but that didn't work either. She vaguely remembered it having two numbers and writing a zero as the second figure, but she had no idea at all what the digit in front of it might have been.

'Park up here,' Nell said, 'and I'll walk down.' Greg insisted on coming with her, which she was grateful for when the octogenarian resident and his doppelganger dog at number ten both growled menacingly at her from their front window. Number twenty clearly was inhabited by either a deeply patriotic Englishman or a member of the National Front based on the St George's flag in both upstairs windows and a rather offensive bumper sticker on the car outside. Number thirty had three cracked tiles on its pathway, a dead fir bush in a pot next to the front door and a gutter held together with duct tape. As Polly had never stepped out of her house without her nails painted since puberty, Nell concluded that this was very unlikely to be where she lived and didn't even bother ringing the bell. By the time they reached number fifty, Nell was starting to wonder why, out of all the roads in all the world, her sister had chosen this one.

Number fifty had an empty parking space right outside it, a dry rectangle on a wet road, showing that one had been recently moved. The pathway tiles were immaculate, the paved area in front of the living room window a paradise for potted plants, the windows adorned with sleek white Venetian blinds.

'Bingo,' Nell said as they stood on the pavement looking up at it.

'How do you know it's this one?'

'I just know my sister.'

'Wait!' Greg said, pulling Nell back by her coat sleeve. 'They've got a Ring doorbell.'

'A what now?'

'A Ring doorbell.'

'What's that?'

'Where did you say you were the last few years? 1985?'

'Believe it or not, fancy doorbells aren't that far up most of the world's priority list. Some of the places I've lived haven't even had doors. What's a Ring doorbell?'

'It records movement outside the front door. She'll see us if we get any closer.'

'So, what now?' Nell walked a few steps further down the pavement and peered down the alleyway between this house and its neighbour. 'I reckon we try round the back.'

'And what then?'

Nell shrugged. 'There might be a window open?'

'In December?'

'Or a key under a doormat?'

'Unlikely, but worth a shot I guess.'

They gently tiptoed round the back, through the unlocked side gate, trying not to look as furtive as they felt. Nell peered in through the kitchen window; her hunch was right, it was definitely Polly's house, one of those family photos taken in a studio was framed on the wall showing Polly, Damian and Beatrice all lying down facing the camera, their chins cupped in their hands in a cute, slightly unnatural, pose that made Nell shudder a little.

'Check under all the pots, see if there's a key anywhere,' Nell ordered.

'Is this illegal?' asked Greg. 'I don't want to spend Christmas in prison.'

'Of course not, it's not like we're breaking a window or anything,' Nell replied, trying to pretend that she hadn't already tapped the glass to see if it was single or double glazed.

A very full colour-coded family planner hung on the kitchen wall alongside the fridge which was decorated with novelty magnets obviously collected from holidays and day trips. Vacations that Nell had sometimes seen catalogued on Facebook. She'd always liked the posts, sometimes even putting a comment like, 'That looks fun!' or 'Looks like you had a lovely time!' to try to keep the fragile thread between the two of them intact. Nell's gaze travelled to the kitchen table, where a stack of placemats lay next to a roll of kitchen roll, and next to them, a neat pile of papers.

On top was her letter, out of its envelope, clearly read.

CHAPTER THIRTEEN

'You should leave a note at least.'

'Saying what? Turns out I'm not dead, and none of what I said was true?' Nell buried her head in her hands as they sat on the patio step in Polly's back garden. 'Let me think.'

'I could nip back to the car and get a pen and paper?'

'I honestly don't know what I'd say.'

'How about, sorry if my letter made you upset, good news, it was a false alarm, I'm still alive and would very much like to rebuild some bridges?'

'I told her that Damian tried to kiss me and I once saw him with her best friend.'

'Why did you tell her that!'

'Because it's true! I wouldn't make that up, and I didn't want to carry that secret to my grave.'

'And yet you were happy for your parting shot from earth to be the destruction of your sister's marriage?'

'No, I just thought that she should know.'

'Why? Why did she need to know?'

'Well if he'd tried it on with me, his wife's sister, and her best friend, then who else has he had a go at? I was doing her a favour.'

'I'm not sure she'll see it like that.'

'That's why I was trying to get to the letter before she did.'

'Did you not stop to think at all about the effect the letter would have on her? I mean, I get that you thought you'd be cavorting in the clouds by now, but did not one part of you think this through before cleansing your own conscience? To think of the cost? The impact?'

His words hung soberly in the air, because the truth was, Nell thought sadly, she hadn't. The letter writing had been cathartic, a final last word, a sombre sign off; she hadn't imagined them being opened and read at all. What did that make her? Thoughtless? Uncaring? Self-obsessed? Her stomach lurched at the accusation she'd thrown at Damian like it was confetti at the wedding she never made it to. The volcanic ash cloud was a convenient alibi for missing it; it was all over the news, you couldn't dispute that no planes were flying, but she wasn't in some tropical paradise like she led them believe. She was in Paris. A hop on the Eurostar away. Four hours maximum door-to-door with both feet firmly on the ground at all times. The truth was, she just didn't want to go. She didn't want to pretend to be happy about Polly marrying a man who'd cornered her outside the toilets in a pub and told her 'Don't worry, she'll never know,' then half an hour later seeing him leave through the side entrance with a girl that would go on to be one of Polly's bridesmaids. Nell didn't want to have the same circular conversation from well-meaning and less well-meaning aunts and cousins, and parental friends, and friends of friends, repeating to each of them that, *no, the next one would not be her*. Nell didn't want to feel the same crushing conundrum of whether life would have been better had she stayed.

A metallic clank from the side gate made Nell and Greg

scramble to their feet and dash behind the shed, just as Polly and her dog rounded the corner of the house. The dog started barking as ferociously as a miniature dachshund could in the direction of where the two of them were cowering. 'Sadie, stop,' came Polly's voice. 'Leave it.' Her tone was devoid of authority, of power, of control, but it was laced instead with fragility, and sadness. It was the voice of someone who'd been gulping in air between sobs, breathless from walking and crying. Nell peeked out round the corner of the shed to see her sister just standing there on the patio stones, her hands limply hanging at her side, staring, just staring, at nothing. Making no attempt to go into the house, or to sit down on one of the garden chairs, as though her body had forgotten how to move. Her face was red and puffy, her make-up long gone. She looked smaller than Nell remembered. The poise, the elegance, Nell had always associated with her had completely disappeared. She looked broken.

'Polly—'

The word was out of Nell's mouth before she could stop it, as she stepped out from behind the shed with her arms outstretched, in her mind going in for a hug, but as Nell replayed this moment, and her sister's terrified screaming reaction to seeing her, over again in her mind, she conceded, it could have been interpreted as zombie-like.

Polly shot into the house; the sound of the heavy double bolt being drawn across it violently echoed around the garden.

'Well, that seemed to go well,' Greg said, extracting himself from a potted fir bush and brushing himself down.

'Do you think I scared her?'

'I would say that is pretty conclusive.'

'Should I go after her?'

'Unless you want her to come back out and burn sage in your face.'

Nell gingerly crept up to the window and gently tapped on it. 'Polly,' she said loudly, adding unnecessarily, 'it's me, Nell.' When she was faced with silence she turned back to Greg for encouragement, who gave her a few eager nods and shooed her with his hand.

She knocked on the glass again, 'Polly? I need to talk to you.'

'Go away!' came the quivering shout from within.

'Polly, please, I'm still alive, it was all a massive mistake, please, open the door.'

Silence.

'I shouldn't have sent that letter,' Nell shouted through the glass, 'I'm so sorry, I really didn't mean to upset you, I don't know what I was thinking—'

'You weren't,' muttered Greg from behind her.

'Please Polly, talk to me,' Nell begged. 'I'm not moving until you open the door.'

At that exact moment Nell felt a drip of water fall from the heavens and land down her collar, goading her to see exactly how committed she was to staying put and arguing her case. Another drop fell on her head. And another.

'Polly, please—'

'Nell, we should go, we can come back later when she's calmed down.'

Nell swung round to face Greg, 'No, I can't leave like this.' She turned back to the window and hammered on it again, the rain falling thick and fast now, running in rivulets down the side of her face and neck, 'Polly!'

They then heard a door slam and an engine start up from round the front of the house. By the time they'd run around the side it was disappearing around the corner. Polly was gone.

A few minutes later Greg and Nell were back in his car, sitting on two plastic bags to protect the seat's upholstery.

124

They both stared ahead at the patterns the rain was making on the windscreen, droplets racing each other in tandem before veering off on different routes.

'She's never going to forgive me.'

'She will. She just needs some time to process this.'

'I wouldn't forgive me.'

'Yes, you would. You literally hold a grudge for the time it takes to eat a KitKat.'

Nell turned her body to face him, 'What makes you so sure that you still know me? That I haven't changed in the last twenty years?'

'Because you haven't.'

'You're saying my feelings are all surface-level? That I don't have any deep emotions?'

'That's not what I said, nor implied. I merely said that you don't hold a grudge. Right, shall we go to your mum's now?'

Nell gave a lacklustre nod. A few hours ago, this mission had seemed exciting, fun even, an adventurous challenge worthy of a primetime slot on Channel 4, but the reality of what she'd done was firmly sinking in. These were people's feelings and lives that she had played with. And not just any people either, people she loved, and who loved her. Apart from Tom, she didn't love him, but her letter had implied that if she was granted more days breathing, that she could definitely learn to. Oh God, she was actually going to throw up.

Greg had never been good with vomit. Nell recognised that not many people were, it wasn't a characteristic the majority of people would seek to have, or boast about, '*I'm good with horses, house plants and vomit.*' But Nell quickly remembered that he was spectacularly bad. They'd once both made the poorly considered choice to have a steaming plate of egg fried rice from a man with a gas-powered hot plate in his bicycle basket in Hua Hin on the west coast of Thailand, and she

125

was tasked with cleaning up after both of them after his infant-like wails of woe.

'I think I'm okay now,' Nell said, getting back in his car. 'I managed to do it over a drain.'

Greg started retching in the driver's seat, and held up his hand to stem her from elaborating further. When he regained his composure, he handed her a packet of chewing gum from the glove compartment. Before he slammed it shut again, Nell glimpsed a torch and a mobile phone, exactly the same make and model as his normal phone that was plugged into the car speakers.

'Why do you have another phone? Is it a burner phone? Are you a crim?'

'Don't be ridiculous.'

'Do you do seedy deals in your car? Is it a hotline to the mafia? Do you have a whole other family?'

'If you must know, it's an exact replica of my usual one so that if this one gets lost or stolen or my cloud storage gets hacked, I still have all my contacts, photos and files etc. I back it up weekly so it merges all my content.'

'That is an incredible amount of forward planning.'

Greg shrugged. 'It just means that should I ever find myself in a situation not unlike yours, I wouldn't be scrabbling around for numbers and knocking on doors trying to find addresses, I'd have it all right there.'

'Do you also have a pop-up replica house, a briefcase of cash and a duplicate passport?'

'Why would I have all of that?'

'Well it's just the logical next step of contingency planning, isn't it? Another life just ready to go, should this one go pop.'

'Are you mocking me? I can't work out if you're teasing.'

'I just wonder where it stops? The back-ups one puts in place for things going wrong, the insurance policies. It's a rather negative way of looking at the world, isn't it? Preparing for the worst.'

'It's not preparing for the worst, it's preparing for—'

'Something bad to happen.'

'Something *unexpected* to happen.'

Nell pressed on, 'But surely everything is unexpected. You're not following a script. You don't know what's going to happen in five minutes' time, so what's the point in preparing for it?'

'You're a fine one to talk, if you had been slightly more prepared for the unexpected this week, then you wouldn't be in the pickle you are now.'

'I'm not in a pickle.'

'You are in a pickle. And somehow you've dragged me into it too.'

'I didn't drag you anywhere Greg Gage, it was your idea to come along for the ride! You could be sat right now in front of your multiple monitors moving numbers about, but instead, you insisted on driving me down here.'

'I thought you'd need my help.'

'I don't *need* your help Greg, I *like* your company. It's different. I am perfectly able to sort all this out myself, it's just slightly more pleasant doing it with you than without you.'

'Only slightly more pleasant?' Greg had a faint twitch to his lips as he spoke.

'Just a smidgen.'

'Well in that case, shall we crack on? And can you not put the chewing gum wrapper in the side compartment? There's a dog poo bin over there.'

Julie, who lived next door to her mum, had a spare key. She'd always had a spare key, much like her mum had one for Julie's house and probably Polly's. Had Nell thought through this quest in any more detail than just 'find house, get letter', she might have realised that the simpler plan would have been to have started at her mum's and made life considerably easier for herself.

'But Jenny's not back for another ten days,' Julie said, handing over the key after hobbling back inside for what seemed like an eternity to get it. 'Are you stopping until then?'

Nell hadn't considered that as an option at all until this moment, suddenly realising that would solve every one of her immediate problems. She smiled at the older woman who had babysat her most Saturday nights of her childhood and said that she wasn't sure of her plans yet.

'Of course,' Julie replied kindly. 'Your mum tells me all the time all the exciting places you're going to. What a life!'

Nell smiled. 'I'm sure I'll see you soon, Julie, thanks for the key. Look after yourself.'

You had to pull the handle up while turning the key not quite all the way to the right to open it; it was a knack Nell learned in her last year of primary when she was given a front door key to let herself in after school as her mum had taken on a second job in the afternoons and Polly finished at senior school later. As the door opened into the house Nell breathed in the familiar scent of dusty pot pourri on the semi-circular hall table and her mother's perfume that penetrated every surface. She stood in the neat hallway, once home to school bags, trainers, PE kits, hockey sticks, her dad's golf clubs, piles of coats on top of coats on the hooks that now only housed his and hers matching waterproofs. The silence more than the cleanliness was unnerving. Even after she and Polly had moved out, Nell had only been back here a handful of times, each time greeted by a houseful of people: her nana's funeral, a Christmas, a fleeting flying visit – times when the house heaved with life. But today it was still.

Eeeeeee. Eeeeeee. Eeeeeee. Eeeeeee. *For fuck's sake, when did her mum get an alarm?* Eeeeeee. Eeeeeee. Eeeeeee.

Nell put her hands over her ears as Greg came running in through the door, also covering his ears, 'For fuck's sake, when did your mum get an alarm?' he shouted over the deafening shrill.

Nell shook her head, 'I've got no idea!' she yelled back.

'Run back to that neighbour you got the key off and see what the number is, I'll try and find the box.'

'WHAT?'

'GO TO THAT WOMAN NEXT DOOR. GET THE CODE.'

Nell put her thumb up and ran next door, only to find no answer to her frantic knocking. The alarm sounded just as loud out on the street. The police would surely be here in minutes. Then they'd connect the dots with her being the woman on Wanted posters in the lobbies of every five-star hotel in the country and the game would be over. She'd spend Christmas inside eating leathery turkey sharing a cell with a woman called CeCe the size of a second-row scrum rugby player with a fondness for origami and killing people.

Nell dashed back next door. 'NO GOOD. SHE'S NOT THERE.'

'WHO ELSE WOULD KNOW THE CODE?' Eeeeeee Eeeeeee Eeeeeee.

Her mum had lived on this street for nearly forty years, Nell could have told you everyone on it once, but apart from Julie, the rest of the houses seemed to now be house-shares or young families. She suddenly had an idea: Polly. She ran into the living room, still holding her hands over her ears, to the top drawer of the Edwardian desk that once belonged to her great-grandfather. In it, as Nell well knew, was the well-thumbed address book her mother had always kept there. Eeeeeee Eeeeeee Eeeeeee. She flicked through to P for Polly – no surname categorisation for Jenny Graham, oh no – and there it was, her sister's number and address. Jeez, thought Nell, being a forward planner would definitely have had its benefits today.

Her fingers shook as she dialled her sister's number from her mum's home phone, the deafening siren of the alarm making any coherent thought impossible. Eeeeeee Eeeeeee Eeeeeee.

'Mum! How are you back already? What's that noise?'

'POLLY, IT'S ME NELL, I'M AT MUM'S BUT THE ALARM IS GOING OFF, WHAT'S THE CODE?

'You broke into Mum's house?'

'NO, I GOT THE KEY OFF JULIE.'

'Is she out of hospital already?'

'WHO?'

'Julie. She had a hip replacement and then got a viral infection.'

'SHE SEEMED FINE. I NEED THE CODE.'

'0810 Star.'

'GREG! IT'S 0810 STAR!' Nell shouted through to the hallway where Greg was poised by the small white box on the wall. 'THAT'S MY BIRTHDAY!' Nell suddenly realised. Every day her mum had tapped in Nell's birthday into the keypad. Every day. Perhaps even a few times a day. Nell had gone weeks, sometimes months without even thinking of home, and here was her mum, nipping out to the shops, Nell's birthday, back from the shops, Nell's birthday, a jaunt to the hairdressers, Nell's birthday, coffee with friends, Nell's birthday, meeting Polly, Nell's birthday. This thought hit the hardest. Here was Polly, living less than a mile away, the waterer of plants, the keeper of keys, the reliable one that never moved away, the one that knew when neighbours were having new hips, and yet the one that left without a backwards glance got immortalised as an alarm code. That hardly seemed fair.

'I'M SO SORRY,' Nell shouted, at the exact same moment the beeping ceased, her loud words echoing down the phone line. She heard her sister inhale and exhale loudly.

'Polly? Did you hear me?

'I heard you. Everyone heard you.'

'The letter, I didn't mean any of it.'

'Yes you did.'

'The old me might have done, but—'

'The old you?' Polly laughed sarcastically. 'The letter was posted a few days ago, how much of a personality transplant have you had since then?'

Polly wouldn't have believed Nell even if she told her. So, she didn't.

'Nell, there's a police car pulling up outside,' Greg called from the hallway.

'Polly, I've got to go, I'll call you back.'

'Please don't.' The line went dead.

The two police officers were very understanding after Nell flung open the door to the downstairs loo and pointed at a family photo collage that she appeared on countless times proving that she wasn't an opportunistic grand larcenist. 'Sorry for wasting your time officer, the code completely flew out of my mind.'

'It happens all the time, don't worry about it. Enjoy your day.'

'You too.'

The second police officer was still in the cloakroom studying the photos, 'Nell Graham?'

'Yes?'

'Oh my God, It's me, Karen Filmore! We were in the same year!'

'Oh wow, Karen, gosh, what a coincidence. You remember Greg Gage from our year as well?'

'Oh my God, you two are still together? That's so lovely, you always were a great couple. I'm still with Ian too, how many kids have you got? We've got three. How old are yours? We should get them together. Have you got a National Trust membership?'

'Oh no, we haven't got any kids—'

'Oh God sorry, me and my big mouth. There was a segment on *Loose Women* the other day where they talked about never asking women if they have kids or not because you never know the struggles some people go through.' Karen stuck her bottom lip out a little and tilted her head to the side.

'Oh no, it's nothing like that,' Nell said quickly. 'We're just—'

'Ian won't believe it when I tell him that I bumped into you two! How have we never seen each other around before? Where do you watch the football, Greg? It can't be the Blind Busker because Ian's always there and he would have said.'

'I'm not really into football to be honest—'

'Let me give you my number and when the weather heats up we'll get you down to our beach hut, we've got a gas hob in it.'

Greg started to speak and Nell put her hand on his arm to stop him, 'That sounds really lovely Karen, Greg has a real soft spot for beach huts.'

After they'd gone Nell walked into the kitchen and filled the kettle up from the tap.

'What are you doing? I thought we were going to get the letter and go?'

Nell had completely forgotten about the letter in the mayhem of the last half hour. A pile of post was on the kitchen table and Nell leafed through it but there was no letter from her there. It couldn't have been delivered yet.

'I think I'm going to stay here for a bit to be honest.'

'What? You can't stay here by yourself.' Greg opened the

kitchen cupboard he knew the mugs were kept in and handed Nell two of them. It was such an instinctive, normal act of recall, but it unsettled Nell how comfortable Greg was here.

'Why? Do you think the mean streets of Hove are too much for me?'

'It's Christmas next week.'

'I've spent most Christmases alone; one more won't make a difference.' Nell handed Greg his tea.

'Come back up to London with me, I've got the week off between Christmas and New Year anyway, it'll be fun.'

'You've done too much for me anyway, I can't impose on you anymore. This house is empty for the next week or so, I can hunker down here, figure out my next move—'

'So, you are going to go off again then?'

'I meant my next move in a metaphorical sense, not the next place I *move* to.'

'So, you're staying in England?'

The hopefulness in his voice didn't escape Nell who tried to temper his childlike optimism with a dose of reality, 'I'm not sure yet. All this is so, new. This isn't like other decisions I've made. Everything before now has been temporary, a stop-gap until D-Day, now my whole future is lying ahead of me, like endless calendars with nothing filled in. It's terrifying, and exciting, and I'm so scared of getting it wrong.'

'I think the best thing for you to do would be to come back to London, and I'll help you figure it out.'

He was being helpful, but something about the way he took control prickled at her. He'd always done this, and she'd been grateful for it when they were teenagers, thankful that decisions were taken out of her hands, particularly when he had an instinct for what was the right thing to do, but she wasn't nineteen anymore.

'No, I'm good here,' she said. 'I would say that you can

send my stuff on to me, but I'm standing up in the only things I own,' she joked to lessen the effect of her rebuttal.

'Nell, come on, think about this.'

'I am thinking about this, I need to make some plans, figure out my next steps. There is everything I need right here.' That came out wrong. She realised it had immediately after she said it seeing him visibly wince at it. She quickly followed that up with 'Knowing Mum, there's a freezer full of food, the wi-fi password will be stuck to the wall somewhere and it gets me out of your hair.'

'I like you being in my hair.'

She grimaced. 'That's odd.'

'You know what I mean. I'd forgotten what your energy is like. I like your vibe.'

'Who even are you? Two days with me and I've got you talking about energy and vibes?'

He ran his hand through his hair a little self-consciously. 'Well yeah, I guess having you around again made me realise that maybe I've been a little too focused on work and making money and less on having fun.'

'I'm not sure escaping a hotel, evading arrest, trying unsuccessfully to break into a house, getting caught in a downpour, setting off alarms and making friends with the local constabulary counts as fun, does it?'

Greg grinned. 'More fun than I've had in decades.'

'You need to get out more.'

'Maybe I do. Maybe I need to Be More Nell.'

Nell smiled despite herself. 'That's quite possibly the nicest thing you have ever said to me.'

'Will you spend Christmas with me at my folks? I don't like to think of you being here alone.'

Nell loved his mum, she did, she was a kind and generous woman, with her time, her food helpings and her advice. But

Nell really didn't think she had an entire day of Patty Gage in her. 'Let's see,' Nell said noncommittally.

'Why not? Are you flooded with other offers?'

'A lot can happen in a week,' Nell said, never believing this to be true more than right then.

Greg looked around the kitchen. 'It's really odd being back in here,' he said. 'The amounts of times I've sat at this table with you.'

'I know, it's really weird.'

'It's like the last twenty years haven't happened.'

They held each other's gaze for a beat too long, remembering that the last time they'd been in this room together they'd been a young couple with their whole lives mapped out for them.

Greg coughed. 'Right, well, I'll be off. Let me know if you need anything.' He wrote down his number on Jenny's telephone message pad underneath Karen's. He then put his hand in his pocket and took out five twenty-pound notes. 'It's all the cash I've got on me, but it should see you through the week.'

'You don't need to give me that.'

'I do. You've got nothing.'

It wasn't laced with any malice at all, but the words slapped Nell around the face. *You've got nothing.*

It wasn't until the day had turned to dusk outside and Nell was curled up on the sofa covered by a blanket that smelled of her mum that Nell realised that he was wrong.

She had got something.

She had a second chance.

CHAPTER FOURTEEN

All nostalgic ideas Nell might have harboured of sleeping in her childhood bedroom quickly disappeared as Ray appeared to have commandeered Nell's old room with a rowing machine and a set of weights laid out in front of the mirrored wardrobe doors for him to check his sagging biceps in, so Nell begrudgingly opened the door to Polly's old room instead and gasped. The whole room had been made over to be a child's paradise: a giant sticker of a hot air balloon soaring among clouds spread across one wall, while a canopied single bed came down from another wall into the room. A stack of children's picture books lay by the bedside table, a bookmark in the top one. It must be Beatrice's room for when she came to stay, the way Nell and Polly used to at their nana's. Nell bet Jenny was a wonderful granny, all apple crumbles and games of Ludo.

It might have been the feeling of being beneath mosquito nets again that made Nell sleep for nine hours straight, or more likely, the sensation that she just couldn't shake of being home. She had a shower and then dressed in a pair of her mum's jeans and a jumper, taking her own thrifted clothes down to the washing machine for a well-deserved bathe of their own. She then took her mum's laptop from the sideboard in the kitchen, made herself a cup of coffee and settled back on the sofa.

Nell was both relieved and perturbed by her mother's lack of cyber security on her laptop. No password, no two-step verification, no naming of files in obtuse and misleading ways. Just a simple click of the on button and you were in Jenny's world of Bills, Work, Holidays, Family, Admin, Hobbies. Nell clicked on the latter as it seemed so incongruous to the mother she knew, the woman whose life was a conveyor belt of good deeds for other people. She never knitted, or jogged, or painted or did anything remotely classed as self-care, she simply didn't have time, so Nell was fully expecting the folder to be empty. But here was a folder on her desktop crammed full of photos and website links containing every wild and wonderful pursuit you could think of, images of middle-aged women with backpacks standing on mountains, pictures of older women sitting around drinking wine with an open book on each of their laps, another photo of two women, both with short grey hair, beaming directly at the camera while in a canoe, oars aloft. Nell peered at each picture in turn, trying to spot her mum, but none of the women were her, who were they then? She then spied a watermark on one, an image library stamp on another, and realised that these weren't Jenny's hobbies, it was a wish list of Google images that appealed to her. Nell hastily closed down this folder and felt guilty for trespassing on her mother's dreams. She must have been collecting these for years. At least she was on a cruise now, she'd have felt worse for her if Jenny wasn't currently soaking up the sun on the deck of a liner as it weaved through the Caribbean. She might not be conquering the wilderness, but the buffet spreads on those things were meant to be legendary.

Nell drummed her fingers on the table as she opened up Google. Now that she had the whole internet laid out in front of her like the yellow brick road she had no idea what to look for first. There was no point going for housing without the money to pay for it, therefore it had to be a job first. But then she'd need an address and bank account. Was it terribly poor form to contact the charities she'd donated the proceeds of selling all her stuff to and asking for a refund? It might not be poor form, but it was certainly bad karma, and she felt she had enough of that running away from the hotel. What else? She could set up a new email address, that was a step in the right direction. Good. Excellent. She was about to rebuild her friend lists on Facebook and Instagram, before stopping and wondering if New Nell needed them. Aside from the fact that New Nell didn't have anything to post of any worth, perhaps linking with people from the past wasn't the right thing to do. Until she figured out for herself what this second phase in her life looked like, seeing conflicting messages from friends and acquaintances spread thickly across the globe all merrily getting on with their lives, in whatever form, would surely only highlight how empty hers was?

Not empty, she tersely reminded herself. Full of possibility. Nell started biting her cuticles. What could she search for that would be helpful?

Average life expectancy for women

82.6 years. That seemed a lot. Maths wasn't really her strong point so she opened up a calculator tab and typed in the sum. 82.6-38.2=44.4. Oh, dear lord. She potentially, probably, hopefully not, had forty-four years to plan. That was loads. She'd never taken a multi-vitamin, so that would probably knock off a couple of years, and she'd about ten years of smoking roll-ups among other things in the bag, so again, maybe another five could come off that. She was reasonably fit, lugging a 20-kg backpack around for twenty years had cultivated an impressive core strength, so maybe that would cancel out the bad stuff. But then that hallucinogenic barley wine she'd had in Guatemala that knocked her out for forty-eight hours straight surely must make the number plummet again. Forty-four years. How the hell was she going to fill forty-four years?

She started typing again. **How to have a meaningful and happy life**

Practise gratitude. Find your passions. Do conscious acts of kindness. Connect with the like-minded. Nurture relationships. Cultivate optimism. Nell read the phrases again. If ever there was a rulebook for living life to the full, here it was right in front of her. She wrote these phrases on the pad next to her, determined to remember them when she felt unsure about what next steps to take. She did recognise, however, that she had manage to break all of these rules in some way in the last week alone. She had ripped off a hotel that treated her like royalty, banished the man that tried to help her, broken up his relationship, bartered with a charity shop, made an old woman who had just had a hip operation and a life-threatening viral infection get up from her bedrest, broken into her mother's house, worn her clothes without asking, eaten freezer meals she might have been saving for a special occasion, reconnected with a girl from school she pretended to remember but really didn't, severed a sibling relationship pretty conclusively, all the while thinking that the rest of her life was definitely buggered and the future was incredibly bleak.

Average age to have a baby UK

30.6. She didn't know why she asked that one. She'd never even considered having children. But the speed at which Hayley had decided that marriage and babies were the future that she immediately wanted once she knew that she *was* going to have a future made Nell reassess things. Might she want a family? But children needed stability, didn't they? And she was hardly the poster-girl for putting down roots. But then again, she'd met plenty of parents on her travels who had strapped a rucksack to their front and a baby to their back and wandered off down the Inca Trail or wherever. Life with a child was whatever you made it, there was no rulebook about where or when it had to happen. Greg had made it clear that he'd want his kids to have the childhood they did, in Hove, complete with beach hut. She reckoned Tom would be the type of dad that would suggest taking the kids out of school and sailing around the Galapagos.

How much money does a single person need to live UK?
£26,000 per year. Right, thought Nell, that made her decision whether to stay in England or not pretty easy for her.

What is the happiest and cheapest country in the world?
Bhutan. Interesting, she thought. She'd never been.

Flights to Bhutan
19 hours 45 minutes, three connecting flights. Flights from £650.

Jobs in Bhutan
Software engineer, travel consultant, agricultural labourer. This might have legs.

Tom comedian The Bedford comedy pub Balham. What? Where did that come from? Her screen was suddenly filled with a catalogue of photos of him, all promotional pictures of him smiling cheekily underneath his mop of curly hair. Some from the right, some from the left, one of him looking up, a few of him on stage holding a microphone stand. Seeing him brought a medley of feelings to the surface. Of all the letters she'd written, his was the one that she shouldn't have. Her mum needed a letter of love, so did Greg, to know how important they had been to her; Polly needed to know the truth too, perhaps not in such a blunt way, but Nell still stood by her decision to call Damian out to save her sister more hurt in the future; and she had no regrets with her dad's letter at all. But Tom? Nell had known the guy for less than three hours. She shouldn't have messed with his head like that, even if she did mean all of it. Over the years she'd felt instant connections with people, and normally acted on them, so that part wasn't so unusual, but it wasn't just lust that made her make the giant leap from selling her bed to rolling around in it. He just seemed to get her, and he made her laugh, in the week that she thought she was going to die, and that was no mean feat. Nell clicked on the first photo.

Tom Radley is a favourite of The Bedford with his sharp wit, observational nous and aura of 'bloody good blokeness'. His last five shows have been instant sell-outs, he returns in the New Year with his new, hotly anticipated show 'Bucket List' touring theatres across the South. Bucket List. Bucket List! Nell could feel a rampant rage growing inside her as the cogs all clicked into place and she realised that he'd made a whole show around her planning her non-death. It was bad enough to have it as a fleeting segment in the gig she saw, but to monetise it for a whole tour? Oh, that man! He'd even had the audacity to apologise for it in his note. He must have thought that she was long gone by now, and the coast was clear for him to ridicule her again. All thoughts of a new life in Bhutan *cultivating optimism* and *practising gratitude* instantly evaporated as she started plotting how to find the man she was passionate with and *do a very conscious act of **un**kindness* to him.

The shrill ring of her mum's landline made her jump. She stared at it for a second thinking through whether she should answer it or not. A) it wasn't her house. B) in the unlikely event it was for her, it could only be Greg and she didn't know

141

what to say to him yet, and C) it wasn't her house. The answer phone clicked on.

Her dad's voice came through the machine. 'Jenny. It's um, Tony. Can you call me back when you get this. I've, um, heard from Nell, and—' His voice cracked. 'Just call me back please, on my mobile, not the home phone. '

The hairs on Nell's arms stood on end hearing his voice. She was frozen to the spot with how sad he sounded. The red flashing button on the machine taunted Nell. She closed her eyes to block it out; this week was a rolling tidal wave of emotion after emotion: shock, elation, surprise, exhaustion, disappointment, regret, rage, and guilt, mostly guilt. An hour ago she'd jauntily been looking at flights to the other side of the world again, reverting back to her tried and tested coping mechanism of putting as much distance between her and the problem as possible. But these problems were entirely of her own making. Why had she felt the need to poke her family's sore spots? To make *that* her lasting legacy? Her dad clearly was more sensitive than she ever gave him credit for. She'd call him back and explain. She lifted her hand to pick up the receiver when it rang again. *Not her house*. She put her hand down again. After four rings the answer phone sprang into action again.

'Jenny. I just want to say that I am really quite sad about you going home and leaving me here alone. I felt like a complete pillock at dinner by myself last night until that nice table of couples took pity on me and asked me to join them, they were really fun, you'd have enjoyed it, I don't know why we didn't sit with them before. It's not like you being there is going to change anything, is it? Nell's gone. You rushing back there is only going to upset you more, it's certainly upset me, and I don't know what you thought was to be gained by it. By the time you've come to your senses and want to fly back the cruise will be over and I'll be home. So, I just wanted to get that off my chest. And make sure you delay Nell's funeral until I'm back so I can support you, but it probably won't be until the New Year, I would've thought there'll be a big backlog over Christmas.'

What did Ray mean, *Nell's gone*? How did he know? And her mum was coming home? Nell looked around her mum's living room in a panic; last night's dinner plate was on the coffee table next to half a bottle of wine she'd helped herself to, two half-empty coffee cups – *Cultivate optimism*, no, they were definitely half-empty – and her laundry was drying over all the radiators in the house, which she'd cranked up on the thermostat without thinking of the effect on the smart meter just to make them dry quicker. Evidence littered everywhere around the house, a house she'd been in for less than twenty-four hours, proving that far from maturing and learning lessons, and using her second chance to be a better person, she was still a slovenly, selfish middle-aged woman acting more like an entitled sixteen-year-old than someone who had been given the opportunity to reinvent themselves for the better.

An hour later, the central heating was back to an acceptable, affordable level, the circular watermark on the coffee table left by her glass had been painstakingly scrubbed away, and all crockery she'd used had been washed, dried and put away. She'd put her own clothes back on and folded her mum's back in her wardrobe. She still had her mum's pants on, but needs must. Both messages on the answer phone were deleted: her mum didn't need to hear Ray's and Nell would deal with her dad's one soon. She'd even called Julie next door to see if she could pick up anything for her from the shops. She'd also called Polly twice but the line rang out. Nell paced the kitchen nervously. If Ray was right and her mum was on her way back here, that threw up so many questions. Her letter certainly hadn't been delivered: not yesterday when Polly's was, nor this morning when the mail only contained pamphlets about stair lifts and wills, so how could she have assumed that Nell had died? And judging by Polly's horrified reaction to seeing Nell rise from the dead out of her fir bush in her back garden, maybe Nell shouldn't just be sat at her mum's dining table when she walked in after a two-day journey home, it might terrify her. Nell checked her watch; it was just coming up to midday. With her stomach in her throat, she picked up the phone to call her dad. It rang three times before it was answered.

'Yes?' came the impatient voice of a woman who hadn't signed up for her husband's histrionics, just the proceeds of his business.

Katie had come into the picture about eight years ago. She had been the paralegal on her dad's legal team overseeing the sale of his property development business. He'd started with one student house when Nell was around sixteen; they had a painting party, her, Polly, her mum and dad, radio cranked up, rollers in hand as they transformed the dingy terrace into a magnolia wonderland over a weekend. It snowballed from there, one or two more houses a year until around ten years later he teamed up with a construction firm and built seventy-two executive homes on a prime piece of land between Brighton and Hove. Within weeks her dad had a shiny new car in the driveway, brochures of million-pound properties he wanted to move to coming through the letterbox each day, while her mum had dug a trench for herself around her beloved home and refused to move.

Nell had been so preoccupied with her own life that she hadn't even noticed on a fleeting trip home that her dad had got his eye-bags surgically removed, grown a designer beard he had trimmed weekly by the local barber, and had a whole new wardrobe. She might have made a couple of passing comments like, 'Oh wow, Dad, I can't believe the leather seats in your car warm up, that's so weird,' or 'Did you fall in your aftershave?' but that's all they were, passing comments, said one minute and gone the next.

Nell had been living in Seoul when her mum's email had come through telling her that he'd moved out to be with Katie. The wave of acute disbelief followed by crushing disappointment that had washed over her was like nothing Nell had ever felt before. How could her wonderful dad have done this? This was the marriage-story of those real-life weekly magazines, not her own parents'. How could he have done something so hackneyed, so clichéd as to leave the wife who had supported him for more than thirty years without a backwards glance? The lovely, caring, gentle wife who had put her own career on hold to raise their two children, to pack the lunches, to remember the PE kits on the right days, to listen to the daily dramas and offer advice, to drive to bowling alleys and shopping centres and cinemas and parties, to wash and dry and iron his shirts, and his golfing outfits, and to host dinners and laugh at all the right moments, and do everything that meant that his life ran on oiled rails, and then as soon as a tall blonde just a handful of years older than his daughters put her manicured hand on his arm and said, 'You're so clever,' he packed a bag and drove his warm-seated gas-guzzler into the sunset.

As Nell sat there in her mum's living room – the house Jenny now shared with Ray, another man's belongings pushing Jenny's once again to the back of the shelf – hearing Katie's clipped Hampshire accent on the other end of the phone demanding to know who was there, Nell realised that her anger all these years wasn't on her mum's behalf, not really, but more for a fairy-tale being smashed to pieces. The Prince Charming turning out to be the villain.

'I know you're there,' came Katie's high voice. 'You have to stop calling. Do you know he's married?'

'Could you give Tony a message for me please?'

'Who is this?'

'It's Nell.'

'Nell who?' Katie still sounded suspicious, as though this wasn't the first female caller she'd intercepted.

'His daughter.'

'Oh?'

'Yes, hello. Congratulations on the wedding.'

'That was years ago.'

'Well yes, but better late than never.'

'Your dad isn't here at the moment, he left his phone behind. I wouldn't normally answer it.'

'It's fine, can you just pass on a message to him that I didn't die.'

There was a second's pause. 'You didn't die?'

'No.'

'Were you meant to?'

'Yes. Well, I thought so. But I didn't. And he thinks I did. So can you tell him that I am very much alive, and in Hove right now, and would actually really like to see him.'

'I'll tell him. Does he have your number?'

'I don't have one, but I'm staying at my mum's house.' Nell winced as she said that; here she was having a perfectly pleasant exchange with the woman who broke up her parents' marriage, now mentioning his first wife.

'Oh, is she back from the cruise?'

'Um, no, not yet.' How did Katie know about that?

'I'll get him to call you there then. Nice to speak with you finally, Nell.'

146

Nell couldn't bring herself to parrot the same back, even though that's what the silence demanded, so she just replied, 'Yes. Take care,' which was sort of the same.

The house was still and silent. Nell sat on the sofa just staring at the fireplace that had once housed photos on the mantlepiece and two stockings every Christmas. She squinted her eyes and could just make out the two little dots where the hooks had once been.

She didn't know what flight her mum had got, or even from where so she couldn't track it, and she still didn't know if it would be better if she was here or not when she walked in.

Greg would know what to do.

He answered the call on the second ring, almost as though he'd been willing it to ring.

'The way I see it,' he said, after she'd explained her quandary and various options, 'it's actually quite simple. You use this time to do something special for her, to make it clear that you do care about her, and that you intend to spend what's left of your time on this earth, whether it be short or long, rebuilding bridges and being as close as it's possible to be.'

'And that's why I called you. I knew you'd know what to do.'

'I'm guessing if your mum thought she was going to be away for Christmas then there's no decorations or anything up? You could do that for her? Make the place look pretty and festive, no one can argue when there's fairy lights everywhere. Use the money I left you to Christmas the place up. Get some nice food in, cook her a meal, she wants *you* Nell, to spend time with *you*. Don't run away from this, okay?'

'But maybe I should just leave her a letter.'

'No more letters. You need to face this in person, not hiding behind a piece of paper while you jet off somewhere again. You're not thinking of going away again, are you?'

Beautiful Bhutan, happiest cheapest place on earth. . .

'No,' Nell sighed, 'I'm not.'

'Good. You've got this, I've got complete faith in you.'

'I don't know what I've done to deserve you being so nice to me, but thank you.'

'What for?'

'For the advice, for not turning your back on me in the hotel stairwell, for making this week a lot better than it could have been.'

'It hasn't all been one-sided you know, meeting you again made me realise that I've turned into my dad without even realising it. So. . . I'm going to start making some changes in my life.'

'What?'

'Yep. I've arranged a three-month unpaid sabbatical. Life's too short, isn't it? I don't want to blink and another ten years have gone by, and all I've got to show for it is a bigger bank balance and a bigger indent in my office chair where my arse has been sat. Life's for living, you had the right idea all along, I couldn't see that at the time, but the scales have lifted from my eyes and I see it all now, so clearly. I don't want to be like everyone else anymore.'

'Just slow down and think things through properly. You're not me, I had reasons for living the way that I have—'

'As did I! You showed me that! We could even go travelling together, once everything is sorted with your family; the world is literally our oyster.'

Nell didn't pick him up on the misuse of the word literally, it wasn't the moment, but equally, now was certainly not the time for big decisions that would alter the direction of his life forever. She couldn't be responsible for yet another life veering wildly off course.

'Right, go, go, you've got to get to the shops before she comes back.'

'Please don't do anything mad before I see you on the twenty-third,' Nell begged.

'I'd like to say no, but I feel like a new me is just around the corner!'

Nell closed her eyes to the ceiling when she put the receiver down. How much destruction could one person wreak in four days?

CHAPTER FIFTEEN

When Nell first left England to go travelling she was sure that a hundred pounds could have bought a pretty decent car and fed a family of five for a week. She recognised that nostalgia had a tendency to blur the accuracy of memories, but a hundred quid certainly went further than a five-foot Christmas tree, a box of fairy lights and a raw chicken. She looked sadly at her spoils; this was not the glittering welcome home slash sorry for everything slash please forgive me and let's live happily ever after extravaganza she had envisioned. After deliberating for a moment, she put the tree back and picked up four more boxes of fairy lights instead. Greg was right, if in doubt, put a tiny flashing bulb on it.

Greg was not right, however, about potentially throwing his entire career away on a badly thought-out whim. Nell hadn't been able to stop thinking about it since their call. His pension, his health insurance, his security, his salary, everything hung in the balance in the name of spontaneity. It was utter madness. She had to be more careful with what she said and did. It had happened before, never to such extremes, but she'd often persuaded people without even trying, to abandon their plans to scale Machu Picchu and instead head to a dive course in Fiji with her, or to give up their ardent veganism and try her lovingly marinated king prawns fresh off a barbecue. She never set out to manipulate people, that would be the very last thing she'd ever want to do, but for some reason people sometimes forgot their own plans and followed hers instead. She must have been too aggressive with Greg, she should have toned it down, and not been quite so Nell about it all. She'd have to try to make him see that her way was, in most situations, not necessarily the best way, it was just *her* way and he had to follow his own path.

There was a family in front of the milk fridges blocking the way both physically and audibly, two young children red-faced from screaming now sat inside the trolley, angrily throwing out whatever their parents had put in it. The dad was scrambling around on the floor gathering up each item that had been chucked out, somewhat foolishly then popping them back in the trolley so this circle of fun could continue once again. The mum had her phone tucked between her shoulder and her chin having a conversation while holding open the fridge door to retrieve a four-pint milk bottle. There was no way those kids would be able to chuck that out. Nell hung back, unwilling to enter the scene until the other characters had left the stage, hopefully taking all their props with them.

The woman swung round as she ended her call, screamed at the kids to behave, screamed at her husband to leave whatever he was reaching for under the shelving unit and saw Nell. Her face contorted into a wide smile. 'Nell!' she shouted over the screams of her offspring. 'I was just telling Ian I saw you yesterday. Ian, it's Nell, you remember Nell? From school?'

Ian confirmed by a smiling nod that yes, he did indeed remember Nell and offered his hand out. As it had just been feeling around under supermarket refrigerator cabinets and wiping bodily fluids off the face of children, Nell shook it reluctantly, while considering swapping the milk for some anti-bac.

'Is Greg here too?' Karen asked, looking theatrically over Nell's shoulder.

'No, he's gone back up to London for a few days.'

Karen raised her eyebrows. 'London?' she said, impressed. 'What's he doing in London?'

'He works there.' *For now*.

'What does he do?' Ian asked.

'Something in finance, I think,' Nell replied, screwing her eyes up at the two children then popping them open making them chuckle.

'You mean you don't know,' laughed Karen.

Nell smiled. 'Well you know, I was never great with numbers.'

'We were in bottom set maths together, weren't we?' Ian said. 'Now I run my own carpentry business.'

'What do you do, Nell?'

'I'm sort of between jobs at the moment,' Nell said diplomatically.

'The force is always looking for new recruits,' Karen said. 'Especially women.'

'Interesting,' Nell replied, 'I might look into it. Right, well I better shoot off now, lovely seeing you both.'

'Wait, when is Greg back down?'

'The twenty-third.'

'A group of us from school always go out to the Connaught on Christmas Eve, you should join us – Billy, Lee and Catherine, the other Karen, Timmo and Kate, they'll all be there, you should both come. It'll be fun!' Karen emphasised quite how fun it would be by doing jazz hands.

'It certainly does sound fun,' Nell enthused. 'I'm not quite sure what our plans are at the moment, but we might see you down there.'

'We'll be there from about eight, bedtime permitting,' Karen nodded her head in the direction of the two now quiet as mice children who had opened a packet of unpaid-for chocolate biscuits and were merrily destroying the evidence.

On the walk home Nell thought more about Karen and Ian's life, setting up home in the town they were born in, still friends with the people they'd all known as kids. The names of the shared schoolmates Karen had reeled off in the supermarket were familiar to Nell in exactly the same way former colleagues were who she'd shared shifts with in bars and restaurants over the years, the names lodged somewhere, but with no real connection attached to them. Greg was the only person she'd stayed in contact with from school, and she'd only been back in contact with him for four days after an eighteen-year hiatus. She had very little memory of who she sat next to in maths or who she played on the netball team with. Her entire school experience was centered around her friendship with Greg, everyone else was always hovering on the periphery. Nell's initial instinct was to feel sorry for Karen and Ian's small circle of friends, their life experience that was confined to the Sussex seaside town, their community that didn't go beyond the town's borders, but her sympathy was quickly, and, surprisingly, replaced by something else that took Nell completely by surprise. It was an emotion she rarely felt, which is why it took her a second to even place it: Envy.

As Nell rounded the corner of her mum's street with the shopping, an empty airport taxi sailed past. Nell stopped and stared at its retreating tail lights, deliberating which direction her next step should take. She heard Greg's voice saying *don't run away from this okay?* Fighting every one of her natural instincts, for the first time in her life, she walked towards the trouble, and not away from it.

A suitcase lay in the hallway, still padlocked, still with the distinctive yellow ribbon her mother always insisted tying on the handles for easy recognition at baggage claim. She'd tied one to Nell's backpack the first time she and Greg left to travel the world after their exams. It had stayed on for the whole year, getting grubbier and more frayed, but it was a lasting reminder of home that had always made Nell smile.

'Mum?' Nell called tentatively up the stairs.

'I'm in my room, Polly,' came Jenny's weary reply.

Nell faltered and bit her lip. 'Shall I put the kettle on?'

'That'd be nice.'

Nell berated herself as she waited for the water to boil. She should have shot up those stairs as soon as she walked in, banishing her mum's misery as soon as she could, not prolonged it by making tea. It was a delaying tactic Nell recognised in herself and despised.

Nell was shaking so much she could only manage to carry one cup upstairs, not two, holding the mug gingerly with two hands. She paused again on the landing, gathering courage. *Don't run away from this, okay?*

Pushing open the door with her foot, Nell saw her mother's body curled up on the bed facing the window, away from her, her face reflected in the dressing table mirror in the bay. Jenny's eyes were closed, her chin tucked down, 'Just put it on the table love.'

'Mum?' Nell said, sitting down on the bed alongside her, gently touching her mum's back. 'Mum? It's me, Nell.'

Nell felt her mum's body stiffen under her touch, her eyes sprang open and met Nell's in the mirror and Jenny gasped at her daughter's reflection, taking big gulps of air. She reached around and put her warm hand over Nell's, twisting her body round to face her. 'Oh my God, Nell.' Big heaving sobs fell from her mother's body as she grasped Nell to her tightly, rocking back and forth on the bed, wailing and crying and laughing, every possible emotion bubbling to the surface with no hope of separating them. Grief, relief, joy, misery, exhaustion, energy, regret and gratitude, deep, deep gratitude all woven together in an ugly beautiful mess.

'I'm so sorry,' Nell cried into her mum's shoulder. 'I'm so sorry, I put you through this, I'm so sorry.'

'Ssshh, it's all okay, everything's okay now,' her mum soothed, stroking Nell's hair, still rhythmically rocking. 'It's all alright.'

Jenny then ran her hands all over Nell's face, her hands, checking, making sure she was real.

'I honestly thought. . .' Nell started. 'I wouldn't have sent the letter if I hadn't thought it was going to happen, I would never want to upset you.'

Jenny smiled at her daughter weakly. Nell recognised that the numbness of the journey that no parent should ever have to make was catching up with her. It must have been bone-numbingly exhausting going through the motions of saying 'excuse me' as she squeezed past the passenger sitting next to her on the plane, saying 'thank you' to the cabin crew when offered a drink, tipping the taxi driver, empty pleasantries, when every pore of her must have been screaming, 'My child is dead! Why don't you care?' Her body and mind must have suffered a torture over the last day that made it impossible for her to stay awake any longer. 'You must be really tired, why don't you have a little rest Mum?'

Panic flashed across Jenny's face. 'Don't go.'

'I'll just be downstairs, I promise.' Nell pulled the cover over her mum, and quietly left the room, pulling the door to behind her. She hadn't gone through the same pain as her mum had, but she could imagine it; she made herself imagine it, so she would never do something like this again.

While her mum slept upstairs, Nell draped fairy lights all around the living room and kitchen and put the chicken, now sprinkled with herbs, in the oven. She didn't know what else to do so rummaged in the cupboard under the sink for some cleaning products and deep cleaned the fridge and de-scaled the kettle. She was sitting at the kitchen table looking out at the garden when her mum came in behind her, freshly changed from her travelling clothes and with hair still wet from a shower.

'It looks lovely, Nell, I love the lights.'

'I wanted to do something nice for you.'

'And something smells good.'

'Roast chicken, it's got another half an hour. Do you want another cup of tea?' Nell started to get up from her chair.

Her mum waved her back down. 'I'll make it, you must be exhausted doing all this.'

'It was nothing.' *Not compared to what I put you through.*

As they sat together at the kitchen table, a warm teapot between them, Nell didn't ask about how Jenny knew about the letter, nor did she enquire about Ray, or what the next week looked like for them both; they just chatted about Jenny's plans to have the kitchen painted, and how pleased she was that Julie was back home safe from hospital. They laughed about Nell's brush with the police after the alarm incident, and Nell told her mum how she had recently bumped into Greg.

'He was a lovely boy,' Jenny said. 'You always brought out the best in each other. Whenever I run into Patty, down the shops or at the doctor's, we always say that.'

Jenny's next sentence made Nell wince. 'He's doing terribly well for himself. Well on his way to being a director in his company. He paid off Patty's mortgage a few years back now, and he's doing the same for his brother too. Heart of gold that one.'

'Certainly sounds like it,' Nell replied, really hoping that there wasn't too much left outstanding on his brother's house loan or he might be in for a shock soon.

'You could do a lot worse than getting back with Greg Gage, that's for sure.'

'Oh my God Mum, stop,' Nell said, smiling, 'I'm not up for making any big decisions just yet. I'm just happy to be alive and sitting in your kitchen with you.'

Jenny reached over and put her hand over Nell's. 'I'm just happy about that too.'

They'd had so few moments like this over the years, just the two of them together. The last time was when she had surprised Jenny with a ticket to Istanbul for her sixtieth. Nell had just finished a six-month stint working in an English language school in Izmit, a town about two hours' bus ride away from Istanbul. She'd even done what she'd never done before and booked a hotel room ahead of arriving in the city, and dinner for their first night. She'd left the other three nights unplanned because she couldn't change the habits of a lifetime. She'd met her mum off her flight. Jenny was a quivering, but jubilant, wreck after navigating Heathrow airport alone, not to mention the confusing arrivals procedure in Turkey, but all this fell away as she hugged Nell so tightly in the airport, the rest of the world swirling noisily around them as mother and daughter were reunited.

That night in Istanbul, they'd chatted, and laughed, and drank wine, and her mum's eyes danced like Nell hadn't seen in years. They didn't talk about anything deep, not yet, there were another three days to delve into feelings and regrets; that first night was just about the sheer joy of being reunited.

They linked arms back to the hotel like two old friends kept apart for too long. Ray was waiting in the lobby to surprise them. Nell ended up leaving Istanbul the next day, heading onwards to Greece a few days early, three's a crowd and all that. Her mum had cried, Ray had stood on the step of the hotel as Nell's taxi drove off, one arm around his tearful new girlfriend, the other in the air waving victoriously.

'Do you remember that evening in Istanbul?' Nell asked her mum. 'We could dig out some Turkish recipes and recreate it tomorrow night?'

'Are you going to fly in a hunky waiter too?'

Nell laughed. 'Oh I forgot how besotted you were with Hassad.'

'How on earth do you remember his name?'

'We talked to him for ages, his sister was called Alara and she was studying to be a child psychologist in Swansea.'

'Your memory of people is insane, Nell.'

'I seem to remember you saying the same about his eyes,' Nell teased. Jenny squealed and pretended to swat Nell's arm and lost her balance on her chair, making them laugh even more.

'Oh well isn't this lovely and cosy?' Sarcasm dripped off Polly's tongue as she entered the kitchen. She held up a pint of milk and a loaf of bread. 'I thought you might want a cup of tea and toast when you got back.'

'Oh, thank you love, but Nell already got some.'

'She did, did she? That was kind.'

'There's still some in the pot,' Nell said. 'I'll get you a mug.'

'No don't bother, I'm not stopping.'

'Polly, please, I'm really sorry, I never meant to—'

'Save it. I'm not interested in anything you have to say. Bye Mum, I'll call you tomorrow.'

'Polly wait, please, come and sit with us,' Jenny begged.

Nell stood up facing her sister who hadn't moved from the doorway. 'Please Polly, I know I've hurt you but I just want to explain—'

'You don't know anything Nell. You have zero idea of what you've put us through—'

'I said I was sorry, Mum understands, it was all a misund—'

'I don't just mean for the last day, I mean for the last twenty years when you were off enjoying your life leaving us here, you have no idea, literally no idea how hard it's all been, with Dad leaving, and Nana dying—'

'I came back for the funeral.'

'Oh well done, congratulations. Good job on getting dressed in black and eating some vol au vents. You weren't here when she didn't know who we were though, were you? You never changed her incontinence pads on her bed or held a water glass to her lips or sat at this very table with mum, both of us in tears praying the end would come soon, did you? Where were you when I went into labour with Beatrice two months early and sat next to her incubator every day?'

'I sent messages. . .' Nell said weakly.

'Or when Katie announced she was pregnant the week after Mum had a hysterectomy? Were you there then? Making tea for Mum then, were you? No, no you weren't. You've dipped in and out of our lives like a stray cat that only comes home when it remembers that it has a family, gets free food and shelter for a few days then buggers off again.'

'Polly, stop it please,' Jenny said, holding her hands up as if to ward off any more words.

'No Mum, she needs to hear this. Your letter has ruined my life.'

Jenny turned to Nell. 'What did you write in hers?'

'Hang on, I've got it here.' Polly dug her hand into her coat pocket and retrieved the crumpled envelope, angrily taking the letter out and shaking it open. '*I don't know how to say this next part without blowing your whole world apart, but I'm your sister, and I love you and so I have to. It's about your husband. He tried to kiss me at your engagement party and later that night I saw him and your friend Lauren round the back of the pub together. I have kept this secret for years because you seemed so happy, but I can't die knowing what I know,*' Polly said, reading aloud Nell's words. '*I've learned over the years that it's much better to be alone than with someone who doesn't see how amazing you are, and if I can leave anything with you, it's the thought that you are strong, you are powerful, and you can be happy by yourself.*' Polly's hand holding the letter dropped, 'Isn't that nice? Some words of wisdom from beyond the grave.'

Jenny stared at Nell. 'Is that true? Did you see that?'

Nell nodded bleakly, wishing for all the world that it had been all lies.

'What are you going to do, Polly?'

'Nothing! She's just trying to make trouble, to make everything all about her again. I actually feel sorry for you,' Polly spat. 'Look at you, you're thirty-eight years old, single, no kids, no job, no home, you've got absolutely nothing. You've always been jealous of me, and your parting shot from earth was to make sure that I was unhappy too.'

'That's not why I said it, I thought you should know.'

'Why? Has it made me happier? Am I doing a little dance of joy? You have put me in an impossible situation. If what you're saying is true, either I need to pretend I don't know what I know and just get on with it, or I confront him and potentially end my marriage.'

'So, you would have preferred me not to say anything?'

'I'd have preferred you to tell me when you actually saw it happen!'

160

She was right, and Nell honestly didn't know why she hadn't.

Just then the oven timer pinged, 'Why don't you stay for something to eat, Polly?' Jenny asked. 'We can work this out.'

'No thank you, I have to get back to my *family* while I still have one.' Polly slammed the kitchen door before slamming the front one, just to make completely sure Nell understood quite how angry she was.

After her mum and Nell had eaten, largely in silence, loaded the dishwasher together, again without conversing, and Nell had excused herself to lie down, she realised sadly that everything Polly said had been true. Nell hadn't been there for any of it. Every moment Polly had described had been nothing more than headlines in her mum's letters, something Nell had read over breakfast, given a couple of minutes of her day to digest, and then forgot. She always thought that her life was moving on at top speed, and everyone's life back here stayed still, but it hadn't. Life moved and changed for everyone, regardless of what hemisphere you were in. And coming back, being here again, was both familiar and completely unrecognisable at the same time. And it was terrifying.

Jenny was already in the living room when Nell got up the next morning, a hot pot of tea on the coffee table. 'Help yourself love, I've put some frozen croissants in the oven too. They'll be ready in a couple of minutes. Did you sleep well?'

She hadn't. But she also knew that saying so would only cast a momentary shadow over their breakfast, so just nodded and said, 'Like a log,' which made Jenny smile and pat the sofa next to her. During the night Nell had decided to leave Hove first thing, once the off-peak train fares kicked in. She'd reasoned in the early hours that her mum would understand, she'd agree with Nell that Polly would calm down once Nell wasn't around. And it wasn't running away to leave her mum to clear up her mess, not really. Polly clearly needed time to cool off, and that had always happened so much quicker when Nell wasn't there raising the temperature. But now the sun had risen, and Nell was sitting drinking out of a mug that had a golden '18' embossed on it that she'd received for her birthday a lifetime ago, running away for good seemed like a really bad decision.

'Do you think Polly will come round?' Nell asked her mum.

'Polly's a stewer, she always has been. She just needs a bit of space to mull things over.'

'She was right about a lot of things,' Nell admitted.

Jenny took a sip of her tea.

'But also wrong about some. The last thing I wanted was to make trouble, for her, and you, and everyone.'

'She didn't mean that. She was going through a thousand different emotions and the one in that moment was anger. She probably already regrets saying that.' Jenny's phone pinged with a message from Julie, which she read and immediately stood up, 'I've got to go and help Julie get off the toilet, she's stuck. Hold that thought.'

'About Julie on the loo?'

'No you loon, about Polly. I'll be back as soon as I can.'

'I was actually thinking of going back up to London today for a couple of days. I need to make Greg see sense about something, and I think with me out of the way for a bit, Polly will have some space.'

Jenny paused by the door. 'Do what you feel you need to do, sweetheart. But it would be lovely if you were back here for Christmas?'

'Try and stop me. Now go and help Julie, her bum must be freezing by now.'

CHAPTER SIXTEEN

Nell didn't lift her eyes from the view outside of the window once as the train sped through the Sussex countryside and neared London. Could she be happy staying here? She'd never thought so before; whenever she thought of England from abroad she pictured grey oppressive skies, thick blankets of cloud, downturned faces, upturned collars as people hurried, always hurrying. But today, a few days before Christmas, a Christmas she never thought she'd see, the sky was piercing blue without a cloud punctuating it anywhere. A thin layer of frost sprinkled the fields, looking like snow, birds ducked and swooped overhead, coming to rest in the majestic bare branches of trees that had stood sentry for hundreds of years. It was breathtakingly beautiful and Nell felt bad for ever thinking otherwise. And the people weren't hurrying unnecessarily, they had a purpose, people to get home to.

As Jenny had dropped Nell to the station she'd promised that she'd try her best to get Polly and Tony to come round. Maybe she should write them a letter, Nell thought before swiftly kicking that idea firmly out of play. No, Nell told herself firmly, no more letters. Thinking of the letters led to her stomach tightening again as she thought of the other letter out there: Tom's. She imagined him happily going about his day planning his next tour about bucket lists, where she was the butt of every joke in it, patting his pocket where a humiliating love letter from her now probably nestled, telling him that had things been different, he'd be her person. She didn't yet know how she was going to deal with Tom, she'd tried to go down the heckler route before and proven that she wasn't great with words under pressure. Maybe she could visit him backstage before a gig, do her best ghost impression and frighten him into changing his routine. She could wear something flowing and white, make a few noises, wave her arms around a bit and scare him into submission. Yes, that could work. Of course, new Nell, she thought with a sigh, new and *improved* Nell would simply find him, sit him down, calmly explain the situation, say how her feelings had been hurt, and ask him if they could possibly find a compromise whereby they both keep their integrity and yet respect each other's positions. Nell sighed. She really hoped that new Nell wasn't going to always be this boring.

'You didn't need to meet me off the train!' Nell said to Greg who was waiting patiently by the ticket turnstiles at the end of the platform, 'A lovely old man just gave me his one-day travelcard that he didn't need anymore, so I was going to get the tube.'

'How does this stuff happen to you?' Greg moaned. 'I've lived in London for twenty years and that has never happened to me.'

'You have to manifest it.'

'I don't even know what that means.'

'I'll teach you.'

Greg tried to take her small bag from her but she tightened her grip on it. 'It's fine. I can hold my own bag.'

'I was just trying to be nice.'

'I know, but if I was your brother you wouldn't have tried to carry his bag.'

'No, he can carry his own!' he scoffed.

'Exactly. And I can carry mine. Having breasts does not impede me in any way.'

'Okay, okay,' he held his hands up. 'I forgot you were such a feminist.'

'Aren't you?'

'Aren't I what?'

'A feminist. Surely everyone should be a feminist.'

Greg rolled his eyes. 'Nell, it's too early for politics.'

'A feminist believes that everyone should be paid the same, with equal rights, regardless of gender. Put like that, I'd be pretty embarrassed to admit that I wasn't a feminist.'

'I haven't even had lunch yet,' Greg replied. 'Can we leave the soapboxing until after we've eaten and I've replenished my reserves.'

It wasn't his fault, she happily used to let him carry her rucksack when she was nineteen and didn't know any better, or stand aside while he paid the bills, checked them in places, took the last seat on the train or bus while he stood, before older, wiser, women had talked with her into the early hours in various hostels, around various campfires, along various walking trails, gently changing her perspective.

'So,' Nell said brightly, 'I have thirty pounds in my pocket.' She clocked his sideways questioning glance at her. 'Mum gave it to me, don't worry. Now I can either stick to my original plan of hiding it in your coat pockets when you weren't looking to try to chip away at the amount you've loaned me, or, and choose wisely here, I could buy you a bacon sandwich and a cup of strong coffee with some of it.'

'The latter. Because I've wiped your loan off the slate.'

'No! Greg, honestly, I will pay you back.'

'Look, the way I see it, if we'd stayed together, you'd have cost me tens of thousands in birthday and Christmas presents—'

'Don't forget sorry presents for when you screwed up.'

He smiled. 'Yes, and sorry presents. So actually, you're massively in credit. You've saved me loads of money by leaving me. So don't think about the money again, it's not a loan it's a gift.'

'I'm not arguing about it Greg, I will absolutely pay you back.'

'Well I won't accept it.'

'Well you'll have no choice because I'll hide money around your house where you least expect it. You'll go to your medicine cabinet, to take out a paracetamol, open the box, no tablets, only money. You'll look at your curtains one day and think, gosh, they're hanging a bit strange lately, and I'll have sewn a hundred pound coins into the hem.'

'You're such a weirdo.'

'So do yourself a favour, and cut the charade and when I've earned enough money to pay you back, do the decent thing and just accept it. Because we both know I will absolutely follow through on my plan otherwise.'

Greg broke out in a grin. 'I've missed you.'

'I've missed you too.'

He then looked down at his feet, and shuffled them as if seeing them for the first time, 'I was going to ask you something, and tell me if I'm being massively presumptuous, I mean, I hope I'm not, the fact you've come back here today maybe shows that I'm not, but then you can't tell—'

'Spit it out. Remember, life's short,' she joked.

A tiny hint of a shadow passed across Greg's features. 'I've got my work's Christmas party tomorrow night and I wondered if you wanted to be my plus one?'

'Sounds fun.'

'It's in a fancy London hotel—'

'Not the one—'

'No, not that one. London has more than one posh hotel.'

'Okay phew, continue.'

'And I thought that it would make more sense to stay over at the hotel rather than try to get a taxi home the week before Christmas when everyone's going to be at works parties, so I called the hotel and they have a room, rooms, one room, or two, and before I booked, the one room, or the two, I wanted to ask you what you thought.'

'About staying in a five-star hotel? I say hell to the yes.'

'So shall I book the two rooms then, or. . .' He coughed. 'The one?'

'I would imagine, being Christmas, they're probably pretty pricey,' Nell said matter-of-factly. 'So, it seems a waste to get two.'

'Is frugality the only reason you're saying one?'

Nell smiled. He was so easy to wind up when he was being this earnest, she couldn't help herself. 'We are in a cost-of-living crisis Greg. It seems like the only humanitarian thing to do, doesn't it? Take the hit for our fellow man.'

'You're teasing me.'

'Yes, I'm teasing you. I think one hotel room would be lovely. What time's check-in, because I think we should make the most of the free toiletries?' Nell stood on tiptoe and planted a full kiss on Greg's mouth. It happened before she thought it through, just an instinctive act between the two of them. It was the first time their lips had touched in nearly twenty years, and every cell in Nell exploded with familiarity, with a love forgotten. She pulled away and saw her confusion mirrored in his eyes.

'Well, I er, better go and get a party dress,' she said hastily, walking quickly away before even more of their bodies could be reintroduced to each other. She had no idea how or why she'd done that, it just felt so natural.

The dress rental company didn't have a massive selection left. Greg had told her that most of his colleagues' wives were wearing black cocktail dresses, but the shop had been stripped of everything in that category. Nell was quite relieved, she never wore black and cocktails were fun, and black cocktail dresses were the opposite of fun. Her eye was immediately drawn to a coral one-shouldered long gown with a slit up the leg just the right side of indecent and a coral feathered trim on the single shoulder. She loved it instantly, and as she was now such a great customer – second dress in a week – she got a sizeable discount too.

She refused to try it on for Greg when she got back to his, keeping it in its white covering, wanting it to be a surprise until tomorrow. They had a simple dinner of cheese and hams and overpriced focaccia bread from one of Greg's neighbourhood bakeries in front of a film, before chastely saying goodnight to each other on the landing and going to bed in separate rooms. She lay in her bed staring at the wall opposite. Had she made a mistake about tomorrow night? Would it be really awkward? Was it too soon? Was this going to ruin everything?

She had no idea that just the other side of the dividing wall Greg was having exactly the same thought.

She definitely had feelings for him; since their kiss earlier, butterflies had taken up permanent residence in her belly now, showing no signs of moving on; if anything their colony was getting larger as the hours ticked by. But that could just be nostalgia, couldn't it? Feelings from the past tricking ones from the present?

She got an overwhelming urge to go next door and climb

into bed with him. Not to do anything saucy, just to curl up to his warm body. She'd spent her life giving into urges, not stopping to work out the pros and cons, just having a thought and following it. Tom was a prime example of that. If she'd just stopped and considered the various potential consequences before flinging her clothes on the floor then she wouldn't have become his unwitting muse. But Greg was different. Greg was a known quantity. Greg was Greg. She slipped out of bed and tiptoed out onto the landing, listening at his door for any low snores or signs of him being asleep. Silence. She pushed open his door and padded over to his bed, gently sliding in next to him, curving her pyjama-clad body around his under the thick duvet. He reached down to find her hand and brought it up to his mouth, kissed it and held it close to his chest as they both fell asleep.

They arrived at the hotel at 3.01 p.m. the next afternoon, precisely one minute after check-in opened. If they were going to pay through the nose for a last-minute hotel room then they were sure as hell going to get their money's worth. Nell had a pang of guilt as they passed the cheery concierge and the housekeeping staff, reminding her of the bad karma of running out of the other hotel without paying. She made a silent pledge there and then to try to pay the hotel back everything she owed them, no matter how long it took; she didn't want that bad juju hanging over her for the next 44.4 years. Every month she'd anonymously send them money, probably for the next 44.4 years, but that was beside the point, she'd right her wrong.

'So, what do you reckon? Shall we put on the fluffy dressing gowns, attack the mini bar and watch a movie?' Greg said, opening and shutting every door and drawer in the room to check the contents.

'Sounds perfect. I might have a shower first. You get the snacks and sort out the drinks.'

Nell had another urge in the shower. This time she didn't waste time weighing anything up, just stepped out onto the bath mat, dried herself off and wandered back into the suite completely naked. *Nurture relationships.*

Greg was just about to open a bag of salted caramel popcorn, but after seeing her, he decided, on reflection, that it could wait.

CHAPTER SEVENTEEN

Judging from Greg's slack-jawed, wide-eyed reaction to seeing her all dolled up in her coral feathered glory, she either looked absolutely sensational, or was dressed completely inappropriately for the occasion. It turned out it was both.

'But, but it's black tie,' he stammered. 'I told you everyone else was wearing black cocktail dresses.'

'Yes, you told me what everyone else was wearing. But I thought this was lovely.' Nell swooshed it around a little so the feathers danced to really hammer the point home quite how lovely it was.

'It is lovely, but everyone else—'

'Greg, listen to yourself. You said it yourself a couple of days ago, you're fed up being like everyone else. Am I or am I not wearing an evening dress?'

'Yes but—'

'Does it state anywhere on the invitation that women have to wear black?'

'Well, no, but it's an unwritten—'

'It's an unwritten rule that sex with an ex is a bad idea, but was it, or was it not pretty damn good?'

'It was amazing but—'

'No.' Nell put up her hand as though she was stopping traffic. 'Enough. You've lived by unwritten rules for too long. I'm liberating you. Be free. Be the Greg you've always wanted to be.'

'You do look really beautiful.'

'Thank you. Now, shall we go and enjoy the free bar?'

The room was a sea of black and white, as Nell knew it would be, and the dark waters parted as they walked in, a dash of orangey pink in a monochrome world. Outfit aside, she was also the only woman to have her hair down, loose and unstyled. It was lucky the ceiling wasn't magnetised or every woman bar her would be stuck to it by their heads the amount of hair pins there were in the room. The quantity of hair lacquer also meant being around naked flames was probably a no-no too.

Greg guided her over to the bar and handed her a tall glass. 'Thank you,' she said accepting it. 'I love prosecco.'

'I think you'll find it's champagne,' a man alongside her corrected.

Nell put it back on the bar. 'Oh what a shame, do you have any prosecco?' she asked the barman with a wink; he couldn't contain his smile as he got a bottle out of the fridge. She liked champagne as much as the next person, but she hated extravagance for extravagance's sake, deliberate displays of wealth and success measured in monetary value, and she also hated pompousness. And she had a horrible feeling that tonight was going to stretch every ounce of patience and self-restraint she had, but for Greg's sake, she would really, really try to behave.

'Greg! So pleased you could make it, you remember Marta, my wife?'

Nell was introduced to Greg's colleague and his wife. Nell

duly complimented the wife on her black cocktail dress, who smiled but chose not to return a pleasantry.

'I hear you're taking a sabbatical! Well, that's a shocker,' the colleague boomed. 'You're a VP, you'd be a director within six-to-eight years, a partner within fifteen, what are you thinking?'

'Well, I thought it's time for a break, travel the world.'

'Good for you, good for you. You're still keeping the stock options though?'

'Of course. Not letting those babies go.'

'We love travel, don't we Marta? Soaking up the local culture and all that.'

'Oh we do, we do, I always say that you can't let the tan fade, so we've even been known to book the next holiday while we're still on holiday!'

'We did six of the seven continents last year alone.'

'Which was your favourite?' Nell asked, glad to be on familiar ground.

'Definitely Asia.'

'Oh, that's my favourite too,' Nell gushed. 'Where did you go? Thailand? Cambodia? Philippines?'

'The Maldives. And it was glorious. We'll have to give you the name of the all-inclusive resort we stayed at,' Marta said. 'Honestly the resort had everything you could ever want, we didn't leave the hotel for the whole time we were there. We didn't lift a finger for the entire fortnight, well only to get the staff to bring us another round of mojitos to our sun-loungers, hahaha.'

Nell and Greg laughed politely.

'And the staff were great, what was that girl called who served us breakfast and dinner every day, Camile? Clementine? Something like that—'

'Oh, who knows, it doesn't matter, they were all great. Plus, you don't even need to tip them! But this resort had five different restaurants, all serving local produce—'

'I've often found that the local produce at the *actual* local restaurants tastes even nicer,' Nell said amiably.

The colleague and his wife moved away quite quickly after that.

'That was quite rude,' Greg said.

'I was merely pointing out that spending two weeks in an all-inclusive resort isn't soaking up the local culture.'

'I don't know, I'd love a fortnight at a resort like that, getting my glasses cleaned by the pool, and eating a fruit kebab that's appeared next to me by the pool as if by magic.'

'Given to you by someone supporting their family on minimum wage.'

'The hospitality industry gives people jobs.'

'Yes, but they also need to pay them a decent and fair wage, don't they? Not to mention tip them where you can. It just makes me really sad that there's what, three, maybe four hundred people here tonight, every one of these women have spent more on getting their hair done today than each waiter will earn for a twelve-hour shift. That's not right. The wrong jobs are valued more all over the world.'

'Can you keep your voice down?'

'Don't worry, no one can hear me over the harp.'

That was a phrase she'd never said out loud before.

Greg took her elbow. 'Come on, let's find our table.'

They were on a table of ten in the centre of the room. Nell's seat had her back to the dancefloor and stage, which was fine, she was quite happy not to witness the dancing that was almost certain to happen in a couple of hours. The seating arrangement went boy, girl, boy, girl, as per protocol, God forbid that more unwritten rules got broken tonight. The man next to her was very pleasant. They ascertained very early on that not one single strand of commonality existed between them, so they gave up trying to find one after a couple of minutes and started tucking into the starters instead.

'Are you having fun?' Greg said, finally turning back to talk to her after spending the main course and dessert talking about how to maximise his investment portfolio from abroad with the man two seats to his left while the other man's wife sat daintily in between them.

'Not especially,' Nell admitted. 'They're not really my kind of people.'

'But I'm your kind of people, and they're my kind of people, so give them a chance.'

'I am, I just had a lovely conversation with the man next to me about school fees. Excuse me, I need to go to the loo.'

It was a bit of a faff trying to hoist her dress up to perform her ablutions, you'd have thought she'd have learned her lesson on renting unfathomably complex evening dresses, but she hadn't. She was just washing her hands when a woman wearing a long black dress joined her at the neighbouring sink. Nell gave her a polite smile in the mirror.

'I just wanted to say that you look absolutely joyful,' the lady said. 'I've been admiring you all night. I wish I had the nerve to wear such a beautiful gown.'

'That's so lovely of you to say. . .?' Nell left a gap for the woman to fill in her name.

'Jess. My name's Jess.'

'I'm Nell. And there's no reason you couldn't wear something like this, Jess.'

'Oh, I could never carry it off.'

'You absolutely could. You'd look sensational.'

'My husband would think I was having a midlife crisis.'

'Maybe start small then, and build yourself up.' Nell reached up to her head and unclipped a sparkly comb that she'd bought for a pound at a charity shop that morning. 'Here, this would go really well with your outfit, and would really bring out your lovely eyes.'

'Oh I couldn't—'

'You can and you should. Let me fix it in for you. There you go, oh you look amazing.'

Jess put her hand up to her short brown bob, and fluffed her hair out at their reflections, smiling. 'Thank you so much Nell, this is honestly the kindest thing that a stranger has ever done for me.'

'It's no problem at all, enjoy your evening.'

Nell retook her seat in the ballroom just as the compere left the stage after introducing the act. The room applauded whoever was walking on stage. Nell reached across the table to top up her water glass. As the clapping calmed down, a man's voice said through the microphone: 'I love doing corporate gigs like this for two reasons: one they pay my rent, and two, it makes me thank fuck I'm a comedian and not a banker.'

Nell snorted water out through her nose. The rest of the room laughed too, self-deprecatingly, completely unaware of quite how truthful the comedian was being. Surely everyone would choose to be them, he was indubitably being ironic. Hilarious.

'I'm sure you're all really lovely people,' the comedian continued, 'individually, but en masse you're like a colony of rich penguins, with, unusually, what can I see here? A beautiful flamingo at its core. I applaud your individuality madam, you are quite clearly my spirit animal, I demand that you leave your millionaire financier husband immediately and come and live in my house-share in Clapham. We even get a whole shelf of the fridge to ourselves. You'll love it.' Nell laughed; this guy was really funny. She swivelled round in her chair to see what her spirit animal looked like and she gasped as the colour drained from both their faces.

The audience waited impatiently for the next joke. The pause was too long to be intentional. It was a shame, they collectively thought, he'd started off so strong. He was probably intimidated, they'd seen it happen before, a confident patter that tailed off to incoherent mumblings. He'd come highly recommended by Iris in HR who'd seen him at a golf club do the month before, he was just the right side of blue and was a couple of hundred pounds under budget, which no one needed to know about.

Tom stammered his way through the next gag, but the audience were already lost, conversations restarted, others were taking the opportunity to visit the bathroom. Nell sat at the table in the centre of the room statue-still, her cheeks flaming.

'Poor guy, he was quite funny as well,' Greg said. 'Anyone for more white? It's not bad, this one.' He turned it round so the label faced him. 'Chablis. I thought so.'

'I'm going to the loo,' Nell said, 'excuse me for a moment.' She weaved her way to the back of the room, her chest heaving in her tight bodice. She was either going to cry, be sick or pass out and she wanted to be away from the busy ballroom when she did any one of them.

'Nell, wait!'

She turned in the carpeted corridor and came face to face with a breathless Tom who just burst through the other double doors.

'You're in the middle of your set,' she said. 'You can't just walk off stage.'

'You're not dead! Are you dead? Are you actually here?'

'Are any of us actually here?' she replied, deadpan.

'I thought you'd died.'

'I thought I did too, but then I woke up.'

'I can't believe this. It's so good to see you again.'

'I wish I could say the same.'

'Why are you angry with me? I apologised about that night at the club, I never meant to upset you, I wasn't making fun of you or anything, if anything the opposite was true, I was in awe of you, your strength and courage, and I was just sad, really sad that I'd met someone so amazing and then you were gone. And then I got your letter, and I realised that you'd felt it too.'

'Felt what too?' She was not going to make this easy for him.

'This,' he gestured first to his own chest, then to hers. 'This chemistry.'

'I don't know what you mean, I literally just wrote a few letters thinking I was dying, tying up any loose ends.'

'I don't believe you.'

She crossed her hands over her chest. 'I'm not asking you to believe me, Tom.'

'I love the way you say my name.'

'It's just Tom.'

'Oh, there it is again.'

'Tom. . .'

'You're doing this on purpose now.'

She smiled in spite of herself. 'You're such a dick.'

'I never pretended to be otherwise.'

'I'm still really angry with you. I saw the name of your new tour, is it based on me?'

'Loosely.'

'What is that supposed to mean?'

They stood to the side then to let two women dressed in almost identical black cocktail dresses walk past. Nell realised that one of them was Daisy, who immediately started whispering to the woman next to her. They gave Nell and Tom sneer-laden second looks as they walked past. Tom nodded and said, 'Evening ladies, enjoy your wee.'

Nell stifled a giggle as the women looked horrified and waddled faster in their matching black stilettos to the bathroom. She playfully hit Tom in the chest. 'You're awful.'

'What? I was just wishing them well for the next adventure in their lives.'

'So how is the tour "loosely" based on me?'

'It's about how meeting you changed my life.'

Nell rolled her eyes. 'Changed your life?'

'Yes. It made me reassess how I've lived my life up until now, and if I died next week, or next year, would I be happy with what I'd done and where I was, and the answer was no, so I've started to change it.'

Nell sighed, she seemed to have that effect on people. 'I hope you haven't done anything drastic?'

'Not really, apart from renamed my entire tour, scrapped all my original material and had to do a rush job on new promo posters, given notice on my house-share, started court proceedings on my ex-wife for joint custody of our son, given up my day job teaching at a local college to do comedy full-time and taken out a lease on a narrow boat to live on.'

'Oh good,' Nell said sarcastically. 'You had me worried there for a minute.'

'You're like a life-coach, but instead of charging for advice you make people buy your crappy furniture and give them amazing sex. It's a very unique business model.'

'I doubt they're going to pay you for tonight,' Nell said, changing the subject.

'Now I know we're friends again I'll offer to go back on and finish the set.'

'Who said we're friends? Again, or in the first place?'

179

'I'd like to be your friend.'

'Did that sound just as creepy in your head?'

Tom nodded. 'Actually yes.'

'You'd better go and make amends with whoever booked you.'

'Are you here with your boyfriend?'

'Ex-boyfriend. I told you about him, the guy I went travelling with.'

'The one who's living until he's a hundred and three?'

'Yes. Except now that I didn't die, his very long life is now in question, isn't it?

Tom blew his cheeks out, 'Poor guy. Look at you starting fires all over the place.'

'I know. It's been a busy week.'

'Can I see you, after this?'

Nell paused. This afternoon she'd rolled around on Egyptian cotton hotel bedding with Greg, and now here she was, really wanting to see Tom again. Turned out New Nell might be just as promiscuous as Old Nell. Some of the secrets of happiness floated into her mind: *Connect with the like-minded. Nurture relationships. Cultivate optimism.* Surely the first one backed Tom, while the second was cheerleading Greg. The third, well the third put everything in the hands of fate. 'I think if we're meant to see each other again, we will,' she said cryptically.

'What does that mean?'

'London's a small city.'

'No, it's not,' he said, 'it's bloody massive.'

'Look, our paths have crossed three times now, in just ten days. Chances are, we'll be in the same tube carriage or waiting in line at the same Starbucks before too long.'

'Do you think I can afford a Starbucks now that I'm an unemployed comedian? And I prefer independent coffee shops anyway, those big American chains just aren't for me.'

Connect with the like-minded.

Tom sighed. 'But I like your way of thinking. Coincidences have certainly been on our side so far.'

'Exactly. Now go and make some more money so you can afford to pay your share when we go out together.'

Tom moved to open the door for her.

'I can open my own doors you know,' Nell said haughtily. 'Having breasts does not impede me in any way.'

Tom tried to hide a smile. 'I didn't think it did. Apart from maybe limiting your choice of fancy-dress outfits.'

'Like what?' Nell asked as they walked back in the ballroom.

'A caterpillar.'

'True, true. Or a pencil.'

'Or a millipede.'

'Or a finger.'

'A centipede.'

'I see we're focusing on the long thin insect category.'

'It's a multi-legged goldmine.'

'Bye Tom.'

'Ooo say it again.'

'Bye Tom.'

'See ya Nell. Take care of yourself.'

CHAPTER EIGHTEEN

'Hey you,' Greg said sleepily alongside her. He was naked, she was not. The reasons for said nakedness were embarrassingly transparent as last night when they got back to the suite, he quite clearly expected a re-run of the afternoon's events and appeared in their bedroom fully prepared for the afterparty. She, however, after her chance encounter with Tom – *I love how you say that* – Radley, pulled on her T-shirt as quickly as she could while Greg was in the bathroom and feigned a deep, noisy sleep as soon as she heard the door open. She'd heard him sigh a loud sigh of disappointment and reluctantly climb into bed next to her; he was in dreamland within seconds. Nell didn't have the same luck, tossing and turning while rehashing, replaying and relishing her conversation with Tom.

There was no doubt that he made her laugh, but that was his job, and he was patently very good at it, but was there more to him than that? He said that he had a child who he wanted to co-parent, was that something that she could take on? He clearly had a complicated life, was there even room for her in it? And then there was Greg, lovely, Greg, who'd been standing uncomplaining in the eye of her storm, as she set about systematically destroying his perfectly ordered life. But apart from the same school blazer still hanging in both their mums' spare wardrobes and a box full of photos of a shiny-faced couple that bore little resemblance to them now, did they have anything in common at all? If Nell hadn't known Greg before last night, and he had just been put next to her as the seating plan dictated, would he have entertained her any more than the man complaining about the travesty of school fee increases to her right? And would she have entertained *him* more to the point, or would she have just been a little bit annoying to him? She'd have thought he was very handsome, if a little too groomed for her normal taste, but she might have asked him a few more questions just to completely ascertain that they were orbiting different planets. Was a shared experience enough to keep people together for a lifetime?

'Morning!' she replied. 'Breakfast ends in forty-five minutes, so do you want to hop in the shower?'

'Uuuuh, my head. Can't we sleep and grab something from the place next door on the way home?'

She realised that his bank balance was vastly different to hers, but deliberately missing a pre-paid meal for a few minutes' extra shut-eye was a ludicrous suggestion. 'Come on,' she said, hitting him with a cushion, 'Spit spot.'

'I could get used to this,' Greg said, twenty minutes later, as they were seated in the grand dining hall and a waiter placed a napkin on Greg's lap with an exuberant flourish.

Nell put hers on her own lap before the waiter could try to.

'I love breakfasts in hotels,' Greg said. 'I can't wait until we go travelling again and have breakfasts like this every day.'

Nell had never had a breakfast like this before in her life.

Her only other experience of five-star living had been the week before and she hadn't left her room the whole time in fear of her death coming about in an inglorious way involving a lift shaft or a particularly slippery marble floor. The breakfast she'd had on a tray was lovely, but not a patch on the tables in front of her laden with every type of pastry and fruit and ham, and condiment choice you could ever wish for.

'Oh good, they have fresh watermelon juice,' said Greg, following on behind her. 'Can you believe that the hotel I met you at didn't have any?'

'Watermelon season is May to September,' Nell replied. 'So why would they have it in December?'

'It was a five-star hotel!'

'That doesn't change the fact that watermelons only grow in warm climates; being rich doesn't mean that you can control the weather.'

'No but it's always sunny somewhere, isn't it? They could have imported it from somewhere that's hot in December.'

Nell opened her mouth to mention carbon footprints and refrigerated truck costs, but chose instead to help herself to some lovely in-season cranberries for her yoghurt and carry it back to the table.

They both sat quietly eating their breakfasts for a moment or two, then Greg said, 'I'd like you to move in with me.'

'I'm sorry, what?'

'Look, you probably think this is moving really fast, but we've been given a second chance here and I really think we should take it. Move in with me. I completely understand if you want to still keep the spare room as yours, and we can take that side of things as slow as you like—'

That side of things? Was he from the 1950s?

'But I really like having you around, and it'll be so much easier to plan our next adventure if we're living together, won't it? I mean, it'll probably only be a couple of weeks or so until we're off again, won't it? I'll contact an agent tomorrow to get them round to value the house for rental and get that ball rolling, then we can fly off once we decide the route we'll take and get a few hotels booked.'

She was stunned into silence with the overload of information to take in, to respond to. She opened and closed her mouth; she literally had no idea what to say.

'I was thinking let's start in Hawaii and work our way around the world going left.'

'We'd hit the rainy season in every country we'd go to then,' said Nell, still slack-jawed from his outpouring of information. 'And we'd cross the dateline, which would ruin us for days.' Her words might have suggested she was entertaining his idea, but her tone made it obvious, or at least she thought it did, that she was not. She'd only just come back. She wasn't ready to get her passport out again. She had to spend a bit of time thinking about her next steps, not do what she always did and head for the airport departure lounge. 'Look Greg, I don't think you've thought this through really, we're not kids anymore, we're forty in two years, you're giving up a really lucrative, stable career on a whim—'

'I'm not giving it up, it'll still be there in three months, if I want it. And it's not a whim!'

'It is a whim! Be honest. Before bumping into me again, had this idea of taking three months off and travelling the world ever crossed your mind?' She held her finger up. 'Be honest.'

Greg squirmed in his seat, and nodded to the waiter for a refill of his coffee. 'Well no, not exactly, but things were different before, weren't they? I thought I had years ahead of me.'

'But you still might live until you're over a hundred, we don't know, do we? And you're planning on frittering away a big portion of your savings on a few months of travel, and then what? You might still have another sixty years to pay for? What then? Just think about this.'

'But I'm exhausted Nell, I need a break.'

'So, book two weeks at the resort in the Maldives Marta and her husband loved so much, go there, rewind, relax, and come back to your ridiculously overpaid job full of energy and vigour.'

He looked like he was considering it. 'I mean it did sound lovely, didn't it?'

Nell didn't answer that.

'Do you think I should call my boss and take back my sabbatical?'

Nell nodded. 'For now.'

'And then I'll book us a fortnight in the Maldives leaving in a couple of weeks.'

If she went with him it would end one of two ways. They'd either get swept away by the romance of the island; after all, that was the Maldivian trademark: candlelit dinners on the beach, rose-petal hearts on the king size beds, floating lily pads and breakfast trays in the infinity pools – actually that did sound pretty great – no, she told herself firmly, that was only one outcome of the trip. The other was that they'd infuriate each other so much one of them would get fed to a passing giant porpoise and this easy truce they'd managed to rebuild would be forever gone.

'No Greg, I think you've misunderstood, I think *you* should go to the Maldives, I've got to try to sort out Dad and Polly and find a job and work out what I'm going to do.'

His face fell. 'You want me to go alone?' He said the word alone as though it was quite possibly the worst thing he could imagine. 'What would I do alone in the Maldives?'

'Swim, snorkel, dive, sunbathe, venture out of the hotel

occasionally to eat some *real* local produce. Read books, start drawing again, perhaps start writing that science fiction time travel novel you were always talking about.'

'I'd get really bored by myself.'

'Did you not hear me reel off the things that you could do? Anyway, you always looked really sexy with a tan.'

He perked up. 'Really?'

'Absolutely. So, at the very least, go and bronze your body and by the time you come back I'll have figured out my life.'

'But you promise you'll stay at mine while I'm gone?'

'Of course, if you don't mind, it'd be a real help.'

'I'll bring you something nice back.'

'Just promise me it won't be from the hotel gift shop.'

He laughed. 'I'm not promising anything. Right, we'd better get home and get packed ready to go back down to Hove tomorrow for Christmas.'

Mentioning Christmas in Hove brought Nell back down to earth with a jolt. She'd received a text from Polly during the party last night saying that if she had nothing better to do, there would be room for Nell at hers for Christmas lunch. It was undeniably loaded with historic resentment, but it was a glimmer of a breakthrough nonetheless and Nell had immediately replied with a *Yes please, sounds lovely*, which she was nauseously regretting now.

There wasn't the same banter between Nell and Greg on the journey down as there had been a few days before because the enormity of the impact of Nell's letters had now sunk in. She knew she was past the simple apology stage, and had crawled into the deep rebuilding and resolution phase, a phase she'd never lingered in long enough to complete before stuffing her belongings in her rucksack and buying a one-way ticket to literally anywhere else.

'Do you want me to come in?' Greg asked as he pulled up outside Jenny's house.

'No, I've got this.'

'Just stay calm and listen to what they say before speaking. You've said your part, now let them say theirs.'

'I know.'

'You can do this.'

'I know.'

'So why aren't you getting out of the car?'

'Because I don't want to.'

'Nell. Get out of the car.'

'Two more minutes.'

'Your mum's standing on the doorstep looking at you. Get out of the car.'

'We're still meeting the old crowd tomorrow night?'

'I'll pick you up at seven-thirty. Now go.'

'It's a really lovely car air freshener you've got, what is it? Lavender?'

Greg unclipped Nell's seatbelt and leaned across her to open the passenger door. 'Go.'

Nell was looking forward to an afternoon curled up in front of the fire in her mum's lounge, but within minutes of Nell walking through the front door, mother and daughter were walking back out of it again to have a stroll on the beach, despite it being December, and the mercury hovering around zero. Every time Nell had a childhood issue to work through, or showed the slightest indication of wanting to talk, off they went to the pebbly shoreline to tell it to the sea. Nell handed Jenny a cup of coffee she'd bought from a snack van parked up along the seafront road and they sat down on a stone wall.

'How did you make Polly invite me for Christmas?' Nell started.

'I didn't, she came up with that olive branch on her own.'

'But you must have said something?'

'Not really. We had a walk along the beach with Bea and the dog and were talking about how funny life has a way of pulling the rug from under you unexpectedly, but sometimes that it's for the best.'

Nell studied her mother, stroking the cardboard cup with her thumb. 'Like Dad leaving?'

'Yes, like your dad leaving. I thought it was the worst thing that could possibly happen, I'd tried so hard to keep the marriage together over the years when I probably shouldn't have done.'

'What do you mean?'

'Katie wasn't his first affair. I hope she'll be his last, for her and Ruby's sake, but I doubt it.'

Nell could feel her face draining of colour.

'He doesn't know that I know about the others, well, not all of them. I thought that if I ignored it, and focused on you two girls then it wouldn't matter that he always had one eye somewhere else. But then Katie came along, and she was much more difficult to ignore. And with you and Polly both off having lives of your own, I didn't have a reason to fight for him to stay. And I'm glad I didn't, because him leaving has been the best thing.'

'Has it?'

'I think so. It's given me possibilities of what I can do by myself.'

'Does being with Ray let you do those things?'

Jenny sighed. 'He's not a horrible man, Nell.'

'I never said he was a horrible man, Mum, just one that might not be right for you.'

'I've got to be honest, the first couple of years after your Dad left were okay because I had Polly nearby and then Nana to look after, but after she died I was pretty miserable, Nell, and Ray came along at a very bleak time for me, one where, if I'm being totally truthful, I didn't see much of a future for myself.'

'You don't need to explain or justify anything to me, Mum, we're all living our own lives, aren't we?' Images of her mum's hobbies folder and wish list of escapades flitted into Nell's mind. 'Just as long as you are living the life you want to live?'

'What does that even mean?'

'I mean, you don't have to settle for someone else's idea of the perfect life, do you? Like I said in my letter, you can do and be anything you want.'

'Of course, people have dreams when they're younger – you know that I've always wanted to see more of the world and have some adventures of my own. But really, I'm too old for all that now. I'm quite happy here in my own home, honestly Nell, I don't need a big adventure or a great love. I'm just happy here in Hove, with Polly and Bea down the road, and you, hopefully, around a lot more, that's all I really want.'

'Of course I'll be here. How's Polly doing? Has she decided what to do?'

'She's still thinking about it. She doesn't want a marriage like I had, but she's also not ready to walk away from it.'

'So, in two days' time when we're all sat around her dining table playing happy families, we all have to pretend we don't know what we know?'

'Can you do that?'

'I can, if that's what Polly wants. Equally, if she wants me to call some members of the Sicilian mafia I know after working on their lemon farm for a month last year then I can do that too. Marco and Renato owe me a favour.'

'Let's keep that option in your back pocket for now.'

'Va bene.'

'Now, about your dad.'

Nell groaned and slumped back against the wall.

'It's sunny, and the golf club is shut after today for the next three days, so if I know him the way I think I do, he'll be halfway round the course round about now if you want to go and find him. Go on, it'll make you both feel better.'

'I'll do that on one condition.'

'What?'

'You move Ray's weights and reclaim the spare room as your own space, with a lovely desk under the window and inspirational pinboards of lovely pictures and photos and places you'd like to go to and things you want to do.'

'But where would he work out?'

Nell's eyes twinkled. 'What do you keep in your shed these days?'

Jenny was right. By the time Nell had found the right bus and walked down the long snaking drive to the club house, Tony was propping up the bar chatting to the girl behind it who was young enough to be his granddaughter.

'Hi Dad,' Nell said, sliding onto the bar stool alongside him. 'Good round today?'

'Nell.'

They hadn't spoken in eight years. Not a phone call, an email, a Christmas or birthday card. Nothing. From Nell's side, the silence was powered by abject anger, and she'd guessed that Tony's was an interesting combination of stubbornness, sheepishness and forgetfulness now that he had a new toy.

'What are you drinking?' he asked her.

'Just a tap water please.'

'Have something more than that, I'll pay.'

'No, you're okay, just a tap water please,' Nell said to the girl. She needed a clear head for this conversation, and definitely didn't need him buying her anything.

'You're alive then.'

'Yes. Look I'm sorry about the letter, for making you think that I'd. . . you know. I didn't mean to upset anyone, it wasn't a cruel trick or anything, I honestly thought I was going to die.'

'But you didn't.'

'No.'

A few seconds passed as they both considered the implications of this. Tony looked so much older than Nell remembered him. The deep lines around his eyes looked more like the results of exhaustion rather than laughter. She hoped the last week hadn't contributed to that, but he had sounded so broken and bereft on the message he'd left on her mum's answer phone, perhaps he cared more than he let on.

'How long are you back for this time?' Tony asked finally.

'I don't know yet.'

'If I were you I wouldn't hang about for too long, it's miserable here.'

'From where I'm standing your life isn't that miserable. I'm assuming the Range Rover with TON 1 on the numberplate is yours?'

'Yes, nice motor that.'

'You parked in a disabled bay.'

'They're always empty. I don't know why they have them, there's no disabled members. Grass and wheelchairs don't really mix.'

Nell bit her tongue before it moved furiously with all that she wanted to say. *Just stick to why you're here*, she told herself.

'About the letter I sent you. . .' Nell started, thinking that was as good a place as any to begin with. 'Did you understand what I was trying to say?'

'Not really. I showed it to Katie and she said that it was a metaphor.'

'I was just really angry Dad, I still am, if I'm honest with you, possibly even more now. I just don't understand why Mum wasn't enough for you. She's amazing.'

'I thought you'd get it more than anyone, Nell. You've spent your life as a black sheep hopping around desperately trying to find something that's better than what you're doing. Even as a child you stuck at something for about five minutes before getting bored and moving onto something new; at least I stayed with your mum for thirty years before looking for greener grass.'

'Did you?' Nell couldn't help herself saying what she was thinking.

'Did I what?'

'For thirty years did you just stay mowing mum's grass? Or did you occasionally mow other people's?'

'I'm not sure that's really relevant, but I did sometimes mow Julie's, when Andy's back was playing up.'

Nell wasn't sure if her Dad's grasp of metaphor was, actually, really bad or whether he was now admitting to an affair with their elderly neighbour.

'Julie always said that my mower did a much better job than Andy's as it happens. His extension lead wasn't long enough to reach the top borders.'

'Stop it! Stop talking! I don't need to know any of this!'

Tony looked really confused and shrugged, 'Well, it was you that brought it up.'

'Look, Dad, I can't begin to pretend that I understand your decision to leave Mum for Katie. I know I don't know Katie, but I can't imagine her being any kinder or gentler, or more loyal than Mum.'

Tony shuffled uncomfortably in his seat. Nell could tell

from his inability to meet her eye that those weren't the qualities he was necessarily looking for in new lawns.

'Were you unhappy with Mum? Did you argue? I can't remember you arguing?'

'We didn't argue,' he conceded. 'Perhaps that was the problem. It was just, well, a bit ordinary.'

'Ordinary?'

Tony nodded. 'You've said it yourself, every time me or your mum asked if you could stay in England for longer, "Life's short Dad, there's so much to see and do." I suppose that's the crux of it, isn't it? I spent years and years being ordinary. Then the money came in, and then women like Katie came along, and I didn't feel ordinary anymore.'

'Mum never thought you were ordinary.'

He took a long swig of his drink and put the empty glass wearily back on the bar. 'Well, maybe not. But you can't look back, can you?'

'Do you miss her?'

Tony motioned for the server to fill up his beer glass. 'I don't know what's to be gained from thinking about that.'

'It would help me understand a bit more. I've always thought that you packed up and left without a second glance, onto someone new and young and exciting. To know that you've doubted your decision, or sometimes missed Mum would make it easier to like you again.'

'Of course I miss her. I never intended Katie to be more than a fling to make an old man feel alive again, but your mum found out, and things snowballed from there. And now look at me, I'm sixty-three with a five-year-old. I'm spending Christmas Eve with my in-laws who are two years younger than me, and my wife's sister, who was in the year below you at school, and my wife's friends who look at me as though I'm their pervert old chemistry teacher, thinking about you and Polly together with your mum all having fun and chatting and laughing and yes, I'll wish I was there.'

Tony paused and Nell knew that he was fully expecting her to fill the silence with something like, *oh you poor thing, that does sound hard*, but she didn't. He didn't need to make 'ordinary' into a bad thing. He could have embraced the stability, the loyalty, the known, and been really happy. That was his choice. And if he was now feeling regret, or self-pity for putting a fleeting moment of excitement above a lifetime of unconditional, steady love, well, that was on him.

'But I would have thought that out of everyone, you should understand.'

'Me?' There was no mistaking the look of disgust on Nell's face.

'Seize the day, live for the moment, life's short, isn't that what you're all about?'

'Not at the expense of other people.'

'You and me Nell, we're the same.'

'I am nothing like you, Dad.'

'Sure. Sure.' Tony drained his glass and tipped it towards the server. 'Another one in here when you're ready, darling.'

CHAPTER NINETEEN

'It's not even seven yet, and he said he'd be here at half past.'

Nell dropped the corner of the living room curtain back down and turned round to face her mum. 'I'm not waiting for him if that's what you think.'

'No, that's not what I think at all,' Jenny grinned. The time they'd spent together in the last couple of days had opened the floodgates of their shared mother-daughter memories: choosing Christmas presents, having lunch in town, even Jenny buying Nell a pay as you go mobile. It was as though twenty years had been stripped away and Nell was just a teen again, needing her mum. And sitting eagerly by the lounge bay window waiting for Greg to arrive, was just the latest déjà vu. Nell caught Jenny smiling at her; she obviously felt like the last twenty years hadn't happened either.

'If you want to bring him back tonight, you know you can. And he doesn't need to sleep on the sofa like he used to.'

'Thanks Mum, but no, I will not be bringing him home tonight.'

'No need to decide that now, see how the evening goes. You might want to by the end of the night.'

'No, no I won't.'

'Just keep an open mind, that's all Nell, see where the mood takes you. I thought you were spontaneous.'

'I am spontaneous.'

'Well then, don't plan. Anyway, I'm a really heavy sleeper.'

'Please stop talking.'

'Or you can stay over there. Just be back mid-morning for your stocking.'

'You've got me a stocking?'

'Of course I have.'

The doorbell rang, startling them both into action. Nell rushed to the over mantle mirror and fluffed her hair up a little, while her mum gave her two thumbs up and moved to open the front door. Greg stood there holding two flower pots, one red poinsettia that he handed to Jenny who gave him an exuberant kiss on both cheeks, and the other, a pot with three crocus bulbs in it, each one with a vibrant green shoot poking through the moss which he handed to Nell. 'It's supposed to symbolise rebirth,' he explained awkwardly, blushing.

'I love it,' she replied, leaning forward to brush his cheek with hers. 'It's really thoughtful.' She placed the plant down on the hallway table and exchanged wide-eyed glances with her mum who mouthed, 'Wow, he has aged well!' to Nell behind his back.

'Right, let's be off,' Nell said before her mum could be any less subtle about how pleased she was.

'Remember what I said Nell,' Jenny sang as Greg and Nell walked down the path towards the gate.

'What did she say?' Greg asked.

'Oh, you know the usual, don't drink too much, don't stay out too late, yadda yadda yadda.'

'Am I the only one having a serious flashback?'

'Oh don't, every minute back here is one massive flashback. I literally feel like I've stepped into a time machine and I'm seventeen again, you've just picked me up and we're off to meet our friends in the pub.'

Greg gently shoulder barged her. 'Will we also be taking a detour home like we used to down to the seafront behind the last beach hut?'

Nell was incredibly thankful that at that moment they were between streetlamps and he couldn't see the scarlet hue of her cheeks.

A rowdy roar went up when they walked in the pub. After Karen's 'bedtime permitting' aside in the supermarket, Nell had thought that they'd be the first to arrive while everyone else sorted out babysitters and read bedtime stories, but it turned out that parents of young kids were the most eager to start a night out. 'Young kids' was a little inaccurate, as it transpired that Lee and Catherine, who got together in Year Ten, same as Nell and Greg, were dropped off at the pub by their son who had just passed his driving test.

Nell stayed on the periphery of the group for the first couple of drinks, unable to join in conversations about other people they all knew and she was supposed to, old teachers she had only vague recollections of, British current affairs she had no idea about, the *Strictly* final she hadn't watched. She was in her home country, and yet it felt more foreign than most of the places she'd ever lived. Greg seemed completely at home, however, reverting back to being the enigmatic rugby captain that boys aspired to be and women aspired to be under, judging from the reactions from the female contingent of the group.

The gin and tonics were starting to relax her, she could feel the silky spirit soothe her nerves and she leaned into the feeling. As anecdote after anecdote was shared, memories that had been pushed to the back of her mind with things piled on top of them started to resurface: concerts they'd all been to, festivals on the beach, school trips, camping trips, shared firsts – drinks, kisses, spliffs, sex. Ten people bound together by a shared adolescence. Nell quickly realised that no one was judging her, or questioning her life choices, they weren't even that interested in the places she'd been or what she'd done since the last time they saw her. They were more excited about the fact she and Greg were there together, with them, the old crew, on Christmas Eve in the Connaught.

Apart from the other Karen, and Timmo and Kate, who had to all get back for babysitters, the rest of the old gang picked up a bag of chips each from the chippie – Nell had been gone from England too long to opt for curry sauce on hers, so settled for good old-fashioned ketchup – and the remaining six piled on down to Karen and Ian's beach hut. Like so many things that Nell had been quick to pour judgement on, it turned out she rather liked beach huts. Ian deftly unclipped a hook from the wall and hey presto a table appeared, likewise, two fold-down chairs slipped out from underneath the sofa, which Karen proudly proclaimed with a lascivious wink, 'was also a bed'. They sat there amiably on the concrete slipway outside the open doors of the hut, Nell and Greg next to each other on deck chairs, Billy, Lee and Catherine on cushions from the sofa and Ian and Karen on the fold-up dining chairs. Sitting together like they had hundreds of times before, on different seats, in a different part of town, quietly eating snacks as though it was breaktime and they were waiting for the lesson bell to ring. The sound of the sea gently lapped at the pebble shore a couple of metres below them, a reminder that the tide comes in and goes out again, the moon full and round casting dancing shadows on the water. Nell looked up from her salty vinegar-soaked chips and caught Greg's eye. He smiled his wide lopsided smile and she smiled back. He reached over and took her hand in his on the wooden arm of the deckchair, brushing her fingers with his thumb, in a way he'd done thousands of times, engulfing her smaller hand in his, slowly stroking it, telling her silently to trust him, that it was all going to be okay.

It caught her quite by surprise, but for the first time in a week, seven days to the day, since Nell had woken up in a hotel room wearing a rented ballgown, her shoulders weren't bunched up around her neck and she wasn't thinking, what next? In fact, if she was being totally honest, she couldn't remember a time in her life when she hadn't thought, what next? But that Christmas Eve, surrounded by old familiar faces, with Greg, charming, lovely Greg sitting next to her on the seafront, she was quite happy being in the now. And if this was what ordinary was, she'd happily take it.

CHAPTER TWENTY

Beatrice stood at the top of the stairs looking down on them as Polly ushered a present-laden Nell and Jenny into the hallway. 'Nanny!' The little girl hurtled down the stairs and flung herself at Jenny who scooped her up and buried her face noisily in her granddaughter's neck as Bea excitedly reeled off what Father Christmas had brought her. Nell lingered behind, taking in the features of her niece, who was a carbon copy of Polly at this age with her short, bobbed strawberry-blonde hair and neat fringe. Bea paused and looked over Jenny's shoulder suspiciously at Nell. 'You're Aunty Nell.'

Nell nodded.

'Did you bring me a present?'

Nell nodded again, smiling this time, wishing that adults were as easy to thaw.

'Do you want to see my room?'

Nell let herself be guided upstairs to Bea's room. She was ceremoniously introduced to every teddy, doll and stuffed animal, was shown how bouncy Bea's bed was, how tall she was by the new pencil mark on the door frame, which certificate went with which good behaviour, and Bea was halfway through listing everyone in her class and what they usually had in their snack-boxes, when Polly stood by the door telling them that it was time for lunch. The faint sketch of a smile on her face told Nell that her sister had been there a while before she'd spoken.

Nell had already decided that the best, nay the only, plan for the day was to disarm through unbridled optimism and joy, starting with the exuberant reunion with Polly's husband. 'Damian! Lovely to see you again, happy Christmas! Yes, I know, bit of a surprise. . . not sure how long I'll be staying, probably for a while. . . how's work. . . fantastic, great news, hasn't Bea grown? Ooh, red cabbage, lovely, shall I sit here?' It was exhausting, but necessary, and Nell's one summer working at Disneyland Paris came in very useful in cultivating an aura of positivity when all she wanted to do was pick up the gravy boat and deposit its Bisto goodness all over Damian's lap.

Polly hadn't had the same Disney training as Nell though, and Nell sensed the effort it was taking her sister to smile and felt so guilty that she was the reason for that. Every nuanced movement Polly made displayed a rampant hatred of her husband, right down to giving him the two least-crispy roast potatoes and driest-looking piece of turkey. He seemed merrily unaware of any undercurrent, though, and Nell wasn't aware that he'd had any theme-park training, so his levels of jollity were quite impressive. She did clock him looking at his phone quite a lot when it buzzed, and turning it over on the table so the screen wasn't visible. On the third time this happened, Nell looked over at Polly who was staring at it too, nostrils slightly flaring.

'I think after lunch we should go for a girls' walk on the beach and leave Daddy to clear up, what do you say Bea? Would you like Aunty Nell, Mummy and Nanny to take you and your doggy for a walk?' Nell asked her niece, smiling.

'Yes absolutely,' Damian said, jumping on Nell's suggestion a beat too soon. 'Happy to clear all this away. I'll probably have a nap too, so don't rush back.'

'Actually Mum,' Polly said, turning to Jenny, 'would you mind staying here and helping Damian?'

'Oh no need,' her husband hurriedly said, 'you girls go and get some fresh air, I'll be fine doing this by myself.'

Jenny looked between her son-in-law and daughter, and obviously realised what Polly was asking. 'No, I'll stay, I think Polly's right, we can do this between us together in no time, and then we can play a game of cards or something, can't we Damian?'

Damian's hand was on top of his phone on the table as it buzzed underneath.

'You should get that Damian, it sounds important,' Polly said. 'Don't worry about leaving the table, you can answer it here.'

He flushed red, and muttered something about it being his fantasy football league just wishing each other a happy Christmas.

'I think that Christmas is no time for phones, not when you've got family round,' Jenny said. 'Come on Bea, I'll help you put your wellies on. Damian, you make a start on the dishwasher, but turn the phone off first eh? There's a good lad.'

The wind whipped round Nell's hair and burned her face with its icy bite, while the sun bathed the tops of their heads with its warm winter rays. 'I don't think the beach has ever looked more beautiful,' Nell breathed, looking at the vast expanse of sun-glinted pebbles, and frothy waves lapping the shore.

'Coming from you, who's seen more beaches than most, that's quite the compliment.'

'None will ever match this one.'

'Really? Even Fiji?'

'Fiji didn't have our initials carved into the harbour wall, or have memories of windbreakers getting blown away, or thousands of Mr. Whippys eaten, or best pebble-finding competitions.'

Polly smiled as they walked. 'That was a brilliant move of Dad's inventing that game, kept us quiet for hours.'

'I saw him the day before yesterday.'

'Oh?'

'At the golf club. I asked him why he left Mum.'

'And?'

'She was too ordinary.'

'Ouch.'

'It made me think, of how many times I've used that excuse to move on from where I am. As soon as things started to feel settled, I packed up. I've spent eight years hating him for the very thing that I do without even questioning it.'

'You didn't leave a thirty-year marriage.'

'No, but I did leave Mum, and you. What you said the other day, about me never being around for the hard stuff, you're right. I don't think I did it on purpose, I don't remember ever thinking, oh Christ, Nana's really sick, better stay away, I just don't think that it ever really occurred to me that I might be needed.'

'You weren't, we had it covered.'

Nell stopped walking. 'Can you just stop being defensive for one minute, Polly, and listen to what I'm trying to say?'

'I know what you're trying to say Nell. But you're not hearing what I'm saying.'

Greg's parting words to her when he dropped her off a couple of days before ran through Nell's mind. *You've said your part, now let them say theirs.*

Polly looked a little surprised when Nell didn't try to argue. She left a second or two to leave room for her sister to interject, but Nell stayed resolutely silent. 'Leaving is so much easier than staying put,' Polly said. 'You think that you were the braver one because you strapped on a backpack and went into the unknown, but it took a different type of strength to stay and deal with everything without running away.'

'If you had told me to come back, that you needed me, I would have.'

'I shouldn't have needed to.'

Her sister was right; she shouldn't have needed to spell it out explicitly. Nell should have known that just her presence was needed next to Beatrice's incubator to weave her hand through her sister's, or to take her turn next to her Nana's bed, to give her mum and Polly some rest, or to be there watching movies with her mum in the early lonely days of her being divorced.

'You're the strongest person I know.'

Polly looked at her sister. 'So why am I not packing up Damian's things and telling him to get the fuck out of my house?'

'I don't know. . . Katie wasn't Dad's first affair,' Nell said after a while.

'I know.'

Nell put her arm around her sister's shoulder and felt her sister tense a little under her touch. A beat, when she could either shrug her off, or lean into it. Polly's shoulder slowly dropped and she put her arm around Nell's waist. The two sisters stood at the water's edge, watching Bea giggle as she ran in and out of the froth in her little wellies, with Sadie the dachshund barking joyously round her legs.

*

'You'll let me know what you decide,' her mum said, misty-eyed, 'where you'll be staying?'

'Of course.'

'There are worse places than Hove to set up a life you know,' Jenny said hopefully.

'I know that. I love Hove, I'm just not sure I'm ready to put a pin in the map and say "here", that's where I'm going to settle down.'

'There are some lovely rentals about at the moment.'

'Mum,' Nell said with a smile. 'I've got a lot of figuring out, and earning money to do, before I start signing any contracts. But I promise that I'll call you in a couple of days and let you know where I am. And you can message me any time, and I'll be facetiming you all the time. You're going to be overwhelmed with Nell-ness, okay? I promise. It's not like before.'

'Overwhelmed with Nell-ness. I like it.'

Nell pushed her kitchen chair back, got up and kissed the top of her mother's head 'Right, let me call Greg, tell him to pick me up in an hour, and get packed.' Thanks to her mum's generosity on the high street during the Boxing Day sales, Nell had a couple more items to call her own, and she begrudgingly, but gratefully, accepted a loan of a hundred pounds to pay for the transport to any interviews if she was lucky enough to get any.

'I'm glad you're back with Greg.'

'I'm not *back* with him.'

'He's good for you Nell. And you're good for him. You'd have a lovely life together.'

'We'll see what happens.'

PART THREE

*Life is what happens when you're busy
making other plans*

CHAPTER TWENTY-ONE

Nell settled down on Greg's sofa with a ready meal from the new batch that had just arrived for the week. Ever the hospitable host, Greg had kept the subscription to the organic ready meal service going even while he went away for New Year's so she wouldn't starve. He'd tried to persuade her to join him on his trip to Bristol with some university friends. It was an annual tradition apparently; they'd all rent a big house and fill it to the rafters with olives and Pinot Noir. Not usually one to say no to a spontaneous party, Nell even surprised herself with the speed at which she declined the invitation. She had had no time for any sort of concrete planning over Christmas and she really needed to just knuckle down and sort her life out.

Sweet, wonderful Greg had also left her an envelope of cash that she was determined not to touch and his computer password. She had a pad and a pen alongside her on the sofa, ready to start brainstorming her next move. The trouble was, her brain was as blank as the paper. What should she do? What did she like? She tapped the pen on the paper a few times, willing the cogs to start whirring.

Books. She liked books. She could work in a bookshop.

Coffee. Maybe a café.

She liked being outside. So, nothing in an office.

She liked plants and flowers. But not wasps. But she did like bees. She wrote down 'honey'.

She'd love a dog. But dogs cost money. A dog could be in phase two of the plan.

Did she like children? She did like children. Very much. Did she want her own one? Not sure. Probably not. She put a question mark next to children.

She loved growing her own herbs and vegetables. She could get an allotment and a market stall and sell her own produce. Strictly seasonal though. No watermelons in winter.

She liked doing bad watercolours, she put the word '*hobby*' next to painting, '*not job*.'

She liked chatting to random people. So, some sort of community role.

Nothing with computers. Didn't trust them.

Did she need it to be hot? She bit the end of the pen. Not especially, she loved the sun, but had just as many happy times in the snow. And her shoulders had a tendency to peel, which wasn't a good look.

Did she want to stay in London? At that exact moment, like a scene from a movie, a siren screamed past answering that question for her.

Hove? She shuddered involuntarily, her body obviously responding to that question before her brain could.

She didn't want to live in a high-rise, hearing people above and below her simultaneously freaked her out. One of the worst nights of her life was in a Cantonese hostel on the second floor of a tower block in Hong Kong. Imagining the thousands of tonnes resting on her ceiling completely freaked her out and she didn't sleep a wink.

She didn't want to share a fridge with anyone, not again. She remembered Tom's joke about that at the Christmas party and winced. There was a time and a place for writing your name on the milk and that time and place was not now.

Remembering Tom made a narrow boat pop into her mind and she was suddenly flooded with happiness. She didn't know if it was the man or the boat that had prompted that particular fizz of excitement so she wrote both *Tom* and *Boat* down, with a question mark alongside both of them. Then felt guilty and added Greg with a heart around it on the other side.

She looked at the filled pad in front of her. That was a good evening's work. Probably the most productive New Year's Eve she'd ever had in her life, and what's more, tomorrow morning held zero possibility of a hangover, or extracting herself from whatever situation her New Year's shenanigans got her into. She felt like a grown-up, making mature decisions to take control of her life. She should open a bottle of something or go out to celebrate. No, she told herself, stop it. If she could stay in tonight, when the rest of the world was going out, then she'd know she had indeed changed. Looking at the scribbles on her pad again, her stomach lurched. It was all very well narrowing down her dreams to this vegetable-growing, bee-keeping, outside-living, dog-owning, people-meeting, book-selling, coffee-making, countryside-dwelling existence that she quite clearly craved, but how was she going to make it a reality? Just then the streets outside erupted with bangs and fizzes from fireworks being let off in gardens up and down the street. She walked to the window and pulled the curtain back to see the sky alight with colour in all directions. She watched the patterns take shape in the inky sky, punctuating the darkness with dots and squiggles and life. Excited whoops of happiness blended with the bangs, singing through the walls of 'Auld Lang Syne', and Nell smiled. She'd made it.

Most of the world was waking up on 1 January determined that this would be the month/year where they'd lose weight/ stop drinking so much/do more exercise/learn a new skill/ end that affair/start that affair/endless variations of adopting new hobbies and pastimes. Most of which would be discarded without a backwards glance two weeks into the new year. For Nell though, the advent of a new year promised something more than a chance to get better at gardening or to learn Spanish. Never expecting to see this year, let alone plan resolutions for it, meant the dawning of this day was hugely symbolic. Whatever decisions she put into place now could, should, really mean something. Today was, quite literally, the start of the rest of her life.

She spent the first morning of the New Year sending off email after email enquiring about jobs. Her CV went on for pages, cluttered with short-term roles in every industry imaginable. Even she could recognise that it wasn't a great look for a potential employer. After hours staring at a screen Nell pulled her coat on and set off with a purpose. She was going to clear her mind with a walk. An aimless walk with no set destination. A walk in which she would mull over last night's life-planning and come up with a concrete plan of action. With no set route in mind, she felt free, taking random right turns because she felt like it, weaving down narrow cobbles that opened out onto noisy thoroughfares that she quickly tried to deviate from, opting for the quieter back streets rather than the busy main roads. After an hour she found herself on a path next to the Regent's Canal and tried to tell herself that this was a fluke, a surprise, yet another twist of fate that had presented itself to her. It wasn't as though Tom had actually told her what waterway his boat was on, London was filled with canals; this was in no way a romantic pilgrimage, it was merely a life-affirming stroll.

She ambled along the towpath, marvelling at the colourful narrow boats lining the walls of the canal. Some painstakingly decorated with fresh, lovingly polished paint, others wearing their rust like proud armour. *Serendipity, Liberty, Seas the Day, Salty Dog, One Moor Time, The Queen Hilda, Nauti-buoy.* Nell smiled at the ingenuity and personality of the boat names as she walked past them. Some had solar panels on their roofs, others pot plants and cat litter trays on their bow. Some had fairy lights and Christmas decorations that hadn't been taken down yet, others looked empty and abandoned, while others looked like they had been a loving home for years.

Nell had to swerve off the tow path to avoid a blackboard. She stopped and read the chalky writing. *Teas, coffees, sandwiches.* An arrow pointed to the adjacent narrowboat. This boat was neither as fancily adorned as some of its neighbours, nor so battle-scarred as to be unwelcoming. She felt in her pocket for money and as her fingers brushed a five-pound note she climbed onto the boat's stern and opened the little wooden door, bending her head to walk through it.

The inside of the boat had been cleared of the sofas and beds that Nell guessed used to be there, and now had a mismatched array of tables, some small seating one or two, others bigger for four or more. A little pot of flowering shrubs sat on each one along with a handwritten little chalk board detailing the choice of drinks and food on offer.

'I'll be out in a minute,' came a friendly call from a cabin beyond the café area, which Nell supposed would be the kitchen.

'No problem, don't rush,' Nell called back. She settled herself at a small table for one. No point taking up a bigger table that someone else might need in a bit, although it seemed as though she was the only one seeking respite on the canal that day.

'Hello love, what can I get you?' An older, grey-haired woman came out behind a screen, wiping her hands on a clean tea towel tucked in her jeans pocket.

'Just a cup of tea would be lovely,' Nell said. 'And maybe a toasted teacake,' she added, choosing the least expensive option on the board.

'Would you like jam with it too?'

'Is it extra?' Nell asked.

The woman shook her head kindly. 'Nope, all included.'

It wasn't until Nell was halfway through her teacake, lavishly spread with melted butter and thick strawberry jam that she noticed the little '50p Jam' on the board under Extras.

'I love your boat,' Nell said.

The woman looked up from the last table in the café where she'd sat down after making Nell's drink and food. 'Thank you, it's a labour of love.'

'I can imagine. How long have you been here?'

'In this mooring? A couple of years.'

'It moves?'

The woman laughed. 'Yes, it moves. Just about. It's a bit creaky in its joints but aren't we all?'

Nell laughed with her. 'I think it's wonderful. You're so lucky.'

'I think so. Fancy a top up?'

Nell would have liked nothing more, but the five-pound note had been alone in her pocket, so she reluctantly shook her head.

'Refills are free.'

Nell looked up at the blackboard to see where it advertised that, but saw nothing. The woman followed Nell's gaze and quickly followed that up with, 'I don't promote it, it's an offer I only extend to customers I like the look of.'

Nell smiled. 'In that case, I'd love one, thank you. Only if you join me though?'

The woman's name was Andrea. She had bought the boat just over ten years ago after a heart attack in her early fifties which made her reassess her way of living. As soon as she said that part Nell knew exactly what she meant. She'd moored the boat up near Peterborough for a while and then brought it to London to have a faster pace of life.

Nell looked around her, smiling at the boat's cosiness. An idea popped into her head, fully formed and completely cooked. 'Can I work for you? Here on the boat?'

Andrea laughed. 'I've been open for three hours already today and you're my only customer. Actually, no I tell a lie, a man popped in to ask for water for his dog, you're my only paying customer, so as much as I'd love to say yes, I barely make enough for myself, let alone to hire anyone.'

Nell's eyes twinkled. 'Well maybe stop giving away free cups of tea and pots of jam to random strangers then.' The two women laughed.

'Can I give you my number?' Nell urged. 'And then if you ever have an emergency, you can call me and I'll step in. I know you've only just met me, but I'm very honest.' *Unnecessarily so sometimes.*

'Go on then,' Andrea sighed good-naturedly. 'Pop it down on this piece of paper and stick it up on the fridge.'

Her phone pinged on her walk home, and Nell excitedly took it out of her pocket, Andrea must have remembered the holiday she'd booked or the knee replacement she'd overlooked. But it was a photo from Greg, standing on the Clifton

215

Suspension Bridge with the words 'Happy New Year!' typed below.

Nell made sure she looked in every window of every shop and café on her walk home, searching for Help Wanted signs. She wasn't in dream job territory, but she needed to start paying her way with Greg, set up the repayment plans with the five-star hotel and ultimately find her own place, so any casual waitressing or shop work would do for now. There was one grubby sign in a kebab shop window, but it was half minimum wage, cash in hand, pot-washing in a tiny airless kitchen and the man behind the counter actually ran his tongue over his lips and teeth as he was talking to her, like the wolf eyeing up Red Riding Hood. She made a hasty retreat, without a kebab. It had started to rain, and Nell ran to the nearest bus shelter to stay dry. A bus pulled into the stop and Nell looked up at its destination; it would literally go past Greg's door. Her change from the teacake and coffee jangled in her pocket, and she decided to hop on.

'What do you mean you don't take money?' Nell asked the driver when he shook his head at her outstretched palm of coins. 'When did that happen?'

'Over ten years ago.'

'Oh. So quite a long time ago then. So how can I pay?'

'Contactless bank card or Oyster only.'

'But I don't have either,' Nell said miserably. 'Okay, no problem, I'll walk.' She was about to turn to step off the bus when a bank card was thrust in front of her, landing on the payment machine.

'I'll pay for it,' came a female voice alongside Nell.

Nell looked round at her benefactor – an older woman, in her eighties, wearing a peacock-blue silk coat, her long white hair falling a few inches below her shoulders, held back from her face by a diamanté tiara, her lips the brightest pinky red.

216

Nell beamed with appreciation, both at the woman's generosity and her dazzling appearance.

'You don't have to do that,' Nell said.

'Too late, it's done,' the woman smiled, grabbing hold of the pole to steady herself back to her seat as the bus lurched forward into the traffic. Nell followed her and sat down alongside her. There were other seats, even pairs of seats that were empty, but Nell didn't even consider those.

'That was very kind of you, here's the money,' Nell said, holding out the coins.

The woman shook her head and waved it away.

'My name's Nell.'

'Are you an Eleanor?'

'On paper, but not in spirit.'

The woman smiled at this, 'I'm Juno. Pleased to meet you.'

'Juno? That's the goddess of love, isn't it?'

'And marriage. Which might explain why I've had six of them.'

'Golly. That's a lot of gravy boats. Which one was your favourite? Husband, not gravy boat.'

Juno cocked her head on the side to consider the question. 'One and six. First loves are always special, aren't they?'

Nell smiled as Greg floated into her mind. Lovely, kind and gentle Greg.

'Doesn't mean that you should marry them though,' Juno said, breaking the spell.

'Are you still with six now?'

'No, he died.' Juno looked wistful for a moment. 'You say goodbye a lot when you get older. More goodbyes than hellos. That's why I like meeting new people. To balance it out a bit.'

Nell stuck out her hand for the older woman to shake. 'Hello Juno.'

'Hello Nell.'

217

'I'm glad I got on this bus.'

'Me too.'

'I like your hair.'

'Thank you,' Juno smiled. 'I grew it myself.'

'And your tiara is very pretty. Have you been anywhere nice today?'

'The library.'

'Well if that isn't cause for celebration, I don't know what is.'

'Exactly. I got two books of poetry, I'm particularly excited about the new collection of short stories by this fabulous Japanese writer I've recently come across and a book about Judaism because I really don't know enough about it.'

'I think I love you, Juno. Marry me, I'll be your seventh.'

Juno laughed, a beautiful throaty laugh that made her blue eyes sparkle, 'I had a lovely girlfriend once, when I lived in Morocco, in the mid-Seventies. She was glorious, long black hair that shone like a still river. We were together for nearly a year, but she had to get married and I was absolutely heartbroken. I married number two not long after that.'

'Do we like number two?'

'Not especially. He liked the horses a bit too much.'

'Number three?'

'Liked the scotch a bit too much.'

'Ah,' said Nell knowingly. 'I have a good feeling about number four though?'

'Number four was lovely. For a while. Got me away from three.'

'Good chap.'

'Five's a lovely Lithuanian man, still pops round to help me out with bits and bobs, but that marriage only happened because he needed a passport. He's got a lovely wife now, who he met here, which he wouldn't have done if he hadn't been allowed to stay, so that was definitely the right thing to do.'

'And six?'

'Six was the best.' Juno tapped Nell's hand lightly and turned her head to the window so Nell couldn't see her eyes turn misty. 'Worth the wait, and the heartbreak along the way.'

'I think you're the most interesting person I've ever met, Juno. Everyone should say hello to you.'

'I'm old and invisible to some and an eccentric to others, it takes a special person to see me.'

'I see you. And meeting you has made my day.'

'What sort of day has it been?'

Nell considered the question as it wasn't phrased like a typical enquiry. *What sort of day have you had?* A life is just that, a string of days tied together. That's why she'd been finding it so hard to think about the homework Greg had set of mapping out a five- and ten-year plan. How on earth was she going to set out a plan for 3,650 days, in the next week? It was impossible. Take today, she'd met two interesting women she didn't know when she woke up this morning, spent a lovely couple of hours on a boat, got lungs full of fresh London air, and now had the prospect of a warm shower and a ready-made, beautifully packaged, lentil bake to look forward to. No one knew what was waiting with each sunrise, so how could you possibly plan for it?

'It's been a really illuminating day,' Nell said honestly. 'I've had a bit of a strange time recently, and today everything just seemed to make sense. I was where I needed to be at each moment.'

'Well, that's lovely.'

'Apart from the kebab shop. I could have done without that little interlude in my day.'

'I've found that there's a time and a place for kebabs, and mid-afternoon on a bank holiday probably isn't it.'

'You are a wise, wise woman Juno,' Nell laughed. 'Oh, we're coming close to my stop, have you got much further to go?'

Juno's face suddenly twisted from the easy, open smile she just had to a flash of panic, her eyes swiftly darting left and right, left and right as she searched for the answer. 'I don't know,' she said breathlessly in a whisper. 'I've forgotten where I was going.'

'That's okay, calm down lovely, we'll chat a bit more and you'll remember.'

'You'll miss your stop.'

'Oh, don't worry about me, I was being lazy getting the bus anyway, I can walk back from anywhere.'

Juno was biting her lip now and pulling on her ear. 'I can't remember where I live,' she said again, starting to rock a little.

'Do you have a phone on you, Juno? Maybe we could call someone you know to help you?'

'I put it down at the library, on the desk, to get my library card out. Oh no, I forgot it.'

'That's fine, don't worry. Oh no, don't cry lovely, we'll sort this out. Right, why don't you get off the bus with me now, and come back to mine, we'll warm you up and have a nice cup of tea and when you remember where you live, I'll take you back there?'

'Do you have peppermint? I like peppermint.'

Nell vaguely remembered some green teabag boxes in Greg's cupboard and hoped for the best as she nodded. 'Come on Juno love, let me carry your books.'

Juno seemed to have shrunk by about a foot, and aged by about a decade in the last few minutes. She held onto Nell's arm as they walked the few metres from the bus stop to Greg's front door. Nell hadn't thought through her plan for helping

Juno beyond making her a tea and sitting her by a radiator. But what if she couldn't remember where she lived, what then? She couldn't let her stay, that would be kidnapping. And while Greg seemed like he was still a charitable sort of guy – he had a *Big Issue* in his recycling – this might not extend to octogenarian lodgers wearing tiaras and reading Japanese poetry in his living room.

'I expected your house to be more colourful,' Juno said, looking around the lounge. 'I hope you don't mind me saying so, but it's a bit, well, bland.'

'I don't mind at all, in fact, I absolutely agree with you. But this is my friend's house, I'm just staying here for a bit while I work out what to do next.'

'Oh good, because I thought for a minute that I'd misread you, I'm pleased I haven't.'

'What's your house like, Juno?' Nell asked, keeping the theme of the conversation going while dropping breadcrumbs to lead her home.

'Oh, it's lovely, I live with my son and my daughter-in-law, so it's their house, and it's a bit like this, all white and minimalistic, I think they call it, I call it boring and lifeless. But my part of it is lovely, it's like the walls have been dusted with a peacock feather, all purples and blues, and orange.'

'Orange? On a peacock?'

'A very unique peacock,' Juno laughed. 'Like me.'

Nell smiled, tentatively pressing on, 'Is it on a busy road? Like this one, or somewhere a bit quieter?'

'It's got a smashing view overlooking the park.'

'That does sound nice, parks are lovely. Which park is that one then?'

Juno's face clouded over again.

'Regent's Park maybe? Or Hampstead Heath?' Nell named the two closest ones that were on the bus route. Juno was looking down at her cup on the coffee table. 'Well, we don't need to work that out now, do we? Tell me about your son, what's his name?'

'William, and his wife is Willa.'

'William and Willa? You're making this up,' Nell teased.

'I'm not! Those are their names, honestly.'

'What do they do? Apart from Waft around Wandsworth in Wonder?'

'They're both actors. William's on television. He's on a medical show in a hospital and she's doing something in a theatre at the moment, on Drury Lane.'

Nell reached over for Greg's laptop which was on the arm of the sofa, and typed this information into Google. It came up immediately with William and Willa's life stories, but obviously not their address. Willa was appearing in a play in the Theatre Royal. 'Okay, I'm just going to call Willa's theatre and see if I can get hold of her, and we'll get you home. Are you alright there Juno, do you need anything else?'

'I might just close my eyes for a moment if that's alright with you?'

'Of course! I've been a right old chatterbox wearing you out, haven't I? You just stay there lovely, back in a minute. There's a blanket on the back of the sofa, put that over you.'

Nell took her phone into the kitchen and dialled the theatre, which went through to the box office. Nell quickly explained that she didn't want theatre tickets, but to speak to Willa urgently about her mother-in-law. The sales clerk clearly had no idea what to do with this request and the line went silent for a couple of seconds while they leafed through their training manual looking for this scenario. Nell's brain whirred. If this didn't work, she could try calling the production company who made William's medical drama, and try to get him that

222

way. The sales clerk came back on and gave her a number of the stage manager who might be able to help. Nell had just pressed end on the call when her phone rang again with a number she didn't recognise.

'Hello?'

'Nell, hi, it's Tom.'

Nell's stomach lurched. 'Tom?'

'Yes, Tom Radley, bed-buyer, great-lover, sometimes funny-man.'

'I know who you are, you just took me by surprise.'

'Sorry, is this a bad time?'

'I'm trying to track down a West End actress to return her mother-in law to her, who is currently asleep on my sofa while wearing a tiara.'

'Fuck me, Nell, you have the best life.'

'Don't I just?'

'But well done on getting a sofa, things are obviously looking up for you.'

'Oh no, sorry, let me clarify, I still only own the clothes on my back, I'm staying with a friend.'

'The ex?'

'Yes but he's not here. He's in Bristol.'

'I love Bristol, it's got a great arts scene.'

'Yes. But look Tom, as nice as this is, I have a lovely pensioner called Juno to return to her rightful place.'

'Would you like some help?'

'I wouldn't say no.'

'Where are you? I'll get an Uber.'

Nell gave him Greg's address, and asked him to look up who produced William's hospital show on his way over and try to track down a number for him. Nell stuck her head around the living room door to check on Juno, who was dozing happily on the sofa, her purple ballet shoes kicked off on the floor next to her. Nell smiled and carefully closed the lounge door behind her.

The stage manager wasn't answering. She called Tom back, 'Do you mind diverting to the Theatre Royal Drury Lane and seeing if Willa is there? You'll need to go round to the stage door and just say—'

'I know what to say, don't worry, I've got this. Missing mother-in-law, tiara, sleeping, safe.'

'In a nutshell.'

'Tom?'

'Yes?'

'How did you get my number?'

'My neighbour on the canal told me about an inspiring woman she met today with wild hair and green eyes called Nell and I knew it was you. And you left your number with her. You don't mind, do you?'

'No, I don't mind. Not at all.'

'I'll call you when I've found Willa.'

'Brilliant, and thank you, Tom.'

'My pleasure.'

See, this, thought Nell as she hung up. *This is why you can't make ten-year plans. Because the universe clearly doesn't work like that.*

CHAPTER TWENTY-TWO

'Who's that in the background? Hang on, is that the comedian from my work's Christmas party?'

'Yes, that's Tom.'

'Who are the others?'

'Willa's the one dressed like a Medieval peasant villager, she's in a play, and Juno's the one wearing a tiara. Say hello to Greg everyone.' Nell swung the phone behind her and everyone gave an enthusiastic wave at the screen.

'And, er, why exactly are they in my house?'

'It's a really long story, I'll fill you in on it later, but no need to worry, everything's under control, have a lovely evening, speak tomorrow. Bye, bye. Okay,' Nell said to the trio assembled in Greg's lounge once she'd hung the call up. 'Anyone for a cup of tea?'

Willa looked at her watch, 'I've got to get back and get my make-up done, I'm so sorry about this Nell, she knows she's not allowed to go out without us.'

'Oh no harm done at all, honestly, I've really enjoyed my afternoon.'

'But I had to go today, Willa, the library had ordered me Murakami's book specially, and I needed to pick it up.'

'It could have waited until the weekend,' Willa said, a tinge of impatience in her voice. 'We could have taken you then.'

'But I wanted to read it as soon as I could,' said Juno sadly, her demeanour taking on that of a chastised child.

'Right, we've taken up enough of your time, Nell, thank you again, really, you've been very kind. Juno, you'll have to come to the theatre with me, and William will pick you up from there once he's finished at the set.'

'I'm happy for her to stay here if you like until he's finished,' Nell said. 'I'm not going out again and I can make her something to eat. Save her going out in the cold again.'

Willa deliberated for a moment and Nell could sense that she was weighing her up, sensing that there was something inherently trustworthy about her. Juno clearly seemed to like her, but then again, she was a complete stranger and you couldn't be too careful with vulnerable people like Juno.

'I'd prefer to stay here,' Juno said, taking her ballet pumps back off again. 'The theatre's far too noisy and the toilets backstage are really not very nice.'

Willa checked her watch and clicked her tongue. 'Okay, Nell, if you're sure? He shouldn't be here too much after seven, he's filming in Elstree today, but finishes at six, are you sure that's alright?'

'Honestly, we'll have a lovely time. Tell him not to rush, we're absolutely fine.'

Willa turned to Juno, 'Juno, you're so lucky you met Nell today, things could have turned out really badly if you hadn't.'

'But they didn't,' Juno smiled.

You couldn't beat her logic.

Once Willa had gone, Juno turned her charm onto Tom, flicking her long white hair about, regaling him with stories too fantastical to be true, but conveyed too earnestly not to be. 'I think she's lining you up to be husband number seven,' Nell whispered to him half an hour later in the kitchen as she was fixing Juno a snack.

'I think she's marvellous,' Tom smiled. 'But then she is basically you in fifty years.'

'I would be absolutely delighted if I turned out like that.'

'It's almost a given.'

'Thank you so much for helping out today, I hope I didn't pull you away from anything important?'

Tom shook his head. 'I'd just dropped Arlo back to his mum's and so it was perfect timing. I needed a distraction from my misery.'

'Is he your son? How old is he?'

'Four.'

'It must be hard being away from him.'

'The worst feeling ever. But hopefully she'll agree to joint custody and then I'll see him much more. To go from being there with him every day to just once or twice a week for a few hours or one night is unbearable. But now I'm more settled, with my own place, it's much easier for him to visit.'

'I can't believe you and Andrea are neighbours, what a coincidence.'

'It is, if you believe in coincidences.' His eyes twinkled.

'What do you mean?'

'Nothing, nothing, just that I mention that I live on a narrow boat, and a few days later, you happen to be walking through London's biggest collection of house boats.'

Nell shrugged. 'I was out for a walk and ended up by the canal. Simple coincidence.'

'Isn't it?'

'Anyway, it was very lucky I was because otherwise I wouldn't have been on the bus that Juno was. So, all's well that ends well.'

'Indeed. Now can you show me how to use your ex's very complicated and expensive-looking coffee machine, because the schadenfreude in that would make me very happy.'

'You're a terrible person,' Nell laughed.

'I know.'

William messaged to say that he was leaving the studio and would be there soon, which cast a blanket of doom over the three of them, because they'd all forgotten their time together was only temporary. Nell answered the door to him a short while later with a yellow Post-it note on her forehead which read 'Mohammed Ali' and showed him into the living room. His mother had a similar yellow note on her forehead. 'So I'm a lady, who likes animals and chocolates, but not very fond of clothes – Lady Godiva!' Juno shouted joyfully, clapping her hands together. 'William! Come and join us, this game is super fun.'

William stood in the doorway, surveying the scene wearily, 'Come on Mum, you've taken up enough of these nice people's time.'

'Honestly, it was no trouble at all,' Nell said, helping Juno to her feet. 'We've had a lovely time with Juno, she's a wonderful woman.'

William gave Nell a tired smile. 'She is.'

'I'd love to see you again, Nell, if you're ever free?' Juno said hopefully.

At the same time Nell replied, 'Of course,' Juno's son said, 'Leave her be, Mum.'

'Let me write down my number for you Juno, call me any time, I'd love to see you again soon.' Nell got up to get a piece of paper and a pen.

'Honestly, you don't have to give her your number, she'll be calling you all the time, when you're at work—'

'It's been an absolute pleasure hanging out with Juno this afternoon, and I'm between jobs at the moment, so she wouldn't be interrupting anything.'

'Only if you're sure?'

'A hundred percent.' Nell flashed him a smile and then enveloped Juno in a big hug. 'Now you look after yourself okay, and make sure you polish your tiara ready for tomorrow's adventures.'

'No adventures tomorrow,' William said. 'Willa's at the theatre all day and I've got a couple of heavy days filming that I can't get out of.'

'Who's staying with Juno?' Nell asked.

'She'll be fine at home, as long as she doesn't leave it.'

'She can't stay locked up in a house for a couple of days by herself.'

'It's a very big house,' said William.

'It might be Buckingham Palace, but she's a beautiful peacock. She can't stay inside or she'll get really sad and all her feathers will fall out.' Nell realised as she said it that she might have taken the analogy a little too far. 'I'll come round and keep her company.'

'You've done enough already.'

'Honestly, it's no trouble. I'll bring my freind's laptop round to job-search from yours, and we'll hang out together. Would you like that, Juno?'

'I'd absolutely love it. We could do some Reiki together.'

'Now that sounds like a plan. William, text me your address and I'll be round at about eleven.'

William hesitated for a moment, and Nell suddenly realised why. 'Look,' she said, 'I know you and Willa are famous, Juno told me, I'm sure you're very good at what you do, but I don't

229

own a TV, have never seen you before in my life and have zero stalker genes in me. I really like your mum, she seems to like me, I'm at a loose end tomorrow and I promise not to go through your rubbish and sell stories to the tabloids.'

Her brazen honesty seemed to take William aback, which Nell thought was odd being the offspring of Juno. There were a couple of moments when he considered what she said, before he nodded gratefully and took his tired mother home.

'You're really lovely.'

Nell narrowed her eyes at Tom.

'You are. The vast majority of people would have seen Juno on that bus and given her a wide berth and you went towards her, not away from her.'

Nell shrugged. 'I like interesting people.'

'Have dinner with me. Tonight. I can't promise to be as interesting as Juno, but I'll give it my best.'

'Tonight?'

'Why not?'

'I have a lentil bake in the fridge.'

'As appetising as that sounds, I'm not ready to say goodbye to you yet and I'm starting to feel odd about being in your ex's house.'

'You drank his coffee without complaining.'

'I did drink his coffee, it was excellent coffee, but now I'd really like to get to know his ex-girlfriend a little better and I feel very odd about that happening in the poor guy's house.'

Nell smiled. 'Well in that case, I'd love to go out with you.'

They must have walked past about ten, twenty, even thirty, restaurants and bistros in Greg's neighbourhood, some white and glass boxes, others appertaining to be cosy trattorias with prices for their pasta that would make an Italian weep into their Salad Caprese (£22). Neither Nell nor Tom even paused to look at the menus.

Soon after leaving the house, Nell had punched out two quick text messages, the first to Jenny:

Hi Mum, Happy New Year! All good here, met two lovely women today and now heading out for dinner with a friend. Speak soon, love you, Nxx.

The second to her sister:

Hey Polly, hope the new year is a happy one for you. Please call me whenever you'd like to talk, I'm always here. LY, Nxx.

'All okay?' Tom asked after Nell had finished typing the last message and put her phone back in her pocket.

Nell nodded. 'Yep. Or it will be, I hope. Yours wasn't the only deathbed letter I wrote.'

'Ah.'

'Yes.'

'Bad?'

'The clean-up operation is taking longer than hoped.'

'Do you need outside agencies to offer assistance?'

'Not yet. But thanks for the offer.'

'Not me, I feel I've done enough. But I have a mate called Bob who's very good.'

Nell smiled. 'I'll bear Bob in mind.'

'That's all he ever asks for.'

They strolled in silence for a minute or so, weaving through the lamp-lit London streets. The shopfronts were becoming less polished as they walked towards an area of the capital they both felt more comfortable in.

'Can I ask you something?' Tom asked after they'd just navigated a rather complex six-junction set of traffic lights. Nell nodded, so Tom carried on talking, 'You seemed remarkably sanguine about dying the first time we met. You

231

don't need to answer that, I'm just curious. If someone told me now that my time was nearly up, I'd fall apart I reckon.'

'I had nineteen years to prepare for it. How old are you now?'

'Thirty-five.'

'Okay, so that's like me telling you that you're going to pop off the planet when you're fifty-four. You'd think, "oh, that seems a bit young, but that's ages away and that's still loads of time to do all the things I want to do." It's not the same as finding out you're ill and only have months left. That must be heart-breaking. So, for me, it just sort of created a nineteen-year calendar to start filling up. By the time it came around, it was almost as though it was just another event in the diary. I know that sounds odd, but I'd made my peace with it.'

'Did you ever doubt it?' Tom asked. 'The prediction? Were there moments where you wondered if you were wrong to believe it and let it dictate everything?'

She could tell him about the nights of deep loneliness in hostels, surrounded by couples making plans, families she'd met along the way, so confident in their immortality they would have three, four, sometimes six children, not even considering if the unthinkable happened. She could have told him about her own niece, Beatrice, who she'd deliberately stayed away from so the fragile little girl would never have to face the sharp, confusing stab of grief at the age of six when her aunty died. Or the gradual severing of ties with her mum, her sister, her childhood friends, the slow and measured edging away from anyone that might be affected by her not being around. It was much harder to miss someone you never saw. For them and her.

She'd be lying if she told Tom that all these deeply deliberate decisions to cut herself off from any kind of love hadn't poked her in the ribs when she was least expecting it over the years.

An inner voice, quiet at first, then gaining strength and power, inviting her to consider if she was, after all this, wrong. If Mandy had been wrong. If the life she'd chosen to lead was the wrong one. The voice wasn't there all the time, she wouldn't have been able to bear it if it was, but it came for her at her lowest and highest moments. Would she ever have found herself in the plaza in Chimbote eating the best anchovies of her life caught a hundred metres off the Peruvian coast if she'd never visited Mandy? Or fallen deeply, but very temporarily, in love with a beautiful Uruguayan man and lived with him in his crumbling studio in Montevideo overlooking the ancient citadel gate for a couple of months? No. But then again, if Mandy had never been part of Nell's story, Nell would probably still be top of her sister's Recent Call list on her phone, and there would be more up-to-date photos of herself in her mum's downstairs loo and she might have a place at her dad and Katie's table for Sunday lunch every other week. Her dad might not have even had his affair in the first place if she was still around able to spot the signs of boredom or restlessness earlier than her mum did. She definitely knew that her mum would never have settled for Ray. Jenny admitted on the beach that he appeared at a time when she was incredibly lonely after her dad left and her nana died. If Nell had been there, to fill that gap in her life, to make her feel loved and valued, then there would have been no void for him to slip into. And Damian definitely might not have tried it on with her if she hadn't been the wild and unpredictable one, back home for a night or two before disappearing again. And if he had, then Nell would have been much more inclined to tell her sister there and then if she knew that she'd have been around to pick up the pieces. The whole family could be different, could be happier, had she never left.

There was no denying though, that Mandy's prediction had

233

opened as many doors as it had shut, and for the most part, Nell chose not to query it, or it hurt too damn much. But there was no doubt in Nell's mind that those ten minutes in an Australian woman's garage had changed absolutely everything.

'I think it's human nature to question whether we're making the right decisions, but for me, I knew that I could only take my last breath if I knew that I'd had a full and varied life, and for me, that meant travelling to really obscure places, having conversations with as many different types of people as possible, eating every type of edible thing on the planet, dancing to every type of music, reading every type of writing, and being open to every new adventure. To others a full life might mean something entirely different. If there's one thing I've learned over the last twenty-odd years it's everyone is the same and everyone is different. Does that make sense?'

'More than you know.'

'I don't set out to change other people's lives though,' Nell said. 'It worries me that you've made all these decisions off the back of meeting me.'

'Believe me, they were a long time coming. You didn't brainwash me into doing anything, you just gave me the kick up the backside I needed to make the changes. My day job sucked the life out of me, sharing a house with weed-smoking housemates who never bought their own milk was doing my head in, not seeing Arlo enough, sleeping in a third-hand bed where my feet stuck out the end—'

Nell coughed, 'I'd like to remind you of your audience.'

'To be honest my bed was the only thing keeping me sane—'

'That's better.'

'But seriously Nell, you may not set out to be, but you are an inspiration.'

'No, I'm not. I've been inherently selfish with the way that

I've lived my life up to this point, I realise that now. And if I'm being completely honest—'

'Circle of truth,' Tom said.

'I don't quite know how not to be. This whole being mindful of others' feelings, opting in, not opting out, sticking around, not moving on, it's all completely alien to me. And I don't know if I like it yet.'

'I understand that. You've lived your whole adult life pinging the bell and shouting "next!" when life's got a bit boring, or hard, and you've just packed a bag and moved on to the next thing, but there are adventures everywhere if you look for them, you don't need to be in the Amazon rainforest to have a good time. You could be here, at the. . .' Tom looked up at the sign swinging above the door of the pub they were standing outside. 'The Rat and Parrot.'

'I do like parrots. Not so much rats.'

'Well one is better than none. Shall we?'

They had two pints each and a steak and ale pie and chips and it was delicious. Nell ran her finger round the outside of her plate to catch the final bits of gravy. 'Can I be nosy?'

Tom shrugged. 'Sure.'

'Why did you and your wife split up?'

'It's too clichéd to be funny.'

'Not everything needs to be funny.'

'I'm a comedian. Everything needs to be funny.'

'Give me the non-humorous highlights.'

'In love. Then we weren't. Arlo happened in the second stage, to try to get us back to the first stage. Didn't work. She then found the first stage with someone else.'

'Ouch.'

'Yep. He's a nice guy, has a hair transplant though. Got it done in Turkey.'

'Each to their own.'

'Odd choice though, isn't it? What does that say about society's expectations of beauty that you feel the need to go to Turkey, have a piece of the back of your head removed and sewn onto your forehead?'

'I got a great hummus recipe in Turkey,' Nell said.

'Which is exactly what you should leave with, not a skin graft.'

'The key is never to use tinned chickpeas. You've got to cook dried chickpeas.'

'Is there anything you don't know?'

'I don't know why I ever thought the Amazon was better than the Rat and Parrot.'

'See?' Tom said with a smile. 'Adventures on your doorstep are sometimes the best kind.'

They were nearer Tom's barge than Greg's house, so when the subject of coffee was raised, it was purely a matter of geography that made them turn right out of the pub rather than left. Tom's last words leaving Greg's house about not wanting to get to know his ex in his own house were still dimly resonating in both their minds though, so it was likely to be a mixture of both reasons that led them to the river.

His boat wasn't as far down as Andrea's, and as it was a rental, it didn't have the welcoming accoutrements of its neighbours: no potted plants, or bounteous mini greenhouses containing salad ingredients on its roof. But as they stepped inside and he turned on a few lamps and lit the log burner, the boat looked every bit as warm and homely as Nell had hoped it would.

'I have gin or tea?'

'Gin please.'

'Are you warm enough? There's a blanket under that seat if you want to get it out?' Boats and beach huts really had

236

this multi-functional furniture vibe sorted, Nell thought as she lifted up the seat cushion before settling back down on the banquette with the blanket over her lap. Tom joined her with two gin and tonics, tucking his own legs underneath the blanket too.

Nell gazed around the boat, taking in the little windows with linen curtains, the small galley kitchen with colourful mugs on hooks, the flickering flames of the log burner. 'I've been worrying that I made you change your life, and now I'm here, I'm pleased I did. This is really lovely.'

'I honestly love it. I've been coming up here for years, just to walk along the river, clear my head, and I saw the To Let sign on this boat literally two or three days after I met you, and I didn't even think twice. I put the deposit down there and then.'

'I'd have done the same, it's so relaxing.' Nell leaned her head back on the cushion, 'Do you want a lodger?'

'There's only one bedroom.'

'That's fine by me.' It was meant to be a joke, but she realised as soon as she said it that it neither sounded like that, nor was it received as such. But as Tom leaned his head towards hers, she was quite pleased about that. Not everything needed to be funny.

CHAPTER TWENTY-THREE

She'd slept with two men in just under a fortnight. It wasn't a first, but it made Nell feel uneasy. She'd more or less decided that Greg was her future, and yet with Tom everything just seemed so effortless and natural.

'The freckles on your left boob look like Orion's belt.' Tom traced his finger along the skin on her breast as though there was a dot-to-dot inked on it.

'How have I lived for thirty-eight years not knowing this?'

'Beats me.'

'What other constellations have I got on me?' Nell threw back the cover to reveal her naked body.

'Let me see,' Tom blew out his cheeks, to really emphasise how seriously he was taking this task, 'Well it's not a constellation, but this birthmark looks like an otter. Now this, this I haven't noticed before,' he said, 'and it will require a closer look; make yourself comfortable, I may be here a while.' No sooner had he pulled the cover up over his head than there came a sharp knocking on the boat's hatch followed by a woman's voice calling him.

'Oh shit!' he said, jumping out from under the duvet and grabbing his jeans. 'It's my wife.'

'Ex. Ex-wife,' Nell called out after him as he ran the length of the barge, pulling his clothes on as he went.

Nell leaned her head back on the pillow and looked up at the curved ceiling. Life was an odd, odd thing.

As the minutes clicked on, she didn't know whether she should get dressed, or just stay there; as mood-killers go, exes turning up unannounced was second only to dysentery. She reached for her clothes and put them on, just as Tom came back into the cabin.

'Everything okay?'

'Arlo forgot his monkey,' he said, lifting up first one corner, then another, of the mattress to retrieve where it had got trapped. 'Back in a second.'

'I can go if it's easier?'

'No honestly, let me just give this back to Leah and I'll be right back.'

Leah. The ex had a name. Of course she had a name, it would be very odd if she didn't.

Nell tiptoed into the main cabin. The door to outside was ajar, and she could see Tom was standing on the bow of the boat. Leah must still be on the canal path. Nell didn't intend on eavesdropping. People's business was their business, not hers. But if anything was a great indicator of what type of human a person was, hearing them converse with an ex-lover was gold.

'Here you go,' Nell heard him say. 'Sorry I didn't notice he didn't have it.'

'You know he can't sleep without it.'

'Maybe we should get him another one, so he keeps one at each of our houses.'

'This isn't a house Tom, it's a boat.'

'It's a house-boat.'

'It's a piece of rusty junk in a really rough part of London.'

'It's a beautiful piece of engineering in a down-to-earth community.'

'I feel really uncomfortable about Arlo staying here. What if he sleepwalked and fell in the canal?'

'When has he ever sleepwalked?'

'That's not the point, he could wake up in the night, feel disorientated and fall in the water.'

Nell anticipated his response along the lines of, 'What's stopping him becoming disorientated at yours and falling out of the second-floor window?' But instead, he said gently, 'I double lock the hatch door at night, and he sleeps in my bed with me, he's completely safe.'

'I'm just not sure that this is the right environment for a little boy to spend half his time in. The odd weekend is fine, but I can't see that you can really be serious about the joint custody thing.'

'Lee.' Nell winced at hearing Tom shorten his ex's name. 'It's late. You said that Arlo is upset about Monkey, why don't you take it back to him, and then we can continue this conversation during daylight hours.'

'Arlo's with my mum. He'll be asleep by now. There's no need for me to rush back. I could come in and we could have a glass of wine and chat about this now.'

'Won't Rob be wondering where you are?'

'He's staying with friends for a while.'

'Oh?'

'Yes, we're going through some things.'

'Okay.'

'So, shall I come in?'

'No, I really think it's better if we continue this conversation tomorrow.'

'I think I've made a really horrible mistake, Tom. I miss you. Arlo misses you.'

Nell flattened herself against the kitchen cupboards the other side of the wall. This was why eavesdropping was never a good idea. No one ever overheard something that made their life better. She debated whether she should just put her coat on and go out the rear door, or even push past them, cheerily thanking Tom for the use of his bathroom because hers was broken, or some equally plausible platonic reason for her to be on his boat at nearly midnight. The pause between Leah saying what she said and Tom responding was unnervingly long. Was he communicating to her in sign language? Frantically miming out, 'Sshh. Woman. Inside. But hold that thought.' Were they kissing? Oh God, this was so awkward.

Tom coughed. 'Look Leah, you have what you came here for.'

No, she hasn't, thought Nell.

'Come on Tom, for old times' sake, invite me aboard, Skipper.'

Nell desperately looked around for a cupboard big enough to squeeze into, but narrow boats weren't famous for their roominess.

'I didn't want you to find out like this,' Tom started, 'but I've met someone who I really like. Like, *really* like. And for the first time in a long while I feel like I could be happy again. I'm sorry for what you and Rob are going through, I think he's a nice guy actually, odd personal grooming choices, but a nice guy, so I hope you sort out whatever you've got to sort out. Did you drive here or do you have a cab waiting because it's late.'

'My car—' Leah said weakly.

'Okay great. Look, I'll give you a call tomorrow and we can have a proper chat about Arlo. Take care of yourself.'

Of all the conversations Nell expected to overhear, that was not it, from either side. Tom's quickfire banter and repartee had completely disappeared; he was mature, honest and kind. And unless he was talking about someone else, which would be deeply awkward, he was quite clearly very fond of Nell. So much so, tonight he chose her over reconciling with his wife and putting his family back together.

Nell grabbed her coat, ran through the bedroom, her heart plummeting as she rushed past the rumpled sheets to the back of the boat, opened the door to the stern and slipped out of it as quietly and quickly as she could into the dark night. She'd done it again. She'd bowled into a stranger's life, gaily knocking bits of it about, severing relationships beyond repair and making people question things they'd never doubted before. If she hadn't been there tonight, with Tom, he could have said yes to Leah, they could have rekindled their love and Arlo would once again have two parents living together. Having fun with Greg and seeing where it would go was completely different to doing the same with Tom. She was not going to be the reason a family split up. She was not going to be Katie, she just wasn't.

CHAPTER TWENTY-FOUR

'It's a shame you ran away. I liked your boyfriend.'

'He wasn't my boyfriend. And we won't be seeing him again.'

'You suited each other.'

'Not really.'

'He really likes you.'

'You've only eaten half your sandwich.'

'You like him too.'

'Juno, stop it.'

'I have a sixth sense for these things. I think you'd make each other really happy.'

'It's complicated.'

'Good things often are. If you had an uncomplicated life at your age I'd think something had seriously gone wrong.'

'I don't like complicated. Complicated makes me uneasy.'

'How complicated is complicated? My sixth husband, God rest his soul, had two ex-wives, four children, nine grand-children, and could never transit through the United Arab Emirates or he'd get arrested.'

'Okay, not *that* complicated.'

'Is that him now?' Juno pointed at Nell's phone which was

vibrating on the side table next to them. Nell picked it up, looked at the screen, sighed and put it back down, face down.

'So that's a yes then?'

'At what point in your life did you feel like you had all the answers?'

'I'm yet to feel that.'

'And how old are you?'

'Eighty-four.'

'Wonderful. So, you basically have to wing it until you die.'

Juno nodded. 'Basically.'

'Do you want to play backgammon?'

'I want to talk about your love life.'

'I'm too sober for this talk.'

'I know where William keeps the good stuff.'

'We are not getting drunk at lunchtime.'

'I thought you were fun.'

'I am fun. But I'm also slightly scared of your daughter-in-law.'

'Oh, Willa's alright. She didn't ask to have a madwoman in the attic living with her when she fell in love with William. If you want to talk about complicated, that's complicated. She's basically a stepmother to an octogenarian.'

'I'd love to be your stepmum. That sounded weird, was that weird?'

'Not especially.'

'Are you going to eat the other half of the sandwich? No? Can I have it?'

'I told you to make one for yourself too.'

'I know, but it's William and Willa's food.'

'They wouldn't mind.'

'I'm just fed up of eating other people's generosity. I need a job Juno, where can I find a job?'

'Have you thought about escort work?'

Nell started choking on her tea. 'Jesus Juno, I did not expect that to come out of your mouth. I'm not that desperate yet.'

'What's desperate about it? I watched a programme on Channel Four about it. You get a free meal and a thousand pounds all for keeping a lonely man company. Sounds like easy money to me.'

'But then you have to have sex with them.'

'Sex! No, it's just getting dressed up and going for dinner.'

'I feel you may have missed a vital part of that programme. Did you fall asleep during part of it?'

'I may have done. Oh, that's a shame, even I was considering doing it.'

Nell's phone buzzed again.

'Answer the damn thing and put the man out of his misery.'

Nell stuck her tongue out at her, picked the phone up, angrily jabbed the screen without looking and said, 'I'm really sorry but please stop calling me. I don't want to be the reason you ruin your life. You're better off without me. I think it's best if we go our separate ways.'

'Fine. I was calling to just have a chat, but screw you, Nell.'

'Polly! No, not you, I thought you were someone else.'

'Wow, you have been busy going around pissing everyone off.'

'Is everything okay?

'Yeah. Well sort of. I just wondered if you're free to have lunch with me next week? I can take a half day next Thursday or Friday and come up to London if you're free?'

'I'd love that!'

'Really? Okay then, great. Shall we say Thursday? A week today.'

'Fantastic.'

'Great.'

'Polly? I'm really glad you called me.'

'Mum said I had to.'

Nell smiled. 'Well, whatever. I'm pleased you did.'

'So, what's new with you? Who did you not want to ruin their lives?'

'It's complicated.'

'It's not complicated,' Juno said very loudly in the background. 'It's really rather simple.'

'Who's that?'

'Just some batty old woman,' Nell winked at Juno. 'Take no notice.'

'Was it Greg? Mum told me you're back together.'

'We're not back together. And it wasn't Greg.'

'Give me the phone,' Juno demanded, holding out her hand. 'Come on, pass it over. Hello? Hello? My name's Juno, I'm a friend of Nell's. You're her sister? Well can you talk some sense into her? She's got a lovely chap on the go, who's very handsome, funny, kind, and thinks that she's absolutely smashing and for some unfathomable reason she's not having any of it. She's not listening to me, so please try and make her see sense. Nice speaking with you.' Juno then held the phone back out to Nell.

'Sorry about that Polly, I'm doing a spot of community service today, and I've been paired up with this barmy old woman who talks complete nonsense. Oh dear, she's just peed herself, better go. Can't wait to see you next week, lots of love.'

Juno stuck out her bottom lip at Nell. 'Why did I have to be incontinent as well as barmy? That was mean.'

'Sshh, time for your nap, old lady.'

The landline on the coffee table next to Juno rang then, and she was still laughing when she answered it, 'Oh hello William, yes, I'm having a super time with Caroline—'

Nell's blood ran cold.

'She's teasing me something chronic though, but we're having a lovely day. . . You want to speak to her? Sure, hang on.' Juno passed the cordless receiver over to Nell. 'He wants to talk to you.'

Nell took the phone from her, eyeing Juno carefully, but the older woman was sitting smiling back at her. 'Hello?'

'She called you Caroline.'

'Yes.'

'Is that your other name?' William asked, hope in his voice.

'No,' Nell answered carefully. 'I don't know where that came from.'

William sighed audibly, sounding tired. 'Caroline was her sister who died, years ago now.'

'Oh no.' She'd seemed so lucid all morning, but talking about Nell's own sister must have confused her.

'I'll come back,' William said.

'No, honestly, it's no problem, I can stay here all day, I have nowhere else to be. Please, she's fine with me.'

He hesitated for a moment, then obviously heard his name being called and said, 'Are you absolutely sure, Nell? It seems a massive imposition.'

'I promise it's okay.'

'Thank you. Really. I'll come back as soon as I can.'

William and Willa's house was amazing. It was one of those old double-fronted Victorian houses on a wide, leafy avenue that looked quite normal and unassuming from the front and then all strip lighting and a white shiny kitchen with an island the same size as an average suburban kitchen in the back of it. Bi-fold doors ran the width of the back of the house, leading onto a paved garden dotted with tall trees in pots and a beautiful dining area under a pergola. It was tasteful, charming, and Nell was absolutely terrified to touch anything. She tried to limit her time in this part of the house to a three-second dash to get more supplies to take back up to Juno's wing on the second floor, which was much more to her taste and comfort levels. Obviously once the servants' quarters, the top floor was a warren of smaller rooms, with ceilings pitched at odd angles and narrow original fireplaces in each one. Juno had given her a grand tour, proudly pointing out the oversized embroidered poufs from Indonesia that peppered the floor space, their mirrored sequins projecting little dots of sunshine over the carpet, complemented by colourful wall hangings, some painted canvases, others more eclectic – a silk kimono on a wooden hanger on one wall, next to four mounted wicker serving platters from Malawi. Photos adorned every surface, some black and white, others faded coloured ones, Juno on a camel, in swimwear, kaftans, next to a small two-prop plane – hundreds of memories. If Nell had had a home to send things back to from her travels, these were the things she'd have bought, and this was the home she would have.

They spent the afternoon talking about bar and bat mitzvahs, the trick to keeping cut tulips upright in a vase (a penny in the bottom of the vase) and the time that Juno had sung in an all-girl trio hopping from oil rig to oil rig to entertain the offshore workers with cover hits of The Ronettes and The Supremes. The television stayed resolutely off in the corner, and despite Juno's continued reference to it, William's cocktail cabinet stayed firmly locked.

'Well, this looks like it's been a very successful day,' William said when he got home, his lanyard from the BBC studios still around his neck.

'She's a very easy person to spend time with,' Nell said as he showed her out.

William smiled gratefully at her. 'For the most part. But thank you. She's the happiest I've seen her in ages.'

Greg was back from his New Year's Eve house party in Bristol and was busy booking his holiday to the Maldives, determined to start his adventuring as soon as possible when Nell let herself into his house. She got two wine glasses out of the cupboard and the least expensive-looking bottle of wine from the wine rack and joined him at the dining table. She had to look away from his laptop screen as Greg made the booking because the figures involved could have funded Old Nell for a few months. She had a fleeting moment of regret that she wasn't going too as she watched him gleefully scroll through the hotel website's photos of beach cabanas with their white chiffon curtains billowing in the breeze, the water bungalow on stilts where he'd be staying with a glass floor in its veranda so you could see the fish below, and its own pontoon where you could dive off into the crystal-clear water for a quick swim before breakfast.

'It's not too late for you to come too,' he said, reading her wistful expression.

She smiled and shook her head. 'I've had my fill of paradise for a while, but thank you.'

'I still want us to go on our own adventure,' he said. 'I'll come up with some ideas when I'm away, you have a think too, and then when I come back we'll make a plan.'

Nell nodded. 'Right, you best go pack.'

It was odd being the one sitting on the bed watching the other person fill a suitcase, reminding them every so often what to put in it. 'Remember to pick up mosquito repellent and sun cream at the airport.'

'Yep.'

'And put all your toiletries in a freezer bag.'

'I have travelled before you know.'

'You had to blow the dust off your suitcase.'

'Well, maybe I took another bag,' he teased.

'Of course. A man about town like you wouldn't just have one suitcase.'

'Nope.'

'Which would also explain why this one still has its price sticker attached to it. From a store, which, if I'm not mistaken, went bust about five years ago.'

'An oversight,' Greg smiled. 'That label's been all over the world.'

Nell reached into his suitcase and stroked one of his folded shirts. 'I'm going to miss you.'

Greg paused folding a T-shirt. 'I'm going to miss you too. But we've got lots to think about; being apart will actually be quite good I reckon. We both still need to make our one-year, five-year and ten-year plans and we'll compare them when I get back.'

He might as well have been talking a foreign language: five-year, ten-year plans? She loved his positivity, but she couldn't envisage their plans for the future being similar at all.

Cultivate optimism.

'That sounds like a great idea,' she said cheerfully, trying not to dwell on the fact that she didn't even have a five- or ten-*hour* plan at that precise moment in time. Last night she absolutely thought that she could have a future with Tom, and today, she'd spent the day ignoring his calls and feeling guilty for getting in the way of his family life.

Greg must have mistaken her downcast expression as one of regret because he immediately sprung up from the bed, and said, 'Right, I'm not taking no for an answer, I'm booking you a ticket to come with me.' He put up his hand to stem her rebuttals. 'No, I've made up my mind.'

'I can't, Polly's coming up to London next Thursday to have lunch with me, and I can't cancel on her when she's just extended this olive branch.'

'Fine. Come for the first week. Five days. Come for five

days, we'll eat and drink and laugh and enjoy each other's company, you come back here and have lunch with Polly and make some plans, and then when I get back a week later we'll take it from there.'

'But Greg, that'll cost a fortune, I can't pay you back—'

'It's my treat. Late birthday present.' He got his phone out and started tapping away on the travel website. 'Oh, that's really lucky, there's only one business class seat left. Oh, but it's not near mine. I'm sure we can get people to move.'

Nell put her hand out over his phone to halt him booking anything and eyed him with a serious expression. 'Greg, if I agree to this I'm not going business class. Book me the cheapest seat you can. And I don't need luggage, I can wear layers. Actually, what am I saying? I don't even have layers.'

'But I can't be in business while you're in cattle?'

'Well, you'll be going alone then. I don't even want to go; I need to be here—'

'Fine. One economy ticket, luggage included, now I just need to message the hotel.'

'Greg please, think about this, we've only just met up again, it's too soon to be—'

'Too late, it's booked. Right, best get packing, the taxi's coming soon.'

'I don't have anything to pack. I don't own any summer clothes at all, or a swimsuit. Unless you've booked a naturist resort, I'm going to be woefully underdressed.'

'There'll be shops at the airport.'

Nell raised her eyes to the ceiling and let out a big sigh. She'd forgotten how gung-ho Greg could be given the tiniest bit of encouragement. Part of her was thrilled to be heading back to the sunshine after nearly two months in wintry England, but the other part, the much larger part, was filled with trepidation at what this might mean. Was she choosing

Greg? Now that Tom knew where she was living, there was every chance that he'd just turn up here, and she definitely didn't want to be here for that confrontation. She had no choice, she had to remove herself so he and Leah could make a fresh start without her complicating everything.

'How's the leg room?'

Nell stretched out her legs, trying to ignore the crushing sensation as her knees pushed against the seat in front, 'Absolutely great, look.'

'And your meal?'

'Splendid. Who knew that mashed potatoes could have that texture? Yours?'

'I had a tablecloth.'

'Fancy.'

'I don't mind swapping for a bit? You could watch your movie on a bigger screen?'

'Nope, grand here, thanks though.'

'Is that poo on the seat next to you?'

'No, chocolate mousse. There's a toddler in that seat who knocked it out of my hand when they sneezed and her dad took her to the toilet to clean her up.'

'Nell seriously, swap with me for a bit, I feel really bad I'm up there and you're here.'

Nell looked up at Greg who was standing in the aisle holding onto her head rest and the one in front. 'Greg, go back to your quiet fancy cabin and eat some more caviar. This is how I've always travelled, how I will continue to travel, and I am really happy here. Honestly. There are some things in life that I absolutely think are worth splashing out on – decent footwear and skilled tattooists being two of them – but thousands of pounds for a ten-hour flight is not one of them. I am very happy here, you are very happy there, don't think

252

of me again until we land, by which time please do think of me again because I have no idea the name of the resort and so I will need you by that point to find the right hotel bus. Now go. GO.'

She wondered as she watched him walking back up the plane to the business cabin whether she was just being difficult for difficulty's sake. She had once been upgraded for free, on the only occasion she had turned up to a check-in desk not wearing flip flops and an inflatable pillow around her neck, and she had to give it its due, it was a very lovely experience. She didn't see the need for the anti-ageing moisturiser in the amenity kit – it had been a twelve-hour flight, not a twelve-year one – but she still used the sleep mask now, and the little salt and pepper shakers were a lovely touch, even if the cabin crew had politely asked her to remove them from her bag and return them to the empty tray when they collected it. It was so tricky working out what was a freebie and what wasn't on these things. But she enjoyed all the perks and luxury knowing that it hadn't cost her a penny more than her economy ticket; she doubted she'd have relished the Moët quite so much if she calculated its eye-watering cost-per-sip. So no, she was quite happy where she was, thank you very much: covered in chocolate mousse and toddler snot, and contorted into the space of a rabbit hutch.

Nell absent-mindedly picked up the in-flight magazine and flicked through it: pages and pages of perfumes, overpriced smelly water, compact cosmetics and handbags. A feature called *24 Hours in. . .* held her interest for slightly longer, agreeing with their picks for Budapest, deeply disagreeing with their suggestions for Moscow, and feeling her chocolate mousse rise up to revisit her when she turned the page and saw Tom smugly smiling up at her from the page about London. *Round off your day of shopping and sight-seeing with a front row seat at Tom Radley's new comedy show 'Bucket List', a sure-fire hit and one definitely not to miss!* Nell slammed the magazine shut and crammed it back in the seat pocket with such ferocity the man in front turned round to glare at her over his headrest. Of all the men she had to have one last fling with, she chose him. Why didn't she pick the guy who delivered her last takeaway? Or the man who walked his four Irish wolfhounds past her house twice a day. Why a scruffy comedian with a wife, kid, bad taste in socks, who seemed to be sodding everywhere?

As they emerged from the airport seven hours later, Greg was doing his best Man from Del Monte impression, sauntering out into the sunshine in slip-on Tod's, white linen shirt and new Panama hat, fresh from an enjoyable rest and recuperation, pushing his suitcase on a trolley, while Nell was next to him, wild-haired, dirty, smelly and with a rucksack strapped to her back. It was sadly not her trusty one that had travelled the world with her, as she'd ceremoniously burned that in an emotional cleansing ceremony the day before checking in the hotel in order to check out; it was actually Greg's old one he'd found in the bottom of the spare room cupboard.

'I don't think it's a rucksack sort of resort,' he'd said as she squealed with glee upon finding it.

'And I'm not a suitcase sort of person,' she'd retorted. 'So, if you want me to come with you, then you have to accept how I travel.' She'd gone through the side pockets of the rucksack before filling it again with toiletries and a few of the T-shirts he was lending her. She planned to head straight to a local market and pick up a few sarongs. While cleaning the rucksack out she found the bar bill for Long Bar in the Raffles Hotel in Singapore, one of those few times that Nell had swallowed her aversion to splashing the cash and thrown herself into stepping back in time to 1920s Malaya. The price of their two Singapore Slings had outweighed the cost of their overnight hostel, but perching on a bar stool, brushing peanut shells off the counter onto the floor, sipping the sweet pink drink while soaking up the history of the place was totally worth it.

'Greg, look, do you remember this?' She'd shown him the twenty-year-old receipt.

'I remember having a wash in their toilets,' he laughed. 'And filling our pockets full of their peanuts for later.'

Nell had smiled. 'Happy days.'

'Hungry days.'

'But mostly happy.'

'I came back from that year about two stone lighter.'

'You can't measure memories on the scales,' Nell reminded him.

Greg patted his flat stomach, 'I plan on coming back from this holiday two stone heavier.'

Nell had another pang of apprehension then, what on earth had possessed her to go along with this plan? Did she and this Greg have anything in common at all? He quite clearly just wanted to set up camp next to the buffet table and she had a complete inability to sit still for more than twenty minutes.

'Do you reckon they'll still be serving lunch when we get there?' he said, looking at his watch as they sat down on the airport shuttle bus.

'Haven't you just eaten your body weight in business-class treats?'

'Calories consumed in the air don't count as calories.'

Nell looked out of her window as the bus weaved its way through the Malé streets to the port where the speed boat transfer to their resort was waiting. Houses and shops and people and life, all crammed onto one tiny island surrounded by ocean. Thousands of tourists landing here every day just to quickly jet back off by seaplane or boat, not making it anywhere near the town. Nell made a mental note to come back here one day during the week to support a few of the local shops and cafés.

'Hi,' came a voice from the seats behind them, followed by a hand through the gap between the seats. 'We're Jack and Sophia, are you guys on honeymoon too?'

Nell replied no at the same time Greg said yes, prompting Nell to swivel to face him, horrified.

He smiled and shrugged his shoulders. 'You get loads of free stuff,' he whispered back in explanation. 'We used to do it all the time, fake birthdays, anniversaries, at the very least you get a free glass of bubbly, but once I ticked the honeymoon box on the booking form, we got an immediate upgrade to a water villa and a couples massage!'

'Greg! I can't believe you'd do that!'

'Uh-oh, first married tiff?' Jack laughed.

Nell swivelled round to face the couple behind and smiled a wide, unnatural smile, 'First of many, Jack, first of many.'

'Seriously,' she hissed back at Greg. 'What possessed you to do that?'

'You did. I haven't done a single outrageous thing since we broke up, and that frisson of excitement I got when I realised all the freebies we could get, all for a little white lie, it was amazing!'

'We'll have to tell them it was a mistake when we check in.'

'We will not! We even get a fruit basket.'

'I can't believe you.' Nell crossed her arms and turned towards the window.

When they got to their room after three more cold hand flannels and a fruit kebab, there was a fruit basket, a cake with *Congratulations Mr & Mrs* iced on it, a big rose petal heart on the bed and a handwritten note from the manager personally congratulating them on their nuptials and inviting them to enjoy a complimentary dinner for two on the beach that night.

'Too much Greg, too much,' Nell seethed as she threw the note down on the bed and stormed out onto their swimming pool deck.

'They said a fruit basket and a massage, I didn't know about all of this stuff! I promise!'

Nell stiffened as Greg sidled up behind her and pressed his body into hers, wrapping his arms around her. She continued looking out to sea, wishing that their hotel room overlooked a car park or a four-lane motorway junction, which would make being in a bad mood so much easier.

'It was only a bit of fun, sorry, I thought you'd find it funny. We used to do things like this all the time. You even made me pretend to propose to you in that restaurant in Bali so we'd get free champagne.'

'I was so much younger then. I didn't realise that it was people's businesses we were cheating.' Nell closed her eyes. Running out of the London hotel without paying had been weighing on her mind constantly.

'This is a chain hotel,' Greg said, wrapping his arms around her from behind. 'It has an eight-billion-dollar revenue, their profit margin went up sixty-one percent last quarter, they're not going to miss a cake and a dinner.'

'And a fruit basket and a massage.'

'And a fruit basket and a massage. Now, let's have a swim.'

'I need to buy a swimsuit first.'

Greg kissed her shoulder. 'No you don't.'

CHAPTER TWENTY-FIVE

There were about ten other honeymooning couples already sitting at tables for two on the beach when Nell and Greg got there, their skin still soft and slightly crinkled from an afternoon exercising in their pool. He had always been very good at exercising, Nell recalled, but she'd put that down to her never having had any exercise partners before him. But now she had exercised with many, he was still one of the best. Second only to Tom who had exercise moves she'd never even heard of before, let alone done. Five times on two different occasions.

She felt a little lightheaded even thinking about that, so took a deep breath and kept her eyes focused on the horizon as they walked towards their table, waving joyfully at Jack and Sophia as they passed them.

'You okay?' Greg said, after pulling her chair out for her on the sand. Nell decided not to berate him for the gesture, it was sort of sweet. 'You look a little flushed.'

'No, fine, sunburned probably.' Nell looked around them. 'This is lovely.' The beach was dotted with flaming torches stuck in the sand, billowing white chiffon curtains around the pagoda where the food was being cooked on an open grill by two chefs in starched whites. A violinist stood to the side, beads of sweat slowly dripping into their collar as they traversed through the canon of romantic ballads for all the honeymooning couples.

'Do you think he does requests?' Greg asked Nell.

'Dare you to ask for Meatloaf's "Bat Out of Hell".'

Greg laughed, 'How about "Another One Bites the Dust"?'

'Tammy Wynette's "D.I.V.O.R.C.E".'

'U2's "Still Haven't Found What I'm Looking For".'

Nell almost spat out her cocktail. 'That's brilliant. Do it. Double dare you.'

'No double dares.'

Smiling, they both looked down at the menu. 'If you get the octopus I'll get the tiger prawns and we can share them?' Greg said, reverting back to their tried and tested method of ordering food in restaurants.

'Perfect, and how are you feeling about the sea bass and the fillet for main?' Nell added, running her finger down the listed dishes.

'I'd prefer the lamb rather than the fillet if that's okay?'

Nell scrunched up her nose. 'I don't really eat lamb.'

'Since when?'

'Since I worked on a farm in New Zealand.'

'But you'll eat a cow?'

'I couldn't eat a whole one.'

Greg didn't crack a smile. 'Same logic though, they're both animals.'

'Not really, one's big and loud and just sort of stands there for years and years. The other skips and hops and has big plans for their lives that they'll never get to realise.'

'Fine, we'll have the fillet.'

'You can have the lamb and I'll have the sea bass. We don't need to share.'

'But we always share.'

'But if you really want the lamb, have it.'

'No, it's fine.' Greg took his napkin off his plate and smoothed it over his lap once he realised no one was going to do that for him. 'I'll have it next week when you're not here, if you're still insisting on only staying for half of our honeymoon.'

'The other couples will think I've left you. Especially if you hook up with someone else in the second week.'

Greg's brow furrowed. 'Why would I hook up with anyone else when we're back together?'

'We're not back together, Greg. We're just enjoying each other's company again and getting to know each other.'

'I already know you.'

'Um, I don't think that's necessarily true. You *knew* me, absolutely, but I'm a very different person now to who I was then.'

'Not really.'

'What do you mean? I'm completely different!'

Greg shrugged his shoulders. 'Your hair's longer. You've got a couple more piercings than you had before. You don't eat lamb now.'

'Not how I look or what I eat, I'm talking about who I am. In here.' Nell prodded her chest and then pointed at her head. 'And here. And you've changed too.'

Greg adjusted his cutlery so the fork and knife were straighter next to his plate. 'Not really. I mean my circumstances have changed, but I don't think I've changed at all.'

Nell put her head to one side. 'Really?'

'Really.'

Nell decided to test his theory by saying excitedly, 'Let's order some shots, and after dinner swim naked in the sea.'

'I know what you're doing. You're trying to shine a light on

260

how fun and spontaneous you are and how middle-aged and boring I am.'

'No, I'm trying to remind you how to have fun.'

'I have fun. We had fun this afternoon.'

'We did. After you drew all the drapes around the swimming pool and checked the temperature of the water with your elbow.'

'Cold water does things anatomically to men that you wouldn't understand.'

'What do you want to do tomorrow?'

'Well now I feel like you're going to judge me if I say nothing except sunbathing and eating.'

'To be honest, I think you deserve a day of doing nothing. You work way too hard and so tomorrow can be your day. You call the shots all day. But then the day after is my day.'

'No bungee jumping.'

'Okay.'

'Or drugs.'

'Deal.'

'Nothing illegal. It is still a Muslim country.'

'In that case, we broke a few laws a couple of hours ago.'

'Doesn't count.'

'Okay then. Cheers.'

Greg tipped his glass of wine towards hers, 'Cheers.'

Nell was awake at least two hours before Greg, old habits of rising with the sun difficult to shake off. She slowly slid her body off the white sheets onto the floor and gently padded over to retrieve her dressing gown before heading out to the sun deck. The morning sun danced on her face as she upturned her chin towards the sky and closed her eyes, breathing in the salty air. She'd done this in countries all around the globe, sometimes leaving someone sleeping inside, often with an empty cabin behind her, but always with gratitude for waking up to a new day full of possibilities. This sense was sharper now that she was living and breathing through days that she never thought she'd see. The need to make each day count hadn't lessened with this second chance; if anything it had made it even more important. Could she feel this sense of purpose in England? With Greg? It would be so easy to just slot into his ready-made life. There was definitely space for her, unlike in Tom's filled-to-the-brim existence where she'd be jostling for room with a cute little human and a larger-than-life ex-wife. Greg was lonely, bored, wearied, and she could definitely change that. And he'd provide the stability and love that she hadn't felt for years. And on a practical note, half his cupboards were already empty, not that she had the means to fill them with her stuff, but he was generous to a fault and would make sure she always had everything she needed. But did he get her? Like really *get* her the way that Tom seemed to? Greg didn't seem to accept that nigh on twenty years was enough to completely change a person, and while she herself was often infuriated with the decisions she made and the situations she found herself in, for the most part she liked this version of herself so much more than twenty-year-old Nell who devoured guide books and read reviews before doing anything, unable to make a decision unless someone else said it was a good idea first. And that someone had usually been Greg.

The breakfast tray floated on the pool. Which Nell always thought looked absolutely lovely in Instagram pictures, but in reality, it meant that every time she took her hand out of the water to grab another croissant, she got a side order of chlorine with her food. She was about to say as much when she clocked Greg's look of closed-eyes ecstasy as he savoured his slightly soggy pain au chocolate and decided to stay schtum.

'So, when was the last time you went abroad?' Nell asked.

'I go away all the time with work. Last year I was in Hong Kong twice, Frankfurt, Moscow, Madrid.'

'Wow, and how many times did you eat outside of the hotel?'

Greg looked a little sheepish. 'That would be none, but I do stay in really nice places, so the food is always excellent. But I'm on the go twenty-four-seven when I'm away, so there'd be no time anyway. I literally fly in, have meetings back-to-back and fly back out.'

'Could you try to tack on an extra day or two, to have an explore around?'

'I don't know, probably, I've never thought about it. Here, have a guava.'

Nell took the fruit from his wet fingers, 'Yum.'

'This is the life, isn't it?' Greg leaned back against the pool's tiled wall. 'We should put it in the plans that we go on holiday at least three times a year.'

'With what money?'

'I have money, Nell. And what's mine is yours.'

'We're not married, Greg.'

'But we could be. We were planning to be once before. I drove past the hotel we were going to have it in the other day, they've had a conservatory put on the side, it looks really nice. Our mums would be thrilled.'

'They would,' Nell agreed, picturing the smiles as wide as the brim of their hats, the linked arms and shared laughs, the clichés tossed about like biodegradable confetti of 'good things come to those who wait', 'absence makes the heart grow fonder' and 'patience is a virtue', all uttered within the UPVC glazing of a brand-new conservatory of a hotel just off the A27. Nell shivered and it wasn't even cold.

After breakfast they settled down on a pair of adjacent

sun-loungers on the beach – Nell under the parasol, Greg just outside it in an attempt to get the bronzed body Nell had said was so sexy. Their fruit juices were constantly refilled and they even had their sunglasses cleaned, which Nell felt was slightly unnecessary, but when they were handed back to her she begrudgingly admitted that she felt like one might after cataract surgery.

All day the conversation about marriage was playing on a loop around Nell's brain: *he wasn't serious, he can't have been.* In the three weeks they'd been reunited she'd wreaked havoc on his carefully ordered life, he surely couldn't be keen for a lifetime of that. And she had serious concerns of whether they were actually right for each other. Take today, she thought, this was his day, where he called the shots, made all the decisions, and so far, he'd only strayed from the sunbeds three times, once to have a swim in the sea, and twice to use the bathroom, because he refused to wee in the ocean. She readily recognised that holiday Greg might well be far more lethargic and relaxed than everyday Greg, but she was really bored with his chosen pace of life. Even walking to the hotel restaurant was too much for lunch, so he ordered it to their loungers. He'd shaken his head at her suggestion of snorkelling – 'the sun will burn my back' – and said a firm 'no' to parasailing, water skiing or anything that demanded a risk assessment form, which left Nell sitting on the sand at the water's edge under a big floppy hat she'd just spent an eye-watering amount of Greg's money on in the hotel shop, sifting sand through her fingers, wondering, not for the first time this holiday, how different this experience would be if she was here with Tom.

The next morning Nell didn't wait for Greg's own body clock to rouse him; as soon as her own eyes were open she jumped astride him and twerked him awake. 'Wake up, wake up, we've got a fish market to get to!'

'That is not an appealing prospect right now,' Greg groaned and put a pillow over his face.

'Wake up Greggy!'

'That's not my name,' came the muffled voice from under the pillow.

'Greggy Greg Greg, wake uh-up.'

'You are so annoying.'

'I know-ow.'

'Can I have a coffee first?'

'One espresso coming right up, then we'll get the eight a.m. speedboat back to Malé.' She hopped off him and danced her naked body over to the coffee machine, ignoring the groans of discontent from the bed.

'Tell me again why we're in a fish market when we don't have an oven to cook anything in?'

'Because it's got a great atmosphere! I love fish markets; I try to go to one in whatever country I'm in.'

'It smells.'

'Look how fresh they are!'

'Seriously Nell, can we find another market? One that sells things without eyes?'

Nell consulted the piece of paper that she'd scribbled some place names on the night before, 'Okay, next stop Majeedhee Magu Road.'

'Is it too much to hope for that there'll be a Starbucks or a House of Pancakes there?'

Nell ignored him as they ventured back out into the sunshine onto the busy road, pulling Greg back onto the pavement milliseconds before a moped floored him to the ground. 'Look where you're going!'

'I did!'

'You looked the wrong way! You haven't got your "I'm invincible" armour on anymore, remember?'

A look of thunder flashed across Greg's face, making Nell think that maybe it was still too soon to joke about his new mortality.

A couple of hours later, Nell was armed with some handmade necklaces made out of tree resin, a couple of batik sarongs for herself, two beautiful peacock-coloured ones for her mum and Greg's mother, and a deep burnished orange one Nell thought Polly would like, and Greg had bought a fridge magnet. Baby steps, thought Nell. They stumbled upon a beautiful little store selling items made out of coconuts, and she convinced Greg that his life would be a lot better with some salad servers; he was reticent at first and then got swept away with the coconut ingenuity and ended up buying something from every shelf, making the old lady behind the counter beam with the idea of shutting up shop and going home early.

Lunch was from an unassuming café on the beach, a whole fish for each of them, served simply with lemon and rice. This was the most comfortable Nell had felt for days, weeks, months even. She looked at Greg as he devoured his food, his skin glowing with three days of sun, his hair flopping into his eyes, and the years fell away. A different beach, the same them. If you looked closer you could see the new laughter lines around her eyes, the growing-fainter-by-the-day grey circles under his eyes denoting too many late nights at work, a slight hunch on his back from being glued to a screen all day every day for years, and a new posture for her too – more upright, relaxed, assured. But still them.

On the boat on the way back to the resort later that

afternoon, with their shopping bags tucked safely behind their legs, Greg's arm around her as they crashed over the waves, Nell was still smiling. Today had been a good day.

'But why do you have to go?' Greg sat next to her half-filled rucksack on the bed, stopping short of taking each item out as soon as she put it in.

'We always said that I would just come for five days, I need to go back and sort things out.'

'But you could do that from here. There's internet and phones, you can apply for jobs from here.'

'Greg, it's been great, fantastic even. I'm so glad I came, but it's time for me to go back to reality and start making some plans.' Nell rolled up a T-shirt.

'Do those plans include me?'

'Of course!' She wasn't lying; these last few days had brought feelings that were buried far below, so far below in fact that she'd thought they'd completely disappeared, right up to the surface. She'd almost even told him she loved him last night; the mix of nostalgia and negroni was never a helpful one. If anything, the near-miss declaration made her even more determined to get on the return flight as soon as possible before the heady blend of sun and sentimentality addled her brain even more.

PART FOUR

*What the universe wants,
the universe gets*

CHAPTER TWENTY-SIX

The next morning, after an arduous flight home where the inflight magazine stayed resolutely in the back pocket of the chair in front, Nell sat on Greg's sofa waiting for Polly to arrive for their lunch. She looked around the white room, wondering if she could be happy here, if she could slot into this room, this house, Greg's life, or if the space wasn't Nell-shaped after all. It all seemed too easy, and yet possibly too hard all at the same time.

Her phone started ringing on the arm of the sofa. She assumed it would be Polly asking for directions from the tube – she didn't come up to London much – but to her surprise, it was William, Juno's son. Nell's stomach lurched. She answered it with trepidation and only allowed herself to breathe once he'd assured her that Juno was 'absolutely fine.'

'Look,' he said, once he'd ascertained that yes, she did have a lovely holiday, and no, she didn't bring the weather back with her, 'I have a proposition for you, Nell. We're at a crossroads with Mum, she's wandered off too many times, let random people in the house—'

Nell shifted the phone to her other ear, unsure of whether that description included her.

'Signed up for all sorts of things from cold callers, and she's forgetting, or confusing things every day now, and I feel really uncomfortable about her being here alone. We've looked around a few homes for her—'

'Who's we?'

'Sorry?'

'You said "we".'

'Er, Willa and I.'

'Okay.'

'And, um, the ones we've seen just seem a bit soulless and she's so full of life and colour, I'm not sure she'd be happy there.'

Nell didn't feel that she needed to say anything at this point; it seemed as if William had got to the right train of thought on his own.

'So, I, we, want to keep her here for as long as we can, but that means getting some help in. And I wondered if you'd like the job? I was thinking. . .'

He then named a daily rate that made Nell wonder if he was quite well, but it was what he said next that had her palpitating.

'There's also a little self-contained one-bed flat in the basement where you could stay if you wanted to? That doesn't mean that it's a twenty-four-hour job, it would just be five days a week, until we're home, the odd evenings when we're out, but the job's yours if you want it?'

'Have you asked Juno?'

'I'm sure she'd be delighted.'

'I'd really rather you ask her first. If she says yes, then I'd love to.'

The kettle hadn't even finished boiling when he rang back

to say that Juno was thrilled with the suggestion, and she could move in later today if she liked. Nell paused before answering, standing once again at one of life's junctions, weighing up the views of the future in both directions, before replying that she'd love to.

The doorbell rang, conveniently giving her no time to second guess herself, not that she was particularly prone to doing so. There was no point lamenting a decision after it had been made; that just took energy away from making the most of whatever it was she'd plumped for. Nell smoothed down her hair before answering it, wishing that her elasticated maxi skirt wasn't quite so crinkled. Polly was wearing tight navy trousers tucked into knee high leather boots, a crisp white shirt and a beige trench coat. They embraced awkwardly, and Nell ushered Polly inside. 'Oh, this is lovely,' Polly said, running her hand along Greg's fireplace, its shelf unadorned with paraphernalia of any kind. 'It's so clean.'

'He has an agency come in.' He hadn't warned Nell of this; she'd only found out by wandering into the kitchen once completely naked after her shower and being greeted by a couple of really lovely Hungarian ladies.

Polly pivoted in a circle, admitting the expanse of white walls and stripped floorboards. 'This is not what I was expecting. Greg Gage has grown up.'

'He has.'

'The flat you shared together was nothing like this.'

'No.'

'Is this where you live now?'

'I'm actually moving out this afternoon. I've just got a job.'

'In England?'

'In London. About three miles away.'

'So you're staying?'

Nell opened her mouth to say 'for now', but closed it again

and just nodded. 'Do you want a coffee here, or shall we go and find a café?'

'Let's go out.'

It was a crisp day, the rare type of January day where the breeze didn't bite and the sky was bluer and higher than normal. The two sisters walked in silence for about ten minutes, which felt to Nell so much longer. Every opener she thought of wasn't right. They sat on a pavement table on the side of the street and ordered two coffees.

'I just want to know something,' Polly started.

'Okay, ask me anything.'

'When you woke up, you know, the day after, and you were alive. Why didn't you call us then and tell us that you were okay? Why let us believe that you'd died?'

'I didn't have a phone, or any of your numbers—'

'Bullshit. In this day and age you can contact anyone within seconds.'

'But I didn't even think you knew the date of the prediction; whenever I'd tried to talk about it before, you cut me off and told me it was rubbish. I honestly didn't think that any of you had any idea when it was.'

'But *you* did. You actually thought that you were going to die and didn't call or come and see us and say goodbye. You were just happy to disappear from our lives.'

'Well I thought because I hadn't been home in so long you wouldn't be that upset,' Nell said weakly, realising how much she'd misjudged everything.

'Even if we hadn't realised the date, you let the letters be delivered, announcing your death, and didn't even try to stop us reading them.'

'I did! That's why I came down to Hove!'

'The day after you woke up!'

'I completely forgot that I'd even written them, to be honest,

274

it was such a shock to be alive, my whole mind was just scrambled with what to do next, where to stay, what to eat, where to go. It wasn't until Greg got his letter that it all came back to me and I came down straight away to try to intercept all your letters before they were delivered. I really am so sorry Pol, I would never have wanted to put you all through that pain. I wish I'd never written them, I really do.'

Polly took a deep sigh, 'Well, turns out you did me a favour. Bea and I are staying at Mum's for a while. I've left Damian.'

'Oh God, Polly, that's a huge decision.'

'After I got your letter, saying what you said, some things started to make sense, and I started tracking him, and turns out he and Lauren have been having an affair for the entirety of our marriage.'

'Oh God Polly, I'm so sorry.'

'Don't be. If you hadn't written what you did, then I'd still be living in a complete sham of a marriage.'

'How are you feeling?'

'Stupid. Numb. Did I say stupid?'

'You're not stupid. It's him. And her. For letting such a great person slip through their fingers.'

'Yeah well. It was what you said about Dad that made me realise that if it wasn't Lauren, it would have been Bella, or Kerry, or someone he hasn't met yet, and I'm better than that.'

'Yes you are.'

'So there it is. I'm a single mum, living with my mum and her weird boyfriend.'

'Oh God, he is really weird, isn't he?'

'He eats cornflakes dry in the evening as a snack while he's watching TV. Who does that? Mum has to hoover the sofa before she goes up to bed.'

'That's the least offensive thing about him. I'm worried he's far too controlling.'

'I'll keep an eye on it. Mum made noises the other day about wanting to do an evening class in Spanish, which he thought was ridiculous, but I'll make sure she looks into it.'

'It's good you're there.'

'I'd prefer to be in my own home.'

'I realise that, I just meant that some good can come out of your horrible situation, that's all. The universe gives—'

'The universe, the universe. Do you ever stop to consider that everything isn't preplanned by the universe and we're all just muddling along until we die?'

'That is a possibility, yes,' Nell said carefully, taking a sip of her coffee. 'Or, we find ourselves in circumstances that seem pretty shit at the time, and then it's only afterwards that we realise that we were exactly where we needed to be.'

Polly stared across the street where two women, who looked to be in their eighties, sat outside another café, both bundled up in heavy coats and scarves. One was smoking a vape. On the table in front of them were not two coffee cups, like on theirs, but two lurid orange Aperol Spritzes, despite it being a few minutes shy of noon. 'Do you think they're sisters or friends?' Polly said.

'Who?'

Polly nodded over the road at the two women. 'Them. They have the same chin.'

'Can't you be both sisters and friends?'

Nell's question hung solemnly in the air while Polly considered it, then said, 'Let's get drunk.'

During the first round of cocktails they decided, while perched on two barstools at the bar, that Polly should tell Damian to move out of their house and put it on the market. 'I am his wife,' she said adamantly, 'not his doormat housekeeper. Do you know what? I even washed the shirts he wore when he took her out? And called an Uber for him while he was in the shower once, so he wouldn't be late for his very important dinner. He was having a complete laugh at me, wasn't he?'

'I don't think he was,' Nell replied. 'He's stupid, he's not mean. I think he's just a very selfish person, doing whatever he wants whenever he feels the urge to do it. But you are worth so much more than that. You're amazing, and there will be someone that sees that, and appreciates you. Or you can just be a fabulous twosome with Bea. But in the meantime, pack up everything he owns in black bin bags and put them in your front garden.' Nell remembered the state of her sister's street and thought to herself that it might even make Polly's smart house fit in more.

During the next round, they decided that Ray could also do one: 'You're right,' Polly conceded after Nell voiced her concerns about him, 'I think I was just pleased that Mum had someone to take her out to dinner and on holiday, but they only go away once a year, they always go halves, and I can't remember the last time they went out for something to eat, and I'm pretty sure he doesn't pay Mum any rent or anything towards the bills.'

'I found some pictures on her computer,' Nell admitted, hoping her sister wasn't going to judge her for snooping. 'Of places she'd like to go to, walking holidays and things, it was in a folder called Hobbies. I think she wants a much bigger life than the one she's living.'

'So what can we do?'

The two sisters brainstormed some ideas as they drained their second cocktail. During their third, they came to the conclusion that Aperol made your teeth feel sticky, and they should probably move onto a gin-based one for their next round. The fourth, an aromatic elderflower gin concoction made them declare that London was, without a doubt, the best city in the world and Greg was still incredibly handsome, but was he right for Nell?

'No offence,' Polly said, pointing her finger at Nell, to really hammer the point home that what she was about to say was not meant to be offensive, 'but you're a bit too colourful for him.'

'Colourful?'

'You're Dolce and Gabbana, and he's Max Mara.' Seeing Nell's confusion, Polly attempted to expand her analogy further, really getting into it. 'You're a tie-dye T-shirt, and he's a pair of linen trousers. You're Morocco, he's Monaco. You're The Rolling Stones, he's The Beatles, you're—'

'Okay, okay, I get it,' Nell said laughing. 'He's much more refined than I am.'

'It's not about refinement, it's about being too different to be compatible.'

'I know loads of people that like The Stones and The Beatles, can't the two live harmoniously side by side forever?'

'They can, they can. But at some point, Jagger's going to look at McCartney and tell him to loosen up a little. And McCartney's going to tell Jagger to get a haircut and stop dancing so crazily all the time.'

'I wish you'd met Tom,' Nell said, 'then you could tell me where he would fit into all this.'

'He doesn't fit anywhere,' Polly said, hopping off her barstool and signalling to the barman that they would like their bill. 'He's still married.' She'd walked about ten steps to the toilet before stopping and calling over her shoulder, 'And his sock-gloves sound really weird.'

After piling back to Greg's flat to pack up Nell's paltry belongings, they took a taxi to Juno's to settle Nell in. The flat in the basement of Willa and William's home was absolutely perfect. Previously probably the kitchens and larders of the Victorian house, it had since been carved up into a pretty decent sized bedroom, living room with dining area, galley kitchen and bathroom. Polly set about brightening up the walls of the lounge with one of Nell's new Maldivian sarongs while Nell bustled about putting homely touches to all the surfaces: the coconut husk fruit bowl in the middle of the little fold-down dining table, a family of soapstone carved sloths from Central America on the mantlepiece, and she hung a handwoven dreamcatcher from the window in the bedroom. They both then flopped down on the little two-seater sofa in the lounge looking at Nell's new home, which was suddenly very Nell.

Practise gratitude. Find your passions. Do conscious acts of kindness. Connect with the like-minded. Nurture relationships. Cultivate optimism.

'I've loved being with you today,' Nell said. 'Thank you for coming up.

'I didn't know how today was going to go if I'm honest with you. I had a return ticket booked hours ago.'

'I'm glad you didn't use it.'

'Me too.'

'It's going to be alright, you know. Going it alone.'

Polly sighed and laid her head on the back of the sofa. 'I know. Can I give the opposite advice to you?'

'Opposite how?'

'It's going to be alright, you know. *Not* going it alone.'

'What do you mean?'

'Hitching your life to someone else's for more than five minutes. It's often a really lovely thing to do.' Polly shoulder barged Nell as they sat together. 'However complicated they are.'

'But you're a living breathing contradiction to your own advice.'

'Not really. Damian and I had some good times, we made Bea, and just because we're not going to be ending our days sat under crocheted blankets on rocking chairs together doesn't mean I wish it didn't happen.'

'Do you want to know one of my biggest regrets about the way I've lived?'

'Go on?'

'Not being more involved in Bea's life. I honestly thought I was doing the right thing, staying away. I rationalised it so many times to myself, that I was protecting her from feeling really sad after I died; you can't miss what you don't know, can you? And she's so young, I didn't think she'd be able to understand why Aunty Nell stopped video calling, or visiting, she might have thought I didn't love her anymore, or that she'd done something wrong, and so I thought that *not* bonding with her was better for everyone.'

'It really hurt me actually, you not being that bothered about her.'

'But I just couldn't. I couldn't let myself forge these deep connections, with anyone. You saw how upset Mum was when Grandad died, and then Nana, she was racked with grief, barely ate for weeks, and if I learned anything from that, it was don't let anyone too close.'

'That sounds like a pretty lonely way to live.'

Nell shrugged. 'I had friends, and lovers, just no one that ever stayed around long enough to know my middle name.'

'As it's Agatha I'd say that was a plus point.' Polly smiled and laid her head on Nell's shoulder. 'Now that you've been given a second stab at life, why don't you make some changes. Come down to Hove more, be part of Bea's life, of mine, of Mum's, and when you're ready, be open to the idea of meeting someone, who's not Greg or Tom, someone you can have a real and deep relationship with.'

'Absolutely to the first part, I'm going to be down in Hove all the time, but the second part? I just don't know how to do that,' Nell said truthfully. 'I don't know how to say to someone, okay, this is me, you're you, let's now spend all our time together.'

'You don't need to spend *all* your time with them.' Polly smiled. 'You can still have a bath alone.'

'That's the one thing I *wouldn't* be doing alone. Baths are so boring when you're in there by yourself.'

'Can I ask you something very personal, Nell?'

'You once showed me how to put a tampon in, it doesn't get more personal than that.'

'Have you ever been in love?'

'Only about three times a year.'

'I'm serious.'

'So am I. From what I understand, love is when you can't stop thinking about someone, you want their smell on you constantly, you crave their laugh, you can't sit next to them without reaching out and stroking their beard—'

'Gross.'

'So yes, if that is love, I have felt that.'

'If that is what love is, I don't think I've ever felt that,' Polly laughed. 'I thought love was depending on someone else completely and being able to show them the sides no one else sees, your fears and insecurities and hoping they never use that against you.'

'I've definitely never had that. But I really don't think love can be defined in a certain way and everyone feels it the same, that's impossible. Human connections are so complex, it can't be put into a neat little box labelled Love surely?'

'Just as long as you're open to having deep connections with someone past the moment when you don't want to stroke their beard anymore?'

Nell knew what she was saying. And in truth, as soon as the moment came when her hand didn't reach out involuntarily to touch whatever part of her partner's body was nearest, that was always her cue to pack up her rucksack. She didn't know what stage came after that because she was always already on a plane, eyes facing forward.

Polly took her sister's hand in hers. 'Look, I get it, you're faced with this big expanse of life that you didn't know you'd have. But just consider making a few changes so you don't always have to be alone.'

'But I like being alone!'

'So keep doing that then!'

'Why are you shouting at me?'

'You shouted first!'

'Is there more wine?'

'I saw a welcome bottle of prosecco in the fridge from the two Ws.'

'That'll do.'

Nell picked up her phone when she was in the kitchen getting the bottle and two glasses. She had a missed call from both Tom and Greg. She was about to ignore them and just put the phone down again when she remembered Polly's words. These were nice men. They just maybe weren't right for *her*.

Hey Greg, how's life in paradise? The tan is looking sharp my friend. I just wanted to let you know that I've got a new job! And it comes with a flat, so I moved out of yours this afternoon. It's all spick and span waiting for your return next week, I've even bought you a plant, I've named him Wilberforce. He likes indirect sunshine, twice-weekly watering and songs by Nina Simone. Thank you for absolutely everything. See you soon, Nxx

Hi Tom, so here I am. Sorry about the running away thing. I do that. By now you and Leah have probably had your big chat, and I think it's for the best if you try and make another go of it with her, for Arlo. I bring nothing to people's lives but mayhem and disorder, and you, and he, don't need that (well maybe you do, for material). You're a magnificent human being, and I'll never regret selling my bed to you. Nell x

CHAPTER TWENTY-SEVEN

A routine appeared without much fanfare at all during the first week at Juno's. Nell popped up the three flights of stairs around 9.45 each morning, revelling in the delight of only wearing socks to work. Not only socks. Socks with clothes, but no shoes. She'd been on a few naturist beaches in her time and loved the feel of the sun on bits that had rarely seen daylight, but she had to be honest, the sand had been an issue.

She made Juno a cup of tea, one sugar, each morning, placing it gently by her bedside one minute before her body clock woke her at ten. After Juno had wafted potions about in her bathroom for half an hour, while Nell made Juno's bed and tidied round, the two of them had another cup of tea and made plans for the day, which invariably included chatting, visiting a nearby coffee shop, the library, a little post-lunch snooze and a couple of games of cards in the afternoon. At the end of her first week, William gave her an envelope of cash that seemed extraordinarily heavy for the lightweight 'work' she'd been doing, and she said as much to him, but he merely replied that she deserved every penny. As ways to make large amounts of money went, this was the type of escorting Nell could get on board with.

Back in her flat that night, she took the notes out of the envelope and divided them into three piles, one for her to open a bank account with, the next to start paying back the hotel she ran out from, the final one to repay Greg for all the handouts he'd given her. She'd invited him round to see her new flat the night before, he'd brought a bottle of wine and an expectation of a sleepover which she swiftly batted away with the excuse of an early morning, and he'd left looking like a child leaving a birthday with no party bag. One word from her would be all it would take to set up a lovely life together: a life of luxury holidays, of lovely food, of movies, of jokes, of great sex, of incredible coffee, but it would also be a life of limits, of always stopping shy of excess. For a blink and you miss it moment she'd glimpsed a different type of life with Tom: one of genuine warmth, and passion, and acceptance. But she was never going to be the other woman in his relationship; she didn't want Arlo decades from now to be sitting with his partner, his friends, talking about 'a woman called Nell who ruined everything'.

The next morning, her phone buzzed on the table alongside her. As she read the message she couldn't help smiling. Tom had written it out like an old-fashioned telegram.

Hey STOP Big chat done STOP Divorce papers signed STOP She's agreed to joint custody STOP. Nell. Just STOP it. STOP being ridiculous. You and I should quite clearly never. . . STOP. Call me.

'What's put the smile on your face this morning?' Juno studied Nell carefully as Nell put her tea down on her nightstand.

'What are you talking about? I always have a smile on my face.'

285

'True, true, but this one is different.'

'You are very astute, old woman.'

'This one is about a man.'

'Two for two. Well done.'

'Is it the comedian?'

'He did message me, yes.'

'Doesn't surprise me. You are fabulous. I'd marry you if I was forty years younger.'

'You and me Juno, would be hashtag couple goals.'

'I don't know what that means, but yes, we would.'

'What are you thinking today?' Nell asked, opening Juno's heaving wardrobe. 'The turquoise or the purple?'

'Is it sunny?'

'Does it matter? You bring your own sunshine.'

'Turquoise then. With the orange vintage fur. And the feather headdress.'

'Excellent choices. I'm going to take you somewhere new today. We're going for a walk along the river, to a little café on a boat.'

'Great. I love cafés and I love boats.'

The canal path was busy, considering it was midweek in the last week of January. The two women walked with linked arms, both as a symbol of friendship, and also to stop the older one falling into the canal. Juno seemed oblivious to the looks she got from everyone that they passed, but Nell watched each one with interest. Some quickly glanced then looked away, unsettled, at Juno's turquoise and orange outfit complete with the extravagant feathered fascinator that admittedly might look to some much more in keeping with Ascot's Ladies' Day than a London canal path. Most took an unabashed, dramatic second look; others didn't, or couldn't, draw their eyes away from her until their shoulders had passed each other, and with a few, Nell was sure that if she'd looked back, they'd still be looking. What was it about non-conformity that made people so uncomfortable? The world needed more Junos, not fewer.

Nell's eyes darted constantly, looking for Tom; they did normally anyway, but they were actually in his neighbourhood, making it more likely that they'd bump into him.

Andrea was thrilled to see Nell again, greeting her instinctively with a hug, which, to anyone else apart from Nell, would seem a little forward after only meeting her once before. But Nell wasn't surprised by the gesture at all; in fact, if Andrea hadn't, Nell would have instigated it herself.

The three women settled at one of the empty tables, which, considering all of them were empty, took a moment of deliberation to choose. 'Quiet day?' Nell said.

'Every day is a quiet day,' Andrea sighed. 'I'm thinking about moving on to be honest, I'm just not getting the trade. There's a Starbucks, a Costa and a Caffè Nero two minutes away on the high street. Why would anyone want to come and have a coffee here?'

'Because it's amazing? And you're amazing? And we're floating. Right. Let's do some brainstorming. We're three highly capable creative women, we can come up with a plan, except let's not call it a plan, because plans are rubbish. Let's call it an ideas board. Have you got any paper? Good, okay. Juno, look lively my lovely, we need your genius on this too.'

Juno's eyes sprang open amidst much protesting that she wasn't asleep.

'So, the issue is, getting people through the door. What have you tried?' Nell asked Andrea.

'Buy one, get second half-price; lunch deals of sandwich and soup or soup and salad, or sandwich and salad. . .'

'All good ideas,' Nell said tactfully. 'But how about hosting

287

events? Workshops? Each afternoon you could have a different activity? Painting classes, you could set up easels next to each porthole and get a local artist or art student in to teach it? Writing workshops, poetry, each desk has some paper and pens, and you provide the coffee and cake, and off they go? You could have gardening talks, how to grow your own veg in small spaces, you could even grow your own salads to use in your food, bird watching groups, provide little binoculars next to each porthole and get a load of twitchers in? Slam poetry nights? Parent and baby groups? Might be tricky getting buggies on board, but you could have a waterproof canopy out the back that they can leave them under and then have a post-school drop-off special of a coffee and croissant between nine and ten a.m.? What about having a drop-in hour from ten to eleven for anyone who wants to chat; word gets around that if you're by yourself and fancy a coffee with someone, then they can come here and sit at a random table and people can just start chatting to each other.'

'That's how we met,' Juno said. 'On a bus. We were both by ourselves and Nell and I started talking, and now look at us, I'm like a queen and she's my lady-in-waiting.'

'You are a queen, my darling.' Nell kissed Juno's hand.

'You could have singles nights,' Nell said, 'where like-minded people come for a glass of wine, some tapas, possibly meet their next great love. You could meet the man of your dreams, Andrea, you never know.'

'Andrea's not interested in men.'

Both women looked at Juno, who shrugged her orange shoulders and took another sip of tea. 'I mean, I could be wrong, but I don't think I am, am I?'

Andrea laughed. 'No Juno, you're not wrong.'

'You really are some sort of voodoo maestro,' Nell said admiringly.

'Not really. I just know people.'

'Talking of knowing people,' Andrea said, and Nell immediately guessed where this was heading, 'what a small world, you knowing Tom. Did he call you?'

Nell nodded. 'He did indeed.'

Andrea clapped her hands together, 'You two would be perfect. My only two customers getting together.'

'I'm not sure that's enough to have in common.'

'He's such a lovely man, he brings his son in sometimes. He has a mini hot chocolate with all the trimmings, and they watch the swans.'

'Is that the complication?' Juno asked Nell. 'The child?'

'Well sort of, I'm not really a mother type of person.'

'He doesn't need a mother. He already has one. He does have one, I assume?'

Nell nodded.

'Well then. He just needs someone to like him, and to make his dad happy. Seems pretty un-complicated to me.'

'And to me,' Andrea chimed in.

'Well quite clearly you two don't know what you're talking about. I'm a really bad role model for young children to be around. I'm flighty, I'm unreliable, I run away at the slightest sign of trouble or conflict, I have a tendency to make people do weird out-of-character things without meaning to, and I swear a lot.'

'I don't think you're any of those things,' Juno said. 'You do swear a lot, but I quite like it, it reminds me of when I was in the territorial army. But you've also got a massive heart, and the most optimistic disposition of anyone I've ever met.'

'Wow, coming from you Juno, who seems to have met half the world's population, that means a lot.'

'Would you both like a free refill?' Andrea started getting up.

'Stop giving stuff away for free!' Nell said. 'We will stay for another one, but we are paying for them. In fact, we're paying more than it says on the board because your prices are too low.'

'I can't get anyone on the boat when I'm charging less than half of Starbucks, how am I going to get them through the door if I put my prices up?'

'Look, I've been away from England for a long time, but even when I left twenty years ago, the price for a cup of tea wasn't this low.'

'But it's just hot water and a tea bag,' Andrea said.

'Yes, but it's also your electricity, and your mooring fee, and your beautiful view, and your sparkling hospitality, and the free biscuit you put on the side.'

'If I charge for the biscuit then it's not free anymore.'

'You can still say it's free, just build the cost of it into the cup of tea.'

Andrea looked doubtful. 'I'm not sure I'm cut out for this cut-throat world of industry.'

'It's not cut-throat, it's just about making enough of a profit to keep you here and in business. I'm saying this selfishly, I don't want you to go anywhere. So, if I can help make things easier for you to stay, then I will. What did you think about my events ideas?'

'They sound terrifying but good.'

'Hat making. You could have hat making classes. And basket weaving,' Juno added. 'And Christmas wreaths in December. You could get a local florist in, provide the space and the mulled wine, and charge five pounds a head.'

'Fifty a head. At least. But great suggestions Juno, keep them coming. Honestly Andrea, you'd be so busy in no time, let us help you.'

'Help her with what?' came a familiar voice from the

doorway as Tom stepped inside, a small boy, who must be Arlo, holding onto his hand. 'What brilliant scheme is Nell concocting now? Hello Juno, lovely to see you again.'

The fact he'd remembered Juno's name, and greeted the older woman with a fist bump, which she actually returned, made Nell like him even more.

'Nell,' he said, with a small, reverent bow.

'Tom.' Nell tried to keep her voice level despite her heart racing. She couldn't tear her eyes away from his son. He was so small, and looked so much like Tom: his brown hair had a little wave to it, he had a matching dimple in his chin, and even though he was a little shy, leaning ever so slightly into his dad's leg for comfort, she could see his mouth twitching with a smile.

'How are you doing?' Tom asked Nell.

'Very well. Just taking Juno out for her daily constitutional.'

Juno huffed. 'You make me sound like a spaniel.'

'More Bichon Frisé,' smiled Nell.

'Nell's been giving me ideas about how to entice more people into the café,' Andrea explained, motioning towards the piece of paper on the table which was filled with scribbles and arrows.

'Wow. Good work.' Tom leaned down, gently unzipped the boy's coat and said quietly in Arlo's ear, 'Go and sit down, bud.'

Nell watched this interaction with his son with awed interest. How did he know how to do that?

'Did you get my message?' he said to Nell once Arlo was settled in his seat, his legs swinging underneath him, colouring with some pencils Andrea had put in front of him.

'I did. This morning actually.'

'Ah. So, is it too much to hope for that receiving the message prompted you down to this part of town?'

'Purely coincidental.'

'Another coincidence?'

'It wasn't coincidence at all,' Juno said, looking up at him. 'I wanted to go to Borough Market to buy falafels but she was having none of it. She can be really bossy when she wants to be.'

'I remember,' he said, his eyes twinkling.

Nell could feel her cheeks flaming. For a boat in winter, it was very warm in there. Arlo sneezed, and Tom reached into his coat pocket for a tissue and leaned over to wipe his son's nose, then put the tissue back in his pocket.

'Well, we should probably be off, Juno,' Nell said, reaching behind her for her own coat.

'Why don't you come and meet Arlo?' Tom suggested quietly.

Nell floundered. 'I wouldn't know what to say.'

'Just say Hello Arlo and see where that takes you.'

'But he's four.'

'Imagine he's me,' Juno adds helpfully. 'Kids and old people are very similar.'

'It's too soon,' Nell said.

'Too soon for what? Saying hello?' Tom asked. 'Arlo buddy, come here and meet my friend Nell. Nell this is Arlo, Arlo Nell.'

Arlo put out his hand the way Tom had taught him to, 'Hi Nell. Did you know that capybaras eat their own poo?'

Tom interrupted, 'We're big into poo facts at the moment. By we, I mean him, he's into poo facts.'

Nell shook his hand and said, 'I did not know that, Arlo. That's a great fact. Did you know that the Chinese soft-shelled turtle pees out of its mouth?' Arlo jumped up and down with glee at this new golden nugget.

'Wow. Just wow.' Tom whistled. 'I knew you were good, but that's genius level good.'

Nell smiled. 'Right, we really do have to go. Lovely meeting you Arlo, high five. Give me a kiss Andrea, and let me know if I can help put any idea into action.'

'Do I get a kiss too?' Tom asked.

'No, you get a fist bump.'

'When can I see you again?'

'She has no plans on Valentine's Day,' Juno said.

Tom put his head on the side. 'Is that right?'

Nell pushed Juno lovingly behind her. 'Don't listen to her. She's quite clearly unhinged.'

'But I do still have full faculty of my bladder,' Juno said over Nell's shoulder.

'Good to know,' Tom smiled. 'If you do find yourself free on Valentine's Day, there's a great jazz band playing that night, if you fancy it?'

'I'll have to see if William and Willa want to go out that night,' Nell said. 'I'm living with them now, keeping Juno company when they're not there.'

'So, you're not at the ex's anymore? Interesting.'

'Daddy. . .' Arlo pulled on Tom's jumper. 'Ask Nell if she knows about koalas?'

Nell knelt down to be at eye level with Arlo. 'Know what about koalas?'

'The babies eat their mum's poo.'

'Well, doesn't that sound yummy.'

Arlo giggled.

'I'm going to go away and find out some extra good poo facts for next time,' Nell said, straightening up.

'Next time?' Tom asked quizzically.

Nell smiled. 'In case there's a next time.'

CHAPTER TWENTY-EIGHT

The doorbell went at 6.30 p.m., shortly followed by Willa knocking on the door to Nell's flat, 'Nell, it's your date.'

That was odd, Nell thought, she'd agreed to meet Tom at the bar at nine. She wasn't anywhere near ready yet.

'He's gorgeous, you didn't tell me he was so handsome!' Willa whispered to her as Nell followed her up the stairs from the basement to the kitchen where, standing in the middle of the kitchen having a chat with William, was Greg. A beautiful bouquet of flowers wrapped in layers and layers of coloured tissue paper lay on the island. She looked from the flowers, to Greg, who was in a black suit, with white shirt and thin black tie, and Willa was absolutely correct. He looked amazing.

'What are you doing here?'

'I couldn't have you sat here alone on Valentine's Day, so I'm taking you out to dinner.'

'But, um. . .' Nell faltered, her brain not working quick enough to work out how to work this out.

'The table's booked for half past seven, so go and put on something fancy. We're going to. . .'

He named a restaurant then that meant absolutely nothing

to Nell but Willa and William both responded with a grati-
fying and simultaneous 'Ooo' which seemed to please Greg.

'You'll need to wear something really special,' Willa said,
'We went there for my fiftieth, and it's incredible.'

'But I don't have anything nice,' Nell said. 'I only own jeans
and sarongs. I normally rent my fancy stuff.'

'Come upstairs with me, we'll find you something. William,
keep Tom company.'

'Greg. My name's Greg.'

Willa gave Nell a blink-and-you-miss-it glance of utter
confusion, but covered that up with, 'Oh I'm so sorry, of
course, Greg, sorry, Tom's the name of the main character in
my play, I'm so used to saying it. William, pour *Greg* a glass
of wine, there's a Chablis open.'

'Don't ask,' Nell said as the two women walked into Willa's
walk-in wardrobe. Willa pulled out a few dresses, all utterly
gorgeous, all very classy and elegant, all the absolute antithesis
of Nell's style. 'These are lovely,' Nell said, running her fingers
over the silk. 'Really beautiful.'

'Try anything on you like,' Willa said. 'We're about the
same size.'

Nell stripped down to her underwear, while Willa hastily
turned her back and busied herself straightening the handbags
on the handbag shelves.

'What's happening here?' Juno said from the doorway.

'God knows, Juno,' Nell said, putting one leg and then the
other in a camel-coloured Max Mara evening dress. 'Greg's
turned up out of nowhere to take me to a fancy dinner, and
I'm meant to be meeting Tom in two hours to go and see a
band. I'll have to cancel Tom.'

'No! You can't do that. Tell Greg you can't go.'

'He's booked. . .' Willa said the name of the restaurant
again, but Juno's blank look told Nell that she wasn't the only

one to have no idea what that was. 'And he brought the most beautiful flowers. And he's wearing an Ozwald Boateng.'

'Well in that case, you've only got one option,' Juno said. 'You'll have to go on both dates.'

'I can't do that!' Nell said. 'How would that even work?'

'Where's Tom taking you?' Juno asked.

'Some jazz bar below a hotel.'

'Which one?' Willa said.

'Uh, one near The Strand.'

'That's where this restaurant is too! You could have dinner, by nine o'clock you'd be on dessert, nip out and meet Tom, excuse yourself for a bit and come back to the restaurant for coffee, Greg goes home, you finish the evening with Tom.' Willa clapped her hands together in jubilation at coming up with such a fool-proof plan.

'I think you've been in theatre too long,' Nell said. 'There is no way I can pull that off in real life.'

Willa completely ignored her and instead shuffled through the rails of clothing, 'Right, we're going to need something that's good for a Michelin restaurant and a dive bar.'

'I say we get the former from this wardrobe, and get the latter from mine,' Juno said. 'I have just the thing.'

'Why does that not surprise me?' Nell laughed, following Juno up the stairs to her flat. A few minutes later, in a black jumpsuit of Willa's with accessories courtesy of Juno, she twirled around in front of them. 'Well?'

'Oh Caroline, you look wonderful, doesn't she, Mum?'

Nell's eyes snapped to Willa, who nodded gently, and said, 'She certainly does Juno dear, she does. Have a lovely time Caroline, we can't wait to hear all about it tomorrow, can we? Come on now, let's get ready for bed.' She put her arm around Juno's shoulder and guided the older lady upstairs.

*

'Why are you bringing such a big handbag?' Greg held open the taxi door for her outside the house.

She could hardly tell him that in it were a pair of Converse to replace the nude high heels she was currently wearing and a denim jacket to swap with the black velvet bolero. She had a silk scarf of Juno's around her neck at the moment, which she'd use as a headscarf to tone down the expensive black jumpsuit and turn it into something boho and quirky for the bar along with a pair of long feather earrings to swap in with the delicate drop pearl ones of Willa's. She had tried to call Tom to rearrange, but his phone was off, and she wasn't a cancel-a-date-by-text kind of woman. There was an outside chance of this madcap scheme actually working, but definitely not worth risking a bet on.

The universe had helped Nell out quite a few times over the years: delayed trains when she was also running late; the perfect travelling companion staying in the same hostel heading the same way; being told about a job just as her last pound was about to be spent – but never had fortune smiled on her to quite the extent as it did that night, as Greg's restaurant was standing proud on the fifth floor of the hotel, while Tom's jazz bar languished in the basement. This mad scheme started to look a lot more feasible.

'Oh look,' Greg said once they'd been seated at their candlelit table for two overlooking the London skyline, 'There's a seven-course tasting menu, we should definitely do that.'

Nell's heart sank, they'd be there until midnight if they did that. 'It's £200 a person!'

'But it is with wine-pairing too.'

'I'd want it to be served alongside next week's lunches and a monthly travelcard for that price.'

'This is on me.'

'Greg, I feel really—'

'Sshh. I invited you. I am paying, and anyway, it's a special occasion.'

'We've never really gone in for Valentine's Day before.'

'We did when we were teenagers. Don't you remember? I spent ages making a basket full of love notes under that helium balloon I floated up to your window when we were in Year Eleven.'

Nell laughed, 'And then it got caught on the branches and the love notes went all over the garden, and then my dad saw a really rude one when he was mowing the lawn the next day.'

'He didn't let me come over for weeks after that.'

'And then in sixth form, wasn't it Valentine's Day when we got the tattoos?'

Greg put his index finger out over the table and Nell did the same so their fingers touched and made a small blue heart. They both looked up smiling and locked eyes.

Nell shuffled in her seat and studied the menu. 'We could just go for mains and dessert?'

'No, it's my treat.'

Nell sniffed; she smelt smoke. She looked down and the corner of her menu was over the tealight and on fire. 'Oh fuck!' she said, desperately blowing on it and fanning it, spreading grey ash all over the white tablecloth. A waiter rushed over and couples at other tables were looking over and pointing. Nell started laughing with the hilarity of it, but Greg remained stony-faced. 'Come on Greg, that was funny.'

'Everyone was looking.'

'Chill out dude, it was an accident.'

They had the first three courses, but they weren't courses in the way that Nell would define courses, more mouthfuls, but she reasoned that not many people would pay £400 for two dinners if that's how the menu described them. Their wine glasses were only filled to half as well, so all in all, it was a bit of a swizz. She glanced at her watch, again, it was ten past nine. Hopefully Tom was running late: not with anything too serious, she didn't want the universe to reward her with one hand and take away with another; no, she wanted the delay to be because of something simple, like broken brakes or something.

The waiter brought the next mouthful, a palate-cleansing raspberry granita, which Nell finished in one gulp. 'Right, I'm going to the loo a sec, back in a bit.'

'Why are you taking your bag?'

'Er, women's issues. Bye.'

She glided out of the restaurant as elegantly and rapidly as possible, rounded the corner to the lift lobby and jabbed the button repeatedly until it pinged and opened. Once inside, waiting a few more seconds for another couple also going down, she pulled off her heels and flung them in her bag, pulled her trainers on, shook her hair out, pulled the scarf up over her head, changed the earrings, pulled off the bolero and tugged on the denim jacket just as the lift doors opened into the noisy bar. If she had looked up at all during this rapid transformation, she'd have seen the couple exchange wide-eyed looks of surprise. Tom was already standing at the bar, wearing jeans and a black long-sleeved T-shirt, his sleeves rolled up, handing the barman his card.

'Hey,' Nell said, sliding in next to him.

'Hello you.' He kissed her cheek. 'You look amazing. I got us some shots.'

'Great.' Nell picked the small glass off the bar, clinked it against his and downed it in one. 'Shall we sit?'

'Wow. Shall I get another one?'

'Why not?'

Nell found a table for the two of them at the side of the crowded bar, a little away from where the band were tuning up, but near enough to the door to the lift lobby so she could keep escaping.

'You were great with Arlo by the way. Although he is now calling you the turtle-wee lady.'

'I've been called worse.'

'So, you're working with Juno now?'

'I am. It's working really well. I have a lovely little flat under their house, which is insanely beautiful, all glass and Italian marble,' Nell tried to picture Tom at Willa and William's, in the same easy way that Greg had just slotted in there earlier, and couldn't picture it. But then she wasn't a natural fit there either, she supposed.

'She's great, it must be awesome just hanging out with her all day, talking about that time she lent Marilyn Monroe a white halter-heck dress.'

Nell smiled; he'd quite clearly got the measure of Juno the two times he'd fleetingly crossed paths with her. 'It is, she's a real character. How's your tour coming along?'

'It's going well. You should come and see the show. I'll give you tickets for whenever you're free.'

'Am I in it?'

'Indirectly.'

'Do you mention sleeping with me?'

'Indirectly.'

'In the tiny segment of the show in Balham I saw before I stormed out, you said it was the best sex of your life.'

'I'll say anything for a laugh.'

Nell flicked him in the arm.

'Can I have a percentage of the profit?'

'You can have another shot on me?'

'I'll get them, but the bar looks really crowded, so I may be a while.'

'Why are you taking your bag?'

'It's got my wallet in.'

'You could just take your wallet—'

She didn't hear the rest of his sentence as she pushed through the crowd to the lift lobby, banging everyone she passed with her bag. As luck would have it, the lift was already waiting in the basement, and Nell swapped her shoes, jacket and earrings as quickly as she could, taking a deep breath before the doors opened into the serenity of the restaurant. Her fish was already waiting on the table for her. Greg's plate was empty, his fork and knife pushed politely together.

'Where did you get to?'

'Oh sorry, they were cleaning the toilets up here so I had to go all the way to the basement.'

'Oh, that's a nuisance. You've moved your scarf.'

Nell put her hand up to where her scarf was on her head, not around her neck.

'It looks nice.'

Nell cut her seabass in two and put one half in her mouth. It was very good, she conceded, so popped the second half in too.

'Whoa, easy tiger.'

'Sorry, just a bit hungry.'

'You're meant to have the Albariño white wine with this one.'

Nell took a large swig out of the glass in front of her. 'Yes, it goes really well. They really know their stuff.'

'So, I have something to say.'

Greg reached into his suit jacket pocket and Nell's heart fell into her stomach. No. He was not doing this. She closed her eyes, willing his hand to be holding a tissue, not a ring box. Not now. Not here. Not tonight.

'Nell. Open your eyes.' He held an envelope out to her. 'Open it.'

She gingerly reached across the table, all the while calculating how long was an acceptable amount of time to be queuing for a drink. Inside were two pieces of paper designed to look like airline tickets; one had Greg's name on it, the other hers. 'I don't get it,' she said, turning them over to see if anything was written on the back.

'They're one-way tickets to Bangkok. Well, they're not yet, I just made them look like they are.'

'But I don't get it?' Nell repeated.

'I've been offered the chance to head up the Asia side of the business, based in Bangkok. It's a five-year contract, and I'm seriously considering it. And I'd like you to come with me.'

Nell blinked.

'I know it's a bit of a shock, but everything's that happened in the last couple of months has made me realise that I don't like my life here anymore, I want to do something exciting with the time I have left, and this opportunity just landed in my lap. They'd asked me before about it, but the timing never seemed right, but now it really does. And I really want to do this adventure with you. They'll put us up in an apartment in the city, and we can spend our weekends exploring the country, heading to the islands, down the coast, up north to the countryside. Say something, Nell.'

'Why wasn't the timing right before? You had nothing keeping you here? You could have done it then?'

'You made me realise that you have to take chances and be brave.'

'What if you get there and hate it?'

'Well, that'd be all your fault then – joking!'

'I need to go and have a smoke.'

'You don't smoke.'

'I do now. Excuse me.'

'I'll come too.'

302

'No, I need to process this for a second. Can you tell them to delay the meat course? Back in a tick.'

'Leave your bag.'

'No, I need it.'

'Are you leaving? Is this too much?'

'No, I promise, I'll be ten minutes max.'

'Did I scare you? Am I being too full on?'

'No, honestly, I just need some air.'

She was still putting her feather earrings back in when she reached the table where Tom was sitting, 'Sorry, massive queue,' she explained.

'Where are the drinks?'

Oh shit. 'It's um, table service.'

'You queued all that time and it's table service?'

'I know, nightmare. Okay, so, what were we saying?'

'We were talking about my tour, oh excuse me, could we get two tequilas, and do you want a gin and tonic as well? Okay great, two tequilas, and two gin and tonics, oh and a big portion of cheesy chips, do you want anything else? No? Thanks so much.'

'I have a question,' Nell said. 'Why do you like doing comedy so much?'

'Because I have a narcissistic need to be loved. And everyone loves funny people. Don't raise your eyebrow at me, it's true!'

'Were you always funny?'

'I came out of the womb wearing a fez and a fake moustache.'

'Can you be serious for one minute?'

'Unlikely. But I'll try. Let me see, classic story really, middle sibling of four boys, I'm number three, very loud house, everyone was hilarious, I'm actually the least funny of the bunch. But I never thought that comedy was a career choice, until I met you, and you reminded me that life is short and you need to go all in for things that you love. It had always been something I enjoyed, who wouldn't get off on the thrill of crapping your pants trying to turn hundreds of stony faces into smiling ones, but talking with you about how you'd lived your life, always choosing the path you'd enjoy the most, dodging the things that didn't bring you joy, I decided to just go for it.'

'Does it pay the rent?'

'It does at the moment, who knows after the tour ends? Why do you ask?'

'Well, it's a big responsibility to be the reason someone changes their life.'

'People rarely do things they don't want to do. You're merely the butt-kicker that propels them to do it. Don't take all the credit,' he smiled.

'Phew. So, if it all goes tits up?'

'Totally not on you.'

'I'll drink to that,' she said, picking up the just-delivered shot glass. 'Cheers.' She downed the tequila. 'For the record though, it's not going to. You're really good. And if you want a dream enough, you'll find a way to make it work.'

'What's your dream?'

What was her dream? 'To have a purposeful life.'

'What does that mean? To you?'

'I used to think it meant to be happy all the time, but you can't be. Bad things happen, people leave, people die. So, if you think that to have a purposeful life you need to always be happy, then you'll be disappointed and think you've failed, and then you'll feel shit and feel like your life has no purpose.'

'True. So, what is your purpose?'

'To not feel as though I'm standing still, I guess. I don't mean geographically, although I used to think that's what it meant, but just to always be moving forward, doing something good, useful.'

'I'm really glad you don't want to move geographically.'

'Are you?'

'I am. Because I'm not going anywhere. I can't. Arlo's only four. Realistically I'm not moving anywhere for another fourteen years, and even then, I can't imagine I'll want to ever be more than a few hours from him. Does the idea of staying in one place for that long scare you?'

'What are you asking?'

'I'm asking if you think you might be content staying in one place? Because I like you, Nell. I really like you. But I'm scared of liking you too much because I'm anchored here. And you, historically, don't like being anchored.'

'Excuse me a minute, I just need to make a quick phone call.'

Greg wasn't at the table when she got back to it, but their single lamb chops were, alongside a glass of red wine to accompany it. She took a swig to take away the taste of the tequila and felt her eyes involuntarily cross over a little due to the vast amount of alcohol she'd been consuming. She hastily filled up a water glass and put her lamb chop on Greg's plate.

'You're not going to believe it,' Greg said, moving his napkin from his chair and sitting down. 'I've just bumped into that comedian from the Christmas do in the bathroom! What a small world!'

The blood drained from Nell's face.

'I went down to the basement bathroom as you said the ones up here were out of order, and there he was at the next urinal. It sounded really fun in the bar down there; we should go there for a drink when we finish here. That reminds me, was it him you had round that day when I called from holiday? The old woman you look after was there—'

'Juno. Her name's Juno.'

'Yes, her, and Willa, but how did he end up there too?'

'He drives an Uber,' Nell heard herself say. 'He dropped Willa off to collect Juno.'

'That makes sense. He was quite good though, I remember, but you definitely couldn't make a living from it.' Greg chuckled, 'Probably why he's down in the pub on Valentine's Day and we're up here.'

Nell didn't laugh along with him, and instead looked him straight in the eyes and asked him, 'What's your dream in life, Greg?'

'My what?'

'Your dream. Your reason for getting up in the morning. What are you working towards?'

'I told you; I want to move to Bangkok with you.'

'But why? What drives you?'

'I like having nice things, knowing that I have the means to do what I want. Is that a feather in your ear?'

'Yes. It is a feather.'

'Why have you got a feather in your ear?'

'Because I like it.'

'Where did you get it from? You weren't wearing it earlier? Why is there just one?'

'Doesn't matter, tell me about your dreams.'

'Why are we spoiling the dinner with all this deep soul-searching stuff? This lamb really is incredible.'

'Talking about dreams is not soul-searching, Greg, it's the essence of who we are. If I'm going to consider moving across the world with you, then I need to know that our dreams are aligned.'

'Keep your voice down, people are looking, I think someone's enjoyed the wine pairing a bit too much,' Greg laughed.

'What about after Bangkok? What would you want to do then?'

'Probably move back here, get married and have kids.'

'But I don't know that I want them. Or marriage.'

'Why wouldn't you want that?'

'Why would I?'

'But that's what everyone does.'

'Doesn't mean we have to. Our lives can be whatever we want them to be. We don't need to follow any path at all.'

'But at some point in your life you need to settle down, don't you? You can't live the way you've lived up until now forever.'

'Why not?'

'Because it's not real life, is it?'

'It's my real life.'

'Going from country to country, job to job, forever.'

'I like my job now. I'd be really sad to leave it.'

'You can't honestly tell me that you're happy wiping the arse of an old woman, and that's your ultimate dream?'

'Well firstly, again, her name is Juno, secondly she wipes her own arse, and yes, actually, I am very happy there. For the first time in a long time, I feel like I'm where I should be.'

Greg leaned back in his chair; his arms folded. 'Is that a no then? You don't want to come to Bangkok?'

'I'm not saying that, but you can't just spring this on me and expect me to answer right away.'

'It's not right away, you had a cigarette to think about it.'

'And now I'm going to have another one, excuse me.'

'Aren't you going to take your bag?' Greg said sarcastically.

'Not this time, no.'

'Either I'm really drunk, or you're suddenly much taller,' Tom said.

'I'm wearing heels.'

'Speak up, I can't hear you.'

'I'm wearing high heels!'

'Did you buy them when you were on your phone call? Good multi-tasking.'

'I've got to come clean.' Nell said, sinking into the seat alongside him, suddenly too drunk and feeling too guilty to lie. 'I'm on two dates tonight. One upstairs in a poncy restaurant, and one down here, with you.' She held her breath and winced, expecting him to get angry, or worse, just get up and leave.

Tom leaned his head back against the wall of the booth, closed his eyes and laughed. 'Jesus Nell, you really do make every situation as bizarre as you possibly can, don't you?'

'It wasn't intentional, I promise, it just sort of happened.'

'Which date's better?'

'What?'

'Are you having a better time down here with me or up there with your ex? I assume it's your ex you're on the other date with?'

Nell nodded. 'Aren't you angry?'

He stopped concentrating on the beer mat he'd been fiddling with and looked up at her. 'I'm mildly jealous, but it would explain why you keep disappearing.'

'I didn't mean this to happen. I promise. I was really looking forward to just going out with you tonight, and then Greg turned up at the house with flowers and a dinner reservation and I didn't want to reject him completely, and I thought I could do both, but I can't, especially as someone's been sick in the lift, I'm pretty sure it wasn't me, and I can't run up and down five flights of stairs.'

'Not in those shoes you can't.'

'I'm a terrible person.'

'No, you're not.'

'You hate me.'

'No, I don't.'

'I'd understand if you do.'

'Nell, have you moved into the self-loathing part of drunkenness?'

'A little bit,' she admitted.

'Dance with me.'

'What?'

Tom motioned his head at the dancefloor at the end of the bar in front of the band, where lots of couples were dancing to 'My Baby Just Cares For Me'. 'You might want to take the heels off though.'

Nell kicked the shoes under the table and allowed Tom to lead her barefoot through the tables to the dancefloor, where he spun her round before pulling her in and dipping her back. She squealed and threw her head back laughing as they sashayed round the floor, weaving in between the other couples in an exuberant display of just enjoying being alive.

'What stage of the meal are you at up there?' he asked once the song ended and they returned breathlessly to their table.

'We're about to have dessert.'

'Right, go back up there, have dessert, say thank you for a lovely evening, give him a chaste peck on the cheek – no tongues, you hear me? And then come back down here to finish your evening.'

'Why are you being so nice about this?'

'I'm a nice guy. But even I have boundaries, and being on a double date that I didn't consent to, is sort of a no-go for me, but I'll be here when you get back and we can have another dance. Or, if you feel that after dating both of us for an evening you actually don't like either of us in that way, then bring the poor guy down here and buy us both some shots to take the edge off the misery.'

'Are you going to put this in your show?'

'Haven't decided yet. I mean, it has legs.'

'Back in a minute.'

'You're not wearing any shoes.'

Nell looked down at her bare feet and painted toenails, and agreed with Greg. She did indeed seem to not be wearing any shoes. 'Oops.'

'It's not funny, Nell, this is a really classy restaurant. Why are you so drunk?'

Nell hiccupped and picked up her water glass to try the age-old trick of drinking it backwards, but she managed to spill it down her chin and all over the tablecloth.

'Good God Nell, get a grip.'

'You get a grip,' she retorted childishly.

'I think we'd better go.'

'But we haven't had dessert,' Nell whined. Tom had expressly told her to come up here again, have dessert, say thank you for a lovely evening, get her bag and come back to the bar. After climbing five flights of stairs while the lift was being cleaned, she'd be damned if she wasn't going to be rewarded with something chocolatey.

'If you're going to be sick—'

'I'm not going to be sick.'

'I hate vomit.'

'I know you do.'

Greg motioned to the waiter that they were ready for the bill. 'I'll drop you home.'

'I've had a really lovely evening,' she said. 'Thank you so much, but I'm going to go to the bar downstairs and have a dance.'

'No, you're drunk, I'll take you back to mine to sleep it off.'

'No, I'm staying here. I'm not drunk, I'm tipsy, and I'm in

full control of my body and my decisions, and I want to stay and dance.'

'Fine, we'll go for one drink. But I'm not dancing.'

He was supposed to be going home, he wasn't meant to be coming with her, now he'd see Tom, and they'd meet, they might even shake hands, or worse, fight, and her two worlds would collide, like some massive meteorite implosion.

They stood in the lift lobby as it was apparently now operational again. An older couple stood to the right of Greg, both wearing elegant clothing and, Nell looked down just to double check, location-appropriate footwear, while she was now barefoot, feathers in ears, silk scarf tied like a bandana around her hair, which was wild and sweaty from dancing, holding a handbag the size of a holdall.

Greg looked at Nell's reflection in the mirrored doors of the elevator. 'You know what,' he said, 'I think I'd better just take you home.'

'Greg,' Nell replied levelly, 'I love you. I do. And you've given me lots to think about tonight. But I want to go dancing. And drink a lot more. And eat some cheesy chips.'

'Can we do that?' the older man alongside them jokingly said to his wife. 'I'm starving after that meal.'

'There's a live jazz band in the basement.' Nell leaned forward past Greg to speak to them. 'And they're really good.'

'I love jazz,' the woman said. 'Come on Ted, we haven't seen a live band in years!'

'Go on, Ted,' Nell urged. 'Take your lovely wife dancing.'

The lift arrived and the four of them got in. Nell pressed the button for -1 and looked round at the others in the lift to ascertain their desired floor. She received one excited nod and one thumbs up for the basement, while Greg reached across her and pressed the zero.

CHAPTER TWENTY-NINE

'You seem to have swapped an ex-boyfriend for two pensioners?' Tom said after Nell arrived and introduced him to Ted and Margaret, before the couple headed straight for the dancefloor, waving their hands in the air as they went.

'It seemed like a good exchange.'

'Where did you find them?'

'In the lift. They were heading home and I told them about the band. Why are you smiling?'

'You. You find adventures wherever you go. You found Juno, and a new job, and place to live, on a bus in the rain. Literally on a bus in the rain. You've just convinced two random people to go dancing rather than home to a cup of cocoa and bed. You're astonishing.'

Nell leaned in nearer him so he could hear her over the music. 'What you said earlier, about staying in London. I don't know how I feel about that.'

'What do you mean?'

'I don't know if that is enough for me. I'm worried I'll get bored and break your heart. And Arlo's. And mine.'

'Look, I'm here. I'm not going anywhere. If you choose

me, then you choose this. You choose to have fun on your doorstep.'

'But I don't know if I can do that.'

'You find the sublime in life so well already. You don't need a boarding pass and a typhoid injection to find your purpose.'

He was right. She'd always assumed that adventure meant being far from home, but perhaps it didn't. Maybe this could be enough. She watched Ted and Margaret giggle their way around the dancefloor, clutching onto each other, and wondered what kind of life they'd had? The kind that still made them want to dress up and head out on Valentine's Day to a posh restaurant, and end the evening in a jazz bar being swept along by the moment. If you offered them the chance, right then, of changing this, and told them that they could be on a beach on Zanzibar or a houseboat in Kerala instead, would they take it? Would they heck, because from where Nell was standing, their life looked pretty wonderful.

She nuzzled in closer to Tom. 'Shall we go back to yours?'

'Not tonight, I have Arlo.'

She pulled away slightly, and looked quizzically at him. 'Arlo's at yours, now?'

He nodded. 'Andrea's babysitting, I said I'd be back by midnight, so I'd better make a move, it's quarter to already.'

'If you call her, do you think she'd stay overnight and you can come to mine?'

'I wouldn't leave him overnight, he'd be scared in the morning, and he might wake up in the night.'

'But he likes Andrea.'

'He does, when she's serving him marshmallows on top of his hot chocolate. Not at three in the morning when he's had a nightmare about human-sized pigeons – that was the last bad dream.'

Nell didn't really get why he'd asked her out on this

particular day, knowing that they couldn't end the date in bed. It didn't make any sense.

'Why has your face changed?' Tom asked, putting his finger under her chin and turning her face first one way, then the other. 'Are you cross with me?'

'I just thought that we'd go home together, that's all.'

'We don't need to go home together to agree that this evening has been a monumental success. It's been fun, and deep, and bonkers, but brilliant. I've had a really good time.'

'It would be even better if we carried the party on.'

'Look, I drop him back to Leah's on Monday, let's meet up then for some overnight fun.'

'Sure. I mean, that's three days away, a lot can happen in that time.'

'Nell. This is the way my life is. I thought you understood that.'

'I do understand that.'

'I'm not sure you do. I'm not a complicated man, Nell. Sure my situation is a bit complicated, but not me. I think you have far more to sort out in yourself than I do, and I'm happy to wait for you to do that, but I don't think you're ready to start something real.'

'What the fuck do you know about something real? You're the one going through a divorce, and you're rejecting me.'

'Wow, okay, let's call it a night, shall we? I'll call you in the morning when we're both sober and can talk about this properly. Do you want to share a taxi, I can drop you home?'

Nell shook her head. 'No, you're okay, I'm going to go and hang out with Ted and Margaret.'

After searching for them for some time, Nell eventually found Ted and Margaret in a corner booth where they were reintroducing each other to the insides of their mouths. Nell sighed wistfully; their life did look pretty wonderful.

Two dates. She'd had two dates tonight, but somehow, she'd ended up completely alone at the end of the night.

'Can I buy you a drink?'

Nell looked up from the seat that she'd slumped in at a man smiling at her from the other side of the table. 'My name's Ethan.'

'Hi Ethan. I'm Nell.' She stuck out her hand for him to shake.

'Why is a pretty girl like you all alone on Valentine's Day?'

Somewhere in her alcohol-addled brain she realised that it wasn't the universe's fault at all, it was hers.

She smiled up at the man, he looked nice enough.

'Pleasure to meet you Ethan, but I need to go.'

There was a soft light coming from his bedroom window, so he must still be awake. She typed out a message to him asking him to open the door. A few seconds later she could see a shadow in the other windows as he made his way to the entrance. He opened the door in a T-shirt and boxers.

'What are you doing here, Nell?'

'I didn't want to leave it like that. I behaved really badly tonight.'

'Yeah well, I should have been clearer from the start.'

'Can I come in?'

He opened the door wider. 'Shall I put the kettle on?'

'Can we talk in bed?'

Greg followed her up the stairs, brushing his teeth with his index finger as they walked. Nell stripped off to her underwear, opened up the drawer in his chest that she knew he kept his T-shirts in and pulled one over her head before slipping under his still-warm duvet. She lifted up a corner of it to invite him in too.

'I'm glad you came over,' he said, moving his head closer to her to kiss her.

She moved her head back, and said, 'I realise I'm giving you quite mixed signals right now. I want to talk to you, but I also really, really, wanted to lie down.' She took a deep breath. 'I am not, nor never have been, and I know I never will be, a Michelin restaurant kind of person. Nor am I a business-class kind of woman, nor a five-star resort type either. You are. Even though you grew up going on holidays in caravans like me and all our friends, you were always destined for better things. You brought cutlery in your packed lunch box. And a sachet of salad dressing.'

'Plain lettuce tastes of nothing.'

'My point is, you love all that stuff. I really don't. I feel uncomfortable, out of place and I just don't enjoy it. I don't want you to slum it for me, and I really don't want to spend my life pretending to be something I'm not for you.'

'I get that. I do. But what I can't understand is that you chose to die in a five-star hotel. Not just a standard room in one either. A goddamn suite. You wanted to spend your final days in luxury. So why wouldn't you want to spend your life in it too?'

'Five-star hotels cope with crazy shit all the time, rock star binges, oligarch arms deals, a run-of-the-mill dead body would be simple for them to deal with. And there was something quite depressing about dying at a Travelodge. In a tracksuit.'

Greg stretched out his arm to lie his head on. 'I understand what you're saying, I do. I see the differences between us are much greater than they were twenty years ago, but if we both compromise, we can make this work. I love you, Nell. And tonight, by the lift, you said you loved me – before you tried to convince that old couple to go dancing with you for some unfathomable reason.'

There was so much in that sentence Nell wanted to leap on. 'I will always speak to random people, Greg. And I will always want to go dancing. And I will always love you. But if being in a relationship with you means that I can only talk to strangers half the time, or only go dancing half the time, then that's not the life I want.'

'It's been so long since you had a relationship, you don't understand that compromise is essential. You've been focused on yourself for too long.'

'Quite possibly. But compromise, to me, is making room for somebody else's life in mine, and mine in theirs. It's not about chopping both our lives in half and slotting them together and hoping for the best.'

'Come to Bangkok, let's give it a go.'

'Run away again, you mean?'

'It's not running away, it's embracing adventure. You can't grow and experience all life has to offer stuck in one place. The world is out there Nell, let's grab it.'

'You can have fun on your doorstep too, you know.'

Greg rolled onto his back and looked up at the ceiling. 'I really don't understand you sometimes, Nell. I've finally come round to your way of thinking and now you think something completely different.'

'I don't know what I think anymore. I just know that I want to stay in London for a bit longer. Flying off again feels wrong.'

'Fine. I'll tell them I can't take the job and we stay here.'

'No!' Nell propped herself up on her elbow. 'That's not what I'm saying. I've been round the world, a few times, and it brought me back here. And I want to stay. But your adventure is only just beginning. You need to do this. You need to see where your journey will take you.'

'Why does it feel like we never want the same thing at the same time? You wanted adventure when I wanted security, you want a home and stability right at the time when I want to live a little and experience new places. It doesn't seem fair.'

'It's easier to bear if you believe that the universe gives us what we want when we need it, and that everything happens for a reason.'

'I don't know about that. But then again, maybe a few years

of travel will open my eyes and I'll come back a Buddhist, dripping with crystals and a qualified Reiki master.'

Nell smiled. 'I'd like to see that.'

He paused. 'Do you remember when we met?'

'Of course I do. First term of secondary school.'

'No, the exact moment when we met.'

'Not really, you were just always there.'

'I've loved you since nine a.m., on the eighth of September 1998. The first day of senior school, we were both eleven, and because our surnames both began with G, we were always placed next to each other – our lockers, our seats in class, in exams, lining up for lunch, wherever I was, you were there too. We were both new, we knew no one else, and I was so shy, and you just chatted and laughed with everyone – by the end of the first week you knew every dinner lady's name, every cleaner, every kid in our year and the year above. You made fitting in look so easy, and you took me with you. You carried me through school, building me up, showing me how to talk to people in the easy way you did. I watched everything you did and copied it, and when you loved me back, four years later, I just couldn't believe my luck.'

That wasn't how she remembered it at all. He was enigmatic even at eleven. He exuded a quiet confidence of being able to cope with anything, anyone. Any situation was immediately soothed and any wave of unrest or unease was calmed just by him being there. He'd broken up fights at school just by standing serenely between the two warring parties, he'd been the voice of reason to her indecision, and she hadn't hesitated for even a second when he suggested travelling the world after their A Levels because she knew she'd always be protected. Nell knew, without the tiniest doubt, that if she chose him, she would always be looked after, she would always have a home, she would always be safe.

'I was the lucky one,' Nell said. 'The whole way through school, and travelling, I always felt so able to deal with anything because you were there. I felt so proud to be your best friend, your girlfriend.'

'I'm not ready to let you go.' He wiped a tear from the corner of his eye on the back of his hand.

She reached her hand up and wiped his tear away. Was *she* ready to let him go? One word from her and she could stop this; she could either convince him to stay, or she could go with him. They couldn't walk away from all this history, these feelings. She'd shown him once before how to relax, to enjoy life, to be spontaneous, she could do the same again, and God knows, he had so much to teach her. They could be really happy together.

She held him close and breathed him in. His grooming products may have grown more expensive with time, but his scent was as familiar to her as her own. They'd always been opposites, but that hadn't mattered when they were young, but now they were older, compromise didn't come so easily. *Morocco and Monaco. Jagger and McCartney. Tie-dye and linen.*

'You're not letting me go,' she said gently, suddenly very sure of what she was saying. 'We're giving each other room to do what's right for us, right now. You need to move to Bangkok. You may hate it and end up back here, and that's okay, but you may just love it, and it might ignite something in you that's been missing all these years and you'll wonder why it took you so long. Do you hear me?' She wiped her own tears away. 'And for the record, I didn't carry you through school, we carried each other.'

'I love you, Nell.'

'I love you too. Now turn the light out and be big spoon.' *For what's probably going to be the last time*, Nell silently added.

CHAPTER THIRTY

Nell didn't normally work Saturdays, but William was flying off somewhere early and Nell had promised to take Juno to the library to get all stocked up on the origins of Aboriginal art or the history of the ancient Minoan civilisation ready for the weekend. She'd surprised Nell last week by picking out an erotic thriller, and a book on reptiles, so who knew what would make it to the counter this week. Greg had left his house half an hour or so before Nell, with a hug and a promise to accept the Bangkok job. She'd definitely made the right decision. Nostalgia was no reason to walk a path not meant for them. She absolutely knew that leaving her family again was the wrong thing to do now that she and Polly were close again, and she'd built up a relationship with Bea and her mum, and although Greg would have stayed in London if she'd asked him to, he needed to experience the world, meet new people, find out who he really was now that he wasn't the guy who was going to live forever.

Nell checked the time. She should have time for a quick shower and change back at her flat before Juno would need waking; if anyone deserved an extra half-hour lie in it was

Juno. As Nell rounded the corner of William's road, she halted, stood statue-still on the street in front of a tape cordon, blocking the road. Her breath quickened. Two fire engines were parked midway down the street. Without thinking, she lifted up the tape, ducked underneath, and ran. She knew it was their house before she got there, blindly fighting back the tears as she raced between the stationary fire trucks, desperately looking for William, Willa or Juno. There was no ambulance, but had it gone or was it coming? Nell stopped, and looked up at the house, the first two floors untouched, still pure white, but the roof was idly smoking; the white render around the attic window, Juno's window, was charred black.

Nell's hand flew to her mouth and she felt herself unable to catch her breath. Why was no one saving Juno? Why was there no ladder reaching up there? She frantically looked around her for a firefighter, the police, anyone, to help her save them. It was still early, Juno would still be sleeping. 'Help!' Nell shouted. 'Please, someone, help me!'

'Hey, you okay?'

Nell allowed herself to be led to the back step of the fire truck by a female firefighter. Nell gasped, 'Is anyone inside? The old lady?'

'They're safe, and at hospital, I think they were taken to the Royal Free.'

Nell's phone started ringing. Willa. Nell thanked the firefighter and hungrily answered the call, walking quickly away from the house towards the main road where she could flag down a taxi.

'Are you all okay?'

'We're alright. It was a bit of a shock, but it's okay.'

'And Juno?'

'She's drifting in and out of consciousness; she's hooked

up to all these machines, they're monitoring her heart and breathing, but she's alive.'

'Oh my God, it must have been so scary.'

'I'll tell you everything when you get here, but can you stop by an M&S and pick up some underwear for Juno, she likes the—'

'I know which ones, what about PJs and a cardigan or dressing gown?'

'Yes, good, and some clothes for when we get let out.'

'What do you need?'

'A change of clothes would be good. Mine smell like a barbecue.'

'For William too?'

'No, he left really early and is currently on a flight to Belfast to film on location, I've left messages so he'll hopefully be able to get a plane straight back.'

'I'll go to the shops now, and come straight over.'

The terror of fearing the worst had been replaced by a relief that almost made her feel numb. Were these the emotions she'd put her mum through on her journey back to England before Jenny knew that she was still alive? As Nell half-walked, half-ran towards the taxi rank, willing there to be a cab waiting, she dialled her mum's number. Jenny answered after just a couple of rings. Nell didn't even wait for her to say hello before all her words came tumbling out. 'Mum? It's me, Nell. I love you so much. I just wanted to tell you that, because I know I don't tell you enough. But I do. And I'm so sorry, for making you think I was dead, for not coming back more, for making you worry when I hadn't called for weeks on end, all those times when I didn't answer your emails, or texts, and you must have thought that something awful had happened to me, and then I just resurfaced with no explanation, no consideration for the panic you must have felt, and I'm so, so sorry, I really am.'

'Nell, slow down, what's happened?'

'I just wanted to tell you that, I know you know, but sometimes you just need to tell people how you feel, don't you, because they can forget. And you might think that they know, but if you don't say it how can you?'

'Nell darling, what's happened?'

'It's all okay now, but there was a fire, and Juno's in hospital, she's fine, I'm on my way there now. But for a moment this morning I panicked, and suddenly realised what I've put you through, for years. And I'm really sorry.'

'She's safe. And you're safe. And that's all that matters.'

'I love you, Mum.'

'I love you, Nell. Let me know if you need my help in any way. I'm only a short train ride away.' After Nell ended the call she replayed her mum's words. *Only a short train ride away.* For years her mum had been in different hemispheres, conflicting time zones, the possibility of her being of any assistance in any situation was never an option, so Nell had never even considered it. But now she could, and would. And Nell knew that with just one call Polly would be there too. The thought made her smile, and she felt her shoulders drop, and with that, a taxi with its For Hire light on pulled up alongside her.

Nell's shopping basket looked like that of someone with a split personality: vibrant patterns versus silky monochrome. Whatever she picked up for Juno, she chose the opposite for Willa, and as she didn't know if any of her own belongings had escaped unscathed, a few items that sat comfortably in the middle of the two on the spectrum for her so she could finally change out of last night's jumpsuit. She piled snacks on top of the clothes, and some toiletries too, and picked up a range of special interest magazines for Juno's eclectic reading tastes, including ones on model railways, superyachts and a

National Geographic. Using her new bank card gave her a frisson of excitement; she hadn't had a UK bank account in years, as she hadn't had a fixed address before. The frisson of excitement was rapidly replaced by a frisson of fear as she realised that she might not have a fixed address any longer.

Willa greeted her with a hug when Nell put her head around the curtain drawn around Juno's bed.

'How is she?' Nell whispered, nodding at Juno, who seemed to have shrunk against the hospital pillow, wearing a pale blue regulation gown that drained her of all colour.

'Sleeping.'

'I passed a coffee shop on my way in.' Nell put her arm around Willa. 'Come on, I'll get us a couple of cappuccinos, you look done in.'

Once they were settled with their coffees, Willa explained how Juno had woken up early and was cold, and tried to light the fireplace in her bedroom, which had been blocked up years ago. 'Apparently she had a fireplace in her childhood bedroom that was always lit in the mornings, and she thought she was back there.' Willa ran her hand through her unbrushed hair. 'I knew nothing about it until the smoke alarm on the landing went off, and ran upstairs and got her out, but the fire had already spread to the curtains and bedding, and by the time we'd got outside, because her rooms were in the loft conversion, the roof had caught. I have no idea how bad it is, flames were still coming out when we left in the ambulance.'

'They've put it out now, but it's still smoking a bit.'

Willa put her head in her hands. 'Oh Jesus.'

'Where are you going to stay?'

Willa shook her head. 'I have no idea. We'll have to go into a hotel for a few weeks until we get it sorted. But the most worrying thing is Juno, I don't know what we can do with her, she can't be in a hotel room by herself, nor would she want to be, but we can't lock her in, and if she went wandering in the night then she could be in real danger.'

'One step at a time, let's see how she is today and tomorrow, and then we can start making a plan after that. I can share a room with her and make sure she doesn't get up to any mischief.' Nell paused, a small smile playing on her lips. 'Or at least none that we haven't planned for.'

'William's going to say that she should go into a home, I know he will, but she would hate that so much, and I couldn't bear to think of her all by herself waiting for death.'

The thought of Juno sitting in an armchair in the corner of a nursing home lounge was enough to make tears spring into Nell's eyes. 'It will all work out.'

'She was so lucky to have met you,' Willa said. 'We all are.'

'I'm the lucky one; not only did she pay my bus fare that day and get me out of the rain, but you've given me a home, a job and put me back on my feet. I literally had no clue what I was going to do with my life until I met Juno, and then it all fell into place.'

'Because you were open to it. You have to take some of the credit,' Willa smiled. 'I love Juno, but I'm not sure I would have sat next to her on the bus if I didn't know her. And knowing her the way I do now, my life would be the poorer for it. When William introduced me to her for the first time, he gave me this long speech on the way over to her house, she lived in the heart of Chelsea then, about how wacky she was, and "out there" and unconventional, and I was so intimidated by her.' Willa laughed, remembering the hallway filled with taxidermy and hanging Geisha parasols, giving way to a living room of books and film posters, and a record player spinning round with an obscure French singer warbling out on it. 'She made us a jug of Pimm's, at eleven o'clock in the morning, and I remember looking from her to William, and wondering how a man so sensible and, well, normal, had emerged from this woman!' Willa picked up the sugar sachets absent-mindedly. 'We'd go over to hers every couple of weeks for lunch, and it was always a riot, there'd be a motley crew of people, artists, poets, gardeners, the girl from the local Co-op, anyone basically, who had an interesting face or story. She collected people like other people collect coins or postcards. Some days she'd have cooked for hours, the table laden with far too much food for us all to eat; other times, she'd have forgotten that inviting people for lunch should normally contain some lunch, and she'd open a tin of biscuits or call her favourite restaurant to drop some meals round. You never knew what you were going to get with her, and that's what makes her magical to be around.'

'You really love her.'

'I do. But it's taken a while to. And I feel so guilty for that now, but she's not an easy person to be around sometimes. Not only does she make me feel incredibly boring alongside her, worrying about her also occupies a large part of my day. It's probably for the best that we never had children, because we've certainly got our hands full with the one that we've got now,' Willa said. 'I've often wondered how different my life would have been if William had a—' she put her fingers up to make speech marks '—"normal mother". One that never needed to live with us, one that came over at Christmases and Easter and the odd Sunday for lunch. It would certainly be easier. But nowhere near as fun.'

'You would still have a roof,' Nell joked.

Willa laughed. 'I would still have a roof. But you know what as well? It's made me fall in love with William more too. Because I've seen how gentle he can be, how patient. I'd never have seen that side of him if it hadn't been for Juno.'

The image of Tom kneeling down to unzip Arlo's coat came

326

into Nell's mind. The way he ruffled the little boy's hair and helped push his chair in. The easy way he called him 'bud', the way he knew how important Monkey was.

'I'm happy to stay here for the rest of the day if you need to go to the theatre soon?'

Willa shook her head. 'I called the director; my understudy is taking over for a few days. I normally try to catch a cold or something a few times during the run to give my understudy their chance in the spotlight. This is a little more drastic than the sniffles, but she'll be delighted. I once did a two-year run on *Les Mis* as the understudy for Fantine and the bitch never called in sick once.' Willa slapped the table with both hands. 'Right, best get back to the ward, she might have woken up and not know where she is.'

'Do you want me to sit with Juno for a while so you can go and sort things out?'

Willa shook her head. 'No, I don't want to leave her. I can book a couple of hotel rooms from my phone. I think you should be able to still use your flat though, as it's in the basement, but I'm waiting for the fire chief to give the all clear. If you don't mind, could you go back to the house and see what's going on? If you're allowed in, can you get the green folder from the kitchen drawer and bring it in? All our insurance documents are in there, and some numbers I need.'

'No worries. I'll call you as soon as I've got an update.'

'You're an angel.' The two women hugged again. 'I mean it,' Willa said. 'We're very lucky to have you in our lives. I don't know where you came from, or who or what sent you our way, but I'm very glad they did.'

Nell had kept her tears pushed back firmly behind the dam just behind her retinas the whole tube ride and walk to the canal, right up until she was sitting in the stern of the boat on Andrea's bed – the café being far too busy – and then she started crying and just couldn't stop. She really didn't want to disturb the customers – who were currently listening to a talk on wildlife photography – with the loud wailing she desperately wanted to do, so instead she just sobbed silently into her drawn-up knees. Andrea had shuffled Nell into her room after she'd greeted her at the door with a big smile and one wasn't returned, knowing immediately that something terrible had happened.

'Hey.' Tom bent his head to come into the cabin. 'Andrea came and got me, what's wrong?' He sat down on the bed alongside her and Nell just turned and buried her face in his jumper. He didn't say any more, just rhythmically stroked her hair until her sobs subsided.

'Juno's in hospital, she set the house on fire.'

'Oh my God.'

'She's okay, or they think she will be, but she's getting really ill Tom, and I don't know what's going to happen to her.'

'She's okay, that's all that matters. Is the house still standing?'

'I don't know, Willa thinks it's just the top floor and the roof, but I'm heading there to find out.'

'I'll come with you.'

'You have Arlo.'

'He's at school until three, it's only one. Come on you, dry your eyes.' He wrapped Nell in a big bear hug, 'It'll all be alright.'

It wasn't alright. The entire top floor of the house, Juno's sanctuary, her treasure trove, her Aladdin's Cave, was completely decimated. It didn't help that almost all her collectibles, carefully curated from a lifetime of magpie-like magnetism to the sublime, were one hundred percent flammable. 'She is never going to get over this,' Nell said sadly, looking round the charred remains of Juno's life. 'There's nothing left. Nothing at all.'

'It's just stuff,' Tom said. 'The most important thing is that she got out.'

'It's not just stuff to Juno, especially not now her memories are fading; they're her link to her past, of who she was and what she did. In here she wasn't an old woman, she was an explorer, a daredevil, someone who was fiercely loved and desired. Honestly, I wish you could have seen it, then you'd understand. Every inch was covered with moments from her life, it was so her.' Nell put her hand up to her mouth. 'I can't believe it.'

Nell stepped gingerly towards the door on the least blackened floorboards, seeing something catch the light under the charred sofa. She bent down and gasped as she retrieved Juno's tiara, stained black from the soot, but definitely salvageable with some washing up liquid and determination. Nell smiled as she turned it delicately over in her hands. *Juno will shine again.*

'Come on, let's check the rest of the house.'

The first floor had escaped much damage, save for the acrid smell of smoke and some black marks along the wall where Willa had carried Juno down away from the flames. The fire chief said that she was safe to move back into the basement right away but advised against Willa and William returning until the roof was shored up. The top floor was completely uninhabitable.

Nell packed a few more things of Willa's and William's into one of his sports bags and grabbed the green emergency folder from the kitchen. 'I just need to pop down to my flat and grab a change of clothes.' As soon as she said that, her heart plummeted. She didn't want to draw attention to the fact she was still wearing last night's clothes, but thankfully Tom didn't seem to have picked up on that as he followed her down the stairs from the kitchen.

'Make yourself at home for a couple of minutes,' she called out, 'I'm just going to grab a quick shower.'

Ten minutes later, dressed in an outfit that was much more appropriate for daylight hours, Nell walked into the living room.

'Nice flowers,' Tom said, gesturing towards the lavish bouquet Greg had bought her, which were in a vase on the table. 'Very expensive.'

'I guess.'

'Ready?'

As Nell locked the front door of her flat, she noticed a note stuck to it, which Tom peeled off carefully so as not to ruin the paint of the door.

Nell, I guess your date was a hit then as you didn't come home. We're in hospital, there was a fire upstairs, don't go in house. Call me, Willa x

Tom thrust the note at her. 'I wonder which date was she referring to? Oh no, don't answer that, because I was tucked up in bed with a four-year-old by half twelve, so it wasn't the one with me.'

'Tom I—'

'This is what I meant last night Nell, you have so much more stuff that you need to deal with than I do. You're still living like you're running out of time, that you need to keep cramming experiences and lovers in, because you haven't got long, but you never know, Nell, you might live to be Juno's age, and if you don't start living differently you really might die all alone in a hotel room. Or you could choose to step off, and stay put, and actually let someone love you.'

'It's not what—'

'I need to get Arlo, give Juno my best.'

CHAPTER THIRTY-ONE

'What's she wearing that for?' said Nell in horror, seeing Juno lie lifeless below an oxygen mask.

'Her breathing started getting bad about an hour ago,' Willa explained. 'They've put her on a drip too.'

'Is that normal? What have they said?'

'It's the smoke inhalation, it can take some time to show up, but yes, it's a sign she breathed in too much smoke.'

'But she's going to be okay?'

'They don't know. We just have to wait. What did they say about the house?'

'It's not as bad as they thought, but Juno's flat is completely ruined.'

'Sshh, she might hear you.'

Both women looked over at Juno, who showed no sign of hearing, or thinking, or anything. 'I found her tiara,' Nell said, 'it needs a clean, but I'll bring it in tomorrow.'

'She won't need it in hospital.'

'Willa, she wore it on the bus to go to the library. Of course she'll need it in hospital.'

'So she did,' conceded Willa with a small smile. 'Oh Nell, I want her to wake up so much.'

Nell put down the heavy holdall she was carrying and sank into the plastic chair next to Willa at the side of the bed. Willa took her hand in hers and they both stared at the woman they loved, teetering on the brink between two worlds.

William rushed into the ward an hour or so later. Having picked up Willa's messages the minute he landed in Northern Ireland, he'd immediately hopped on a return flight back. Nell slipped away as the husband and wife hugged and cried, pausing for a second to kiss Juno's head before she left, but she didn't stir.

Nell sat on the wall outside next to the people in hospital gowns having cigarettes. This. This was why she didn't stay in one place for too long. This crushing fear of losing someone she loved. Even if she'd received a call when she was abroad to say her mum was desperately ill, she wouldn't have felt this boulder pressing down on her chest; she'd have been worried and sad, but the depth of feelings she now had for Juno, for Tom, for Greg, for her Mum and Polly and Bea, these were new, and she hated it. She also hated that Tom was right. She'd tried protesting that he wasn't, that he'd completely misunderstood her, but he hadn't. He'd seen through everything and read her correctly. She *was* still living against an egg-timer. With every grain of sand that slipped through was a lost opportunity to do something special. *Being here is special*. She thought about what Willa said earlier, how she'd signed up to a life with William, not knowing that his mother would come along for the ride too, and yet look at the ride it had been. Tom was offering the same proposition: happiness with a catch. But was it a catch or a bonus? Nell watched people enter and leave the hospital; the majority were old, walking with sticks, with frames, but hardly any were alone. How many of them had lived a life of no regrets, she wondered, and if they had them, were the regrets for things they'd done, or chances they hadn't taken?

She'd made her peace with dying, but not really with living. She was still standing on the periphery of so many relationships in her life, dipping her toe in, but never fully committing. She had a half-sister and stepmother she'd never met, a niece she'd only met once. A mum and sister who she knew would welcome her into their fray, if she showed that's what she wanted, a dad who she'd seen once in a decade; and then there was Tom, who was offering her a real chance at love and happiness, but she kept pushing him away every chance she got. When you talked about regrets, that was quite a rollcall.

Nell spent the whole of Sunday keeping a vigil next to Juno, taking turns with William and Willa, holding Juno's hand, chatting nonsense, wetting her lips with her finger and feeling a burst of happiness in the moments when Juno would wake and smile at her. On her way into the hospital on Monday morning, Nell bought Willa and William a coffee and pastry each at the café before going into the ward. She told the elderly woman in the queue behind her that she loved her hat, which made the lady beam, and she tipped the barista a pound. She was going to put things right with her own family, starting today.

Juno was sleeping when Nell entered the ward. Her oxygen levels were still concerning, but the doctors had said that as long as her heart stayed strong, then they were cautiously optimistic. Nell chose not to hear the adverb before optimistic and just clung on to that one.

'If it's okay with you both, I'd like to go and see my family for a day or so, I feel like I'm in the way a bit here, and I'd just like to go and be with them for a night if that's okay?'

'You're not in the way at all,' William said, 'but of course, go and be with your family.'

'We'll call you if there's any change at all,' Willa added, standing up to give Nell a hug.

'Please, good or bad, I'll come straight back.'

'Go, go and be with the people you love.'

Nell waited until she was on the train to call her mum to tell her she was on her way. Part of her hoped that by leaving it so late no one would answer, and she could say that at least she'd tried, but her mum answered on the third ring. 'That's a wonderful surprise,' she said, 'I'll start on a bolognese for dinner, I've got some mince in the freezer I could thaw.'

'We could go out for dinner?' Nell suggested.

'On a Monday?'

'Could do?'

'Where would we go?'

'Somewhere local, or into Brighton?'

'Brighton!'

Brighton was three kilometres away, seven minutes' drive on a good day, eleven on a bad one, yet to hear the incredulity in Jenny's voice, you'd have thought Nell had suggested chartering a catamaran and seeing where the wind took them. Nell suddenly had an urge to charter a catamaran and see where the wind took her, but squashed it down.

'Let me call a few places and see if they have space.'

'They're bound to,' her mum said. 'It's a Monday.'

'Can Polly and Bea come too?'

'What time will you be down? Bea goes to bed at eight.'

Nell had completely forgotten, or maybe she never knew, that young children had early bedtimes, much like she hadn't considered that Arlo went to school. There was a vast segment of the population that she knew nothing about. 'I'm getting into Hove at five, so let's eat at six? I'll walk up to yours from the station and we can go from there? What about Ray? Will he want to come?'

Her mum hesitated. 'Ray moved out shortly after Polly and Bea moved in.'

'Oh?'

'It was a mutual decision.'

The next number Nell dialled she didn't know by heart and had to look up.

'Dad? It's me, Nell.'

'Nell! What's wrong?'

'Nothing's wrong, I just wondered if you wanted to have dinner tonight? With Katie and. . .' Oh God, she'd completely forgotten her half-sister's name. *What is it, what is it, come on Nell.* 'Ruby!' she added triumphantly.

'Dinner?'

'Yes.'

'Tonight?'

'Yes,' said Nell impatiently.

'On a Monday?'

'Yes! On a Monday.'

'With all of us?'

'Yes. I know Ruby will have an early bedtime.' Nell was proud of relaying evidence of this new knowledge, 'So, I was thinking of booking somewhere in Brighton for around six?'

'I think Katie's defrosted some mince for tonight.'

'Can it keep?'

'I don't know, hang on, let me go and check.'

Nell heard him pad across his hallway. She'd never been to his new house, but by the length of time it took for his footsteps to stop, it sounded palatial in comparison to her mum's house. She couldn't pick up on the exchange between her dad and Katie but she could imagine its content.

A minute or so later he was back. 'She says we can have the mince tomorrow.'

'That'll be something to look forward to.' Nell bit her bottom lip; she didn't mean that to sound so sarcastic. *Nurture relationships.* 'I'll message you the name of the restaurant once I've found one that has space.'

'Shouldn't be too hard on a Monday,' said Tony.

As much as Nell wanted to prove both her parents wrong, it was remarkably easy to secure a table for seven people at the first place she called. Not wanting to plump immediately for somewhere so evidently undesirable, she called three other restaurants and all of them had space. Damn the British aversion to weekday dining.

Nell's cold feet started to set in around twenty minutes from Hove. She shouldn't be waltzing back into everyone's lives and fiddling about with everything like this. Her mum wouldn't want to sit at the same table as the woman who stole her husband, let alone the husband who willingly got stolen. Polly would probably take one look at the cosy set-up and walk straight back out. The two girls would be hungry and tired and would much prefer to be sitting in front of *Peppa Pig* than being the only diners at a fancy seafront hotel. And Katie, well Nell hadn't given Katie's point of view much consideration at all since her name first got mentioned eight years ago, but Nell imagined she'd feel pretty blindsided too.

Greg would know what to do. He'd be able to tell her if she should cancel the whole thing and go and eat some thawed mince. It didn't seem like only two days ago that she'd woken up at his. So much had happened in the space of forty-eight hours it felt like a fortnight since he'd put down a cup of coffee next to the bed, and asked her if she was absolutely sure he should go to Thailand alone. Before she knew about

Juno, and ruined things with Tom, she was so sure that letting Greg go was the right thing. Now she wasn't so certain. What would he say to her now, if he was sitting right opposite her on the train? *Be honest.* Suddenly Tom popped up alongside him: *Be you.*

'I've invited Dad and Katie and their little girl to dinner as well,' Nell blurted out when her sister opened their mum's front door.

'Hi Polly, how are you? You look well,' her sister replied sarcastically.

Nell stepped inside and wiped her feet on the mat. 'Hi Polly, how are you? You look well. Do you think that's a massive mistake?'

'No, not at all. I see them most days at school drop-off and pick-up. Ruby's in the year below Bea.'

'You know them?'

'Hove's a small place, Nell.'

'Do you think Mum will mind?'

'Do you think Mum will mind about what? Hello love,' Jenny greeted Nell with a kiss.

'Nell's invited Dad and Katie to dinner as well.'

'That'll be nice, I need to give her back the pie dish she left here.'

'We've got Ruby's wellies in your boot as well, remember,' Polly said.

'Oh yes, hang on, I'll get a bag for life and put them in there. Did you give your dad back his binoculars or are they still somewhere about?'

'Yes, Bea and I dropped them round a couple of Sundays back.'

Nell's neck hurt from yo-yoing between the two of them. It was like she'd entered a parallel universe where nothing made sense anymore. 'Hang on, hang on, you know them?'

337

'Who?'

'Dad, and Katie.'

'Of course I know your dad, I was married to him for thirty years.'

'But you know them as a. . . couple?' Nell couldn't help the taste of vomit rising up in her throat at that phrase. But looking at her mother and sister, she was clearly the only one who felt that.

'We live less than a mile away from them, Nell; if we won the postcode lottery, we'd have to split the prize with them.'

'But aren't you angry with them?'

'What for?'

'For splitting the family up!'

'That was years ago, Nell. And they didn't split the family up, you were already abroad and Polly had already moved in with Damian.'

'But he's replaced you with her.'

'No, he hasn't. He left me for her, he didn't replace me.'

'I just don't know how he thought he'd have more in common with someone he'd known for five minutes compared to someone he'd known for thirty years?' As Nell said those words aloud, she realised that she knew only too well that longevity wasn't a strong enough glue.

'Katie's actually quite sweet,' Polly said. 'Give her a chance Nell, you might like her.'

'I invited her for dinner, didn't I?'

'She's really scared of you.'

Nell turned to face her sister. 'Scared of me?'

'Well, she's never met you, has she? You're quite intimidating on paper. Mystical daughter who travels the world and boycotts their wedding.'

'I wouldn't say I boycotted it. I was busy.'

'Aunty Nell!' Bea threw herself down the stairs and into Nell's arms. 'Can you sit next to me at the restaurant?'

'Of course I can! I bought you and Ruby each a sticker book we could do together.'

'Did you?' Polly asked, surprised.

'Yes, I googled how to keep young children amused at restaurants, and sticker books came out top, so I bought two.' Nell had actually bought three, but Arlo's was still in the carrier bag in her flat. She had no idea if it would ever reach him now.

'That's really thoughtful of you.'

'Ruby's got a new rabbit,' Bea said excitedly on the short drive to Brighton. 'Do you think she'll bring it?'

'Probably not,' Polly said, her eyes focused on the road. 'It would poo everywhere in the restaurant.' Bea howled with laughter at the word poo which gave Nell an idea.

'Bea, did you know that koalas eat their mum's poo?' This was met with riotous applause from her back-seat mate, and shaking heads of disgust from the front seats. 'What? It's a fact. And Chinese soft-shell sea turtles pee out of their mouths.'

'You're so funny Aunty Nell.'

'Friggin' hilarious,' said Polly, gripping the steering wheel harder.

'Oh, what a lovely surprise,' Katie said on seeing Jenny, Polly and Bea. 'If I'd have known you were coming I'd have brought back the bicycle pump. Hello, you must be Nell, I'm Katie.'

'Hi Katie.' Mindful of what her mum and Polly had just said, Nell went straight in for a hug, which caught Katie by surprise as she'd already stretched out her hand, which was then flattened against Nell's left breast. It wasn't the most elegant of introductions, but it was very Nell.

'Dad, hi.' They hugged too, but Nell could sense her father wasn't that comfortable with it, his body stiff and demeanour a bit prickly.

'You must be Ruby,' Nell said, bending down to the little girl's height. 'My name's Nell. I've brought you a sticker book.'

'Tell Ruby about the koalas!' Bea shouted. 'Ruby! Aunty Nell has loads of facts about poo and wee.'

Nell made an embarrassed grimace at her dad and Katie, it wasn't the first impression she was hoping for, but it was the hand that she'd been dealt.

'Are you my aunty too?' Ruby asked shyly.

'No, I'm your sister. You're Bea's aunty.'

The other adults all coughed then, flustered. 'They're cousins really,' Tony said.

Nell looked confused. 'No they're not, she's her aunty.'

Ruby looked utterly confused with this revelation, 'I'm Bea's aunty? But I'm in Year One and she's in Year Two.'

'Yep.'

'I told you this dinner was a bad idea,' Tony muttered to Katie. 'Come on, we should go.'

'Hey wait, I don't know what I've said wrong,' Nell said.

'She didn't know, Tony,' Jenny said in Nell's defence.

'Didn't know what?'

Polly whispered, 'Dad thought that Ruby might get teased if people knew that Bea was her niece.'

Nell just stopped the words *well, he should have thought about that before he made a baby at the age of fifty-eight with a thirty-five-year-old*, from tumbling out of her mouth.

'We were planning on telling her eventually,' said Katie. 'Shall we sit down? Gosh, we were lucky to get a table, weren't we? We should eat out in the week more often.'

Maybe Katie wasn't all bad.

Nell checked her phone. There was a message from Willa saying that there was no change, which wasn't necessarily a bad thing.

Throughout the meal, Nell watched her sister being a parent: moving a glass away from the edge of the table, catching a fork before it hit the ground, cutting up Bea's food, all without breaking away from the conversation the adults were having. A mirror image of events was happening on the other side of the table where Katie was doing the same for Ruby. How did they learn that, Nell wondered. How did they know that the glass would have otherwise fallen? Or that the cutlery was about to plummet? Or that the sausage was windpipe-sized?

'So, Nell, how long are you back for this time?' Katie asked. 'And where's next on the list?'

'There isn't a list anymore, I'm staying in London for the moment.' Nell didn't know why she added *for the moment*; force of habit, she guessed.

Polly leaned forward and shouted up the table to Tony. 'She's got back with Greg, Dad, do you remember Greg?'

'Of course I remember Greg. Great lad.'

'Actually, no, I haven't. He's got a job in Bangkok.'

'Why aren't you going with him?' Polly asked. 'That sounds right up your street.'

'I don't want to. I want to stay around. . .' *For the moment.*

'Life's short Nell, you need to grab it,' Tony said, choosing that moment to put his arm around Katie. Out of the corner of her eye, Nell saw her mum stiffen slightly. For all the pie dishes, and kids' wellies, and binoculars, and bicycle pumps being passed back and forth between the two houses, it clearly still stung. Katie shrugged his arm off her shoulder, reading the situation the same as Nell had.

'Speaking of which,' Katie said, 'when you really thought

you were going to, you know, not be around for long, can you honestly say that you did everything you wanted to?'

Nell shrugged. 'More or less. There was a certain freedom in knowing that things weren't going to kill me until a particular date. I might never have done half the things I did, like bungee jumping, caving, climbing, all sorts of things, if I thought it might not work out.'

'I know what you mean, I really regret never paragliding before I had Ruby,' Katie admitted. 'I wouldn't now, you know, just in case, but if I knew that I wasn't going to die for another thirty years or so, I would.'

'Do you know what I'd do? Apart from try some sushi?' Jenny said, with a new level of enthusiasm. 'I've always wanted to see the view from my roof. We're only three streets back from the sea, I bet it's beautiful up there.'

'Oh, that's a good one,' Polly agreed. 'I've often thought about putting fairy lights on my roof at Christmas time, but have been too scared to get up there. If I thought nothing bad would happen then I'd go the whole hog and perch a reindeer up there too.'

'Dad? What would you do, if you knew it was completely safe?' Nell asked, keen to edge her dad into the conversation.

He sniffed. 'I don't think I'd do anything different. I do what I want anyway.'

Nell and Polly's heads snapped towards each other in wide-eyed surprise at their dad's answer. Tony seemed oblivious to the table's reaction and just reached over and helped himself to another handful of French fries.

'Katie,' Nell said brightly, changing the conversation as swiftly as she could, 'are you still working as a paralegal?'

Katie looked at Tony before answering, which Nell thought odd. 'No, I gave it up when I had Ruby. I've been thinking of doing a law conversion course and getting back into it, but—'

'But there's not enough hours in the day, is there love?' Tony finished for her. 'And it's not as though we need the money.'

'That sounds really interesting, Katie. Is there a course you have your eye on?'

Once again Katie eyed Tony carefully before answering Nell. 'Not really, it was just an idea. I probably won't do it.'

'You should!' Nell said. 'What a great thing for Ruby to see too. Honestly, I always found Mum such an inspiration the way that she juggled two jobs growing up when things were a bit hard, don't you think Polly?'

Polly narrowed her eyes at Nell. It was clear that she knew what Nell was doing, but hadn't yet made up her mind whether she wanted to be part of it or not.

'What type of law would you want to specialise in?' Nell continued. 'It was conveyancing you were in before, wasn't it?'

'Yes, but I'd quite like to get into family law.'

'Can you get a move on,' Polly laughed, 'and you could represent me when I divorce Damian.'

'You're not going through with that, are you?' Tony said. 'It was only a mistake.'

'A mistake I won't let him make again.'

'I think that sounds great, Katie, go for it,' Jenny said. 'I'm sure that if I'd had a female solicitor representing me when Tony and I got divorced, I'd have got a much fairer deal.'

The table went silent. There was no malice in her mum's words at all, just good-natured Merlot-fuelled honesty. Nell actually thought that Jenny had forgotten that Tony was even sitting at the table.

Nell looked around the table; this evening was heading for disaster. She had to pull it back from the brink. She searched her mind for a sure-fire conversation changer. 'Did anyone know that sea cucumbers breathe through their bottoms?' She recognised after she'd said it and clocked Polly giving her a slow shake of the head in disapproval, that she might have been hanging out with pre-schoolers a little too much. Bea and Ruby, however, thought she was by far the best adult they'd ever met.

Tom and Arlo would have fitted right in tonight, she thought as Polly drove them back to Jenny's after the meal. She'd started doing this, placing Tom in various situations, working out what he'd say, how he'd fare. She hadn't conjured one up yet that he'd flounder in.

'So, what do you think of Katie?' Polly asked, looking at Nell in the rear-view mirror.

'I thought she was nice actually. She clearly regrets getting with Dad, who gets more obnoxious with age.'

'Why would you say that?' Jenny said, swivelling round in her seat.

'Which part? The fact that she regrets falling for her millionaire client, or the fact that Dad's a massive T-W-A-T.'

'I can spell you know,' said Bea.

'He's not a that thing,' Jenny said. 'He's just a bit stuck in his ways.'

'He's selfish, sexist and you're well shot of him, Mum.'

'Can we remember who we have in the car?' Polly warned, in a singsong voice.

Bea leaned out of her car seat towards Nell. 'She means me.'

'Gotcha.'

'Is Ruby really my aunty?'

'Oh look,' said Nell, pointing out of the window. 'A bird. Did you know that birds poop on red cars the most out of every colour? True story.'

'For Christ's sake, Nell,' Polly groaned from the front seat.

'Sshh, I'm bonding with my niece.'

CHAPTER THIRTY-TWO

Nell kept her phone turned on beside her all night as she slept on her mum's sofa. Polly had offered to sleep in with Bea, but Nell's ability to sleep anywhere meant a two-seater sofa was as good as an orthopaedic mattress. She woke to a beep around 7 a.m. It was Willa. With hands trembling, Nell opened the message.

She's out of the woods. Oxygen levels up, BP normal. She's awake and talking. She said to choose the funny dad, whatever that means.

Nell flung her head back and closed her eyes, grinning a massive grin. She didn't think she'd ever felt such terror followed by such relief. Her first instinct was to message Tom and she didn't even try to fight it.

Hey, have just heard from Willa, Juno is ok! Hope all good with you, Nx

He replied immediately with just:

Great news!

She stayed online for a few minutes more, just in case there was a more effusive postscript coming, but no, that was it.

After promising Jenny she'd visit again soon, and also host

them all back in London once the house got fixed, she walked with Polly to drop Bea off at school before getting the train back.

'So did last night live up to your expectations?' Polly asked as they walked a couple of metres behind Bea.

'I don't know what I was expecting really.'

'Don't lie. You expected Katie to be a prize bitch, so you could legitimately carry on hating her and blaming her for everything.'

'How come you're allowed to swear around Bea?'

'She can't hear me. Am I close though?'

'Maybe. I don't know, it's tricky putting the piece of the puzzle together when you're thousands of miles away. All I knew is that some woman my age had flashed her bits around and Dad being Dad was off without a second thought.'

'And now? Is that what you still think?'

'Yes about Dad, but actually I think Katie really liked him. Loved him. We don't know what lines he fed her, do we?'

'Does he have to have fed her any lines? Can't he just have met someone he had more in common with? That he loved more than he did Mum? And it's not as though we were Bea's age, and him choosing another woman left us fatherless, is it? We were adults.'

This reminded her of what Tom said about Leah the first time he spoke about their break-up. *We were in love, then we weren't.* People change, sometimes marriages aren't meant to weather storms. 'Are you saying that I've basically made up a version of the story that didn't happen?'

'Perhaps. But maybe you just interpreted the situation the way that you wanted to see it at the time. I'm not saying that's wrong, on paper it could read the way that you imagined it, but nothing is black and white, is it? There are a million shades of grey in everything.'

346

'He did treat Mum really badly though. He basically left her with nothing.'

'That's not Katie's fault though, she had nothing to do with the legal side of it all. And he let Mum keep the house.'

'Whoop de whoop. He lives in a flipping mansion.'

'It's not a mansion. It's an executive five-bed on the golf course.'

'Does the footprint of Mum's house fit into his entrance lobby?'

'Maybe.'

'Does she still do odd jobs to get by?'

'Yes.'

'Did you see Katie's handbag?'

'Yes.'

'Join the dots, Polly, and catch up to where I'm going with this.'

'I get it, I do. But when you see someone every day and run the risk of bumping into them at Waitrose—'

'Mum can't afford to shop at Waitrose.'

'A generic supermarket then, when you literally live in the same neighbourhood, you can't keep up a feud, you've just got to get on with it. Mum's been really classy about it.'

'She's a classy lady.'

'She is. But what you or I think is neither here nor there. But for the record I do agree that he's a bit of a twat.'

'I heard that,' sang Bea from out front.

William had pulled in a few favours and there was already scaffolding being put up outside the house when Nell got back to London. 'We can't do the full roof repair for another few weeks,' the foreman explained to her. 'But we'll make it watertight so they can move back into the lower floors.' That was good news, Nell thought. Although it didn't really solve the issue of where Juno was going to live while everything got rebuilt and restored. Once the builders were done for the day, she decided that she was going to spend a few hours sifting through the charred remains in Juno's flat to see if anything else could be salvaged. But first she wanted to check on Juno in person. She stopped on the way to the hospital to buy a few stems of Birds of Paradise from a local florist cart. Juno deserved so much more than carnations or chrysanthemums.

'Andrea! What a lovely surprise,' Nell said, seeing her friend as she pulled back the curtain around Juno's bed. 'And hello you,' she kissed Juno's cheek. 'Will you ever stop causing mischief?'

'Caroline! I asked Andrea here when you'd be in, but she said she didn't know you! Andrea, this is Caroline, you silly billy!'

Andrea looked at Nell in alarm but Nell gave an almost imperceptible shake of her head, telling Andrea with her eyes not to worry. 'How are you feeling, Juno love?'

'Like a right nincompoop. Mummy always told us not to light our own fires, didn't she Caroline?'

Nell stroked Juno's hair. 'She did Juno, she did.'

'Andrea here was just telling me that she's trying to sell her café. And she brought me a fruit basket.'

Now it was Nell's turn to look alarmed. 'What?'

'It's just an idea. I've actually just met someone,' Andrea explained, a little sheepishly. 'At a History of the London Canals lecture that I went to. And Vanessa was there, she's American—'

'Ah.'

'And we've been seeing a bit of each other, but she's leaving soon for a tour of Europe, and she's invited me along with her.'

'But you can't just go!'

'It was actually you that inspired me, Nell, well, you and Juno, the way that you've both lived. I'm sixty next year and apart from meandering up and down the country's canal system I've barely had any real adventures. I haven't even really been abroad.'

'But you can have adventures on your doorstep, you don't need to go away.'

'I think it sounds jolly fun,' said Juno. 'Make sure you go to Split. Everyone always leaves it out in favour of Paris or Rome, but that's such a mistake in my opinion. And when you're there, ask for Tomislav, tell him Juno sends her love.'

'I was actually going to call you about the boat, Nell, but when you came over yesterday in such a state and you told me what had happened, it wasn't the right time. But I haven't started advertising it or anything, I wanted to ask you if you were interested first.'

'That's really sweet of you, and I would love to say yes, but I just don't have the money.'

'How much is it?' Juno asked from the bed.

'Juno, it doesn't matter if it's four thousand or four hundred thousand, I can't afford it. But I'd be happy to babysit it for you when you're away if you like, Andrea? Keep the business running for when you get back? You'd love to hang out on the boat with me, wouldn't you Juno?' Nell's heart started racing with the idea of working on the boat, opening up every day to strangers, filling them with fresh coffee and cakes, being a hub for the whole community, growing her own vegetables and herbs on the roof, anchored but with the ever-present possibility of setting sail.

'No,' Andrea said, shattering all Nell's dreams into sharp shards with a single word. 'I really do want to sell. I ploughed all my savings into her and so I need the money for the trip and if things work out with Vanessa the way I'm hoping they might, I don't think she's a living on a boat kind of woman.'

'I don't think I could ever live on a boat.' Juno stopped eating a peach for a second to add, 'It would make hangovers horrendous.'

Andrea wanted seventy thousand pounds for it. Nell suspected that when the advert came out it would be listed for significantly more, but that was the amount she told Nell she could have it for. In the six weeks Nell had been working with Juno, she'd saved up a couple of thousand, once she'd siphoned off a percentage to pay back Greg and the hotel. So, by that rate of income, not taking into account inflation, she'd be able to afford it in about four or five years. It was a lovely thought though, for about two and a half minutes.

Later that evening Nell was heating up a can of soup, too tired from what the week had thrown at her so far to make her own, when an idea started forming. Reaching for her phone she typed in a few words, waited for the search engine to kick into action, and then turned off the hob and grabbed her coat.

This one was bigger than the last one. Three, four times bigger. And she could see from her seat in the grand circle that the empty seats that were there in the stalls below were rapidly being filled by people carrying pints of beer in plastic cups, or warm wine in beakers. The stage was empty save for a microphone and a table with a bottle of water on it. How he put himself through this every night, she had no idea. She was terrified, and all that was expected of her was to laugh in all the right places and some of the wrong ones.

He was introduced on stage by an off-stage voice so booming Nell almost expected him to emerge from the wings bare-chested in silk shorts and pair of boxing gloves. But suddenly there he was, fully clothed in a flannel shirt, T-shirt and jeans, hair looking luscious and curly, walking on stage in the easy, warm way he walked anywhere, one hand in his pocket, the other waving up to the circle. Could he see her? Nell doubted it, the lights were too dim, but she sank down lower in her seat anyway.

'Hello London! Thank you so much for braving the February misery to come out this evening. My name is Tom Radley, and tonight I'm going to try to make you laugh and reassess your entire reason for being, so strap yourself in folks, it's going to get interesting. . . So my show is called Bucket List. It is not, as the name suggests, a list of my favourite buckets. That would be a crap show. Quite easy to get sponsorship deals for it though, so I may keep that idea in the old back pocket. But no, it's about the things we want to do before we die. Death. That's a funny stage of life, isn't it? It's the only thing we all have in common. I'll give you an example. Hello mate, what's your name?' Tom walked over to the last seat in the front row. 'Tom? You're kidding. Oh mate, you've just messed up my act. Right, I'll try again, hello mate, what's your name?' This time he asked a man with a shiny bald head near the aisle. Tom looked up at the audience. 'For those of you that can see the man I've chosen, you'd be right in thinking that I'm taking no chances with this one. Dave? Okay, good, his name's Dave. Nothing in common so far. What job do you do, Dave? Electrician. Two for two. Great. Is this your wife, Dave? Yes? What's her name? Emily? Okay then, she's not my wife so that's three for three. Happily married, Dave?' The man nodded. 'Great, so that's four things that we absolutely don't have in common.' The crowd all laughed. Tom walked up and down the stage, flicking the wire of the microphone behind him. 'Now I like Dave, I don't want anything bad to happen to Dave, none of us do, he's one of the good ones. But one day, it will. Dave will die. Sorry Dave.'

Dave put his hand up as if to say that it's okay.

'But the one thing stopping Dave's death from being a tragedy – well two things, one is that if he starts wearing rubber soled shoes, am I right Emily? But the second will be if he makes sure that he lives life to the fullest before the day he carks it. There's nothing sadder than a life less lived. I learned this from the most incredible woman I once had incredible sex with. Thank you for cheering sir, incredible sex is certainly something to celebrate. Back to this incredible woman, let's call her Mel. . .'

Nell felt her face flaming and was so grateful for the darkness.

'Now Mel lived her life thinking that she knew the day she was going to die on, and so everything she did either had to be exciting, bring her joy, or bring her a sense of purpose. I'll give you an example. We had the incredible sex, on a Tuesday at about three in the afternoon. I'm sorry, I'm going to say that again because I don't think you really got it. Three. In the daytime. On a Tuesday. If that right there isn't the perfect example of grabbing life by the unmentionables, I don't know what is. People don't even eat out midweek. We did.'

As the crowd cheered and clapped, Nell sank even lower into her seat so she was nearly horizontal in it.

'Since meeting Mel, and being inspired by the way she lived, I have given up the lease on my flat share and now live on a houseboat, I've filed for divorce – I do have to add here that the Tuesday afternoon with Mel happened after my wife and I had separated, I'm not a complete dick – I've become a comedian full-time – how am I doing by the way? Two cheers for making a good decision, two boos for going back to teaching teenagers.' The theatre all cheered. 'Okay, about half and half,' Tom joked. 'Not bad. And I sometimes eat cake for breakfast now, because I'm an adult and why the hell not? Who made the rule that you have to eat cereal or toast when you wake up? Bollocks to that. If I want a carrot cake at eight in the morning, then I will have a carrot cake. What cake would you have, Dave? Coffee and walnut?' Tom pulled a face at the audience as he pulled the cord to the microphone, 'Each to their own Dave, each to their own.'

Nell laughed along with the rest of the theatre and felt a rush of pride that she'd had that impact on him; he'd said similar at the Christmas gig, and they'd talked about it just the two of them as well, but it hadn't actually sunk in until now. She thought of Greg, preparing to rent out his house and move across the world; Polly and Bea starting again just the two of them; her mum firmly choosing her girls over Ray, realising that a life alone is not necessarily a lonely one. It might have just been a coincidence, but maybe she did have a little hand in each of these things. She had changed too, though. She was not the same Nell who had checked into the hotel two months before. Greg had reminded her of the importance of depending on those you love, of opening your home to those who need it; Polly and Jenny had shown an unconditional understanding of her, reminded Nell that should she fall, they'd catch her, and she was now poised with a safety net of her own for them too. She didn't know where her dad and Katie fitted in yet, but Ruby and Bea would always be able to rely on her – for support and new swear words in a multitude of languages.

Tom's show was a complete hit, the audience barely stopped laughing throughout the whole thing, and Nell made no attempt to wipe away her tears of happiness as she applauded along with them. As the theatre emptied, she left the throng pulsing out the front and made her way around the back, to the stage door. There was a lone security guard there. She asked him to tell Tom that Mel was here to see him. He disappeared and a couple of minutes later reappeared, opening the door wider for her to squeeze through. 'Up the stairs, second door on the left.'

The door to his dressing room was closed. She hesitated outside, once again at one of life's crossroads, where either direction offered a different kind of life. She raised her hand and timidly knocked before turning the handle.

Tom was sitting in a chair facing the make-up mirror. He turned to the door as it opened, and sprang to his feet. 'You came to my show.'

'I did.'

'And?'

'And you're a very funny guy.'

'It's the material I have to work with.'

'Yes, that too.'

'How's Juno?'

'She's good. She still thinks I'm her dead sister, and Willa's her mum, but apart from that she's doing well.'

'That's good.'

'How's Arlo? I have a few more poo facts for him.'

'He'll be delighted. Do you want to tell them to me to pass on or will you be delivering them in person?'

'I was hoping to tell him myself. My Google history and algorithms are ruined now, so I want it to be worth it. If that's okay?'

Tom nodded, 'That's okay.'

Nell shuffled on her feet. 'I also wanted to come and tell you that you were right, with what you said.'

'Which part?'

'All of it.' Nell looked around the room and gestured to the two chairs on wheels in front of the illuminated mirrors. 'Can we sit down for a second?'

'Sure.'

'Look,' Nell started, a little unsure of herself, swivelling his chair round so it faced hers, their knees almost touching. 'I don't know how much of the way I am is down to conscious choices of how I've lived, or just my personality, so I don't think I'm ever going to be. . .' Nell searched for the right word.

'Conventional?' Tom offered, smiling.

'Conventional. Exactly. But I do know that I like you, I like you a lot. And not just in a "I want to stroke your beard" sort of way.'

'I don't have a beard.'

'I know.'

'Do you like beards?'

'I do like beards. But I also like you, with or without one. From the first time we met, I got the feeling that you saw who I am, and understood it. I have spent my entire life running away from things, running to things, just running really, and I don't want that anymore. I don't want to spend the time I have left, whether that's days, months, years, being scared of letting anyone in, for fear of them or me being devastated when it ends. Knowing when I was going to die put an expiry date on everything, and made me so careful with my feelings, and the second I felt like someone was getting close to me, I packed a bag. For their sake, and mine. But I am ready to stay in one place now. And I'd really like that place to be very near you.'

'And Arlo?'

'And Arlo. We can all eat cake for breakfast together.'

'Carrot?'

'Of course, I'm not Dave.'

'Hey, don't you be rude about Dave.'

355

'I wouldn't. Dave's great. But if you've still got room in your life for me, now that he's clearly in it, I'd really like to be in it too.'

'I have definitely got room for you, Nell.' He pulled her in closer and wrapped his arms around her. 'Can we always have sex on Tuesdays?'

Nell laughed. 'We can. As long as we always eat out on Mondays.'

'And if you want me to grow a beard, I can grow a beard.'

'We'll have a think about that one.'

CHAPTER THIRTY-THREE

There were around 1,500 hotels in London. And the universe had decided that the one Willa booked would be the one that Nell owed six grand to, after escaping through their kitchens. She half expected there to be a grainy CCTV photo of her pinned up behind the reception desk, or a face recognition alarm to go off as she went through the revolving doors, but the concierge greeted her in exactly the same way as the people before and after her, with polite British indifference.

Nell kept her collar up and her face turned away from any staff she passed just in case, but she seemed to have got away with it. Willa was unable to find interconnecting rooms, so had got a double for her and William and a twin for Nell and Juno along the same corridor, for three weeks while the builders were in. She had toyed with the idea of renting a house or a flat for a month, but felt that it would be safer for Juno to have multiple people to have to shuffle past should she get the urge to make a getaway. That, and the fact that someone else could do their laundry and cooking for a while.

They'd been in the hotel for a few days, and settled into something of a routine, which involved Nell trying to stay in the room for the majority of the time, which being roommates with Juno was nigh on impossible. She insisted on tea in the lobby, a waltz around the empty ballroom, even sliding through the Staff Only doors to the back of house to thank the housekeepers and busboys personally. As she was wearing her tiara, a silk kimono and a pair of cowboy boots she seemed to get away with all of it.

They were sitting in the lobby, Nell with her back to the reception desk, when Nell's phone rang. It was a video call from her mum. Nell hovered her finger over the end button as a matter of instinct, and then remembered that wasn't who she was anymore.

'You're not going to believe this,' Jenny started, 'but I've just had a call from Tony. Katie's made him show her the terms of the divorce and told him that either he pays me what I'm due, or she's leaving him.'

'What?'

'I know! Apparently, I said something at dinner the other night that stuck with her, I can't for the life of me remember what it was, I was half a bottle in by that point, but she never knew what he'd given me in the divorce, and when she found out how little it was she hit the roof.'

'Dad told you this?'

'Yes, he was really apologetic actually, he said that Katie's made him see that he wasn't being very fair, and that after thirty years of marriage and two kids, I deserved a lot more than just a small semi-detached with a leaky roof.'

'Oh my God, Mum, I can't believe it. That's brilliant.'

'Now look, Nell, I'm giving fifty grand to Polly, so she can put a deposit down on a house for her and Bea. And I want to do the same for you.'

'Fifty grand? Don't be ridiculous, that's your money, Mum.'

'He gave me more than enough, it's what I want to do.'

Andrea's boat floated into the forefront of Nell's mind. She'd be twenty grand short, but maybe she could work something out with her, pay the rest in instalments.

'Mum, are you absolutely sure about this? I don't need your money.'

'I am certain. I never thought I'd be able to do something like this for either of you, and there is nothing that would make me happier than to see you doing whatever would make you happy with it.'

'What are you going to do?'

'Well, I'm not going to sell up, that's for sure. This is my home, but I'll fix the roof, maybe put a nice conservatory on the back. Polly said I should go on a singles' walking holiday for the over-sixties once the weather gets better. Ireland maybe. But I'm not sure about that.'

Nell knew that she had to be careful with how much she pressed, or her mum would know she'd snooped through her private files, so said tentatively, 'But everyone's got places they'd love to visit, or things they want to do, don't they?'

'Do they?'

'Yes, like I've never been to Scotland, and it looks rugged and beautiful, and I'd love the Fringe Fest. Where would you like to go?'

Jenny shrugged, 'I don't know really.'

'If you had no work, and the money to go anywhere. . .'

'Oh gosh, I don't know. Bournemouth?'

'Bournemouth? That's two hours down the road, you could literally go there now and still be back for dinner.'

'Sorry if it's not exotic enough for you.'

'No I didn't mean that, sorry, Bournemouth's lovely, I remember we had a lovely holiday there in a caravan when we were kids.'

'That's why I'd love to go back. But I'm probably too old to do half the things I want to.'

Juno motioned for Nell to share the phone with her. Nell leaned in so Juno could also get into the frame.

Juno came really close to the screen and peered into it. 'Hello?'

'Oh hello, you must be Juno? I'm Jenny.'

'Hello Jenny, I couldn't help overhearing your conversation, sorry about that, I wasn't intentionally eavesdropping.'

'Oh, that's quite alright.'

'How old are you, Jenny?'

If Nell's mum seemed shocked by Juno's nosiness she didn't show it. 'Sixty-three,' she replied.

'A baby! At sixty-three I taught myself how to sail and then set up a sailing dhow rental business in Zanzibar. You can absolutely go to Bournemouth. But I think that you can actually go a bit further than that. I heard you talk about a singles' holiday, and I think that sounds like a marvellous idea. Much better than a conservatory that you can only use for three months of the year as it's either too cold or hot. And the birds ruin the glass roof. But I wanted to say, the world is a big place, go somewhere that makes you gasp with excitement and wonder. Now I've never been to Bournemouth, so it might be really splendid, but also, don't spend all your time with pensioners. They only talk about what ailments they have or about their friends who have died. Young people keep you young, and they teach you so much. Did you know that escorts are actually sex-workers?'

Jenny blinked into the camera, trying to pretend that this was a perfectly normal conversation to be having with an octogenarian stranger. 'I'll certainly give the holiday more thought. Lovely to meet you, Juno, can you pass me back to Nell?'

'Nell? Who's Nell?'

'I'll take that, Juno love.' Nell gently prised the phone out of Juno's hands. 'Sorry about that little fact at the end, every day is a new life lesson. But honestly, Mum, do some proper research, go somewhere you've always wanted to,' Nell's eyes started to get a bit misty at the idea of her mum finally living the life she deserved to. 'Take your pepper spray for all those frisky single men, though, you're a right catch, especially now you're loaded.'

'Oh hush. I'll transfer the money over now. Love you.'

A few minutes later, an alert from her banking app showed the deposit of more money than Nell had ever seen into her account. 'I just need to make a quick call, Juno, is that okay?'

'Of course, can I order some rice pudding with a dollop of jam?'

'Well I didn't see that on the brunch menu. . .'

'I'll ask Jorge. I'm sure he'll do it for me.' Juno waved the waiter over, and gave him her unusual mid-morning snack order, then primly crossed her hands over her handbag on her lap to wait for it to arrive while Nell tapped out a number on her phone.

'Hello?'

'Hi, it's me, Nell.'

'Nell.'

'Mum's just called and told me about the money.'

'Yes.'

'You didn't need to do that, Katie.'

'Yes, I did. Tony told me when he and Jenny got divorced that the settlement was generous, and I didn't question it.' Katie's voice faltered, losing its confidence. 'I wish I had at the time, but I have now, and hopefully righted a few wrongs. I know that money can't make up for all the hurt, but at least it might make life slightly easier for you all. I'm really sorry.'

'Look, I get it, I do. You fell in love, and I don't blame you for that. Dad's a very charming man, when he's not being rude and calling his daughter a black sheep. But he also has a way of growing bigger when the people around him shrink a bit.

Does that make sense? So don't shrink. Do your law course. Be a hot-shot solicitor that every woman wants on their team.'

'Thank you, Nell. And for the record, you're not a black sheep. You're not any kind of sheep.'

Juno's rice pudding arrived and Nell smiled as she watched her generously tip the waiter before she gratefully gobbled it up, her tiara slipping slightly down on one side as she chewed. Nell hung up the call and eyed Juno. 'Promise me you'll stay here a minute? Don't move, okay?' Nell got up. 'I mean it, old lady, not a muscle.'

She walked straight up to the reception desk. 'I'd like to speak to the manager, please. Yes, I can wait.'

Nell turned round to face Juno and made the 'I'm looking at you' gesture with two fingers, first pointing at her own eyes then at Juno. Juno did the same gesture back, followed by an unexpected one with her middle finger that made Nell laugh.

'Madam?'

'Oh hello. My name is Nell Graham, I've got fifty pounds here to leave as a tip for a housekeeper called Christina, and I'd like to settle my bill. It's a little overdue.'

Once good karma had been restored, and Juno settled back in their room for a nap, Nell took her phone out to the corridor. It was a different floor, but the same hallway in every way as the one that she had swished her way down in a rented ballgown just over two months ago, not having a clue what would happen next in the life she'd never planned to have. She walked to the end of the corridor where two armchairs and a potted plant stood in front of a window overlooking the city and sank down on one of the chairs and made a call that she hoped would change her life.

'Andrea? Hi, it's Nell. I'd like to buy your boat. I don't have all the money yet, only half of it, but I can pay you that now and then maybe we could work out a payment structure for the. . .' Nell's heart sank as Andrea told her that she was really sorry, but it had already been sold. She told Andrea that it didn't matter, it was only an idea, madcap really, probably for the best. She could hear the relief in Andrea's voice.

Nell didn't mean a word of it. She was absolutely gutted. All the way up in the lift from the lobby after her call with Katie, and every minute that she was taking Juno's shoes off and helping her lie down on the bed, she had been plotting the planting schedule of the vegetables for the roof allotment. If she could take ownership of the boat soonish, she'd thought, she could sow the majority of the salad seeds, along with beetroot and spring onions ready for summer. The boat would need a little refresh, but that could be done in stages. She was no stranger to hard work, so she could scrub, sand and repaint the interior in the evenings after closing the café, and once the weather heated up, along with the takings, she could tackle the peeling paint and salt-stained windows of the exterior. But now, someone else would be making to-do lists for her boat. That was the dangerous thing about dreams: they were only real in your mind, yet the disappointment when you realised that was heartbreakingly real.

Nell could tell that Juno sensed that something was off when she woke up; Nell tried to greet her with the same smile she always had done, but she couldn't help it being slightly lacklustre. Juno did her best to put the shine back in Nell's eyes by recounting her most outrageous tale yet, involving an all-you-can-drink buffet and three members of the Cambridge rowing team, but it barely raised a smile. In fact, just the link to the water made Nell feel ten times worse.

'Right,' Juno said. 'We've got an appointment.'

'Where are we going?'

'I'll tell you on the way. Pass me my tiara.'

The black London taxi from the rank outside the hotel

weaved its way through the streets, not towards the canal, as Nell half-hoped, wondering if Juno might have secretly bought the barge for her, but instead they drove the other way, past Buckingham Palace, through Westminster, and down towards Chelsea. The cab pulled up outside a rather grand building, and Juno let Nell help her out onto the street.

'Where are we?' Nell asked.

Juno pointed at a smart brass plaque mounted on the wall.

Wayfarers Home for the Elderly

'What are we doing here?'

'We've come for a look round.'

With that the front door opened, and a friendly-looking woman around Nell's age came down the steps. 'Mrs Macpherson?'

'Please, call me Juno. This is my good friend Nell.'

Nell was taken aback; it was the first time Juno had called her Nell in weeks. And it happened on the steps of a nursing home Juno was considering booking herself into.

Nell followed Juno and the woman called Stella a few paces behind, peering into each room they passed with interest. A few rooms had old men and women sitting in armchairs, some watching television, others listening to music, a few had friends and relatives there, but most of the bedrooms were empty. It became apparent why when they rounded the corner to the lounge, which had sweeping views over the large garden beyond it through the floor-to-ceiling windows running the length of the room. High ornate ceilings, and this glorious natural light made this a room Nell never wanted to leave. Residents were dotted around the palatial room: some playing cards, others chatting with a tea tray between them. Stella apologised that it was quite quiet today: a few residents had gone out shopping on the King's Road with some staff, while others were at a matinee of *The Jersey Boys*.

'Have you got any questions Juno?' Stella asked, as the tour took them back round to the lobby, and her office overlooking the garden.

'What's for dinner tonight?'

If Stella thought Juno's question was unorthodox, she didn't show it. 'Well, we have a few options each night that you can choose from, I think tonight we have shepherd's pie.' She and Nell both smiled at Juno's obvious distaste for the first option. 'A vegetable biryani, or Vietnamese pork and noodles.'

'Put me down for the noodles, please?' Juno asked.

'Juno, we need to talk to William about this.'

'No, we don't. It's my choice where I live, and I know that it's getting too much for everyone me living at home.'

'It's not at all,' Nell turned to the manager. 'Sorry Stella, you seem really lovely, and the home you have here is absolutely splendid, and doesn't smell of wee at all—'

'Thank you.'

'But we really need to go away and think about this and speak to Juno's son about it.'

'No, we don't.' Juno put her hand gently on Nell's. 'I have done my research, and my research led me here. I have had the most smashing life, Nell. I have filled every minute with as much fun and outrageous choices as I could. I have loved fiercely and with every cell in my body, I have climbed mountains, and sailed rough oceans, and there is nothing left that I feel that I could or should have done. But I am old, Nell, and I am tired, and I have done all the adventuring I could possibly do. And so, you have to let me do this last step of my journey the way that I want to do it.'

Nell nodded. Her eyes filled with tears as she watched Juno get out her chequebook, and make her final rental agreement.

Once everything was signed, Stella took the paperwork and said that she'd go to check if Juno's room was ready. Nell had no idea how she was going to explain to William and Willa why she was returning to the hotel alone. But she couldn't have changed Juno's mind, nor would it have been right to even try.

'I'm going to come to see you all the time,' Nell said, trying to ignore the lump in her throat. 'You're going to get so bored of seeing me.'

'Make sure you phone ahead though, because I saw the sign-up sheets for the excursions in the lobby, and my name will shortly be on all of them. Oh, and one more thing, Nell.' Juno reached into her handbag, and brought out a bunch of keys. 'I'd like you to go and check on something for me. I bought a narrow boat yesterday morning and obviously I won't be able to run it now I'm living here, so I wondered if you could?'

Nell stared at the keys Juno was dangling from her finger, her mouth wide open in shock. 'You bought Andrea's boat?'

Juno nodded. 'Inheritance tax means I can't gift it to you now because I doubt I've got seven years left in me, but I had it put in my will yesterday that it goes to you when I shuffle off to meet most of my former husbands. William and Willa know all about this too.'

'Are you serious?'

'Of course.'

'Juno, I don't know what to say. . .'

'Just promise me that you'll always say hello to strangers.'

'I will.'

'Say it.'

Nell laughed, her eyes filling up again. 'I promise that I'll always say hello to strangers.'

'And you'll never save anything for best. You'll always drink out of the finest crystal.'

'Should I ever own crystal, I will drink out of it every day.'

'Good girl, now give me a kiss and go and live your life.'

CHAPTER THIRTY-FOUR

Eighteen months later. . .

'Are those leafy green things in the vases carrot tops?'

'Yes.'

'Interesting choice of table decorations.'

Nell looked squarely at her sister. 'They're beautiful, and only ever get discarded. People rarely eat them, and they deserve a last hurrah.'

'Sorry I asked.'

'And before you comment on them: yes, the water glasses were once jam jars, the bookcases were once builders' ladders and the mug rack is made of old spoons.'

Polly held her hands up laughing, 'Okay, okay, I was actually going to just pass comment on your ingenuity.'

Nell raised one eyebrow questioningly.

'I was! It looks really great in here, Nell; you should be really proud of yourself.'

Nell looked around the boat, trying to see it through her sister's eyes, through the eyes of everyone who was coming today. She floated her gaze over the mismatched crockery, sourced one plate at a time from car boot sales and charity shops, seeing them not as deliberately different for financial reasons, and instead appreciated their varied and rich histories – the numerous kitchen cupboards across the country that they once sat in. The lower half of the walls had been painted a soft teal colour, halfway between blue and green, almost the exact hue of the canal when the sun hit it mid-afternoon. Vintage postcards were lovingly pinned to sunshine yellow cork boards, each card representing a moment in time of Nell's life, sent to her on request by her friends and acquaintances scattered across the globe, rediscovered by her begrudgingly re-joining the virtual world. Each postcard held a message on the back, hidden from view, but Nell knew they were there.

A newly upholstered armchair that she'd rescued from a skip sat in the corner, where a ten-year-old Siberian husky was lying, now sporting a bright turquoise ribbon in honour of the occasion attached to her collar. Nell had gone into Battersea Dogs Home a few months before and asked for their oldest dog, and the minute they'd brought her out, it had been mutual love at first sight, with much nose kissing on both sides.

'Where do you want the food set up, Nell?' Katie said, ducking her head to shout through the aft door into the main cabin. 'People are starting to arrive with things.'

'On the trestle table set up on the tow path,' Nell called back. 'That way anyone walking past can stop and have something too.'

'Great, your mum says, can you bring up the plates and glasses too.'

'I'll be up in a sec with everything once I've finished polishing them.'

'Tell me again what this ceremony is for?' Polly said, catching the tea towel Nell just threw at her. 'We're summoning a Greek god?'

'Not exactly, we're making libations to Poseidon, saying a few words that I've printed off the internet that basically says "please don't sink the boat", then dropping a metal tag with the boat's old name written in water soluble ink into the canal, along with half a bottle of champagne being poured in after it—'

'Lucky old Poseidon.'

'And that should be enough to stop him sending some bad luck my way now I've changed the boat's name.'

'And the other half of the bottle?'

'We will drink, along with the rest of the crate, that's just been delivered courtesy of Willa and William.'

'Are they coming too?'

'Yes, but later though, after her matinee finishes. Honestly, I'm amazed how many people said they'd pop along. I even had an email from Greg this morning wishing me well.'

'How is he?'

'Good, still loving Thailand.' Nell paused. 'A colleague of his from the London office, Daisy, she moved out there about six months ago, and they've just got engaged.'

'Oh wow. That's. . . quick.'

Nell smiled. 'Well, he can't afford to wait, now that his life might be short.'

'On that subject. I've sort of met someone too. What? Don't look at me like that. It's early days. He's actually Bea's karate teacher. I'm really hoping it works out, not least because she really likes karate, and the only other club is a twenty-minute drive away.'

'I'm happy for you, Pol, I hope you and Mr Miyagi will be very happy together.

'His name is Sensei Darren.'

'Stop it. It's not.'

'It is. What's wrong with that?'

'That is the least martial arts name ever.'

'Shut up.'

'No, you shut up.'

'Sorry to break up this beautiful sibling moment, but are the glasses ready? Most people are here now, and I'm seconds away from handing out straws to stick in the champagne bottles.'

'Hello you,' Polly said, giving Tom a hug. 'Did Arlo see Bea and Ruby upstairs?'

'He did, they're all playing together.'

'I'll take the glasses up and leave you two alone,' Polly said, loading the mismatching glass flutes on a tray and giving Nell and Tom a big knowing smile as she left.

A few months back, Tom had bought his boat from his landlord and moved it to the mooring directly behind Nell's café. They'd installed a custom-made little gangplank linking the two boats. Their roots entwined, but branches free.

Just how Nell liked it.

He sidled up to her, putting his arms around her waist. 'Would you find it patronising if I told you that I was incredibly proud of you?'

'Not if you didn't mean it in a patronising way.'

'Not at all, just in a very proud partner sort of way.'

'Well, that's okay then.'

'Are you proud of you?'

Nell looked around at what she'd achieved, not just the material collections of belongings, but the home she'd created, the relationships she'd worked so hard to cultivate and deepen. 'I think I am.'

'Are you ready to go and see your people?'

'My people?'

'Well, there's a pretty full canal path out there of the most diverse mix of people I've ever seen in one place, and only

370

you could have pulled them all together. Every single one of them is here because you've made their lives better in some way. Me included.'

'Better or crazier?'

Tom pretended to consider the question for a moment. 'Both. I love you, Nell.'

'And I love you.' Nell stood on tiptoe to kiss him.

'Ready?'

'Almost, can I just stroke your beard before we go?' Tom stuck his newly hirsute chin out and Nell gave his bristles a big lick, which made them both laugh as Tom wiped his face, grimacing, before pulling her in tightly and kissing the top of her head.

A moment later a cheer went up when Nell emerged from the depths of the cabin into the sunshine. Most of the other boat-dwellers from along their stretch of water were there, along with lots of her new regulars. Andrea and Vanessa stood laughing with Katie – Tony had flown out that morning to a golfing weekend he 'simply couldn't miss.' Nell took hardly any enjoyment from the fact that while London was bathed in glorious sunshine, Andalusia was forecast to have the worst storms of the year all weekend, which was a shame.

Nell had set up a few bistro tables along the grass verge and prepared little fun bags for Ruby, Arlo and Bea, who were all sitting using their new colouring books and crayons, their little legs swinging underneath them. Jenny sat on a blanket laid out on the grass next to them, her legs outstretched, her face glowing from the canoeing holiday in the Ardèche that she'd recently returned from. Her tan wouldn't have a chance to fade before her next trip to Valencia later in the month.

'Happy?' Tom said, holding out a glass to Nell.

'Very.'

'Juno looks beautiful.'

Nell followed his gaze as it travelled over the boat's new paintwork and the shining brass handrails. 'She does. But it's Queen Juno to you.'

'She'd be very proud of you too, you know.'

'I know she would.' Nell felt a warmth flooding through her as she remembered the day on the bus when they met. A chance meeting between two nomads that led to this life she was leading now. *Always say hello to strangers*.

'She can tell you herself, actually, here she comes.'

Flanked by an elderly gent on each arm, Juno was making her way down the tow path, looking every inch as regal as her marine namesake in a bottle green kaftan and matching turban. She unhooked one of the men's arms to blow Nell a kiss as they approached. Nell made a heart with her two hands and threw it back.

Many hours later, when the afternoon's merriment in the sunshine had morphed into early evening dancing, the last bottles had been drunk, and the final happy guests had staggered safely home, Nell sat in silence cross-legged on the roof of her boat, wrapped in a blanket, and sent a *thank you* both up and out, to God, the gods, the universe. Every place she'd been to, every person she'd met, had brought her one step closer to where she was today: on a boat, on a London canal, celebrating with people whose paths had miraculously merged with hers. Some for years, others for months. Some whose paths would stay joined to hers for many years to come, others for just a short while longer. She'd learned that there was no way of telling what was in store when the sun rose, or how many dawns she had left, but that evening, sitting on her new home, watching the setting sun bleach the sky a gentle orange, who was counting?

Acknowledgements

Years ago, my legend of a dad, Tim Butterfield, told me about an idea he'd had for a comedy sketch set in a pub at closing time where everyone knew the date they'd die on, and when the landlord called 'time' there was an uproar, with one bloke shouting, 'No it's not, I've still got twenty-two years!' and another exclaiming,' 'Shut up, I've got another seven minutes left.' This little nugget of an idea stayed with me, slowly building into the novel you're reading now.

Making the most out of what time you have left isn't a new idea. In fact, it's one that most of us probably grapple with daily, and at the heart of having a happier life is gratitude. It is almost impossible to express mine to my literary agency LBA, who plucked me from obscurity six novels ago; and especially to my agent, Hannah Schofield, who quite rightly deserves the awards she's rapidly amassing – you're going to need a bigger mantlepiece my lovely. Thank you so much for believing in me, championing me, and for finding me a new home at HarperCollins.

Which brings me to the glorious team at Avon, which I am so grateful to now be part of. To my editor, Rachel Hart, a thousand thanks for taking a punt on me, for falling in love with Nell and for your incredible intuition on when and how to sprinkle fairy dust on my words. To Raphaella Demetris for your fantastic editorial support, Maddie Dunne-Kirby and Ella Young for your marketing wizardry, Becky Hunter for your enthusiastic publicity support, Emily Chan in production and big thanks to the creative genius of designer Sarah Foster for my gorgeous cover and publisher Helen Huthwaite for being at the helm of such a genuine, warm and magical team.

A big, heartfelt thank you to my family and friends, who reminded me this year that boy, am I blessed. My mum Carol, and my sisters Hannah and Davinia, my aunties Sara and Julia and the Poultneys, Coopers, Denfords, Haddon-McMillans, Harpers, Harveys and Poulains, thank you for everything. To Lisa, Bev, Catharine, Claire, Netty, Alice, Tabs, Sally and Nina, thank you for choosing me to be your friend. To Emma and Chris, thank you for the loan of your narrow boat – those three days on the Leicestershire canals resulted in Nell's happy ending, so thank you for your generosity! To Natasha and the staff and students at WBS thank you for your unwavering support and encouragement. And to my own tribe, my wonderful husband Ed, and my brilliantly glorious three children, Millie, Rafe and Theo, thank you for always reminding me what's important.

The Second Chance became all the more poignant as during writing my lovely dad had the diagnosis no one wants. He'd had a huge life, bigger than most, and yet in his final few months on the planet he didn't dream of feeling Caribbean sand between his toes or tasting world-famous delicacies, instead he took pleasure from watching the Snooker Championship while drinking his favourite Pinot Grigio and sitting in the garden with his family around him laughing and chatting. Living life to the fullest, it turns out, doesn't have to be big and expensive. It can be done right here, right now, with the resources that you've already got. Losing a loved one throws your own mortality in your face, and the temptation is to give your life a massive spring clean, when all it needs is a light dusting. None of us know when our own 'time' will be called but, until it is, I know that I for one will be drinking my daily coffees out of the posh mugs, and I invite you, my lovely reader, to join me.